About the Author

Michael Jenkins MBE served for twenty-eight years in the British Army, rising through the ranks to complete his service as a major. He served across the globe on numerous military operations as an intelligence officer within Defence Intelligence, and as an explosive-ordnance disposal officer and military surveyor in the Corps of Royal Engineers.

His experiences in the services involved extensive travel and adventure whilst on operations, and also on many major mountaineering and exploration expeditions that he either led or was involved in. He was awarded the Geographic Medal by the Royal Geographical Society for mountain exploration and served on the screening committee of the Mount Everest Foundation charity. He was awarded the MBE on leaving the armed forces in 2007 for his services to counterterrorism.

The Kompromat Kill is Michael's second novel, his debut novel, *The Failsafe Query*, having been published in July 2018. He has started work on his third spy thriller and hopes to publish it in mid-2020.

THE KOMPROMAT KILL

THE KOMPROMAT KILL

MICHAEL JENKINS

Failsafe · Thrillers

ASIN (eBook): B07QFSF44F

ISBN (Paperback): 9781090614193

Cover Design by Mecob

Cover images:

© iStockphoto.com © Shutterstock.com

To my late father, whose creative Welsh genius inspired me.

And in dedication to the close family of British and American bomb-disposal teams and high-risk searchers.

"To touch something that was meant to cause death and destruction and overcome it, to deny it, is the most amazing feeling."

Anonymous bomb-disposal officer, 2006

KOMPROMAT

Compromising information collected for use in blackmailing, discrediting or manipulating someone, typically for political purposes.

Origin: Russian, short for *komprometirujuščij* ('compromising material')

Prologue

East Berlin

1986

Marcella placed a hand inside her dark grey coat and touched the pistol. She reached further inside, just far enough to feel the full comfort of the Heckler & Koch P7 sitting taut and primed within the pocket she had meticulously made for its carriage. With a round chambered, it gave her the assurance she needed to continue with this disturbing mission. Just.

Feeling anxious, she glanced across the dimly lit road, watching the late-night comings and goings of East Berlin's Auberge bar situated right in the heart of Friedrichshain. The bristle of a chilly wind caught her hair and the collar of her coat flapped.

Marcella didn't like the gritty bars here and the depressing facades reminded her that these were the surly masks behind which tyrannical Stasi informers were ready to act. She knew she had to be careful on this desperately cold night. Much more careful than on her previous mission for she knew she had enemies who had been ruffled in recent days.

The street lights flickered as she watched a tiny rodent scurry along the gutter before dashing into a pavement crevice, squeezing its body into the void like a chipmunk into its burrow. She curled her toes, feeling the chill creep into the arches of her feet and wishing now she'd worn warmer boots. She lit a cigarette. Waiting. Remembering. Recalling her actions from three months ago on the inner German border, deep inside a coniferous forest, where she had dug up her communications equipment ready to facilitate the escape of a high-grade defector into the hands of her MI6 colleagues who were hiding on the far side of the heavily defended border.

The man she was helping to defect was a German with the codename BRUMBY. She remembered the lengthy make-up session with an MI6 colleague, who had created the perfect disguise of a lady in her mid-seventies, rather than the forty-one years she was. The immaculate disguises, backed up by forged exit visas, had allowed them to take advantage of the pensioner scheme, which allowed the elderly to cross into West Germany for up to four weeks a year. As they were retired, they were seen by the East German government as economically unimportant and of no great loss if they defected.

She smiled as she remembered how the Americans trusted the Brits to create these genius escape routes, including a tunnel in East Berlin that Marcella occasionally used when security was ultra-high. Marcella smiled again, knowing that tonight she would use a route by road, disguised as a pensioner, to surreptitiously help an East German Stasi officer defect to the West.

Marcella had one primary role in the cold war as a covert member of the British Embassy BRIXMIS team: planning escape routes and helping defectors cross the border. She was secretly embedded in the British Military Commanders Mission in East Germany, living her life travelling between its mission house in East Berlin and the Olympic stadium in West Berlin. The other eighty-odd soldiers and officers of BRIXMIS knew nothing of her missions into the depths of East Germany for clandestine defection operations, nor did they know about her mysterious Czech-born consigliere that she regularly met in East Berlin. The BRIXMIS staff, who knew her fondly as Marcie, were legitimate British military staff operating from their mission house in Potsdam, where they mounted overt patrols to collect intelligence on the Warsaw Pact forces stationed across East Germany.

Back in the street, the psychedelic bar lights cast a series of curious shadows across the road. Marcella moved slowly to the doorway of a cake shop, biding her time. The mist was super fine, small beads of water drifting gently in front of her face, enough to make her strain her eyes as she watched the American officer cross the street and walk into the bar. She touched her pistol once more, felt her mouth go dry, a signature of her stress levels at this stage of a covert operation, and looked at her watch again. A watch that was counting down the last few hours of her life.

Marcella looked over her shoulder, as if to check that her consigliere was watching over her, guiding her. He wasn't. And she knew that. But it was a ritual that kept the fear at bay, allowing her to get on with the job in hand. Mindfully presuming that she was safe, she began the long walk to the bar and the start of another mission with her CIA contact.

As she opened the door to the bar she felt a chilled breeze quell the lingering smell of alcohol. She looked at the clocks behind the bar – one showed the time in London, another that in Berlin and the last that in Moscow. For a moment it seemed as if she was in a cold-war vacuum as she felt the barman's eyes pierce her torso, before she made her way to the window seat where the American was sat with two glasses of dark Alt beer. Medium height, nothing distinctive, a man who blended in well with the nightlife of Friedrichshain, but he did have one distinguishable characteristic when he spoke. A lisp. A lisp so faint it was almost indiscernible, but Marcella noticed it was always more pronounced when he was drinking.

It wasn't a long conversation and the German they spoke was pitch-perfect to anyone listening in that night to what was an intriguing exchange between the pair. Their cover stories had been immaculately crafted by their respective organisations, the Central Intelligence Agency and the Secret Intelligence Service, and each of them was the best of the best of the intelligence officers operating behind the Iron Curtain. Marcella listened carefully as the CIA man explained how they would help a Stasi colonel, a newly recruited agent, escape East Berlin and that it was now up to her how she got him across the border and into West Germany. The CIA would be waiting for her in Helmstedt in the West.

Marcella left the bar first and made for the narrow rear exit before walking down five small concrete steps leading to a makeshift veranda. She walked confidently into the shadows, crossing a small pebbled yard to a pond which was collecting water from a tall aquatic feature gently trickling over green moss.

The sound of running water gave her a feeling of serenity. She sauntered behind the tall water feature and underneath an ornate arbour bristling with ivy that ensured she was hidden from any peering eyes in the bar. She looked at her manicured fingers. No paint. Just trimmed short. She pinched a small brick with her index finger and thumb to carefully release it from the back of the water feature, placed the antique snuffbox inside the void and replaced the brick to complete the dead-letter drop. Inside the snuffbox was a tiny piece of paper that had been carefully inserted under the powder and into a void in the base of the box. It contained an encrypted message. A message for her consigliere, her handler if the operation went awry that night. She had carefully crafted the message in the toilet of the bar following her discreet conversation with the American. The writing was miniscule but precise, the result of years of training to get lots of information onto a single tiny piece of paper.

Marcella shrugged her shoulders and sighed before walking the short distance under the floral archway to the garden gate and then into the darkness of the street. The sharp wind streaming off the river cut through her hair and she pulled her collar up, tightened her scarf and squinted hard to adjust her eyes to the darkness, feeling her eyes water.

She rounded the corner and strode purposefully along the street, looking for a Wartburg 311 with a crack in the top right-hand corner of the windscreen. Within two minutes she was bending down and peering into the car to check that the driver was who she expected it to be: a middle-aged woman with a floral scarf over her head who was now beckoning her to get in. Only a brief nod and smile were exchanged between the two females before they drove off with the defector neatly hidden in the specially adapted boot, which contained a hidden void, breathing tubes and a manual clicker to operate if he was in any trouble.

Two hours later, after an uneventful journey across the East German countryside, they arrived at a small farmstead at the canopied rendezvous point deep in the Bartenslebener Forest. The woman in the headscarf drove over a cattle grid, causing Marcella to accidentally bite her tongue before the car was forced with high revs through deep mud and shale until skidding to a halt outside a small wooden chalet.

Inside the warming chalet, Marcella scrunched up her face, allowing the scarf woman to accentuate her natural wrinkles with make-up. An expensive ultra-light wig was fixed over her naturally short hair, dark brown eyeshadow applied around her nose to age her sharp features and stage paint applied to make her eyes look harsh and sunken. It took twice as long to create a workable mask for the Colonel before he too had the appearance of a seventy-five-year-old. Within a few hours Herr and Frau Schroeder were good to pass muster. Marcella bade farewell to her MI6 colleague and began the process of making sure the exit visas and photographs matched their new pensioner identities. They would cross the border at precisely 8am in their two-stroke Trabant 601 estate car, which was laden with a Zimmer frame and enough clothes for four days to visit a dying sister in Hamburg. Over the last year, Marcella had made good use of the pensioner traffic across the inner German border, which had increased over the years to nearly three million in 1986. She felt confident of another successful defection, but something gnawed away at her from the last words of the CIA officer. Cryptic words from an ambiguous mind.

Marcella peeled off the vinyl gloves to angle a spotlight onto her visa handiwork before glancing across to the Colonel, checking that everything would be OK. Everything would be fine she told herself, despite her mind stoking the fear and her senses dreaming the unknown. Marcella knew she was approaching the most dangerous part of the mission and she took heart that, if she did not return, then one day someone could decipher her message, which would cause bedlam in the intelligence services. She had risked her life to investigate several cases related to East Berlin spy rings and her legacy now lay in that antique snuffbox, a present from her closest confidant.

Marcella walked outside to retrace the route to a buried cache she had taken on arrival that night, confident with her surroundings, pleased with her forgeries. A final radio call to her master would signal that the operation was good to go. She had walked the route a dozen or so times previously, using prominent markers to navigate her way to her secret location in the woods.

A distant owl hooting and the leaves flickering in the breeze were the only sounds she heard amongst the thicket of trees, though she found her mind juggling with the racket of confusing voices in her head. Did her CIA contact know? How might he know? Don't be so silly, you're being paranoid. She touched her pistol one more time before looking to the ground where her stash lay. Below her feet and next to a small tree stump lay a buried cache, the contents of which included an HF radio, two Beretta pistols, a variety of passports, exit visa documentation and a thousand Deutschmarks. Marcella reached under the stump of a tree to pull out a small trowel to break the turf. She began to lift the lid of the metal container to replace the items she had used for the forgeries and to make that final call. She glanced over her shoulder one more time.

Just as she peered inside with a pen torch in her mouth, a tall man stepped out from the shadow of the trees. He approached her from behind, drew his Makarov pistol fitted with a silencer, grabbed Marcella's forehead from the rear and pumped two shots into her head.

Chapter 1

London

June 2019

Fletcher Barrington was an American spy who carried troubling secrets and wore a cleverly developed mask to hide them. Now in his late sixties, he took pride that most secrets in his life remained unknown to others, not even his closest Washington colleagues. Only a handful of people in his esteemed career truly knew the man behind the aging face who now walked with a slight limp. Those who knew Fletcher Barrington described him as charming and domineering, but they knew little of the real man who was walking past the Ritz hotel on his way to a rendezvous at one of London's iconic venues with one such person who knew him better than any.

Two immaculately dressed doormen graced the entrance to Quaglino's in the affluent St James's area of London. A timeless cocktail bar. A jazz club with a buzzing atmosphere. A magnificent venue for the discerning, elite and wealthy of Mayfair. Barrington handed his coat to a pretty Polish woman as the maître d' appeared though a gap in the neatly hung curtains that concealed the entrance to the huge amphitheatre below. A tall woman, she was immaculately dressed in a black cocktail dress with matching high heels and her hair was in a tight bob. She spoke with a distinguished Home Counties accent and held a smile that drew Barrington's gaze for too long. She exchanged courteous pleasantries and led the way to his regular table just below the showcase stairway. The house was full. There was a vibrant mood as the eight-piece jazz band readied itself for the first of its two sessions on a low stage at the far end of the gargantuan hall that preened itself in a colourful opulence that represented 1930s London.

Barrington enjoyed his forays to this special place, lavishly refurbished to recreate its style of yesteryear, and a place of respite from his slavish political routine as an American official visiting London. Fletcher Barrington was a former CIA grandee – a knotty, gregarious figure with a stare as cold as the wars he had fought in.

Barrington stood to welcome his guest. 'Nice of you to come along, Edmund,' he said jovially, gripping his friend's hand before giving him a hug. 'It's been too long.'

'A long time indeed,' his friend replied, bowing slightly. 'We will make up for it tonight. What a splendid location.'

Barrington nodded. 'This is my favourite place in town: great cocktails, fine dining, and magnificent jazz – now complete with my wonderful British friend.'

Edmund Duff was considered one of the reformers of the British Foreign Office. Handsome, just turned the corner of his mid-fifties, single and with an agile inquisitive mind, Edmund had been fast tracked through the diplomatic system following his years in the Ministry of Defence and was widely touted for one of the big five overseas ambassadorships in the coming years. An expert on the Middle East with a particular penchant for Persian history, and a sharp view of Britain's internationalist role alongside America's, he had established a great rapport with Britain's political elite as a senior Foreign and Commonwealth Office official.

Duff's driver, who doubled as his minder, sat at the far end of the cocktail bar above the staircase, with a perfect view of his charge at the table below him. He would be able to see the comings and goings through a single avenue of approach to his man and keep a watchful eye from a discreet position above the main hall. The minder drank lime and water with ice and the barman ensured he was always topped up, having been primed with hard cash to provide both information and drinks for him whenever he needed them.

'Now, where's your lovely Lebanese lady tonight?' Barrington asked in his booming Arizona drawl with the faintest of very faint lisps.

'Overseas I'm afraid, but she asked me to give her apologies and she hopes to meet up next time you're in town. It never stops in her world, and makes my crazy world look like a walk in the park as your lot often say.'

Barrington smirked, unrolled his napkin and replied whilst tapping his fingers on the table. 'I never had such simple walks my friend. Just conflict and wars. It's nice to walk a bit now I'm semi-retired and, anyway, that bullshit New York language is not my kind of world as you know.'

'Your junior officers were always frightened of your bluntness,' Duff said, pointing a finger. 'It's why they ran from you, and why we always got on.'

'You had a fine mentor in me, young man,' Barrington replied superciliously. 'Now, let's drink some good French wine. We have a few things to discuss.'

Fletcher Barrington the Second was the son of a mining magnate and the first in his lineage to join the CIA. He had graduated from Yale in political science in 1976 and went on to earn the George C. Marshall Award as the top graduate of the CIA Command College Class of 1978 at Camp Peary – a multimillion-dollar spy complex nestling in deer-filled woods in Virginia known to CIA insiders as 'The Farm'. A talented athlete and footballer, with a proclivity for young women, wine and classic cars, he subsequently became the CIA station chief in Sarajevo, capital city of Bosnia-Herzegovina, in 1995 - just as war was at its most savage. He was renowned for his no-nonsense, blunt style of leadership, which belied his acute political acumen. In retirement he was recruited as one of a number of retired CIA station chiefs involved in the Pentagon's military analyst program, designed to propagate disinformation across a number of political and military campaigns. Covert propaganda was now his world.

'What about Jonathon Thurlow? How is he these days?' Duff asked.

'He's still a liability, I'm afraid. Drinks himself into depression too much. He's holidaying in Santorini right now, spending top dollar on high-class prostitutes, knowing him.'

'We need to watch him, you know,' Duff retorted. 'He talks too much. Not the kind of army officer I've ever wanted to trust with my life and career.'

Barrington leant across to the younger Duff, just as the jazz band struck up for their first session. The lights glimmered and a pale blue spotlight drew everyone's attention to the trombonist, who was smashing his turn as the soloist in the eight-piece band. Barrington spoke loudly into his friend's ear with striking clarity. 'It's been a risk for us for many years. His bloody West Point education didn't serve him well despite him being made a US divisional chief of staff. I saved him from losing his career after our time together in the Balkans. Fear not though, I'll make sure he knows to keep his mouth shut. The years have been OK for us and I will have no compunction about taking him out of the game if necessary.'

Two hours later a rapturous finale came to a close on the stage. The applause for the band lasted a good three or four minutes, with the best of the cheers reserved for the bald drummer who mesmerised the audience with a string of solo slots in the last piece. He placed his hand on his heart and bowed like a metronome before disappearing through the stage door. Barrington stood and continued to clap as the chants of 'more, more' swirled around the magnificent amphitheatre.

Duff looked up and gave his customary fifteen-minute signal to the minder, who was attentively observing the peripheral surroundings of his charge.

One drink later, at the end of their evening, Barrington gave his friend a hug and slapped him on the back before pulling his head into his shoulder. Barrington was not one for tactile acts but, after a few drinks, he always reverted to machoism to show his strong regard for the closest of his friends. 'Do give my regards to your lovely lady Edmund when she returns,' he said. 'Must be wonderful for her to visit her family again after all these years.'

'Of course,' Duff replied, reaching over to hear a little better. Barrington's lisp had become more pronounced after a few glasses of Chablis and a final brandy.

'She's quite a good-looking woman you know. Keep her on your best side,' Barrington suggested.

'I know, and I will. She's always flying around the globe and I often wonder if we'll ever meet again,' Duff joked, finishing his Saint-Émilion wine.

'Make sure you give me some dates when you're next in Washington now,' Barrington said, before giving him a wide arcing handshake. 'Great night as ever Edmund – I shall send you some details of my current project on Iran, just to see what you think of it. Plenty of influence operations I'm having some fun with.'

'Ah, conditioning your great American public I see.'

'Bon voyage.'

When Edmund Duff visited London clubs it was a long-standing ritual of his that he would give his minder precisely fifteen minutes before walking to the exit. The minder was on his way out of the club to collect the car when he heard an extraordinary alert on his phone. He had never expected to hear such a strange alert and was jolted by its connotation. He grappled with his phone to check the message. The Precipio counter-surveillance software had alarmed from the system installed in his car, indicating that someone had placed a metallic device on its underbelly. A bomb or a tracking device? Someone was tampering with the car – right there, right now. The minder had used the system for well over two years on all of Duff's vehicles, but never once had he received a false alarm. This was a real alert. An alert that was transmitting directly to his phone, indicating that someone had just placed a magnetic tracker on the vehicle or, more frighteningly, an under-vehicle improvised explosive device.

'Shit,' he muttered, pulling his jacket on at the same time as calling in to his ops-room staff. 'It's either a UVIED or a tracker,' he growled down the phone, starting to jog briskly towards the car in Arlington Street. He ran into the street-level parking office, knocked hard on the window and demanded that the attendant look at the CCTV coverage of his car in the last five to ten minutes. The young Ghanaian waved him to the side door, releasing the maglock to let him into the control room. A fifty-pound note helped smooth the proceedings.

The minder studied the high-definition imagery, searching vigorously for any unusual activity at 22.27, the exact time the alarm had alerted him. 'For fuck's sake,' he snarled, looking again at the CCTV coverage. He checked his watch. Duff would be on his way out of the club soon. He cursed, strode out of the car-park office, slammed the door and walked purposefully to the car-park entrance. He sidestepped the barrier and walked quickly down the ramp before turning the corner into the dimly lit lower-first-level parking lot.

Nothing. It was quiet. 'How the fuck has this alerted?' he grumbled. False alarm or a fault? Taking no chances, he approached the car, looked around and then crouched onto one knee to check the underside of the passenger seat. Just as he did so, he felt the hard cold steel of a muzzle on his neck, his eyes flickered and the firearm jolted, sending a bullet straight through his jugular vein.

A couple of minutes later, Duff watched his silver Mercedes CLS approach Quaglino's on the right-hand side of the road. Its lights flashed, the vehicle came to a steady halt and the doorman opened the rear door for Edmund to enter.

Duff adjusted himself in the plush leather seat and started to scour his phone for any new messages. There was just one. A text from his French Lebanese girlfriend: *'Delayed again Darling, will be another few days.'*

He sighed. Then he looked up to see a second man in the passenger seat smiling and pointing what looked like a Taser stun gun at him. It was - and it was fired right into his chest.

Chapter 2

London

Jonathon and Elise Van De Lule had been planning their annual trip to Israel for several weeks, their preparations having been interrupted by a burst of glamorous social occasions amongst west London Jews. Elise, who had recently been elected the President of the Board of London Jews, had somehow managed to battle and survive cancer during this tumultuous period, but had pushed on through it, eager to keep fighting the worrying tide of anti-Semitism she felt was now infesting British shores.

The Van de Lules had arrived at the West London Synagogue at 11am on a glorious Saturday morning, attended prayers and eaten lunch in Kensington High Street with twelve friends and family. They had been careful to choose a restaurant that offered exquisite fare to celebrate their daughter's new role as a patent attorney. After a short walk around Kensington Gardens, they discussed the merits of a leisurely afternoon at home to confirm the itinerary that Elise had crafted earlier that week for their trip abroad. Jonathon had shared the idea of just making love for a while and they both laughed in excited anticipation of an afternoon of pure relaxation.

Elise glanced over her shoulder as they walked to their chauffeur-driven car - an action intimating to Jonathon how exactly do we get rid of our minders for the day? No words were uttered, but they grasped hands, swinging them a little with synchronised joy, relishing the bursts of a summer breeze that cast gentle eddies across the Serpentine.

Around 2.50pm they made their way along Chelsea Bridge Road, having decided to walk from the River Thames and make the most of the sunshine, before turning right into Sloane Gardens.

They had stopped for a moment to take in the views of the new building site that was once the grandeur of Chelsea Barracks, but was now being converted to gargantuan mansions courtesy of hefty Qatari investment. They didn't quite know what to make of the decadent monstrosities. Elise walked first up the few steps to their three-storey house, which was set back into the corner of the huge red-brick Victorian mansions. She inserted a large key and entered the house.

It was ten hours later that the Metropolitan Police detective surmised that they had been killed by more than one assailant, and that they may well have been tortured before their deaths. It was amongst the most gruesome scenes of murder he had ever witnessed in a career just shy of thirty-four years.

Jack H arrived at the mansion block at 7am the following morning and was chaperoned by a young female detective to the homicide team's command vehicle. Jack was MI5's Director of G Branch having been propelled into the role following the sacking of his previous boss, who had become the fall guy for MI5 failing to stop the Manchester Arena bombing a year earlier. He cussed that MI5 were again viewed as having failed to monitor the bomber, a twenty-two-year-old Libyan, when the secret truth of how many they had stopped that year would shock the public to the core. Nonetheless, Jack was making sure he didn't follow suit into early retirement and so kept a tight hand on the tiller of Britain's most potent counterterrorist intelligence arm.

Quite a crowd had gathered at the end of the terrace, held back by the blue and white crime-scene tape that signified the police's outer cordon. With a glance, Jack spotted the congregation of press photographers at the far end of the street and turned his face to avoid any scrutiny by sharp-eyed photographers trying to identify who he was. Just as he stepped into the police command vehicle to change into a forensic suit, he heard the punishing sounds of a helicopter hovering high above him. He didn't look up. Jack had spent too many years on covert operations in MI6, where it had been drilled into him never to look up at airframes that might catch the perfect shot of his boyish looks on high-resolution imagery. Everything about Jack revolved around drills that had been hammered into him to stay alive and remain undetected. His life in the shadows was second nature to him but he had one attribute no other spook of his era had. A sharp intellect and an uncanny knack of plotting the most devious intelligence manoeuvres that allowed him to stay well ahead of the game. He was a genius tactician.

Jack bore no marks on his face or any history of violence despite having spent decades nurturing the most brutal intelligence agents in the fields of Afghanistan, Iraq and, latterly, Libya. For this suited civil servant was the epitome of the modern-day spy. His craft dealt not with weapons, gadgets or high-tech equipment, but with political tactics to achieve an aim. This spy was a master of espionage operations, where deception, guile, coercion and meticulous planning were the tools of his trade. And he was bloody good at it. Or so his boss and mentor had always told him. Jack was the go-to man for the Director General of MI5, or D as Jack always referred to him. D had empowered Jack to lead in a clandestine role acting as the commander of MI5's most secret internal unit that ran deniable operations. It was a highly capable paramilitary organisation known as 'The Court', which had been born out of a need to retain secrecy well beyond the probing powers of political institutions. Too many intelligence leaks over the years had, in D's mind, severely damaged Britain's ability to protect itself.

Jack sat in the homicide vehicle awaiting the arrival of the Senior Investigating Officer. He had been told that the SIO at the scene was a prickly superintendent who disliked MI5 involvement. Waiting impatiently, Jack's mind drifted back to the intelligence papers he had read the night before.

Not a man to excessively waste his criminally low salary, Jack had been sitting in his favourite, but hideously cheap, Ikea armchair trying desperately to catch up on the intelligence of the day. He had put his two young children to bed, praying that Sophia, his eldest, might one day recover from her debilitating multiple sclerosis. It can be a cruel life, he often thought, watching his daughter suffer so badly at only nine years of age, but he countered those thoughts, as the religious man he was, with ones telling him it could be much worse. The fact that she was living – that they were both living - was enough to give this humble man the solace he needed.

Jack had witnessed enough barbarity in his career of nearly thirty years' service to the Crown – a service that had seen him promoted very early on each occasion, and a career that D had mentored closely to ensure Jack got all the right senior posts to groom him for one day becoming Director General.

Jack sighed as he read through the classified file containing his written notes in the one-inch right-hand margin – just as he had been taught all those years ago when analysing high-grade intelligence. What he read saddened him. It was bad enough having the Russians running riot but now the Iranians too. Are we this far into the depths of a new war, he thought? Multiple enemies on multiple fronts, from cyberwarfare to the chaos of Russian influence operations tearing apart Western democracies.

He flicked through the first two pages. How on earth has our world come to this, he wondered? He had long felt that the political uncertainties of 2019 were likely to lead to a deep decline in Western democracy, and the mammoth implosion that no one had yet predicted wasn't far off. But he had. And what he was reading was beginning to confirm it. The darkest days of Great Britain, as the country was faced by its gravest threat this century. It was a 'black swan moment', as he often told his wife, who was sat quietly reading her novel in the lounge next door. The black swan that no one had predicted. But it would come. He knew Britain's security service needed some skin in the game to get ahead of an impending hybrid war.

'Iran is mobilising,' he muttered to himself as he read the INTSUM that D had personally provided him with earlier that day. The intelligence summary was pithy and to the point. The Iranian Ministry of Intelligence and Security affairs, the MOIS, was active in Europe and had identified targets for terrorist strikes and assassinations. The MOIS posed a massive threat. He read the third page, which provided some history on the Iranian threat.

'During ancient times, the dagger was the weapon of choice by Shia Nizaris to carry out assassinations against those who

were out to persecute them. A weapon which is still the preferred tool of choice by today's MOIS assassins, often grotesquely mutilating the body of their victim to strike fear into the hearts of their enemies, reminding them of what lies in store if they cross the Iranian regime.

Today, another way a MOIS agent strikes fear into those he is tracking is to sometimes play mind games with the target. This is all about escalating the victim's sense of fear, just as in days of old, when Nizari assassins would leave a dagger under a target's pillow, as a threat to intimidate them.

The Nizaris were skilled in infiltration; they would set up long-term sleeper cells to allow their operatives to observe enemy strengths and positions, which they would report back to their masters to give an indication of how the enemy operated. Methods that are still used today by MOIS agents.'

Jack read the entire document, which intimated that Iranian sleeper agents had been awoken and were now mobilised on the British mainland. He shivered at the thought, not knowing that the very next morning he would be faced with a mission of mammoth proportions - one that would lead to him crafting a devious espionage plan that might, just might, work.

'Good morning Jack,' the tall, suited man said as he entered the vehicle and closed the door in a single flowing movement, intent on making a strong entrance. 'I'm Detective Superintendent Alan Toombs. Come on, I'll show you around, but I warn you it's not very pretty.'

Jack watched the Superintendent open the visitors' book, scribble something inside it and then ask him to sign it. Jack wrote his name as Jack H and nothing else.

'Just a couple of points before we go in,' Jack said, handing his business card to the SIO. 'This is your primacy as a criminal investigation, but my Director General has asked me to make sure we get full disclosure on any evidence retrieved from these murders.'

The SIO looked down on Jack, whose five-foot-eight frame was dwarfed by the surly Scotsman. A purposeful and lingering stare followed. 'This is a police matter, not MI5,' came the rebuttal. 'If we find anything that relates these murders to terrorism, I'll let you know. I'm not sure why my boss even said you should attend.'

Jack shrugged. 'Very good. Now what have we got exactly?'

'Two dead. Husband and wife. All knife wounds from a frenzied, brutal attack. They broke in from the rear and it's unlikely to be terrorism I'd say.'

'If it's an assassination, it's very much terrorism and I'll let you know when I decide that,' Jack agitated.

The SIO grunted. 'It hardly looks like a clean professional hit to me. Just a messy set of gruesome murders. What on earth makes you think it's a professional assassination other than that they were Jews?'

'I read a lot. Let me have a look.'

The Superintendent pointed to a stack of sterile white suits, gloves and boots on the table. 'Changing room is the tent outside. I'll meet you inside the house.'

'Thanks. By the way, have you recovered any of the weapons at all?'

'None so far. Come and have a look when you're changed. The scene is still pristine.'

What Jack saw of the crime scene haunted him immediately.

Elise Van De Lule, who had suffered a frenzied attack to the stomach with a knife and had been decapitated, was sprawled across her sofa, while her husband lay nearby, his clothing blood-soaked and in tatters from the savage knife attack. According to the SIO, the couple had both been sprayed in the face with an unknown substance, and the attackers appeared to have entered through a basement-level window that was smashed.

The couple had been fighting for years to establish political leverage against anti-Semitism and were the most prominent of the British Jews who were continuously outspoken against the Republic of Iran. That in itself had probably elevated them up the target list of the MOIS, Jack thought, and made them the focus of Iranian surveillance. No matter how much this looked like a savage murder by intruders, only a state-sponsored capability could have pulled this off and defeated the close-protection teams, high-tech alarms and the regular police attendance and patrols around their home.

Jack stood and surveyed the scene closely. Scanning. He searched with his eyes to try and find anything that might confirm his supposition. They must have suffered horribly, he thought, as he looked at Elise's body, whose slash wounds were ferocious. One, or two attackers he wondered? He spotted the broken spectacles of Jonathon Van De Lule next to a large glass table that was sodden with blood and a few small links of what looked like a gold chain that had been ripped from his neck, perhaps to suggest a violent burglary. But Jack's gut instinct was that it was not and that this was an assassination of an intensity and brutality he had never seen before.

He realised that the moment he declared it a terrorist murder, panic would seep into central government. He imagined the flurry of activity in the Chief of Staff's office at 10 Downing Street and the furore amongst the political staffers who would end up working in overdrive to get their media messages woven. A high-profile Jewish assassination in the heart of central London. Would they try and dampen the Iranian threat if he declared it? Quite probably. Would they try and avoid the connotations of a state-sponsored assassination right in the middle of a political maelstrom surrounding the ever-increasing tide of anti-Semitism within the UK? Definitely. This was a professional hit with a message. Talented investigative journalists would be all over it and would soon begin to stitch together the developing trends of Iranian activity across the UK and Europe, activity Jack had known about for some time but had only read in specific detail the night before. He'd already been planning his moves before this hit. Predicting. Staying a few moves ahead of everyone else, including the politicians.

The arrests ten days earlier of two Iranian academics at University College London may have seemed innocuous to most. But Jack had foreseen a trend emerging. The UCL academics had been arrested for undertaking surveillance activity on London synagogues as well as for photographing prominent Jewish families. And then there was the secret intelligence, not known by the wider world and the media, of a very small cache of military-grade explosives found in a garage in Battersea. MI6 had received this intelligence from officers in Bahrain who had cultivated human sources linked to three Iranian caches that were found there in 2017. The investigation included a case where Bahraini security forces had discovered a large bomb-making factory in Nuweidrat and arrested several suspects linked to the IRGC, the Islamic Revolutionary Guard Corps, and its infamous killing machine known as Al Quds. Authorities said the facility contained more than a tonne of high-grade explosives, making it one of the biggest finds in the Middle East linked to Iranian state-sponsored terrorism. Now small caches were being found in south London and the forensics linked them to Bahrain and to an ongoing investigation in Istanbul.

Jack knelt down next to Jonathon Van De Lule. His eyes were open, yet far away. Thick red blood had congealed on the slash wound on the side of his neck and a gaping hole in his cheek had ruptured the bone. His mouth was pursed, and the acrid smell of bodily fluids breached Jack's flimsy mask.

Jack cast his mind back to the '80s and '90s when Iranian state-sponsored assassinations were at their apex - a series of slayings dubbed the 'chain murders' took place across America, with the victims including political activists, writers, poets, translators and ordinary Iranian citizens. The MOIS assassins' modus operandi varied greatly between each murder: some were slain in staged robberies, many were stabbed to death in their beds or on the rooftops of their homes, one doctor was killed by an assailant posing as a patient, others died in car crashes and, most ingenious of all, some were injected with potassium chloride to simulate cardiac arrest.

'Can you come this way Jack? There's something I want you to look at,' the Superintendent asked. Jack followed him into a large bedroom with open-plan closets and a marble floor. The clothes were immaculately hung and a small corridor that led to the bathroom delineated between the male and female wardrobes. A suited and booted forensic officer was searching the bathroom but had been ordered not to move or touch anything until Jack had arrived on-site. Unbeknown to them, the Metropolitan Commissioner had given an order on the advice of the Director General of MI5, who had recommended that the Executive Liaison Group would need to meet if Jack determined it necessary once he had assessed the murder scene.

The Executive Liaison Group is unique to major terrorism investigations and allows decisions to be made between the police, who have primacy for obtaining arrests and public safety, and MI5, who retain the lead for collecting, assessing and exploiting intelligence. The Executive Liaison Group allows MI5 to safely share secret and raw intelligence with the police to decide how best to gather evidence and prosecute in the courts. The two organisations work in partnership throughout the investigation but Jack would make the call on how this would pan out in terms of intelligence collection that could lead to finding wider terrorist cells.

Jack entered the bathroom, where the smell of perfumed soaps and lavender lingered and a circular bath dominated the room. He walked across and peered into the white Villeroy & Boch crucible. Inside the bath were fourteen prominent dots painted in blood and precisely drawn in a shape that Jack immediately recognised. Four of the dots were connected by thick lines of blood. Presumably from the Van De Lules.

'A calling card?' the SIO said questioningly.

'An assassin's calling card.'

'What exactly does it represent? Any ideas?'

'I do. I know exactly what it is. It's the star constellation of Scorpio with fourteen stars, four of which represent the deaths at the hand of the assassin. The rest are his target list.'

'Or hers?'

'Could be. Quite rare though. Most Nizari assassins are male.'

'Nizari?'

'Persian murderers. My guess is we have a Nizari assassin on the loose and he or she has only just begun.'

'How do you know it's not just a serial killer leaving a calling card? A signature killing?'

'Oh, it's definitely a Nizari calling card,' Jack said nonchalantly, before turning to walk back into the bedroom. 'Like any serial killer, it's figurative. A signature to make sure investigators know it's them. And to taunt us. It also shows the modus operandi and how much he took enjoyment in it.'

'Or she,' the SIO ventured again.

'I'm not convinced. Anyway, let's see if he or she is playing any mind games with us. Have a look under the pillows.'

Jack watched the SIO walk around the king-size bed, so that he was facing the photographer. Jack nodded and the SIO carefully lifted the first pillow nearest to the bedroom window.

Sure enough, under the pillow was a curved Persian dagger covered in the blood of the Van De Lules.

Chapter 3

Westminster

Jack immediately made his way to D's office to brief him on what he had seen at Sloane Gardens. D had instructed him to rendezvous at the covert offices of The Court located in the heart of London's legal chambers set back from the Strand.

Jack was certainly no lawyer, and often shunned the advice he was given by lawyers as the Director of Counter Terrorist Operations. They were far too risk averse and too trapped in their world of legalese to make a real difference in the world he existed in, one where he plotted to catch terrorists and spies. Although, if there was one thing he had noticed in terms of a cultural change at MI5, there were now more lawyers in the corridors of the intelligence services than at any other time in history – such was the microscope they had been placed under in these heady days of ensuring transparency.

Jack did however look like a lawyer, which was part of the reason he had chosen the Strand for the covert offices of The Court's operations.

Jack was the archetypal grey man. A person who would never stand out in a crowd. Most often dressed in a blue Marks and Spencer suit and a crisp white shirt accompanied by a drab tie, and always with a foundation of black brogues. Despite being in his fifties, he looked ten years younger and was sporting nothing more than a few strands of grey in his short back and sides. His only vice was the occasional pint of beer at his local pub in the village of Denham in Buckinghamshire and the occasional red wine with dinner at home.

As Jack stepped out of the Tube at Charing Cross station, few would have imagined this was a man who had interrogated the toughest of Al-Qaeda commanders in Afghanistan or known of his citation for bravery in Beirut, when he had shot a suicide bomber who had breached the inner cordon of a British family-housing compound. On that occasion he had taken a set of red-hot ball bearings in a leg for his trouble. Jack was not just a loyal Crown servant, but a spy who operated best in the deserts of the Middle East, the mountains of Central Asia or with the dark gangs of the Balkans, where he had made his name as an MI6 interrogator.

Now the most senior counterterrorist spy in MI5, his expertise was plotting traps and lures for traps. His mind was deep in such a plot when he arrived at a passageway on the Strand. A passageway that started off narrow and rubbish-filled, but soon opened up into a much wider passage with grand buildings looming overhead inside Devereux Court. A court named after a traitor. Robert Devereux, Earl of Essex was once a favourite of Queen Elizabeth I, but he had tried to lead a coup against the Queen, commanding a small force from this location to the City. The layout of Devereux Court dates from around that time, and today the passageway leads from the Strand into the heart of legal London and is lined with the sorts of legal chambers you'd expect in the ancient streets of the capital. One of the chambers had a brass plaque with the words D Winship and K Fenton Chambers on it. A secret court within a court. Home of The Court.

Jack flashed his key fob across the console and punched a six-digit key code to open the door, which led to a second door behind which were a narrow set of dust-ridden stairs. He opened the second door with a key and made his way up the creaking steps to a series of offices that had been maintained in its 1970s decor and style. It was how D liked it.

The offices were small. Four rooms on the first floor and a large expansive room on the second which was situated in the loft. The secret facility had a secure storeroom, a small briefing room with a table and eight antique wooden chairs, a reception room and a central office. Jack stepped onto the landing, where he turned right into the outer reception office that was manned twenty-four hours a day by highly vetted ex-military signals staff. He walked around the wooden veneer counter, placing his briefcase next to the coat stand, and knocked on D's office door.

The Court was D's very own cabal of hand-picked officers who ran the office and its much larger intelligence fusion centre located out of the city, together with a set of core staff who ran what D called his own active-measures campaigns around the globe. It employed a mixture of freelance ex-intelligence officers in the UK, as well as veteran special forces operators and a mix of former MI6 and MI5 specialists, all highly vetted and sworn to keep The Court's operations fully secret.

'Jack, good to see you. Sit down my boy. Did you put the Old Bill straight on all this?' D asked, standing behind a 1970s vintage President desk that was empty except for a large ink blotter and two pens standing to attention in a wooden stand. His half-moon glasses sat at the edge of the curved desk, with a light blue swivel chair contributing nicely to the vibrant colours of the room.

Jack sat on a pale green seat opposite the desk, a battered and beaten high-back chair, its arms now decaying from D's guests gripping them and fiddling with its material.

'What have we got then?'

'A vicious attack. Definitely Iranian and a professional hit.'

'Jesus Christ,' D remarked, slumping into his seat and giving the underside of his desk a fierce kick. 'The Home Secretary's going to be chuffed to bollocks with all this happening on our patch. It's bad enough with the Russians running riot. Now this.'

Jack sat forward to show D a photograph on his phone, which he placed on the desk. 'I think its Department 15 that's been activated. What I saw today had all the hallmarks of an MOIS assassination with a bit of Nizari ideology thrown in.'

D grabbed his glasses and took a look. 'By fuck Jack. This is brutal. Nizaris you say?'

Jack took a few moments to explain that Department 15 of the Iranian MOIS were a team of brutal regime enforcers who, like the ancient Nizaris, carry out assassinations abroad. He explained that victims of MOIS assassins tend to be Iranian dissidents who pose a threat to the regime or key opponents of the regime. The murders carried out are brutal, designed to instil fear into the hearts of any dissenter brave enough to speak out against the regime, and some of the victims of these hit squads had died in the most barbaric way.

D tutted and ran a hand across his chin. 'Iranian assassins. Sleepers waking. Russian chemical attacks and cyber-attacks. All on my bloody turf Jack. Now a missing diplomat to boot as well.' There was a pause while D pinched his nose before bloating his suited posture like a kangaroo puffing out its chest. 'Bloody hell Jack. We're in the shit here you know.'

Jack knew the signal well. A signal that was asking him what to do about all this chaos.

'I know, sir. Deep shit I'm afraid.'

Jack placed both hands on the arms of the seat and adjusted his tie so that it sat perfectly in the middle of his shirt. A deep-seated habit of his. 'We are entering a new dimension with the Russians and Iranians now hitting us time and time again. The intelligence is sporadic at best, and the chatter is rumour more than fact, but it looks like this is just the start of a massive campaign. Nasty stuff ahead I'm afraid, sir. The Iranians have gone dark and we're in the dark.' Jack took a moment and reached for his phone - hardly having to look to see D's irritation. 'It looks like sleeper agents are being tasked with more assassinations and, quite probably, acts of substantial sabotage too.'

'You're damn right as normal Jack. All because of the Americans' impatience and their geopolitical folly. Anyway, let's get to the important stuff.' D pulled out a note from his jacket and laid it on the desk. 'I need you to master this Iranian threat Jack. I need that magnificent mind of yours to plot away and give us a winning formula here. Let's get on the offensive before it's too late. I need someone right inside their crucible of terror.'

Jack fidgeted, making himself more comfortable in the chair. He found himself fiddling with the yarns again. 'I have a few ideas and I've already set a few trains in motion. If you're happy I'll proceed, sir.'

'Damned right Jack. You're the man to make things work here. I'll have to deal with those wretched ministers as they go into orbit over this. They won't know how to handle this at all you know. Bloody useless the lot of them.'

Jack was fond of his mentor. On nearly every occasion that they met, D would use the opportunity to coach him. And Jack enjoyed the man's wisdom. It had served them both well as they entered their later years in HM Crown service. Though D looked much paler than normal.

'Your operations are like a riddle wrapped in a mystery inside an enigma,' D struck up. 'Get me a new enigma Jack. We're forever being hamstrung by our own people and the Russians have been getting away with murder over the years with their hybrid warfare.'

Jack threw a cursory smile, watching D rise before walking to the window and placing a hand on an oak mantelpiece where an antique wooden clock took pride of place. Underneath the mantelpiece was a black 1950s safe cemented deep into the thick wall.

'You know what Jack? I think we've found our true fold with The Court. Our real mission is grasping opportunity in today's world of disinformation, cyber-espionage and the mayhem of the Russians with our political elite not knowing how to lead this nation any more.'

The Court was not the first time MI5 had operated a deniable secret unit. During the '70s and '80s, MI5 had established an inner cadre of deniable operators known as the Inner Policy Club consisting of a group of officers who masterminded deniable operations via contracts with private security companies often run by trusted former MI5, MI6 and military personnel, and whose relationships could all be denied. The Court ran along similar lines with all the missions tasked by Jack being deniable operations outside the legality of traditional MI5 operations. D didn't want to expose crucial intelligence to the nosey goings on of Whitehall corridors, where senior civil servants had, over the years, ensured that national secrecy was shared far too easily with ministers and committees, by way of what they called accountability. Politicians were not trusted to know of such a secret capability, given that leaks and exposés were now de rigueur in the corridors of Whitehall. The Court was the brainchild of D and remained one of Britain's most heavily guarded secrets, the activity of which was known internally as 'The Third Direction'.

'Today we need to be bolder, and more innovative than ever before,' D continued. 'And I need you to conjure up some miraculous operation that can save this country from its own downfall, and that from its own dismissive hand. Where exactly are we right now?'

Jack fiddled with his tie, again lining it up with his shirt buttons. 'My staff are hard at work trying to track down any Iranian sleeper agents we may have on our soil and I've come up with an idea on how we can mount a wider operation using The Court. We know of one assassin so far, and probably one or two sleeper agents, but there will be more being tasked. How far would you like me to go?'

'Go far and wide Jack. Use everything we have at our disposal now. This is the beginning of a war, and whilst we're witnessing some skirmishes right now, it will come to the boil in time and my fear is that the lid will be blown out of the stratosphere.'

Jack watched D clench his fist, walk sharply to his desk and grab his note. 'Coffee or gin?' he inquired.

Jack hated the coffee in the office, feeling that a stiff drink might ease the immensity of the drama ahead. 'A small gin please, sir.'

'Good man,' D said, already pouring it. 'You know, one day soon we must go for a few beers Jack. We've never done that. A good old-fashioned pub, what do you say?'

Jack wondered if D was softening after all these years. He was a battle-hardened grafter as much as a master spy. D had risen to the top of his game the hard way. He wasn't one for civil servant politik, or the new breed of officers who had been coached never to take too much risk.

'Be aware Jack that these killers may have been trained by the Russians you know. A little-known fact is that the Russian SVR trained a number of Iranian assassins and I'm guessing the Russian GRU have probably done the same.'

While Britain was still feeling the aftershocks from Russian military intelligence trying to assassinate Sergei Skripal in 2018, their GRU officers were not all as incompetent as the media made out. D was one of the country's foremost experts on the Russian foreign intelligence service, the SVR, and its military intelligence arm, the GRU. One of his best friends was a source he had recruited in East Germany during the cold war who had provided astonishing intelligence on how the Russian intelligence services operated at a deep level. D had been warning ministers of the threat from the GRU and SVR for some years and was mightily irritated that not enough had been done to rein them in. 'Political bollocks' Jack had often heard him say.

D reached inside a folder on the desk and passed Jack a small black and white photograph.

'Edmund Duff. Kidnapped. I'm not sure if it's the Russians or the Iranians but I want you to look at this too,' D said, pausing to lift his glasses. 'The PM is getting a lot of grief about what's happened to this missing diplomat and wants to know what the hell I'm doing about it. I'm briefing her later this morning and I think his kidnapping might be linked to what's been happening with the Iranian activity we've seen of late. My fear is that the Russians are involved too. They're bloody good at using proxies and this has all the hallmarks of a Russian deception plan to send us in the wrong direction. What do you think?'

'Hard to say at this stage until we've looked at it a bit more. Tell her we have our best agents on this and we're looking into Duff's background and accomplices too. Might be nothing, might be extortion or he might have been talking too much. He might even have been recruited as an agent. He was one of the FCO's Middle East experts you know, travelled a lot there and could easily have been tapped.'

D took a hit of gin before patting the clock, trying to get it to work again. He hit it one more time then turned to pace the room. 'Jack. The problem we face is most grave. The Russian influence operations have crippled our politicians with fear. Fear of not knowing what to do. Of not knowing how this game of disinformation and influence is being played. To an extent, the long arm of Russian active measures has neutered our political class - and they don't have the competence to deal with it. A breed of politicians that knows little of how Putin has changed the game – forever. Do you see that?'

Jack felt himself nodding and feeling similar dismay.

Despite the long speech and the context that he had just heard, Jack fully understood that this was his boss giving him his intent. 'Leave this with me, sir. I've got a team investigating the Iranians and the missing diplomat and we'll see if they're linked. I'm going to bring in Sean Richardson for this job too – it's right up his street.'

'Very good Jack. A fine operator. Do as you need.' D kicked the black safe with a toe punt. 'Now, you remember when I asked you chaps to relocate this safe from the Millbank offices when we set this little place up?'

'I do. We've all had bets on what's inside.'

D roared with a deep laugh and banged the clock again. 'Well I can tell you the secret of that Jack. Up until last week nothing existed inside it. I have never ever put anything in there. It has remained empty during my tenure for many years, until that is, last Tuesday.'

'Go on,' Jack uttered, knowing he was being prompted to ask.

'It now holds some information from the cold war that has only recently come to light. From East Berlin to be precise. It came from an old friend of mine in Prague. A small snuffbox that I'm personally investigating which relates to an incident in Friedrichshain in 1986.'

'Do you need some help?'

'No Jack. Not just yet. You see I have quite a serious heart condition which might require you to step in should I pass away.'

Jack watched him wave his right hand to immediately quell any sympathy Jack may have voiced. Jack remained silent, but a little shocked. He could see D was teeing him up and it had become clear to Jack that his boss was not infallible to the vagaries of health. D was in his mid-sixties now and a life of hard graft, immense stress and never-ending political battles would inevitably have taken its toll.

'I won't give you the key my boy, but you absolutely have my permission to blow the bloody door off if I shuffle off this mortal coil.' D laughed again, banging the desk with his hand. 'Hard to think that my legacy revolves around a snuffbox eh? But rest assured, only you know of this and I'll ensure that any of my findings over the months are also put in there. I really don't know where it'll lead but I have an inkling it refers to some historical foul play and some equally evil bastards. I have a few more interviews to conduct to find out what happened behind the Iron Curtain back on that day.'

Jack felt honoured. Proud in fact. His lifetime coach and mentor telling him that the last days of his life were coming and that he alone would have the authority to take whatever legacy he left forward.

D indicated it was time to close. He summarised and collected his brolly from the brass case of a Second World War shell sat next to the door.

They walked together down the Strand, then turned right at Admiralty Arch to walk through St James's Park. The rain started to fall as they walked across Horse Guards Parade and into the small courtyard where the Coldstream Guards stood fastidiously on parade.

D stopped and pointed with his umbrella to a small doorway under the arch. 'Fond memories of that door Jack,' he said, standing to attention, his umbrella regimentally placed by his side. 'That was the door I passed through many years ago to hand in my military ID card. A fine summer's day as I remember.'

Jack stood silently listening to a man he held in high regard. He was not just a senior civil servant but the first ever military officer since the Second World War to become the Director General of MI5. A highly decorated one at that. He watched D turn and begin to march off down Whitehall.

'Oh, by the way Jack, what about this blood in the bath? What's it all about?'

'Most likely the assassin is showing us their mission. A blood list of his or her targets and the numbers. I'll do some thinking on why, but star constellations and zodiac signs play a big role in Islamic scripture and even in the Quran. They were superb astronomers and mathematicians you know.'

'Keep me updated Jack. I'm just popping in here for a short while to keep them all calm.'

Jack nodded, glancing across to Downing Street and hoping that his tactics would be up to the mark in the coming weeks and months.

Chapter 4

South of France

Sean Richardson stood on his bedroom veranda, wondering what had hit him the night before. He groaned as he walked gingerly past his artist's easel to gaze out at the early-morning views of the Provence region of southern France. The views beyond the swimming pool encompassed glorious spring blooms and the distant forested hills of the Préalpes d'Azur National Park a few dozen kilometres from the Cote d'Azur. The magnificent scenery had all been perfectly captured on his latest canvas.

Sean was a life maker. A man who thrived living right on the edge. Full of energy with a penchant for risk taking, he wasn't the type to be glum or solemn. He just got on with life no matter what it threw at him. A life that had bared his soul on many an occasion and thrown a whole heap of shit at him over the years. It was a life he had only just got back after several years of forced retirement from HM intelligence services, which included a stint in an Afghan jail following a journey that had almost plunged him into self-destruction. To his closest friends, he'd sum up his most recent past as being sacked from HM services for having a fling with an Iranian spy, getting banged up overseas for being an innocent weapons smuggler and being a fugitive on the run from a bunch of Russian thugs who had a price on his head. Luckily, Jack and The Court had agreed that Sean's maverick nature warranted him having a second chance to serve the Crown but very much tucked away from the niceties of formal service.

Sean peered over the balcony to the swimming pool terrace to see his girlfriend, Melissa, sat at a table quietly reading *Le Monde* and taking a light breakfast in the warming French sun. Tucked away on the fourth page was a small piece hinting at Hezbollah involvement in the murder of a prominent Jewish couple in London. It suggested that the Van De Lules might have been assassinated on the orders of Iran due to their anti-Iranian rhetoric at numerous rallies, and that their murders, plus the recent outpourings of anti-Semitism in Britain, were beginning to seriously embarrass the British government. The police had released very little detail, but the paper intimated that the intelligence services were on a high-alert footing for further attacks.

'Meurtre à Londres,' Melissa shouted out, lifting her sunglasses momentarily to see the state of her lover.

'D'accord. Excusez-moi mademoiselle – temps pour un bonnet de douche,' Sean shouted back sarcastically.

Sean had always had a tinge of jealousy that Melissa could speak and read French so well and he was struggling to keep up with her vast language skills. To counter that he'd often make silly phrases up. Her superb grasp of the French language was one of the reasons the location was suggested to them by MI5 when they had both been safely relocated with new lives and new identities in the recent past.

Sean pulled both hands through his greying hair to tie it in a ponytail and walked back into the bedroom, moaning about his hangover. He was half shaven and bleary eyed as the memory of the previous night in downtown Nice began to surface. He was sure that Melissa had managed to coax him into a taxi following a raucous night at the Meridian Hotel, where she had been among her peers at the annual journalism awards. But he cursed that he couldn't remember the journey home. There had been lavish cuisine, long speeches and vibrant dancing in the ballroom. Trays of champagne. God that was good. Stella and French wine, not too bad, he thought. Followed by hours lingering at the casino tables amongst some of their new friends and colleagues. Then there were the shots. Christ. The shots. Sean grumbled as he remembered all of them. He sat on the bed, reached for his shirt and started to look for his phone. After a few minutes searching he found it under his dinner jacket, which was sprawled across the carpet in front of the king-size bed.

There were several unread texts and one message on his TextSecure application. This intrigued him as it had been set up two months ago as the primary means of letting him know of any tasks that MI5 wanted him to carry out. He had wondered how long it would be before Jack contacted him and a wry smile glided across his face as he opened the message. Jack had given him a few clandestine roles in the south of France since he'd been relocated two years ago, but in truth, for Sean, it was just simple agent work. Developing contacts across France was another form of art that Sean enjoyed and one that he was as good at as his steady hand enabled him to be with oil paints. He'd been tasked with finding out who was susceptible to being recruited, who in Melissa's world of journalism was also a spy. Crafting contacts and having dinner and drinks with potential sources who might give an insight into French espionage operations. Where in the world they might be focusing their intelligence efforts. To be fair, Sean had recruited a couple of human sources before formally handing them over, but he always wanted more. Something meaty rather than base-level intelligence officer work in a covert life with no formal diplomatic cover. He wanted a mission that would take him to the edge. Give him the thrills he so badly missed. Little did he know it was coming. And it was coming in a package that Jack would personally deliver.

'Arnie Arnison,' was all the text said. It was the codename Sean had chosen in memory of a friend and legend from the intelligence services who had died suddenly some years ago. He knew immediately that this was the code for a tasking that The Court would leave in a data file on their remote communications portal held on the dark web. Sean had been held on their books as a deniable resource to be used on missions that MI5 required through their highly secretive cabal of veteran officers who became operational only for the most discreet of special projects missions.

It gave him some solace that Jack, who led the operational aspects of The Court, had seen it fit to break Sean out of the Afghan jail and provide him with the means to become a free man again – but only after he had tracked and traced a dead whistle-blower, resulting in a grapple with the Russian secret services before finally exposing a couple of sleeper moles deep within the British Establishment. Sean wasn't very pleased that such a result meant an entire lifetime on the run from the Russian SVR, who had happily laid out a contract on his life after he had exposed and nearly killed their best female spy, who had operated for years within the British parliamentary system.

Sean fought with his trousers, swaying as he tried to get the second leg in, then, once successful, made his way downstairs into the living room. He fired up the computer then dived into the kitchen to make some tea and toast with a large dollop of Marmite to kick his body back into shape. Once the laptop was up and running he entered the dark web via a TOR browser and entered the link to take him into a database. Whilst the dark web was fully secure against prying eyes and provided good protection against state intelligence apparatus trying to track and trace Sean, it still had a few backdoor holes that needed some precautions. If they were able to find this secret file location, they would simply see thousands of academic databases. Rows upon rows of spreadsheets with raw IT metadata – only one specific file held the data that both parties could transmit messages through.

Sean opened the file and was disappointed to see only a very short message. He was eager for more.

'Make your way to the safe location. Something has happened here, and we need your help.'

Sean added a new row to the spreadsheet and answered.

'Roger. Will make headway now – estimated arrival tomorrow morning. Will send details when I'm at St Francis.'

Sean then deleted the first message in the spreadsheet row before logging off and making his way outside with his mug of tea, a wedge of Marmite toast delicately balanced in his mouth. He slipped his sunglasses on, as much to hide his reddened eyes from Melissa as to shield them from the fierce southern French sun.

'Morning,' he said mutedly as he smiled at Melissa and took a seat with the toast still in his mouth. Melissa peered over her sunglasses and put her paper down.

'So, the beast awakens,' she said. 'Show me your eyes Casanova.'

'Nope,' he replied.

'Bloody good job you have me to look after you,' she said. 'You were a walking disaster last night – I nearly slotted you.'

Sean laughed. 'Fear not, someone will surely beat you to that with all these bastards after my neck. Looks like I'll be putting myself back out there and amongst the thick of it in hours few.' Sean grinned before sitting back to drink his tea, knowing what would come next.

'Well,' she said. 'He's been in touch then?'

'Yep.'

'Good,' she replied. 'Only two things from me then. Make sure you get me involved. As much as I love my French journalism, I need something juicier and more investigative to get into. And secondly, keep on your toes because once you start moving you'll be leaving a footprint everywhere and those Russian bastards will be onto you like a rash. Only you could go and expose the deepest, most regarded female spy in Russian history – and the granddaughter of a brutal KGB assassin too. Fucking hell.'

Sean grinned, knowing how right he had been that she'd reply in exactly the manner he had expected. Eager as ever, Melissa had convinced Jack to have her 'on the books' for anything that involved deep research and areas of intelligence gathering that he needed kept secret from those in the not-so-secretive corridors of Thames House and Vauxhall Cross. Her investigative skills and global connections could be useful Jack had surmised.

'All he's said is that they have a problem and to make my way to the bolt-hole. He hasn't given me a clue what it's about.'

'Well, I'm sure you'll need somebody looking at this beyond the normal day-to-day intelligence collection. I'm not sitting here on my arse for weeks on end while you gallivant across the globe.' They both chuckled. 'At least you can test some of the plans that have been set up for us. I look forward to being your investigative source.' She sat back, feeling smug knowing she'd get the call.

'I'm sure you'll hear from me, but you have to play by the rules my lady. You bloody well nearly got us both killed last time. Anyway, I'll take the route that we agreed on and set up from there. I'd have thought the Russians would have better things to be getting on with without trying to take me out of the game, especially as they have all that trouble with that Novichok fiasco in Salisbury.'

'Don't you believe it,' Melissa said. 'Those bastards will always want retribution for Natalie being captured by you.' They grimaced at the memory of the explosive journey and mayhem that had seen them arrive as new people in a new land with new jobs – even if their service to the Crown was only part-time.

Jack and The Court had provided two new homes in France for them, along with new passports, new backstories, new social clubs, new credit cards and a set of communication and escape plans. They had another safe house in Lyon, but their primary safe house, their bolt-hole, was based over the border in a small town called Viola in Piedmont, Italy. It would be here that Sean would transit through whenever making foreign journeys, and then onwards to the small and less busy Turin airport, which provided safer options for covert travel. The safe house was a remote wooden chalet in the hills above Viola set amongst the dramatic pine forests with restricted approach routes and covert cameras that Sean could monitor remotely for any unwanted visitors. Any surveillance footprint had to lead back to this neat chalet rather than their luxury home on the Cote d'Azur.

Chapter 5

South of France

S ean's journey to the safe house in the cool early hours of the morning was uneventful except for a brief incident involving a small fallow deer rushing out from the conifer woods, before rooting itself to the spot in front of his Peugeot 3008 SUV. The enchanting scene of the young deer gazing into Sean's headlights as dawn broke took on an even more bizarre note as two young stags began to fight behind her. Fleetingly, they sparred. Then they were gone, leaving nothing but a burst of dust from the ancient track and the sporadic low-lying fog rising gently across the steep valley road. Sean revved the motor, grappled with the wheelspin and thrust the vehicle up the tight track, glancing across to the open hillside where the elder stags sat protecting their herd.

Sean's bolt-hole was a wooden chalet set deep in the high Alpine hills above Viola located in the upper Val Mongia near the delightful foothills of Monte Bric Mindino. Known by its codeword, *St Francis*, the sanctuary was a place of respite and pleasure for Sean where he'd often spend time alone to continue his passion for drawing and painting. His favourite haunts for setting up his easel were in the village square as well as in the magnificent Chapel of San Giovanni and at the Rocca Dei Corvi or Sfinge, a natural rocky tower some ninety metres high, which was topped off by a Sphinx-like head.

Sean took the right-hand branch of the only fork on the kilometre-long track and headed to a promontory that provided a good view down the hillside to the chalet. He started his ritual of checking the security of *St Francis* and its immediate area before he ventured any closer. He scanned the area through his binoculars before walking through the woods and completing a full circuit around the chalet, which was perched on a small hillock deep in a conifer forest. He checked the vulnerable points and avenues of approach to the chalet before checking for any signs of ground disturbance and any unusual vehicle tracks.

Next, he took out his phone and punched in a password to a CCTV and security application to check for any alerts on the detection measures that he'd installed in and around the chalet. He checked the CCTV coverage from cameras that were placed high in the trees covering the two inward routes, then spent some time checking for any alerts that would have alarmed from the pressure mats he had placed inside the bolt-hole. Any intruder stepping on them would have triggered a silent alarm and produced a camera shot if they placed a foot on the key vulnerable points that he had guarded with sensors and active infrared beams. These would then send a secure text-message alert to his phone.

There were no alerts. No intrusions since he had last been here. He set off on a final walk around the chalet before entering via the back door located on a veranda overlooking the valley basin below.

Within five minutes he'd booted up his laptop, logged onto the dark web and sent Jack a message.

'At St Francis – what's next?'

He had travelled light. Just his mobile phone, a laptop and spare burner phone, a small rucksack with enough kit to see him through a few days and two thousand Euros, along with a French passport in the name of James Le Roux. He was poised but guarded. The treacherous world of espionage had caught him out too often to be too blasé about anything any more. He trusted no one, not even Jack. But he trusted him just enough to dip a toe in the water to see what might come at him.

A few transmissions later and all was set for a rendezvous with Jack at the top of a pine hill at 2pm in a felled clearing offering staggering views of the distant Alps.

It was 1.45pm in a warming sun. Sean sat on his rucksack and waited. He took a drink of water from his flask, hummed a tune and fiddled with his lighter, trying desperately not to spark up a cigarette. But he did anyway. He thrived on his work but needed a nicotine hit to keep his edge just at the right level. Without it he was snarky. With it, he felt he could deal with anything at any time. He put his lighter in his top pocket, checked his watch and then a few moments later heard the familiar sound of a distant helicopter and found himself trying to figure out which direction it was coming from. After years of operating with helicopter insertions and extractions, he still cursed himself that he could never quite work out the incoming direction until it was too late. Same again. Before he knew it, the Italian Forestry Commission helicopter had risen above the hillside from the valley and Sean was cowering for protection as the rotors caught the loose wood shavings and small branches, blasting them fiercely across the high knoll.

Sean dropped to one knee, putting his hand across his face to shield his eyes before peering through his fingers to see Jack open the door and exit the helicopter. He watched Jack run towards him, bent over in a deep crouch, before giving a thumbs up to the pilot to indicate he could engage his gears and take off.

'You really didn't need to wear a suit you know Jack,' Sean said sardonically, before shaking Jack's hand. He watched the helicopter glide off towards the distant Gran Paradiso mountain.

Jack laughed. 'I only have a few hours here, then it's off to a rather boring meeting in Rome.'

'I'm beginning to believe you don't have any clothes other than suits, for God's sake. Here, put this on, just in case any loggers see us down below.' Sean threw his North Face waterproof to Jack before firing up the quad bike. 'Hold tight, time for a bit of fun.'

'What's the job then?' Sean asked, grabbing a couple of beers from the fridge and then placing them on the rustic wooden table in the lounge. 'You flying in means there's something big on the boil, eh?'

Jack poured a beer into a small glass, looking pretty unphased as normal. Sean watched Jack pull three pieces of paper from his inside jacket pocket and place them on the table, each folded in thirds. Sean sat opposite Jack and pushed a small jar of olives towards him, as if to say 'your move first'. He watched Jack take a long drink of his beer and leant forward - poised.

'It's as bad as we ever thought,' Jack began. 'The Iranians have pretty much mobilised and we don't know what's coming next.'

'Mobilised what?' Sean asked, his curiosity piqued.

'Their sleeper agents, and quite probably their hybrid-warfare plans.'

'Christ, for a moment I thought you meant their entire military forces, tanks, air force, the lot.'

'Well, this mobilisation is probably worse. There's no doubting we can deal with them on a battlefield, but this is a mobilisation of their terrorist and sabotage arm, backed up with offensive cyber-capability – it really isn't looking good at all.'

'How do you know? Is this all the fallout from the President killing off the Iran nuclear deal?

'Exactly right,' Jack said, downing his beer. 'I couldn't have some water, could I?'

Sean sensed the stress level in Jack, despite knowing that he rarely showed it. He grabbed a carafe of water and poured some into two glasses. 'Go on Jack – I can see the worry right there in your eyes.'

Jack smirked. 'Put it this way: if I didn't have a meeting later to try to scrape around for more intelligence I'd be staying and drinking plenty of red wine with you. It's as high an alert as I've ever known in my entire career and D is demanding we go into overdrive and gather as much human intelligence as possible on their plans.'

'Imminent strikes then?' Sean suggested with a sigh. 'What's your thinking then? A cyber-strike on critical infrastructure or sabotage?'

'I have no idea. Lots of people in the intelligence services thought it was all a myth that the Iranians had sleeper agents in the UK, but in The Court, we have collateral that they do. D is worried about that. Especially as the Russians may have coached them in this, and we're not quite sure how much support they are giving to them. Now we have a number of incidents showing us that Department 15 is active in the UK too.'

'Department 15? Who are they?'

'Part of their Ministry of Intelligence and Security trained by Al Quds and Speznaz operators who could create havoc on

European soil. Their specialism is assassination and terrorist attacks, of which we think there have been a few already.'

'Hence the three pieces of paper Jack?'

'Close Sean, but no cigar I'm afraid.'

'OK, let's get to the nub of this then Jack. What do you want me to do?'

'Do you remember the Iranian woman you had a fling with?'

Sean sat bolt upright and looked behind him, throwing his head back in despair. 'Jesus Christ Jack, is there nothing you don't know about me?'

'Very little Sean. But hey, treat this as it is. You are most probably the single best person within the entire UK intelligence service to get right in amongst what is happening right now. You never knew it at the time, but she is a high-grade MOIS intelligence agent, and a bloody dangerous woman.'

'You can say that again Jack. Staggeringly dangerous. She messed with my mind and drove me insane.'

It was when Sean had been at his most vulnerable, and still a serving intelligence officer, that a stunning-looking Iranian woman had sat next to him on the Eurostar from Paris to London. A plant by the MOIS. And Sean was her target. Sean had been through hell after the death of his wife, Katy, the year before he was on that train and he was tumbling into deep hopelessness. The fling he had with an Iranian woman named Nadège was the launch pad for him being sacked from the service. A cold chill came over him as he remembered the wild parties, the crazy sex and the hold she had exerted over him at a dire time in his life. Deadly, he thought.

'I need you to find her Sean. And I want you to turn her.'

'You really are taking the piss now Jack. She fucked with my mind and nearly killed me off, never mind getting me sacked from the service. It was a short fling. I never even thought she'd been a spy. She was a model for fuck's sake and I got properly suckered in by it all.'

'Well, if it's any consolation, we didn't know until recently how high grade she is in the Iranian MOIS either. I have a Russian GRU source who has been running her as a double agent. Up to now we simply thought she was a lowly agent provocateur. But

I've received verifiable information that she's probably behind most of the British operations and a high-grade assassin too.'

'What do you mean?'

'There was a murder in Bosnia last month. A former mayor of Sarajevo. His best friend was a paid agent of ours and he told us how the Mayor was assassinated by Nadège and another woman. Both stunning females. Lulled to his death by beauty.'

'OK. But where's the link to the here and now? What's the link to the Iranian threat?'

Jack pointed to the pieces of paper.

Sean unfolded the first piece of paper that Jack had passed to him. It showed two photos of Nadège and a few paragraphs on her background. Sean read it in detail before glancing up to see Jack casually sitting back in his chair with his arms folded. Sean looked into Jack's eyes, irritated by it all.

'You really are taking the piss here Jack. What makes you think I can get her to turn? She's an out-and-out murderer, has been for a while by the looks of it, and is motivated by her own narcissistic lifestyle I'd say. Wealthy, powerful and living the circuit with Britain's elite.'

'That's what we all thought too. But I've been told by my source that she's been making mistakes and might be ripe for turning. I don't know, but I want you to find out as much as you can about the current operations she's running and get close to her. It could give us the intelligence we need to help stop the carnage that is being primed across Europe. My hunch is that only you can get close enough and it might take a while. But, in the meantime, you need to latch onto her and find out what she's up to. Bring your team in as you need.'

'She certainly seems to have kept a low profile for all these years having only just come to your attention.'

'Yes, and we need to know more about her work. My source doesn't have the full picture of what's going on with her, but her direct connection to the Russians is worry enough for me. A lot of the information my source has given us has come second-hand. You know, GRU and SVR gossip and the like. Enough for snippets of information but not detailed intelligence – just broad information. I need you to get the detail. Hunt her down, connect with her again, use your skills and team to find out what she's up to. And see if she might turn.'

'For fuck's sake Jack. This is a non-starter,' Sean said, annoyed by what seemed like a ludicrous mission. He scratched his unshaven jaw furiously. 'It's a suicide mission. She'll know from the start who I am and what you've tasked me to do. Not a fucking hope mate. It'll all go pear-shaped from the off.'

'You'll think of something Sean, I know you will. You always do. You had a connection with her. I seriously think she might turn if you play the right moves.'

'Very fucking funny Jack.'

Sean was annoyed but studied Jack's face quizzically. How the hell does he always know everything about my life, he thought? Sean stood up and walked to the back door leading to the veranda. He waved an arm and asked Jack to follow, grabbing a bottle of his finest red wine from the rack on the wall. Jack brought the glasses.

The view from the deck was stunning. A small trestle table with two canvas chairs gave a perfect line of sight straight down the Mongia valley, with coniferous forests looming large in the sky. Buzzards flew high above, circling for their prey. Another ruse, Sean thought casually. He was dipping his toe in and didn't like what was coming at him.

Sean popped the bottle of wine, knowing Jack couldn't resist a good red and that his stress levels were so highly primed now that he surely wouldn't refuse. The sound of silence broken by the occasional twittering of birds was inspiring. They sat and drank, saying nothing for a good five minutes. Taking a moment in time. A lull before an impending storm. Both sensed the gravity of what was about to come.

'I suppose,' Sean began. 'I suppose you have more than you're telling me. What's the hidden part? Whilst I trust you to a small degree Jack, you lot are a bunch of treacherous bastards and I need to make sure I'm not being set up for a fall again.'

'Nothing hidden at all,' Jack replied, pushing the second piece of paper across the table. 'I don't know enough myself to plot this one out yet. I need you to get me more. I haven't got a clue on the extent of the sleeper threat. That's why I need you to get me actionable intelligence that's far clearer than I have right now – and something I can move on.'

'What's this then?' Sean asked, picking up the second piece of paper. 'Another demon from the past?'

'An incident from two days ago. The results of a professional Iranian assassin.'

'Nadège?'

'Could be. Not sure yet.'

Sean read the details of the murder of two Jews in Sloane Gardens. Jews who were critical of the Iranian mullahs and were now the victims of a vicious double murder. 'May I?' Sean asked, indicating the third piece of paper. Jack nodded.

Sean opened the third piece of paper. It provided the simple details of Edmund Duff being kidnapped outside Quaglino's in St James's and the details of his close protection officer, an ex-Royal Marine, being shot in the neck at a nearby car park.

Sean placed the paper on the table before taking a sip of wine. 'Intriguing, but this bloke is a British FCO diplomat. Why him? Extortion? Bribery? Or what?'

'A noble question and one I can't answer. Other than we need to investigate his disappearance in detail to see if there are any links. This case could be a high-level trigger for other major plays. I've no idea. What I do know from some cursory research is that he was heavily connected to some key American players – neocons. The type that want to take Iran down, not just by subterfuge, but direct military action. They don't care and they're an impatient lot.'

'What about this ex-CIA chief he was dining with? Anything on him?'

'Not sure at the moment. Fletcher Barrington is a former CIA station chief now working in the Pentagon. A neocon that's for sure, but we need to look at all of Duff's acquaintances in detail. See where it leads.'

'What's the focus Jack?'

'Slow time, and long burn. Get Melissa onto Duff and his associates, including Barrington. She can do that remotely and I don't have enough investigators right now. But for you, the focus is Nadège.'

Sean picked up the piece of paper relating to Nadège which provided a snapshot of the intelligence on her background, her role and her most recent whereabouts – Istanbul.

Chapter 6

Sea of Crete

The ship's decks were overflowing with holidaymakers catching a last glimpse of the setting sun as the vessel steamed past the white cliffs of Santorini in the Aegean Sea. Few on board would forget the experience of seeing the sun drop into the clear sea, leaving only the silhouettes of the tiny islets and the blue-domed cupolas of the island churches twinkling in the ship's wake.

On board, walking along the lower-deck footway, was an Iranian intelligence officer who had flown into Crete and paid cash for a one-way ferry trip to the majestic island of Santorini. Her suntanned figure and graceful manner gave away the shape and elegance of an international model – the glances at her were many. She was bejewelled with diamond-encrusted sunglasses and wore a white sleeveless floral dress, canvas wedge shoes and a fashionable Eugenia Kim floppy hat.

Nadège Soulier felt the warm wind tussle with her long black hair as she stopped to take in the dying views of an island beginning to drift into its twilight mode of flickering evening illumination.

The ferry passed the cliff villages of Oia and Fira, majestic white structures precariously perched on the cliff faces like a haphazard collection of giant white and blue Lego buildings placed by a giant's hand. The captain piloted the vessel around the ancient black volcano and into the inner ring of the Athinios ferry port with its sheer cliffs dominating the quaint bric-a-brac stalls at its base.

The ferry reversed into her moorings and the ship's stewards gave the signal for the passengers to disembark into the chaos of jostling crowds beyond. Nadège made her way to a waiting black Mercedes whilst a lone policeman blew his whistle, trying to keep order as the lorries and cars disembarked through the throngs of people on the quayside. Nadège sat comforted by the calm of the leather interior as the car zigzagged its way up the imposing cliff side to her five-star hotel resort.

Her enjoyment came from manipulating men and women into trusting her. What she looked for in a man was enough gullibility to allow her to control him. She looked for the same in a woman.

Now one of the most senior Iranian agents in the Ministry of Intelligence and Security, she was at her happiest with model shoots for glamour magazines: another branch of deception in her character and life. A double life. She had the cover of a glamour model but led a hidden life of being a deadly spy. Her cover gave her access to wealthy targets amongst the European elite but, for now, she was on a mission. A mission she chose to execute for the love of her life. A woman by the name of Petra and the only individual in the world who truly understood her disordered personality.

The men who browsed her photos would not have known that her rise to fame had not come through modelling but by rising through the ranks of the Iranian intelligence system as one of their fiercest and most capable spies. They would not have known about her upbringing in a wealthy Lebanese family in France, her rise to distinction through the '90s as a child model and then a switch when she graduated as the top Iranian MOIS student on their notorious agent-handling course in Tehran. Neither would they know about the tantalising portfolio of men she had met and bedded during a lifetime of chasing intelligence secrets. Including Bosnian political leader Franko Burrić.

It was the summer of 2018 when she targeted him. Burrić was the former Mayor of Sarajevo following a long career in the Bosnian Army. Burrić had made a name for himself during the civil war in the mid-1990s, was linked to Bosnian organised crime gangs, and had fallen for Nadège when she'd arranged to bump into him at a cocktail party in Sarajevo. It would lead to his death.

Nadège had asked Burrić to take her to his beachside mansion near Split for the weekend and to take in some of the city's finest restaurants and clubs.

When they arrived late on the Friday night, Burrić switched the lights on and made his way to his exotic bar in the lounge that led to the swimming pool.

'Can you bring the drinks to the patio?' Nadège said to Burrić, throwing him a seductive glance. Before long, Burrić stepped through the open doors onto the patio. A shot from a pistol. The margaritas smashed to the ground, followed by Burrić. He had been shot in the chest. Shadowed by the incandescent light of the poolside was a woman. Her name was Petra Novak and she was the person Nadège had heard the story from. A story that reeked of gut-wrenching horror for her - and one that started a quest for deep revenge.

Nadège took the pistol from Petra and pumped a further shot into Burrić. This kill was not her first and certainly not her last. She'd enticed him to a weekend of sex where Petra would be waiting to commit her first murder. Nadège had used two weapons that night – an M70 Zastava and her most potent one: her beauty.

As the women left the mansion, they had no idea that Franko Burrić wasn't dead. For now. He'd survived long enough to make a short phone call. On his deathbed, he told his best friend about what had happened: before passing away painfully.

Nadège stepped out of the Mercedes and into the blistering heat of Santorini. The driver escorted her to the largest suite in the volcano-view hotel situated on the west of the island. Perched on the outstanding Santorini caldera cliffs the hotel exuded the finest of Cycladic architecture, with traditional cave houses designed as luxury suites within the cliffs. The majestic canvas of colours and brightness paved the way to her suite lower down the cliffs and she was greeted on the large patio by a man in his fifties. They smiled at each other and hugged before moving into the VIP suite arm in arm.

Nadège was skilled and patient. She felt no compunction to deviate from her plan. She spent two days of sunbathing and fine dining with her companion, interspersed with long periods of somatosensory stimulation, sex and bondage. Whilst she held a deep-seated hatred for the man, she controlled her emotions and acted out the scenes like a professional actress as a means to an end. She was a fine artiste and thrived on the control she exerted and the total dominance she had over her submissive partner. On the last afternoon she set her plan in motion. She had by now gained his entire trust.

Nadège bathed in the infinity pool, peering over the edge towards the volcano steeped in the afternoon haze with the large land mass of Thirasia behind. Her mind drifted back to London. She had been given the mission of assassinating the two Jews in Sloane Gardens: Jonathon and Elise Van De Lule. It was a double kill that had been ordered by her Iranian handler and an act that was conducted to ramp up tensions in the West as part of a series of escalations the Iranians had planned. Her role across Europe and her cover as a model had again helped her. She had befriended Jonathon Van De Lule at a charity event and the rest was easy. The images of her stabbing him to death gave her a heart-pounding feeling of exhilaration, a psychotic feeling, because she loved the planning and the meticulous perfection of her kills. It always had to be perfection. But this next kill, like Burrić's, was not an officially sanctioned kill by the MOIS, like that of the Van De Lules in London – but another one of her own choosing, as an act of revenge. For her lover. Petra.

Jonathon Thurlow was a former American Army colonel. He was single, in his late fifties and had served with distinction across the globe, including in Panama, Guatemala, Bosnia and Iraq. He had a penchant for wealthy ladies, and often chose very expensive escorts to play out his fantasies. He had no idea that his death would be not as the result of an honourable military event, nor from old age – but at the hands of a vicious female assassin, driven by vengeance.

As she stood in the pool, arms outstretched on the glass pane, Nadège felt the arm of her man reach around her waist and they kissed. She was dressed in a strapless yellow bikini as she turned to put her arms around his shoulders, feeling the strain on her stomach as his large paunch pushed her slightly backwards. 'I think it's time we had a little bit of something different,' she said. 'I feel ready for something new now I've got to know you so well.'

'I think I like that idea already,' he replied. 'I'm not sure I can wait too long to see you again. Let's make the most of the time we have left. What's your idea?'

'A very special one,' she said, beginning to uncouple and make her way to the edge of the pool. 'Give me twenty minutes and come along.' Thurlow leant back onto the pool's edge. He smiled as he caught her enticing eyes luring him towards a new experience.

Nadège felt herself falling into a trance. She recalled her latest kill in London. Sex was her way of trying to deal with her awkward mind and loneliness. But killing gave her the real sensation. She remembered how she had entered the Van de Lule household, taking delight in the entire experience of killing and leaving her mark for those who found the bodies.

Nadège felt calm and controlled but moved quickly to set up her apparatus in the lounge area of the suite. She began to fix some chains to the wooden beams above the large dining table and rigged up some black kernmantle ropes and a straitjacket in preparation for his arrival. She had previously readied him for the main feature of their trip through gentle bondage sessions that he had never before experienced. It was his fantasy to play out such roles with a stunning goddess and Nadège had skilfully teased him into trying it. She wanted him to feel vulnerable and helpless. She had concentrated on linking with his inner spirituality and getting him to enjoy the masochistic pleasure of tight restraint and pain. She would now ramp that up a notch.

He arrived back at the room exactly twenty minutes later. Nadège was topless, wearing a pair of black leather high-heeled boots and a small red thong and carrying a black paddle in her right hand. 'Soft to start with?' she asked, feigning a level of empathy he had become accustomed to from his teacher.

'Yes please. And very slowly too,' he said, dropping his white towel on the sofa as he walked towards her smiling with childlike excitement. 'Do with me as you desire, my goddess.'

With that, she struck her open hand with the paddle and demanded he bend over the table. She fitted the straitjacket and began tying the black ropes onto his wrists, smacking him vigorously on the backside – she had practised the art of getting him into a hog-tie position in less than three minutes. She didn't want this going wrong and she worked speedily, strapping his legs back towards his head as he lay on the table. Using a silver karabiner, she clamped his tied wrists behind his back and onto his ankles. Then she gagged him with a ball chain and lowered the rope into position, raising him above the table using the leverage of a pulley and chain strung over the rafter above.

She smiled as she walked around the table, lingering in front of him provocatively. 'Still fine?' she inquired. He nodded and then she began to heave the black rope through the zigzag pulleys, enabling her to pull his heavy torso up above the table with ease. Within twenty seconds he was suspended two feet above the table and entirely helpless.

She placed a black rucksack on the table and began to pull out several items for her torture routine, positioning them carefully on the table so that he couldn't see what was coming. She began to attach the items gently, massaging and stimulating him as she did so. A set of ball chains was placed precariously on a smaller side table and rigged with a piece of rope so that they would drop fiercely if the string was pulled. At that stage she paused to check her rigging.

She walked back to the front of the table to face him, standing tall in front of him. She was only four inches from his face. She smiled. From behind her back she showed him a Persian dagger. A black dagger with emeralds embedded in its handle and a glistening sharp blade. She watched him inspect the dagger with curious and slightly fearful bedazzlement.

'I'd like you to remember a safe word we'll use for this technique,' she said. His eyes were glazed and he hummed in agreement, nodding his head. She inched closer. 'Its High Chaparral,' she murmured into his now-ashen face. The name had sent him into a complete panic, his eyes rolling with fright, as he sensed his demise. 'High Chaparral' was a secret gang known only by a few men. His face was etched with fear now, realising his utterly hopeless position. Every part of his body began to twitch with sheer terror.

Nadège was enjoying seeing him grimace and sway in the suspended hog-tie with sheer dread on his face. She tightened the ball chain and watched him convulse wildly as she leant beneath his torso to pull a rope attached to the small table. She yanked the rope with all her strength and the two balls dropped with horrendous speed, causing the man to shudder with excruciating pain.

She took pleasure and surprise in watching his eyes roll and his body excrete before he simultaneously fell into unconsciousness. She then used the dagger to make a small incision directly in his anterior jugular vein. He was gone from the world very quickly.

Watching him die provided the surge of adrenalin she needed after the long period of manipulation. The tease. The trap. Then the kill. She sat and admired her work, taking a moment to rejoice in her sense of supremacy.

Chapter 7

Italy

The idyllic setting of the chalet gave Sean the peace he needed to think. And to plan. Jack had explained that Nadège was not due back in Istanbul for a while, making him wonder who exactly was the source that Jack had recruited to provide the human intelligence on Nadège. Or did he have more sources? That single-sided piece of paper told the story – he didn't have a lot to go on. Hardly anything at all. And this made Sean wonder if the three pieces of paper were connected? What was the linkage between Nadège and the kidnapped FCO diplomat, and the murders in Sloane Gardens? Or were they all unconnected?

Jack had explained that the Iranians knew that Britain had been helping the CIA to destabilise Iran and try to mount a coup from within. This was being conducted under the radar of a political position in which Britain had declared its support for other EU nations by not siding with the American President to kill off the nuclear deal. Practically, it provided leverage for Britain to retain cohesive European diplomacy within the EU set against the backdrop of a deeply wounded Brexit negotiation that was taking primacy for the British government.

Britain was playing two hands. Quietly supporting the US in their fight against the Iranian mullahs, which included secret intelligence, but keeping a tight hand on the diplomatic tiller to help the EU find a better way to keep Iran from backing away from its nuclear-deal pledges. The trouble was that Iran was so wildly incensed at the nuclear deal being culled that relations had plummeted, and the ruling mullahs now felt backed into a corner and had to either strike out or lose their dictatorship.

In 2015, Iran had agreed a long-term deal on its nuclear programme with the P5+1 group of world powers - the US, UK, France, China, Russia and Germany. It came after years of tension over Iran's efforts to develop a nuclear weapon and, under the accord, Iran had agreed to limit its sensitive nuclear activities and allow in international inspectors in return for the lifting of crippling economic sanctions. It seemed to Sean that all that had now gone bust and that the Iranians were now striking out against Britain and Germany, who had recently banned the Iranian airline Mahan Air from landing in their country. Sean had read that Mahan Air were known to be transporting Al Quds equipment and manpower to conduct state-sponsored terror on targets in Europe.

Sean grabbed his canvas and set up his painting easel on the deck. He had long wanted to capture the magnificent views of the Mongia valley on a new canvas and painting allowed him the peace and time to plot and think. The political situation with the Iranians was fascinating to him. There they were in May 2018 with the nuclear deal culled by the US administration. A deal they saw as useful to disguise their nefarious activity of building their own nuclear weapons. Even better, EU countries were still supporting Iran and refusing to sanction the country at all.

How the tables quickly turn, Sean thought. Within twelve months, even France and Germany were turning against Iran. While EU policy focused on saving the landmark international nuclear deal in 2018, anger had now grown in some EU countries over the Islamic republic's espionage activities, which led to them applying restrictive sanctions following their role in plots to kill political opponents in France, Germany and Denmark. Now in Britain too it seemed.

Sean lunged into a dark brown satchel and scratched around to retrieve some oils and a battered old palette. The sun had risen to its zenith and he revelled in the splendour of his favoured retreat. How on earth would he get into Nadège's tight circle of life though? What were the levers he could pull? What if he buggered it all up from the outset? He cringed at how she had mentally incapacitated him during their fleeting relationship some years ago. He caught a glimpse of a flight of ducks gracing the skyline, sighed and then started to make broad brushstrokes to capture the dense pine forest. He sipped his wine, sat back to critique his work and opened the drawer. A mental drawer in his mind. A single drawer amongst many others sealed shut.

His thoughts drifted back to Nadège and the first time he had met her. He started to quiver inside. Sean rarely brought back memories from his damaged past, preferring to lock them away in his virtual drawers. Every now and again he'd pull one open in his mind. It was never a good experience.

He had met Nadège at a desperately low point in his life following months of depression after the sudden death of his wife, Katy. She was only thirty-three years of age and had died of a brain haemorrhage while he was away on a mission in Moscow. It was a pure accident when he first met Nadège on the Eurostar journey back to the UK from Paris. Or he thought it was an accident. But it was part of a well-planned operation by the Russians, who were using Nadège as a plant to try and recruit Sean. He grimaced as he recalled how that chance meeting, a true piece of serendipity at the time, wasn't true at all. The Russians had spotted an opportunity when Sean was at his most vulnerable and tried to latch onto him using one of the world's oldest espionage tactics. A glamorous woman. The trap had worked. Sean had a crazy sex-fuelled relationship with Nadège for many months, but he never gave any secrets away. That didn't matter to the service though. He was caught fraternising with a foreigner from a country on a list of nations that, as a British intelligence officer, he should have formally declared. That was nearly ten years ago. How on earth did he plummet so far, he wondered? It was no surprise that the intelligence services had placed him in suspended animation for so long. The equivalent of being sacked.

Enough. Sean didn't want to think any more. He closed the drawer in his mind before picking up a twenty-millimetre brush immersed in indigo oil. He started to flick some paint at the canvas, aiming at the light blue sky, when his phone buzzed. It was Melissa. She had sent a text with a code alerting Sean to log on to the dark web and retrieve a message. He stepped inside the chalet to the bright, nicely adorned lounge, with a wooden stove in the centre of the room and a bunch of large cushions sporadically placed around it. He grabbed his laptop and sat on a cushion, leaning back against the leather sofa. After the laptop had booted up, he opened the TOR browser and looked for the message spreadsheets specifically designed for him to communicate whilst on operations.

'Any news? Send Sitrep.'

Melissa was being impatient as normal, and Sean immediately knew she wanted some of the action. Time to brief her.

'You're in. Jack will ask you to investigate the background to a British FCO diplomat who was kidnapped two days ago in London. He'll send details. Met Police are investigating but The Court want you to dig - do a deep delve on his background and the man he was with that night. A former CIA agent by the name of Fletcher Barrington who is linked to neocons. Standby. Jack will send details by this means. I'm tasked to conduct some surveillance on a target who is due in Istanbul soon. I'll be calling in the team.'

Sean leant back and put his hands behind his neck. Jack had instructed him to make his way back to the UK in a couple of days. He remembered Jack's precise words: 'This is too big to have you run off into the wilds of Asia Minor without being properly read in Sean. We need to plan this with accuracy. Follow the instructions in the cache and we'll get you the intelligence you need and a helping hand from our friends over the pond.'

He smirked at the thought of being back in the fold again after all the years of being persona non grata, grateful that Jack had saved his arse on more than one occasion. Most notably by saving him from dying in an Afghan jail after Sean had been framed for being an illicit weapons dealer. Sean ran his hand through his hair, reminding himself that he needed to get it cut, get it dyed and to transform his guise as soon as possible if he was to be on the move. He was still a target for the thugs of Russian SVR.

He wondered how Billy Phish was. He knew he'd need Billy to give him a head start by hacking the relevant friends, businesses and colleagues of Nadège – whoever they might be. And he knew Billy Phish would be crucial in getting the vital leads that Sean needed on Nadège's activities. He also needed more from Jack's source. Something didn't seem right on that score.

Sean waited until dark to make his next move to find the hidden cache located a short distance from the chalet. He pulled on a headtorch and stepped out into the blackness of the forest. He had to use his memory now. His memory of where the small cache of equipment and escape pack was buried. They had been buried by him and Melissa when they had first set up their emergency bolt-hole and the metal battle box contained everything they needed if ever they needed to make a planned escape. The Russians were still after Sean and that contract still lay on his head – but he was certain that, by now, the task of tracking him down would have been sub-contracted from the Russian SVR agents to organised crime gangs. But any move he made internationally might just trigger the state apparatus of the Russian intelligence services and they would home in on him quickly. He needed to make sure his digital footprint and travel measures were sound.

He recalled his route to the battle box. He had to memorise a series of markers to get back to it – day or night – under pressure. He spotted the wooden fence that provided the delineation between the forest and the national park, making sure he kept it on his left-hand side as he traipsed through the mud, over a few hillocks and through a tiny stream until he reached a deep hollow with a tree trunk sat in its centre. A marker that indicated he needed to take a left turn at ninety degrees before heading on that bearing for fifty metres deep into the undergrowth of the coniferous forest. Sean swiftly jumped over the fence and then paced fifty metres until he arrived at a strange-looking tree with a hollow archway at its base. He angled his headtorch to the ground, retrieved a small trowel from the side pocket of his trousers and began to dig, reminding himself to be careful of the explosive booby trap he'd previously armed. A simple pull wire that would initiate two pounds of explosives if anyone opened the lid of the battle box.

Tugging at the undergrowth, it wasn't long before he'd scraped away the peaty soil to reveal a small patch of green painted metal. He carefully ran his fingers around the left-hand side of the box, gently feeling for the wire, which was tightly sprung against a bolt fixed to the base of the container and which, if pulled, would release a small pin that would initiate a detonator placed in the explosives. He slowly unwound the wire and gently pulled it away from the box, releasing all the tension. He lifted the lid three inches before reaching inside with his fingers to unscrew a bolt that would cause the C4 explosives to detonate if the lid was lifted too high. Safe. He was in.

Inside the box, protecting his cache from the damp and rot, was a double wrapping of thick canvas which he peeled away to reveal its contents. A bead of sweat dripped down his temple. He placed a large tin to one side and then checked that the other contents were in good shape. A Beretta ARX160 semi-auto pistol which he'd give a quick oil. Two Beretta 92S pistols wrapped in a tarp, and an HF radio set if he needed to transmit by old-fashioned means. He opened the contents of the tin, revealing bundles of Euro notes wrapped in paper sleeves, two passports with separate identities that he could use on overseas operations and two credit cards with five-year expiries ready to go. He placed Melissa's passport back in the tin, closed the lid and placed a pistol with a ream of ammunition in his rucksack. His thoughts momentarily considered that Russian and Iranian sleeper agents across Europe might be doing exactly the same thing. Tracing their hidden weapons caches in readiness for war.

Chapter 8

Brussels

Sean was up and out of the wooden chalet before daybreak, making his way at speed to Turin airport. He glanced at the open passport on the passenger seat and checked in the rear-view mirror to see if the picture matched his new disguise. 'Pretty bloody good,' he mouthed.

The flight from Turin to Brussels was incident-free and he felt relaxed when he eventually got through border control at Brussels airport unhindered. Jack's preparations had been immaculate so far. Sean knew only too well that the SVR and other intelligence agencies had insights into passenger manifests, sources within border officers and plenty of people-watchers outside airports taking pictures of people, so his disguise was crucial.

He bought a bus ticket and was soon heading towards the Eurostar terminal in the city centre. When he arrived, he bought a monthly commuter's ticket for frequent travel between Brussels and Lille, knowing he didn't have to supply a passport or driving licence. He had no intention of alighting in Lille. He then made a series of counter-surveillance moves at the Gare Du Midi and was content he had not been followed but would be surer of it when he was on the train. He boarded the train with a few minutes to spare and only showed his season ticket to Lille. The train journey to London St Pancras was uneventful and he was glad they had not changed the rules about where they checked passports on the Eurostar routes. He only showed his passport once when he boarded at Brussels, and it was not checked again throughout the entire journey to the UK. This helped him arrive on British soil with a minimal footprint.

He walked down the escalator and into the St Pancras terminal, turned left and walked out of the exit to have a cigarette. He stood with his back against the wall, watching every individual who exited on the same route behind him. Nothing. Anyone following him would have had to have looked left as they exited or have people placed ahead of him looking directly into the area where he stood next to an ashtray. He knew Jack would have a team watching his every move, but he couldn't see them – these were highly skilled MI5 surveillance teams and they were tasked with following Sean, looking to see who else might be following him. It was a nervous journey for Sean as this was the first time he had stuck his head above the parapet for the Russians to have a look at his movements. He wondered if they had given up, having decided he wasn't worth pursuing.

Sean then made his way to Baker Street on the Metropolitan Line, again making several counter-surveillance moves, knowing that the teams who were covering his back would want him to be doing exactly that – to help them spot any SVR followers. Having satisfied himself that he had done his job thoroughly he sat in Pret A Manger on Marylebone High Street and, using his second phone, sent a text using the TextSecure app. It simply asked, *'Can I cross the line?'*

Five minutes later he received a positive response, walked around the corner and jumped into a fast car that took him to RAF Bentwaters in Suffolk.

Chapter 9

Suffolk

The fierce Suffolk breeze ricocheted inside the rear cabin of the Toyota Hilux as Sean struggled to stay awake on the long journey from London. He grappled for the handle above the window to heave himself up into a more comfortable position as the vehicle approached its destination.

RAF Bentwaters nestles quietly in the heart of the Suffolk countryside, close to the Heritage coast and some eighty miles north-east of London. The airfield is a former RAF base that once housed the largest US Air Force fighter fleet in Europe during the cold war. With a combination of A-10 Tank Busters, F84-Thunderstreaks, F-16s and its own nuclear command bunkers for the 81st Tactical Fighter Wing, the air station was once a thriving American community in deepest Suffolk.

The Americans were gone now, but the revetments and toughened air shelters remained, together with a thriving business community run by a local farming family. The air traffic control tower sits beside the breezy airfield entrance, giving superb views across the runway and the local ancient farmlands.

Sean caught a glimpse of the tower's mast, a Union flag flying proudly above it, and could just make out the curious shapes of the aircraft shelters scattered across the former cold war base. Only this time they were being used by small businesses. Some were bonded warehouses, others were used as TV film studios and a vehicle depot, and some creative entrepreneurs had even converted some of the three-feet-thick shelters into high-tech data centres and children's play zones.

Sean watched a Cessna aircraft twist precariously to land on the active runway, which was primarily used by vintage air enthusiasts and hobby flyers. The car came to a halt in front of a concrete command centre complete with a set of huge bomb-proof doors set just behind a blast-proof wall. The entire complex, built in the late '70s, had its own decontamination units and was constructed to withstand chemical and nuclear attacks from Russian aggressors. Sean's mind drifted back to the days of the cold war, and the fond memories he had of living in West Germany as a kid.

Sean was chaperoned through the bomb-proof doors, coming face to face with a polished silver door that provided the biometric entry to the complex from within a secure airlock. He marvelled at the genius of the site and the state-of-the-art facilities constructed behind the cold war facade. The huge outer bomb door began to close automatically. Eventually the lights dimmed, and the second door eased itself open on automated hinges before juddering to a halt, revealing a huge inner sanctum buzzing with activity.

He stepped inside the void, surprised to see a huge reception lobby fully adorned with modern furniture, with French paintings on its walls and small corporate accoutrements, including green planters and a water feature on a semicircular table which dominated the room.

'Over here Sean,' Jack shouted as he appeared from one of the glass-walled side rooms, waving a hand for him to enter.

'Very corporate Jack,' Sean said, gesturing with his right hand and smiling. 'You entertain here as well?'

'In a fashion, yes we do. Now, leave your rucksack in this room and place any phones or devices in the cabinets over there. Compartmented facilities. You know the drills by now.'

'I assume I'm here to be indoctrinated?' Sean said knowingly.

'We need to plan meticulously,' Jack replied, leading Sean to the briefing room. 'You'll be read into a number of intelligence compartments before we let you loose on this one I'm afraid.'

Sean nodded and followed Jack to a double set of oak doors, watching him punch in a numeric code before placing his finger on a biometric console. The telemetry took a moment to kick in before a loud click released the left-hand door, which opened automatically. The lights came on slowly, revealing a large oval table with a dozen leather chairs perfectly aligned and set up for a conference. It had the air of a corporate boardroom, with numerous leather-backed notepad holders regimentally placed in front of each chair. An air of immaculate precision. Sean walked slowly around the table, frivolously running a finger over a long oak sideboard to check for dust. He held his finger in the air, made an approving face to Jack and continued his inspection, admiring the decor and the series of pencil drawings of London's iconic attractions placed around the ovate walls.

'Welcome to the club,' Jack said, taking a seat at the head of the table. 'We'll be joined by a few others shortly, and we have a live video conference at 4pm direct to our operator in Istanbul.

'Some club,' Sean said, as he continued inspecting the room. 'Bomb-proof, nuclear-proof and, knowing you, the place has probably got its own decontamination showers and a fully fledged artificial intelligence hub too?'

Jack, dressed as usual in a navy-blue suit, reached below the table and flicked a switch. Sean heard the motors first, before turning behind him to see a large oak panel divide and slowly open to reveal a data centre with a high-tech operations room taking centre stage. Sean walked towards the glazing and peered into the dimly lit digital void. 'Bloody hell Jack. This is taking the piss. It's bigger than the MI5 hub for Christ's sake.'

'Indeed. There is no such thing as the split loyalties of MI5 and MI6 here. It's a full-capability fusion centre for global operations run by The Court, complete with high-end data mining and artificial intelligence capacity for all of our intelligence collection assets. D is very proud of it, after years of wrangling to get it built in total secrecy.'

Sean studied the huge banks of live-imagery screens, counting twelve operators, who were controlling the communications and command and control stations. The flashing lights of an internal data centre sat behind a glass wall with banks of servers and high-grade IT racks.

'Very neat,' Sean said, swivelling on a leather chair. 'Mesmerising in fact. Cyber-ops too?'

'Everything Sean. The entire building is chemical- and blast-proof, and we have our own air-conditioning units, emergency power supply and protected telecoms cables as well as access to all the intelligence systems we need, including American compartmented intelligence.'

Sean rolled his eyes, puzzled at the US connection. This was his first ever job for The Court and it looked as if Jack was going to fully induct him into the entire secret operation. Jack pointed to the data centre beyond the clear glass walls. 'You see Sean, this was D's vision. Modern intelligence where he could counter hybrid warfare with his own. It's a mix of artificial intelligence and cyber-capability which we simply couldn't operate without the Americans and their investment. After the Snowden leaks the Americans wanted something more secure, recognising the leaky nature of their intelligence agencies and justice systems. D needed the same so, over a few years, he brokered a partnership with them.'

Sean turned in his chair, leaning back to test its weight. 'All makes sense,' he suggested, leaning forward for the coffee Jack had poured him. 'After the fiasco of the CIA scandals and the FBI corruption I can see why this has come to pass. Their agencies can't operate without someone whistle-blowing, leaking data or being indicted for fraud.'

'It's deeper than that Sean. They have no idea who's who in their agencies now and double agents are running amok. That's why D suggested to them a joint fusion centre with actionable intelligence that really is secure.'

'To avoid insider threats too?'

'The threats to our nation are grave Sean. D is a visionary. He foresaw all this. He foresaw the need for an arm of intelligence that we call The Third Direction. Ministers are no longer capable of making the right decisions to protect our nationhood. Take the influence operations of Russia for example. They have done exactly what they set out to do twenty years ago, knowing it takes that long to embed into a nation. They have been successful in every way possible – and D wants us to now become masters of hybrid warfare. To go on the offensive.'

'What offense have we got?'

'Full offensive cyber-capability with the Americans supporting us and a full range of psychological warfare apparatus. Big-data analytics and a compartment like no other – it's not five eyes – just two eyes. It's tight – very tight.'

Sean wondered what would come next. The days of traditional nationhood, warfare and securing national assets really had changed. Forever by the look of it.

'Russia and Iran are our immediate threats,' Jack stated. 'Now, shall we start?'

Jack tapped a couple of buttons on the audio-visual console before a screen lowered itself at the end of the room, the lights dimmed automatically and a picture of a middle-aged man lit up the room. In his forties, Sean thought. Baby-faced appearance. He looked scared. The picture certainly gave that appearance. Sean could see it was a photograph taken by a surveillance team and it seemed to have been taken in London.

'This is Sergei. A Russian GRU colonel who was a walk-in ten months ago.'

'Bloody hell. A live walk-in. To where?'

'A rural police station in Sussex. He covered his tracks well enough. He's the GRU lead officer for their illegals programme. A massive catch.'

Sean sat forward and leant on the table in astonishment. The last time he had met a Russian sleeper agent, a woman called Natalie, she'd nearly killed him in a shootout in France. 'An incredibly lucky catch I'd say. Is he kosher?'

'He is. I've made sure he is by running him myself. I've used him on a few operations to make sure he's not swinging both ways and, so far, he's come out clean. He's ready to trust now and we'll provide him with full defection status once we get what we need from him. A deal we agreed on.'

Sean smiled, rubbed his chin and sipped his coffee, using two hands around his cup. 'You've been plotting again Jack. This bloke better be one hundred percent legitimate, else I'm out.'

'Well, you can judge him for yourself. You're about to meet him. He's sitting outside.'

Jack pressed a button on the console and the door opened. Sergei walked in accompanied by a chaperone, a tall brunette who looked more like a professor than an intelligence officer.

'Sergei, this is Sean, a good friend of mine,' Jack said, pouring water for both of them. Neither man stood to shake hands. Sean didn't feel it was necessary, and a respectful nod sealed the introductions. Nothing more was said but an unspoken connection was made between the two men.

Sean wondered why on earth a senior GRU officer had handed himself in to MI5 after running sleeper agents for Mother Russia probably for a decade or more. The risk to his life if he was caught was immense.

'Sergei, can you let Sean know about the mission you've been working on please?'

A pause. Then a wry smile from Sergei before he started to talk in immaculate English, with no sign of an accent. 'I was instructed by Moscow to find a bomb-maker in Britain.' He stopped abruptly, turning to Jack to check he had permission to carry on. Jack gave an indiscernible nod. 'Not just any old bomb-maker,' Sergei continued. 'An ex-military one. An expert who could make the most complex of explosive devices.'

Sean wondered where this was leading and decided to just listen for a while without asking any questions. He'd judge the veracity of what was being said by observing Sergei's demeanour.

'I've also been acting as the GRU handler for an Iranian agent who became a source of information for us about two years ago and was perfect to use as a feeder for information we wanted to go back to the Iranians. We use her sparingly and recruited her as part of a mutual agreement. She'd provide British intelligence to us and we'd share information with her. She's a very dangerous and hugely complex woman. I don't know - but something is not right with her. Her temperament is chaotic. We gave her the codename *Nochnaya Sova* – NIGHTOWL.'

Sean's face remained still and focused. He knew that Sergei was talking about Nadège but that he wasn't going to share his own background with her. 'What about the bomber?'

'I found one. I was instructed to get him to meet NIGHTOWL's UK facilitator, a Syrian, who spent a while vetting him before whisking him away. I've no idea where he is and the operation has always been a dark one for us. We were always told not to get too close. 'Provide all assistance' was what I was told by the centre.

Moscow does not want to be evidentially connected in any way to the Iranian operations and I've never been privy to the detail. The Iranian operation is sanctioned at the highest levels in Moscow and they keep those elements very secret. I was tasked to facilitate everything she needed whenever she asked.'

Sean's mind hummed with intrigue as Jack threw a picture of the former British Army bomb-disposal officer on the screen. 'Sergei is still operating for the GRU and has not been compromised. We've been careful about that. He's still running NIGHTOWL and we'll be sending her the odd signal or two in the coming days to tee you up with her.'

'As what?'

'Exactly what you were when we rescued you from that Afghan jail. A weapons smuggler.'

Sean rolled his eyes. 'Here we go again. Another bloody ruse likely to end up with me in the can again. What's to smuggle then?'

'All in good time. You'll connect with NIGHTOWL as the man that the Russians have put in place for the weapons she has asked for in exactly the same way that the Russians introduced the bomber to NIGHTOWL. It will work.'

'Not a fucking chance Jack. She'll never fall for that in a million years.'

'She will.'

'Why?'

'Because she had feelings for you Sean.'

'For fuck's sake Jack. How do you know that?'

'I know everything. Trust me.'

Sean laughed. 'Where's this bomb-disposal guy then? The bomber?'

'We're not sure. Nor do we know what NIGHTOWL wants him to do other than to build high-tech devices. Sergei and I think the Russians are now using the Iranians as their own proxies to hit Europe. To cause carnage. But, in so doing, taking every precaution to make sure it is not attributable to them. Hence all the weaponry and IEDs being sourced elsewhere. The Russians, as you know, are smart at this game.'

Sean knew from his previous forays with the Russians that they preferred to use proxy armies to do their dirty work of subversion, active measures and disruption of their foes. Ultimately, he knew their objectives were to weaken Europe and the EU so much so that they would just implode. The fact that the Americans had just killed off the nuclear deal with Iran meant that the Russians could easily arm and weaponise the Iranians to enable them to conduct terrorist attacks as part of Iranian revenge. This was big. The Russian modus operandi was never to leave any evidence that could link their direct provision of arms and equipment to their proxies. Crimea was a classic example, as were Abkhazia and Georgia. It was always planned in detail, and always surreptitious so that it became plausible deniability. No trail. No evidence. Just provide the offensive capability and orders.

Sergei drank some water and asked Jack if he should continue. Jack nodded. A picture of a city flashed up on the screen – a city that Sean immediately recognised.

'This is Yerevan in Armenia. A small country flanking Iran and Azerbaijan, with Georgia to its north.'

Sean lurched forward, placed his elbows on the table and cradled his face in his hands. 'I know it well Sergei. A main staging post for smuggling routes between Russia and the Middle East or Europe via Istanbul.'

Sergei nodded. 'You understand very well. It's also where I learnt that we can acquire fissile material from the local mafia. I was tasked to find out where we could get it from and from whom - using our Armenian contacts in London.'

'A bomb-maker and fissile material? Jesus.'

'We don't know Sean,' Jack chipped in. 'We need you to find out what's going on here. Your role in recruiting NIGHTOWL is vital to us. Or at least find out what she's planning.'

Sean noticed how Jack was careful not to release any details on Sean's previous relationship with Nadège in front of Sergei. 'You think they're planning a terrorist strike using fissile material, right?'

'Yes,' Jack replied. 'We also think that the Iranian sleepers are mobilising, and we need that information from NIGHTOWL. You're the only man likely to get that for us.'

'No fucking pressure then. Thanks mate.'

'Sergei will be available tonight for you to explore what else he knows but, for now, we'll leave it there.' Jack indicated that this part of the meeting was now firmly over. Sergei nodded and walked out with his minder.

'Impressive Jack. A high-grade sleeper agent who's happy to talk and operate on our behalf. What does he want?'

'He's had enough. It's that simple. He's lived in the West for so long that he's pretty much become one of us. His old nation holds no loyalty or desire for him any more. What's more, he knows he's coming towards the end of his usefulness back in Moscow, so he doesn't want to go back to living a life of hell. He got comfortable and we got lucky. We'll get him a new life under protection when we've got what we want out of him.'

'Too right you got lucky. You always have been. What other surprises have you got up your sleeve?'

'You fly out to Istanbul tomorrow morning. The CIA will fly you there and you're already in the terminal building. The runway is right outside.'

Sean sat back and chuckled.

'Oh, and your contact in Istanbul is Samantha. She's arranged everything.'

That startled Sean. He threw his head back in shock. 'Fucking hell Jack. Thanks a bunch for that.'

Chapter 10

Kuwait

The British Airways Boeing 747 jumbo jet struggled with the fierce Persian Gulf crosswinds as it lurched and swayed before landing with a heavy thump at Kuwait International Airport. A recent sandstorm had left an orange fog swirling in the air and it was hard for the passengers to make out the old and decrepit terminal building as the pilot taxied the aging aircraft at speed to its docking station.

Walking down the steps from the upper deck business-class cabin was a man who had last set foot in Kuwait in 1991 in his role as a British Army bomb disposal operator during the repatriation of the country from its Iraqi Army invaders.

Wilson Hewitt had aged. Life on the run at the very edge of living had burnt him and he wore a face that most strangers would shy away from looking at. His pockmarked face, shaven hair and steely gaze projected a man who had seen and tasted depravity at its fullest. He smiled assuredly at the petite air stewardess whose eyes dodged his attention as he walked off the plane and onto the jet bridge. Had she looked closer, she'd have seen that his right ear was completely missing.

Hewitt grimaced as he descended the escalator that provided access to a grim and dingy-looking arrivals hall, knowing he would have to endure the pain of mucking about getting a short-term visa before he could venture into the country. He stepped left and opened the sliding door into a tiny yellow booth which had just enough space to hold three people. He stepped in and lit a cigarette. It was an odd place to have a smoke but a legitimate cubicle nonetheless. He was never enamoured by visiting the Middle East, knowing he didn't like the place, but this was business and his sufferance was generally high when the big dollars were paid. As he smoked, his mind wandered back to the man he had met in Trader Vic's at the Park Lane Hilton in London. A young Syrian man who suggested he needed to meet some people in Kuwait.

He had met the intermediary, who had provided the right credentials to get an audience with Hewitt. After a few checks and balances Hewitt had agreed to meet him to discuss what his people were after. The young man sat opposite Hewitt and so began a short and to the point conversation with him. 'These people are very wealthy and well connected across governments in the region and they need someone to operate for them who can do some real damage,' he had said. 'They pay very well and want you to travel to Kuwait.'

'How do they know about me?'

'Libya,' the young Syrian said. Hewitt carefully observed the young man's words and demeanour, looking for any oddity in his manner and eye movements. Hewitt sensed the lad was somewhat fearful of him. He observed that the Syrian was smartly dressed, had clearly been educated in London courtesy of wealthy parents, spoke excellent English and wore an expensive Rolex watch.

'I need three things first.' Hewitt looked around the cocktail bar, checking for any sign of a stitch-up. He was guarded in who he met, and how they connected with him. 'I need the provenance of who they spoke to about me – to verify they are legit and not fishing.'

'OK, I can tell you that now.'

'No. Write it down here with the location where they met,' Hewitt said, passing across a blank business card. 'I also need a new passport and pseudonym to travel with, and I need a large deposit in the bank before I agree to anything.' Hewitt sipped his water, took the card back and wrote the deposit sum on another card. 'When all that's in place I'll know they are competent and serious – then I'll consider it.'

Hewitt finished his cigarette in the airport terminal and glanced over to the visa desk where three women sat side by side, each clad in a light grey hijab, full-length garments and some sort of immigration badge on their shoulder. He finished his cigarette and walked over to them, slinging his small red rucksack over his shoulder.

A small queue of Western businessmen stood in the queue in front of him and, eventually, the middle woman of the three beckoned him forward. He handed his passport to her, watching her flick through the pile of pre-notified visa documents without any hint of emotion. Her neatly manicured nails and facial make-up belied her modesty, and Hewitt admired her pretty face. She looked up, checked his photo, stamped the visa, remaining po-faced, and waved Hewitt towards the exit.

Hewitt was pleased it had all been pain-free, having previously endured hours of waiting at some airports to get through immigration. He noticed how lax the security was at Kuwait airport as he walked through the exit gate into the baggage hall. He allowed himself a rare smile as he noticed a petite woman looking directly at him. She smiled at him and held up a small sign with the words *Mr Hewitt* on it.

'I'm Nadège. Very pleased to meet you,' she said. 'I shall be looking after you during your time in Kuwait, Mr Hewitt. How was your journey?'

'Good, thank you.' He looked discreetly at Nadège, who he sensed was either Lebanese or Egyptian. More likely Lebanese, he surmised, based on her immaculate make-up, expensive attire, lack of a hijab and the smell of expensive perfume. 'I wasn't expecting this,' he said.

'You mean a female, Mr Hewitt?' She turned on her feet and began to walk, looking back at Hewitt, smilingly with a deliberate allure. 'We do like to operate somewhat differently to your usual clients I suspect.'

'It makes a bloody change, I have to say. Where do we go from here then?'

Nadège stopped but didn't answer. 'Mr Hewitt, just so we know you are who you say you are, how are the conditions in Rockall?'

Hewitt took a moment to recall his meeting with the Syrian facilitator who had employed his services for this task. He had been told that, every step of the way, his employers would need to verify he was not a plant and that he was the real Hewitt. 'I'd say they're pretty much the same as those in Shannon to be fair.'

Nadège smiled and marched briskly towards the exit, weaving between the crushes of people in the busy terminal building. Hewitt took in the scene of a wide mix of people as he walked. Some women he passed were clad in black burqas, many businessmen wore the classic white *dishdāshah* and the manual workers were attired in grey full-length cotton *thawbs*. The mix of different women with differing attires was prominent and it seemed very different to that in Saudi Arabia, where he had worked many times. Here, the women wore elegant *abayas*, some with hijabs, some without, and the more cosmopolitan females wore Western clothes with stashes of expensive jewellery and classy handbags. This was a wealthy Muslim country, and all manner of different people gravitated to it because of its outwardly liberal Muslim culture.

Hewitt felt the searing heat hit his face as he exited the terminal before being quickly chaperoned into a large black Chevrolet with the door held open by a large minder. He sat at the rear of the vehicle, sandwiched between two men who smelt of sweat. Nadège took her seat upfront in the passenger seat.

Hewitt noticed another black vehicle slip in behind them from the terminal exit route. 'Mr Hewitt, please forgive me, but we now have a short drive to meet Mr Alimani, your client,' she said. 'He has received your correspondence and has acquired everything you asked for.'

Hewitt nodded, noticing her searing green eyes, well-groomed eyebrows and immaculate make-up with red lipstick that drew his attention, but he didn't reply.

'Mr Alimani will ensure you are well looked after during your time here, and I shall of course be pleased to assist.' A pause while she checked her phone. 'Of course, you'll understand very well that, as we approach his residence, my helpers next to you will need to blindfold you – operational security, or OPSEC as I believe you say.'

Hewitt nodded. He began to wonder about Nadège's very efficient intelligence services background. She had all the mannerisms of a competent Middle Eastern spy, and was no doubt very handy in bed and equally handy in unarmed combat. He mused about both during the journey.

He wondered who this next piece of highly paid work was for? Mossad? Possibly. ISIS? Unlikely. The Saudis? Very likely. Or was this a false-flag operation lined up by the Yanks, Brits or Russians? He would likely never know but was very guarded about each step of the journey to protect his own OPSEC.

Hewitt felt a grip on both arms as the minders blindfolded him for the remainder of the journey. They were rough enough to let him know who was in charge, but civil enough to let him know that these were professional grown-ups in the murky world of mercenary sales that he was dealing in.

As he was guided out of the vehicle, he heard the very familiar sound of a Sikorsky helicopter firing up its engines ready for take-off.

Chapter 11

Kuwaiti Desert

The Sikorsky helicopter was in the air for less than sixteen minutes according to Hewitt's estimate. He was blindfolded with a hood and goggles throughout the journey and the experience was beginning to piss him off. It brought back memories of his military days when he had experienced the traumas of escape and evasion training having been hooded for hours on end with no sense of spatial awareness. He felt a few twinges of sickness as the helicopter came into a wide arcing approach before touching down, rear wheels first.

Hewitt was confused. Had they flown north and over the border into Iraq? Or south and into the desert expanse of Saudi Arabia? Who were these people and what was their big plan? He felt confident that his preparations and due diligence had been sound before accepting the task – and the $300,000 down payment had persuaded him that selling his mercenary skills in this manner was a pretty decent business transaction. A flicker of doubt remained and would still do so until he saw the way these people operated in detail.

Hewitt was helped off the helicopter and guided to another vehicle, which whisked him away into the desert landscape. He had briefly felt the searing heat on his arms before he had been quickly shipped into the cool air-conditioned wagon. No one spoke, but he sensed the two minders again sitting either side of him and the stench of male sweat had become worse. Within five minutes the vehicle had come to a halt.

'This is it – we're here,' Nadège said. 'Sorry about all the inconvenience but I think you'll find your next few days here somewhat more comfortable. I shall ensure it is so.' She opened the passenger door, stepped out and leant inside the rear cabin to remove the goggles and hood from Hewitt's head. 'Welcome to a hot and dusty place,' she said, helping him out of the vehicle.

Hewitt shook his head a little and winced at the sunlight before dropping his head to escape the searing light.

'Here, put these on and come with me,' she said, handing him a pair of Salvatore Ferragamo sunglasses. 'You'll be ready for some food I expect.'

Hewitt didn't answer but stood for a while looking around the vast complex that he had arrived at. He noticed he was in a large private compound with distant mud walls that constituted the large perimeter of the grounds – about four metres high, he thought. Within its boundary were large expanses of flat desert with two or three large buildings and one hugely expensive villa that he stood and gazed at. The larger of the two minders, clad in a white shirt and expensive jeans, stepped in front of him, nodded and asked him to raise his arms. He gave Hewitt a thorough search before handing over his small rucksack, which had been rummaged. The minder, content with his search, stepped aside, nodded again and, with an outstretched arm, indicated for Hewitt to follow Nadège to the villa.

'Mr Alimani awaits you Mr Hewitt,' Nadège said, leading him into a large dining hall dominated by a palatial chandelier. The home was a palace of sorts, perhaps a seasonal one for his client. It was opulent and lavish nonetheless, causing Hewitt to feel a little more at ease. He found it odd that they would meet at such a personal place for his client, especially when he was buying death on a grand scale from Hewitt.

Hewitt was ushered to take a seat at a large sixteen-place Hampton table. His client had good taste in traditional English oak furniture and Hewitt was sure there was probably an element of respect for the British when he did his business. He wondered how many other British businessmen had sat at this table for more legitimate discussions than the nefarious ones he was about to have.

Hewitt studied the large oil paintings of Arabian horses and one grander frame depicting a desert scene of warriors on horseback armed with long-barrel weapons, a swathe of sand kicking up in their wake as they galloped past distant white Arabian tents. Clearly from good stock he mused, perhaps even royalty.

Mr Alimani walked in and Hewitt stood to greet him. 'Assalamu alaykum,' he said, clasping both hands. 'Welcome to one of my homes Mr Hewitt, I hope this will be a pleasant and welcome stay for you.'

'Alaykumu salām,' Hewitt replied, before sitting. 'Pleased to meet you.' He noticed the slow and deliberate movement of his client, surmising he was in his mid-sixties, but also that he had striking bone structure and was clearly a man of wealth. The most obvious feature for Hewitt though was the man's pot belly. He was dressed in a white black-buttoned *dishdāshah* with gold cufflinks, a plain white *keffiyeh* topped with a double circlet of twisted black cord and a large expensive watch on his left wrist. The outfit, coupled with his age, gave him an air of elegance and charm. He sat at the head of the table, with Hewitt immediately to his right.

'I'm afraid I'm only here for a short time before I depart to the Levant,' Alimani began. 'I have a wonderful second wife living there who does put some curious demands on me.'

'That's fine, I like travelling anyway. And I think you'll make it worth my while,' Hewitt replied.

'Indeed I shall Mr Hewitt, and I'm hoping your travels here will be as welcoming for you as they are for me.' Alimani turned towards Nadège, who was sat three seats away from Hewitt having assumed a position a comfortable distance from the two men, recognising her role in the triumvirate.

'Nadège will be looking after you for the entirety of our mutual business arrangement but I'm sure we can have some civil time together as we develop the plans,' he continued. 'I was once the Head of Military Intelligence in Kuwait and, suffice to say, my work still requires me to travel a lot these days.'

Two waiters began to pour water for each man and Nadège indicated to the female waitresses to bring them the starters.

'As a former head of intelligence, you'll understand that I still retain several enemies Mr Hewitt, perhaps somewhat similar to you.'

'Yep, I have too many,' Hewitt replied, picking up his knife and fork, following his client's lead.

'It's fair to say that, for both of us, our enemies have driven us in a particular direction along our many branches of life,' Alimani said. 'For me I've reflected deeply on the last forty to fifty years of global change and I have to say it's led me to some very clear conclusions.' He began to take small forkfuls of the tabouleh dish. Hewitt began to sense an element of Lebanese linkage in all he heard, smelt and observed.

'The world has changed beyond all comprehension and the West has been lulled into a civil war that we Muslims are fighting amongst ourselves. A war they neither understand nor know how to solve.'

Hewitt listened intently and became engrossed in the compelling narrative, wondering where this might lead. Was he trying to influence Hewitt's thinking? Was he trying to prime him that his motives provided an ethical means to an end – even if it meant death via Hewitt's bombs? Or was he being authentic in his motivations for employing a mercenary mass killer?

'Nadège, would you care to transfer the next sum of money please?'

Nadège opened her laptop and started to type.

'You see Mr Hewitt, the West seems to be under some misplaced illusion that this recreation of conservative Islam should be fought by appeasement and integration, which sadly will never work.'

Nadège indicated to the young female waitresses to clear the first course as they stood assiduously at the door.

Alimani continued. 'I do not wish to see evil prevail across our world Mr Hewitt and so I need your professional help to support my scheme. I have an enemy in the West that needs my attention. Something myself and my friends firmly believe in.'

'So, you have some specific targets you want me to deal with?' Hewitt asked.

'I do indeed. The West has been infiltrated by all manner of ill thinking which has skewed its logic of how to bring the damage it caused to an end – the end will be beyond my years Mr Hewitt, but our friends can help achieve the new dawn that is needed right now. And yes, it will require blood to be spilled. That is an unfortunate by-product, but a brutal strategy is needed I'm afraid.'

Hewitt was eager to learn more, but the luncheon was over all too quickly.

'Now Mr Hewitt, I must take my leave.' Alimani removed his *keffiyeh* to reveal a more informal code of dress. He wore a small *Gahfiah* on his head, a type of skull cap, and Hewitt noticed he still had a full head of grey hair. It made him look more Western and youthful – Hewitt took this to be a mark of respect in his presence.

'I think this job will challenge you to your limits and I hope you enjoy putting this mission together. I will leave you with Nadège, who has arranged everything you have requested of us. She has acquired all the items you listed - just let her know of anything else you need. I shall meet again with you one day soon.'

'Just one thing, sir,' said Hewitt politely. 'Who was it that referred you to me through my broker?'

'Shall we just say a good Russian friend who has been watching you for some time Mr Hewitt. Surveillance I think you might say.' He smiled and walked from the room.

Nadège was pleased that the first element of deception with Hewitt had worked well. He'd be none the wiser as to the true motive for building his bombs and killing the enemies of her country. She explained that she would show Hewitt his workplace and quarters before leaving tomorrow for a few days' business elsewhere. She knew she had to settle this task and cement some trust with Hewitt before taking on the next stages of her mission in Istanbul. She missed her lover and was excited at the prospect of being able to fall into her embrace once more.

Nadège showed Hewitt to a dwelling adjoining the main villa and they entered an underground bunker that was accessed by a flight of external steps to the main abode.

Nadège showed Hewitt his workshop. His bomb-making factory. She watched him walk into the bunker, surprised to see such a large expanse of space and the technical equipment around the room. Some of the heavy-set benches had industrial drills screwed into them, others had electrical cutting equipment and state-of-the-art milling equipment bolted to the floor. In the middle of the bunker workshop was a large square table with four chairs around it and a laptop connected to two seventeen-inch monitors. Nadège watched Hewitt walk around the room, looking pleased, before he stopped to look at the ceiling. The workshop had been designed with ceiling-mounted LED lights suspended by chain-links to provide daylight working conditions in Hewitt's new bomb-making laboratory.

'The list of items you requested is on the table Mr Hewitt,' Nadège explained. 'I believe we have acquired everything you asked for but do have a quick look if you want. Or you can check things a little later after I've shown you your accommodation?'

'It looks pretty good,' Hewitt said, meandering around the room, checking some of the tools laid out on the benches. 'I assume you've taken all the precautions I asked when you got this stuff for me?'

'Indeed. My team have very competent networks. They took extreme care to make sure it cannot be traced.'

'Good. In which case I'll come down later to check it all.'

Nadège led Hewitt up the stairs, handing him an access control card for the workshop. 'It's all alarmed, has full fire protection and only you and I have access to the room. The minders who will be around for your security do not.'

'You're right. I didn't expect this,' said Hewitt. 'Very different to most clients I work for.'

Nadège smiled and threw him a look, making sure he knew what the next stage of the day would entail. She loved setting the pace, laying a little bait and enticing her target with her full-throttled appeal, knowing full well that Hewitt would now be wondering which intelligence service she was working for.

The building consisted of two floors, with Hewitt's living quarters on the first floor, which in turn led to a bedroom via a spiral mezzanine staircase. It was plush. The decor and furniture were expensive Western brands. The lounge was dominated by a large semicircular leather suite laden with azure cushions to complement its dark beige colour. Nadège liked classy decor. There were modern pictures of European cities on the wall. They were vibrant, lively and clean, exuding a sense of bravura and urban magnificence.

'Drink?' Nadège asked, standing with a glass in her hand at the well-stocked bar adjacent to the open-plan kitchen.

'Of course. I assume you'll be having one too?'

'A large one. It's time to relax a little. We have a busy time ahead of us you know.'

Nadège started mixing a couple of whisky sour cocktails, glancing at her inner arm as she mixed them in large oval bowls. The scars were not visible, but she could still feel them there. She had been eight years of age when she first cut herself. It felt like a morbid and forbidden desire, but she found it released her inner pain. There was a lot of blood and, despite that, she cut herself again and again. Her father, a Lebanese Embassy official, was always away on business. It was her mother who was left to cope with Nadège's incessant troublemaking and histrionics. Her mother would often lock her in her bedroom in their luxurious house located in the affluent Banlieue of Neuilly-sur-Seine in Paris and that was when Nadège's mind left her. She never really felt empathy, but nor did she feel pain. She simply washed her wounds, wrapped them in cellophane and wore long cardigans for weeks on end. Her obsession with blades never left her, nor did her fascination for her father's job. All she ever remembered was him telling her that she had Iranian blood and that his masters were the ones who would decide how history would be written - and that one day she might be able to shape that history.

Nadège dropped a few ice cubes into the drinks and ran a finger across her scars. Her mind flickered to how she would one day kill this man in front of her and then commit mass murder on an extraordinary scale.

'So why has Mr Alimani gone to all this trouble to recruit me when there are plenty of others out there?' Hewitt inquired.

'He really can't take any chances,' she said. 'He doesn't want amateurs and you are just one part of a much bigger plan.'

'A state-sponsored plan you mean.'

'Perhaps. Now. About the special devices. I need to go to Istanbul to meet someone who will take me to buy the material you need.'

'Same Russian friends who found me then?'

'Mr Alimani has many friends, and they're all very well connected to the weapon-smuggling markets. It's all been arranged.'

'Well, he'll need to be a very well-known and competent weapons runner to get the stuff we need. Probably with contacts in the Russian mafia. It's been a long time since I worked with fissile material but I'm looking forward to it. I need access to a scientist though. I can't operate on this without an expert.'

'I'll be back within ten days,' Nadège said confidently. 'With everything you need.'

'Tell me. Why are you involved in all this? I'm curious.'

'Ah, but Mr Hewitt, you know the rules here,' she said as she walked over to the sofa where Hewitt was now sat. She stood in front of him and placed the drinks on a glass table. Her white blouse was open enough to reveal her ample cleavage and she leant down, knowing Hewitt was not of a mind to ignore it.

'Wilson. You don't mind if I call you that, do you?'

'I somehow knew you would,' he replied.

'You know full well that in our world we don't ask such questions. We are doers and we have things to fulfil.'

She stood and adjusted her pose to show off her figure, then placed her left arm enticingly on her waist. Hewitt looked admiringly at her body before slowly adjusting his gaze to her face. Standing there in her cage of supremacy, Nadège felt a surge of pleasure. She knew that one day she would have to kill this man and that gave her ripples of the sensation she craved. The feelings that had made her alive and kept her alive. She needed to feed her inner torment, most often with sex, but ultimately with the knowledge she would kill again.

'I see,' Hewitt replied.

'You do Mr Hewitt.'

With that, Nadège slipped off her blouse and undid her red bra to reveal a tantalising body that she knew Hewitt would not resist.

'Time for some doing,' she said, dropping her skirt to the floor.

Chapter 12

Istanbul

The gentle murmur of the Honda outboard motor was all Sean could hear as he was slowly propelled towards the port of Haydarpaşa, which nestled on the southern approaches to the Bosphorus strait in Istanbul.

The approach to the port was unusually calm as Sean looked across to the mesmerising splendour of the Bosphorus Bridge, with the reams of night-time traffic gliding across its magnificent spans. He pulled up his hood and adjusted his rucksack, knowing he had another five minutes or so before he would arrive at the disembarkation point, where he could begin his covert insertion into the dockyard. He was the only passenger on the Rigid Raider craft, sitting just behind a highly skilled CIA coxswain who navigated the inlet by feel and stealth to ensure he could deposit his charge into the highly secure area of the port with little fuss.

Sean marvelled at the late-night dining cruisers, whose customers were being treated to one of the world's most superb maritime views whilst being lavished with expensive champagne and Michelin-star cuisine.

The historic port is a central gem of Istanbul and reads like a quick trip through the ages of an Asia Minor adventure. The Phoenicians had their day, as did the Byzantine and later the Roman emperors, followed by crusaders and sultans. The port, Istanbul's largest, moves materials that have been traded for centuries, including cotton, olives and fruit, but also trades electronics, chemicals and automobiles. Sean knew that Istanbul and its trading locations were also a central bazaar for the world's heaviest trade in illicit materials, from drugs to weapons, furs to jewels and explosives to special nuclear materials. Illegal trade across Asia Minor had many such bargaining markets, where buyers and sellers would come.

Sean felt the spray of the sea slap against his face in the shallow breeze. His mind drifted back to the last planning meeting he had with Jack the night before the CIA flew him directly into Istanbul's Samandıra Army Air Base.

Jack had arranged a final video conference direct with The Court's operating base in Besiktas, one of the oldest districts of Istanbul on the European side of the city.

Jack had invited a number of other operators into the conference room for the highly secretive video call, and the conference room had become the centre stage for the detailed planning of Sean's mission. Had Sean known what the Iranians were planning, he might have asked a few more questions before being inserted into the furore of Istanbul and the kaleidoscope of mayhem that was shortly to begin.

'Hi Samantha, can you hear us?' Jack had said as the screen tried to focus in on Samantha's head and shoulders. The video picture was fuzzy as the satellite picture kept zooming in and out, struggling with the bandwidth. Sean leant forward, somewhat eager to see a woman he had not cast his eyes on for nearly three years. He remained tense. Intrigued. And he wondered what emotions Samantha might release after all these years. He watched the streaming images settle and nearly gasped with surprise at how Samantha had changed. She had dyed her hair from brunette and was now a strawberry blonde. Those piercing green eyes shot out of the screen as if to touch Sean right on the chin. They were great friends, but Sean had always felt hunted by her. Chased. Her quarry. He wondered how it would work out being on the ground with her on an active operation after all these years had gone by. The last time they had worked together was as surveillance officers in Northern Ireland, but both had come a long way since then, and there were many skeletons in each of their cupboards. One thing generally remained the same though. She liked to be the boss.

'Hi Jack. And, well, hello Sean,' Samantha said, making a clear effort to accentuate Sean's name. She paused, smiling widely to reveal her glistening white teeth neatly circled by plentiful red lipstick. She'd changed. The once make-up-free complexion with hair scrappily gathered together in a bun had gone. In her surveillance days she wouldn't get a second glance, she had blended in. She looked more like a schoolteacher, or an artist or even a rural vet - no one would have guessed her true profession. On this occasion she had manicured herself meticulously for this moment to rekindle her long-lost friendship with Sean. It was the moment when she would sear her image right into the centre of Sean's psyche. There was something about her though. Sassy and forthright with a charisma that mesmerised. Sean remained fixed on her eyes, knowing her next line.

'I hope you've been behaving whilst I've been away Sean.' Sean cringed, watching the glint in her eye, which drew a wry smile from him. He sensed the laughter being held within the assembled staff, a type of heat that drew a twinkle of redness to his cheeks.

Jack eased the tension. 'So glad you're still on good form Samantha,' he began. 'It's important to keep our spirits up as we knuckle down for what could be a pretty bumpy ride ahead for all of us. Now, could you keep this brief and give us the bare bones of what you've found out.'

'Of course,' she said, now adopting a fully professional posture. 'This is hot off the press from my signals intelligence teams. The SIGINT we have collected has revealed a lot of interesting activity across Turkey, and we're beginning to see similar activity across the region. We're data mining the signals intelligence we've collected through our US systems, and our analytics will soon provide us with some clues. The main assessment is that the Iranian cell we've latched onto have now initiated their smuggling routes to move equipment and stores transnationally. We'll need to track and trace the mules who are moving this stuff across the region and probably into Europe.'

Sean leapt in, eager to get to the nub of the intelligence. 'Any idea what they're moving?'

'Not yet, no. They've certainly given the order to mobilise their logistics chain and I'll brief you when you arrive tomorrow. I have one more snippet though. Our SIGINT has led us to a single location here in Turkey that needs to be looked at. Probably your first task.'

'How did you get this?'

'By observing telemetry signals.'

'Have you seen it anywhere else?'

'Not yet, we're checking.'

Sean looked at Jack for his views, but he didn't flinch. Samantha carried on with her briefing. 'It looks like they have factories where they're making different parts for IEDs and some of the telemetry suggests that these are not just normal improvised devices - they seem incredibly high-tech. The first target to be searched is the port at Haydarpaşa.'

Sean felt the boat reduce its speed to a niggling crawl. The expanse of a huge container ship was the only thing between him and the dockside and he glanced at its bridge wings to check no one was watching the vessel approach the quayside. The craft glided below the ship's anchor chains, the coxswain skilfully manoeuvring the tiny boat until it sneaked alongside the bow of the vessel. Hugging the vessel's skin, the coxswain deftly steered the craft to make sure it was well out of sight of anyone who might be perambulating the dockside above. He coaxed the Rigid Raider slowly to the rusting pivots of an old ladder that Sean would use to covertly enter the docks.

Sean latched onto the sides of the ladder and started to scale the twenty-foot piece of rust to top out on the flat quayside. He stopped just below the top and waited - listening for a good two or three minutes. A huge forklift truck scuttled past the distant warehouses, its pneumatic arm fully propelled in front of the cab and smoke spluttering into the air from a thin chimney at its rear. Sean scanned the distant warehouses in front of him, spotting the small alleyway he needed to enter that provided access to his target.

The target building was the office of a company called Nadim Zuka - a specialist freight-forwarding company for transits between the EU and Asia. Sean's homework suggested it was a family-run business masquerading as a legitimate business whilst concealing the nefarious activity of state-sponsored terrorism. It was a major hub for Iranian operations across the EU and Middle East. Istanbul was, after all, perfectly located for access to the EU via the porous Balkans borders, which provided easy entry into Bulgaria and Romania and smuggling routes through Kosovo and Albania. Eastwards, it afforded immediate access to Iran and the wilds of the Caucasus, plus the deserts of Iraq and Kuwait.

Sean waited until the designated time to break cover before he would move swiftly across the open expanse of the dockyard roads, across a single-track railway, under two container cranes and directly into the Nadim Zuka offices hidden in the alley just off the main concourse of the dock.

He sat patiently hiding behind a large sea container, biding his time and waiting for the lights to go out. An act that would be initiated from the quiet Suffolk backwaters of RAF Bentwaters by cyber-specialists who would take down the entire infrastructure of the port.

Chapter 13

Istanbul Port

The headquarters of Haydarpaşa Port Authority sit within the fenced esplanade of Istanbul harbour and offers superb views across the bay to the European side of the city and a magnificent view of its famous neighbour, the recently refurbished Haydarpaşa train station terminal located right next to the port.

A fifty-ton ship's anchor acts as the gatekeeper to the headquarters where multiple stories of brown-tinted windows look out across the Bosphorus strait where everything from royal yachts to cruise liners pass through the busy sea lanes of Istanbul.

Below the reception, in the basement, is the port's command and control centre, its security control room manned by security supervisors with a large bank of CCTV screens and a small data centre acting as the port's IT hub.

At exactly 0115, the most silent period in the port's operation, a startled security manager watched all of the office's computers and CCTV camera screens go blank and then reappear with messages in blue and black lettering. His primary screen read '*repairing root file system*,' with a warning not to turn off the computer. The other bank of screens were showing large text. '*We have encrypted your files and back-ups. Click this link to pay 7 bitcoins to retrieve your files.*' Equivalent to £22,000.

The entire site had gone dark. The dock's critical infrastructure had been infiltrated by The Court's hackers sitting at their dimly lit consoles somewhere in the quiet Suffolk countryside. Sean's phone began to vibrate; sure enough, right on time. Samantha texted him on TextSecure and the phone came alive with a green screen showing three dots flickering to indicate that she was writing.

'Worm is in. Lights are out. Time to penetrate. Do it well.'

Sean smirked at her incessant innuendo, stuffed the phone in his inside jacket pocket, pulled his high-visibility vest on and began walking briskly across the dockyard to the alley. He imagined the freaked-out faces of the security officers in the control centre, who would now be making urgent calls to their IT people. He thought of them being awoken and forced to attend the site, where they would be bamboozled by what they saw on the screens.

The Court's hackers had inserted a Trojan worm deep into the servers of the port's data centre, which propagated quickly to laterally burn any server that they wanted it to – from IP phones, to CCTV, to lights operated by computers and even to the cranes and automatic barriers. Across the concourse and down the alley, in a quadrant of the docks well away from the main gate and security control centre, Sean surreptitiously entered his target premises. It was an ornate red-brick building that had previously been used as an historical archive but now adjoined a modern spacious warehouse facility. The magnetic locking mechanism of the main entrance had been disabled by the hackers and Sean simply opened the door and walked in. No one would know of his insertion so long as the IT systems remained cooked and the CCTV dark.

He walked past the semicircular reception desk, jumped over the key-card gates and made his way to the main offices on the first floor. He navigated by memory, having studied the building plans earlier that day, and started searching for the communications hub of the warehouse. It was a server room where a rack of pizza-box-sized computers were connected by a tangle of wires, all neatly marked with handwritten labels. On a normal day the servers would push out routine freight manifests, shipping timetables, client pricings and consignment data. Sean wanted access to all the data on the stand-alone servers and any digital traffic that moved through them, as well as to locate any network bridges to the data they held offsite in The Cloud.

The maglocks that normally provided the locking mechanism to the room were now released but a steel console required a code to release a deadlock that provided additional security for the doorset. Luckily it was a cheap push-button lock that Sean knew how to defeat. He took off his rucksack and pulled out a lock-and-pick set, hoping he wouldn't need it if he could figure out the four-figure code first. He dusted the push-button with a thin coat of talcum powder and, with very little effort, could see the numbers that had been punched the most from latent fingerprints. He tapped the code, feeling a sense of relief when he turned the satin-chrome door-handle and the lock released.

Inside the room, he heard the gentle whir of air-conditioning units that kept the server racks cool. He'd been asked to enable remote entry into the servers if they were not connected to the Internet. The hackers could conduct brute-force attacks on any Internet-connected devices and servers, but devices that were stand-alone required another means of covert entry into the systems by way of a radio transceiver that would provide the signals needed for a carefully modified drone to hover above the port and hack into the servers.

Sean looked at the back of the servers for the telephone jack fittings that would provide cabled access to the Internet. All but two servers were connected to it. Both of these could well be connected locally to a building network and would provide hardened security for the terrorist cell if they were operating here. Sean crouched next to the two servers, opened a small side pocket on his rucksack and grabbed a blue Tupperware box stuffed with small radio-frequency transmitters. He plugged two of these into the Ethernet sockets of the servers, closed the mesh door and grabbed his phone. He sent a codeword back to Samantha indicating that the receivers were in place and could now be exploited by Billy Phish, his cyber-sleuth, using a small drone. Sean smiled at the chance of catching up with Billy Phish, who was now ensconced in Samantha's operations room on the other side of the Bosphorus.

Once the drone was in place, Billy Phish would enable a digital bridge back to The Court's operators in the UK, who would be able to dump records, logs and data from the servers to analyse terabytes of information, looking for any useful intelligence on the Iranian operation.

The port's IT employees were now on-site and yelling to their colleagues to turn off computers or disconnect them from the port's network before the malicious software could infect every office and every business on the site, as well as its power, cooling and operations systems. They needed to deal with this before the port woke for its business of the day at 0500. It dawned on them that every minute lost would mean dozens or hundreds more corrupted PCs, which had now been paralysed by the still-mysterious malware.

Sean headed downstairs to the workshops that intelligence had suggested formed the core area of operation for the warehouse. He knew he had to act fast, but he also needed to search precisely to gather as much intelligence as he could in the short time he had on-site. His most important task was to find any bomb-making equipment or to verify the complex was being used by an Iranian terrorist cell, which would give him some skin in the game.

He walked down the stairs and turned left into the warehouse, sweating a little by now. The small warehouse had a number of wooden crates stacked across the open space, with a few corridors to walk in-between them. There were boxes of all sizes, some cardboard, some wrapped in cellophane and some on pallets stacked ready for shipment with cargo netting strapped tightly around them. To the left-hand side were two large offices that looked like post rooms. The lights were on in both of them. He approached the first door, carrying a clipboard under his arm. He tried the door-handle. Locked. He couldn't see through the door's glazing because of the frosted privacy glass. The high-level windows were also frosted and too high to peer through. He decided to check the other room, hoping its door might be open. By turning his head, the headtorch provided him with the light he needed to grasp the handle but, just as he reached for it, he heard a loud shout from behind. *'Durda! Durda! Ellerini Durdur.'*

'Fuck,' he murmured, taking a moment to process the language. Should he turn? Or play stupid and put his hands up? He didn't recognise the language, so he couldn't talk his way out of this one. Security guard, he hoped. He froze rigid and put his hands up, turning slowly to face his aggressor.

'OK, OK,' he said, turning slowly. 'No need to be alarmed.'

It wasn't what he wanted. He looked straight into the eyes of a bearded man with a handgun, who was pointing it right at his chest.

'Mate, I'm doing some checks,' Sean said, waving his clipboard in the air, blagging it to buy the seconds he needed. 'Don't you know there's been a massive cyber-attack on the whole port?'

The man, broad-shouldered with a slightly bent nose, scowled angrily. He smelt bad. His eyes were flickering as he tried to process what he was hearing and seeing. His answer was immediate. 'Fuck off with the bullshit and keep your hands where I can see them.'

Sean noticed that the man had his trouser zip undone and looked like a gruesome wrestler. 'Go and have a look at your computers – you'll see for yourself. We've been the victim of a massive cyber-attack and absolutely nothing is working. It's in meltdown. I'm an IT engineer checking the network nodes.'

The man looked perplexed, his brow furrowed. 'Turn around, white man, open the door and keep your hands in the air.'

Sean paused, then turned slightly, wondering if the scam might have put a seed of doubt in the man's mind. He rejected that thought immediately. Like a cornered snake, he tensed his muscles, bent his knees and, with all the force he could muster, swung his arm back and launched his clipboard like a frisbee straight at the man's head.

The clipboard hit the man square on the chin, allowing Sean the milliseconds he needed. He launched himself into the man's torso but got wacked by his elbow in a vicious blow to Sean's jaw. Unperturbed, Sean grabbed the man's wrist, bending it with such force that his pistol dropped neatly to the floor. Sean ripped the man's left arm behind his back, grabbing it so hard that he was thrown by the momentum to the floor, where he wrenched the man's arm so violently that it dislocated from its socket. The man was screaming in agony and his body went limp. Sean wrenched the arm again to cull any form of retaliation, knowing he now had to kill the man. Breathing wildly, Sean wrapped his forearm around the man's neck, tightened his grip and ripped it backwards with such ferocity that no one could survive such trauma.

He heard the crack of a broken neck and lay there trying to catch his breath.

Chapter 14

Istanbul Port

Sean didn't lie still for too long. He had a job to complete. He rose to his feet, shaking off his aggressor's clasped hand and rolling the heavy corpse off his chest. Sean's pulse was racing, and his throat was now as dry as a bone. He reached for his rucksack, grabbed his water bottle and swallowed half a litre of water before squatting down to think through his next moves. His jaw throbbed as he checked the bone for any serious injury.

His aim was to get as much intelligence from this building as he could. The levels of forensic collection he retrieved from this location would be the launch pad he needed to tackle Nadège and to find out the degrees of sophistication the Iranians had weaved into their planning. Sean gazed around the room and started to control his breathing. Tonight was the only chance he would get and, whilst he now had a body to get rid of, he was not going to pass up the chance and abort the mission. The mission was simple. Get in, verify the site was being used by the Iranians, grab what intelligence he could, get out. Then move on to Nadège.

He momentarily thought of D providing some sort of award for this mission if he got it right, but then again, he remembered he'd never get any such rewards. His life as a legitimate officer of the Crown had long gone. He was now a rogue agent easily deniable by HM Government and no one would give a hoot if he was killed on this operation. A mosquito buzzing at his ear brought him back to his senses as he realised he was expendable here. Why run the risk of multiple casualties during a normal covert search when a deniable operation and a deniable person could easily be waved away by the British intelligence services? A win-win for Jack and

MI5 if it produced the goods, and zero loss if Sean was captured or killed.

Sean swiped the air a few times to get rid of the mosquito and focused. Where could he dispose of the body? How could he clean up the site? He stood above the corpse, knowing he had to act fast. Dump the body first? Or collect the intelligence he needed? It wasn't long before he was dragging on the cigarette he had vowed not to light. He decided he needed to start the search first and deal with the corpse later.

Sean retrieved some of the technical materials he needed for the search from his rucksack. He placed an explosive trace-detector kit on the ground - the type used to identify whether a room had any occupants who were handling explosives by swabbing obvious surfaces that they would touch. Finally, he carefully extracted a machine that would be used to analyse the trace-detection swabs and provide an indication on the three-inch LCD screen of any chemicals present on the swabs. The equipment was a forensic spectrometer and would determine the types of chemical substances he might find at extremely low trace levels. It had been miniaturised for single-person operation and was normally the size of a desktop computer.

Sean glanced at the body, still wondering how to dispose of it quietly and without it being found for some time. The port basin was the obvious answer but how the hell would he lug a sixteen-stone body across the concourse and roads? He felt beads of sweat drip onto his cheek, wiped his brow and took another swig of water to try and stave off the headache he knew was coming. He spotted a red forklift truck and had a thought.

Sean walked around the large warehouse, looking for a suitable crate or box. One big enough to hold the man's body with additional space for a solid quantity of scaffolding poles which he had spied on the racking. Within minutes he was putting a makeshift coffin together before dragging the dead weight towards the crate, which was placed next to the forklift truck. Sean adjusted his headtorch and sat the body up. He knew the man's face would be etched in his memory if he looked at it once more, so he didn't. He was going to slam this episode shut in a drawer in his mind that he would never ever open again. Just like how he coped with all of life's ordeals. He knelt down, braced his back and then, with both arms under the man's armpits, he grabbed him in a bear hug. Sean groaned, banged out a few short sharp breaths and then forced the man's chest against the crate – a further couple of heaves saw gravity take its course as the body tumbled into the crate. Fifteen minutes later the crate was filled with ballast, the lid nailed down securely and the red truck manoeuvred into place with its forks perched ready to go under the crate. The short drive to the quayside would hopefully not draw too much attention with the port's staff still diverted by the cyber-meltdown.

With a sense of real danger now, Sean knuckled down and got on with the job in hand by heading straight into the unlocked workshop. He needed to act more quickly. He began swabbing the desktops of the laboratory that was open, remembering to swab the door-handle first. Then he went to the keyboards – it was obvious that people handling explosives might touch them. The room had waist-high workbenches around two of its sides, with racking bolted onto the walls that held a variety of boxes and equipment. In the centre of the room were two desks standing opposite each other with a computer on each of them.

Sean placed his spectrometer on the high workbench adjacent to the frosted window, switched on the machine and waited for it to boot up. The workshop was a mechanised freight and sorting room where each workbench had machine wrappers, desktop drills and a variety of packaging on them.

Sean gently inserted the first swab into the receptacle of the spectrometer which would provide forensic data on the traces of particles from the surfaces he had swabbed. The machine took a few seconds to analyse the swab and then blinked for a few seconds before squirting out its analysis onto a red digital screen. He looked at the reading, letting out a long sigh. He blinked a few times, trying to focus on the small text, but he was certain. Certain that what he saw first were the four large letters PETN. The abbreviation for pentaerythritol tetranitrate – an organic compound used in high-grade military explosives. Traces of explosive content had been left on the metallic surfaces and the door-handle. Squinting, he checked the next letters on the LCD screen. He made out the letters TNT, which comprised a smaller percentage of the trace compound. He didn't know it at the time, but this mixture of PETN and TNT provided the compound pentolite, a powerful explosive used in rockets that could penetrate five inches of armour plating.

Sean stood back, knowing he had got a result. The facility was being used by state-sponsored terrorists with the legitimate frontage of a commercial company. He'd already placed transmitters on all the IT servers and surreptitious key-loggers on every computer downstairs, as well as photographing key documents that might be of intelligence use. But if he found any bomb-making equipment it would verify what he thought about this place. That it was being used as a hub to store bomb-making equipment before it was smuggled into Europe or the Middle East and then assembled to strike against the terrorists' final targets. Sean worked through the permutations of how such a bomb-making cell might work. They could build the core parts of a bomb, such as the power supply and timer unit, elsewhere. Perhaps even build the complex electronics in another country before shipping them to where a team could construct the final device before it was deployed at a critical infrastructure target. Sean knew that most of the smuggling routes into Europe traversed the Balkan states of Bulgaria, Macedonia, Bosnia and Croatia and onwards through Hungary into the heart of Western Europe. He suspected that this warehouse played a part in a complex logistics chain that would be using routes where officials had been bribed at border crossings, customs posts and freight stations. The drivers, couriers, money mules and hired labour would all be operating together as a highly organised gang, with the Iranian MOIS officers managing every aspect of the operation.

Sean sat on the leather swivel chair in the centre of the room and began to spin it clockwise. Slowly. He looked around the room, scanning areas he might have missed. What had he overlooked? He hadn't found any bomb-making equipment, hadn't found any explosives and the trace levels of explosive compounds were low. Just as those thoughts crossed his mind he noticed something underneath a table in the corner of the workshop. For some odd reason there was a carpet under the table. Under the table. Why? He reminded himself of his covert-search training all those years ago. Look for the absence of the normal, and the presence of the abnormal.

'Bloody hell Sean,' he mouthed dramatically. 'Get a grip. It's right in front of your eyes. The presence of the abnormal. A fucking carpet under a table.' He sprang to his feet, rushed across the room, heart beating with anticipation, and tugged at the carpet. It took him a few heaves to pull the five-foot carpet away but below it was a large grey lid – about two-foot square with a recessed handle in the middle.

Could it be booby-trapped? No, surely not. His thought process suggested it would be unlikely but, nonetheless, he needed to be cautious. He felt around the rim for any obvious wires or booby-trap triggers. Nothing. Then he had the thought it might be on a pull switch. But where was the means to disarm it if he was the custodian of the void? His threat assessment, made within a few seconds, told him it would be fine. He pulled on the lug and placed the lid to his right-hand side. Grappling for his pen torch he peered inside the void, spotting a number of small cardboard boxes. A dozen or so. He pulled one out and stopped to think. He needed to make sure the occupants didn't know that he'd found this small cache and tampered with the contents. Then he'd need to maintain constant surveillance on the warehouse, its staff and the table with the carpet under it. This he knew could be achieved by hacking into the CCTV cameras that operated within the workshop.

He looked carefully to see how the cardboard box was sealed and took a photograph of it before taking a few shots of the void and its cache of contents. The box was sealed with heavy-duty Sellotape. He looked at the others in the void. Most were sealed but the one furthest from his reach wasn't. He memorised exactly how they were arranged and reached into the void to lift that box out. It had interlocking triangle-shaped wings. Next, he gently pulled the flaps apart, surprised to see a myriad of electronic circuits and batteries. He wasn't sure what it all meant and knew he'd need Phil Calhoun, his explosives expert, to have a look at the photos later to verify it was indeed bomb-making equipment. He photographed inside the box without touching anything, capturing the images of carefully welded circuit boards, two cigarette-packet-sized boxes with a number of leads coming from them and what looked like a couple of small black aerials that were not connected to anything. He was no expert, but everything he saw told him that this was some kind of telemetry manufactured to high precision and likely to be used to initiate IEDs. IEDs that would kill and maim.

Sean was done. He had collected a stash of intelligence on the target-site exploitation but started to feel his headache getting worse, probably from the elbow he had taken in the face earlier. He grabbed his water bottle and downed another half-litre in one go before wiping his forehead with his jacket cuff. He wanted to know more about this Iranian operation and how it was linked to Nadège and her role in it. He knew The Court's cyber-team would begin exploiting and analysing the servers' data and he had a team that might just be able to help put this puzzle together – and hopefully put a damned big nail into what appeared to be a high-grade bomb-making operation.

For now though, he had to extract himself on the forklift truck, dumping a body en route.

Chapter 15

Istanbul

Midday sun. Searing heat. And a pounding headache. Sean walked slowly up the incline of the long driveway that led to a villa that Samantha had managed to acquire from the CIA as the team's operating base in the city. Sean was wearing blue shorts and a white T-shirt, wraparound sunglasses and a black baseball hat and clutching his red rucksack, which was full of goodies from the insertion the night before. He felt sluggish and drowsy, not having slept at all well, and his headache had simply got worse.

He stopped halfway up the incline and turned to admire the views of the city from the neatly manicured grounds of the holiday mansion. He spied the grand domes and elegant minarets of the Suleiman Mosque in the far distance and a flotilla of sea-going vessels in the busy shipping lanes transporting all manner of produce and tourists around the inlets of the Istanbul archipelago. The magnificent views of the Bosphorus Bridge provided the perfect backdrop for some of the world's most expensive seafront hotels a short distance down the road. Parked just outside the gate was a Turkish telecoms van with a dog cocking its leg to take a leak on the rear wheel, its elderly owner tugging on the lead.

Sean walked towards the villa entrance, catching the sensation of water droplets on his face, which were being hurled from garden sprinklers around the immaculate lawns. As he approached the entrance he was pleasantly surprised to see Samantha waiting for him under an ornate porch. She was leaning against a white pillar with her arms folded and a look on her face that appeared to be an impatient grimace. She looked to the entire world to be a disgruntled housewife about to lambast a late and drunk husband.

Sean rubbed his chin, hoping he wouldn't get another blow to it, and smirked. Here we go, he said to himself, head down and trying hard not to laugh, which seemed to produce more pain in the jaw, suggesting it might be fractured.

'Late on bloody parade yet again Mr Richardson' was the first quip from Samantha. Probably the first of many to come, he thought. He couldn't help but love her feisty and impish character. At least she has some charisma, he thought.

Sean kept his head down until he was just in front of her, stopped and took his hat off, doffing it to offer an olive branch. He had evaded her for so long now. 'Good morning Sergeant Major. How's the troops?' he inquired sarcastically, knowing full well that Samantha liked to keep a house in good order with no irksome behaviour.

Samantha threw him a look, then stepped forward and gave him a big hug. It seemed to last an age.

'The troops are inside waiting for you, wanting to know when they will eat and when they'll get paid,' she said, floating an appealing expression. 'You look good by the way. Oh, and it's been too long.'

It had indeed been too long. Sean had managed to keep Samantha at bay for a long time, much to her annoyance. She was indeed persistent. Sean always gave her that. A dalliance or two over the last ten years had seen them remain great friends, lovers on many occasions, but Sean was always happy to keep the relationship at arm's length. Nice and casual. But Samantha was not happy with that. Sean noticed she had taken some time and effort to make herself look good. Classy make-up, outlandish curls in her dyed blonde hair and deep red lipstick, which Sean always liked. He put his arms around her and gave her a firm hug. He felt her breathe across his right ear and the puckered kiss on his cheek. The smell of her favourite Penhaligon's perfume lingered hard. Sprayed just before he'd arrived. He knew it.

'So, let me show you around. It's just what we need and a great base for us.'

Sean watched her turn, momentarily admired her short green dress and began to wonder how this was going to pan out over the next few weeks or months together. Samantha was a specialist. An expert cryptographer and signals intelligence officer who Sean had met when she started her career in the Intelligence Corps in Northern Ireland. She had come a long way since those heady days of the '90s. Speaking five languages, including fluent Russian, she could also turn her hand to managing the logistics of any major intelligence operation with boots on the ground. She liked to be in charge too.

Sean looked around the bright and airy courtyard. He loved the feel of the open-plan villa, which had a small water feature in the centre of a huge courtyard illuminated from the atrium glazing above. He spotted a mezzanine balcony before being ushered by Samantha into a dining room that had a huge captain's table as its centrepiece. The walls were pleasantly adorned with paintings of historic ships navigating the Bosphorus channel and his eyes alighted on expensive silver goblets and urns that took centre stage on an adjacent oak sideboard.

Jugsy was the first to greet him. 'Oi, big man. You haven't paid me yet, what's going on?' he barked sarcastically with a beaming smile, arms outstretched.

Sean laughed, casting his rucksack aside on a nearby chair before throwing out his hand and gripping Jugsy's firmly. 'It's all in wads in my rucksack, you impatient bugger. How's it going?'

'Oh you know, bills to pay, not enough fun and working for idiots like you lot. Other than that, it's all good my friend.' Jugsy was his normal gregarious self, saying it how it was, coming across as a grump, but behind that mask Sean could see in his eyes there was an excited man – excited about being back amongst the team and hoping it would be another adrenalin-filled job.

'Did you bring your toys Jugsy?'

'Of course. Two unmanned air vehicles and a hand-launched one too, plus some new imagery-analysis software. High-resolution stuff and with a great target-tracking capability too. I've already tested them this morning so we're good to go whenever you give me the nod.'

'Great, where's Billy Phish?'

'He's having an old man's half hour,' Samantha chipped in. 'I'll go and get him. Briefing in thirty?'

'Yes,' Sean said, opening his rucksack. 'A quick initial briefing, nothing too much, you guys all know the drills. I'll set up the maps.'

Sean spent a few minutes taking his documents and maps from his rucksack, placing them on the table along with the small file on Nadège. He had his old team back together. His mates. Plus Samantha to keep them all on the straight and narrow.

Jugsy was a former Royal Marine and an expert in imagery analysis, and Billy Phish was his go-to man for anything to do with canine detection and somewhat bizarrely, cyber-hacking. Sean could never get his head around how Billy Phish had become a cyber-sleuth and part-time digital forensics analyst with the FBI, yet his talent and passion were for dogs. Training dogs to detect anything from dead bodies to explosives, weapons and even bedbugs in hotel rooms. Quite a lucrative trade, he had once told Sean.

'What's the target then?' Jugsy asked, impatient as ever.

'Iranians,' Sean answered, checking through his photos of the cache from the night before.

'Weren't you knocking off an Iranian bird all those years ago? I remember you going dark for months on end when you were with her. Got you in deep shit as I remember.'

Jugsy was never one to be diplomatic and always went for the jugular. It was part of the reason for his nickname, that and his huge ears. Jugsy was one of Sean's best mates, and knew everything about him. Sean had known Jugsy for about eighteen years. Hawkeye, as he was also known, was a leading expert in imagery analysis, most often conducting highly secret terrorist surveillance from helicopters and using drones.

'You know it got me in the shit big time,' Sean replied, pointing to the file on Nadège. 'Have a little look inside that file for a wee shock. She's our target.'

'Fucking hell mate. You never ever do things by halves do you? Jeez.' Sean chuckled, slapping Jugsy on the back. Sean thought Jugsy was looking thinner in the face but noticed he was still in good shape. Jugsy was now smack on fifty years of age, with a full shock of grey hair, a noticeably radiant red face and a prominent nose. His lean, strong figure gave some indication of a fit man who had formerly achieved military excellence with the Special Boat Service, but his active social life always took a toll on his facial features. He was the best in the world though at what he did with imagery intelligence.

Ten minutes later, Billy Phish made an entrance. He walked in wearing shorts and a vest with an unlit pipe in his mouth. He said nothing but simply threw Sean a groan and a V-sign before shaking his hand limply. He was clearly still dozy and not in much of a mood for small chat. Billy Phish waved at Jugsy and sat down to light his pipe. Jugsy laughed and started the teasing. 'The grumpy old bugger's just been woken up, so you'll get nowt out of him for at least an hour mate!'

Sean chuckled, watching Samantha place a cup of coffee in front of Billy Phish on a small round table. She tapped the spoon on the table, indicating for him to start drinking his coffee. Billy Phish groaned again and lifted his pipe to show appreciation for her help. He slurped noisily as everyone sat waiting for him to stir.

'Right, let's get on with it you lot,' Samantha barked. 'I'll give you the background then Sean will add the detailed tasks going forward. I can see that getting a grip of you lot will be necessary all the time. So be prepared for that. Now grab some coffee and listen in.'

Jugsy rolled his eyes at Sean and sat next to Billy Phish. Samantha pointed where Sean should sit then gave a short briefing, displaying some photos and maps from her laptop. Sean enjoyed watching her when she briefed staff, admiring the pace of her oratory and her expert precision. He was impressed by her charisma and style and took a few moments to study her face. A face that could melt a man's soul when she talked, whilst she made occasional gestures with her manicured hands. Her nails were not too long, painted bright red, and she used her long fingers to delicately tap the keyboard that brought up the slides.

Samantha explained the assassinations in London, accentuating the savagery of Iranian terrorists and their possible linkage to the Russians too. She covered the Iranian Intelligence Services, the MOIS and gave the background to their active-measures campaigns across the globe. Then she moved onto the US's position which, for the Brits, was stoking too many Iranian fires.

She explained that the US President's new economic sanctions were designed to seriously harm the Iranian regime, and so MOIS assassins were ready to strike, with hundreds of worldwide agents and terrorist proxies under their wing. Most of whom had already entered their target countries under the guise of immigrants, students, journalists, lecturers or construction workers, ready now to strike anywhere across the globe.

Samantha paused for coffee and took a few questions before outlining the intelligence requirements for this operation: to identify the smuggling routes, any weapons caches that might be used and for Sean to connect with one of their top agents, Nadège. That line in particular drew a few murmurs from Jugsy and Billy Phish.

'We've been monitoring signals traffic in Turkey and across Iraq and Kuwait,' she continued, flicking a map of the region onto the LCD screen. 'We've had some really unusual SIGINT signatures emanating from the deserts of Kuwait, with replica signals here in Istanbul. There's much more we need to analyse but Sean managed to retrieve some vital intelligence from his exploits last night.'

'You mean he's been with Nadège already,' Jugsy chipped in, smirking. Samantha threw him an admonishing look before continuing.

'He was busy penetrating, I'll give you that,' she said cheekily, knowing how to hold court with these men. 'Entry into a warehouse with the front of being a freight-forwarding company. All yours Sean.'

'OK. So we now have something to work on. The warehouse is being used as a factory to make precision parts for IEDs, it's effectively a bomb-making factory but without assembly of the components. They'll be moving those parts and assembling the IEDs elsewhere. At the moment our intelligence suggests into Europe, so we need to find their routing and their methods of moving the kit. This is where your drones come in Jugsy.'

'Full surveillance on the warehouse then?' Jugsy asked.

'Exactly right. The cyber-team back at Bentwaters have taken control of the CCTV coverage inside and around the port, but I need you to carry out airborne surveillance on the warehouse and hack into their stand-alone IT servers with Billy Phish. He'll need your drones to get him close enough to the RF transmitters I fitted last night.'

Billy Phish raised his hand. 'Have we got a payload on the drone to receive the signals?'

'Exactly right Billy. There are also a few RF keyloggers in place for you to exploit. Do you think you can get into the data?'

Billy nodded. 'Are they networked?' he asked. 'Linked to the Internet too?'

'I think it's a mixture. Possibly a local-area LAN within the warehouse which you can look at while the team back at Bentwaters analyse the Internet-based traffic. I'm looking for anything that leads us to where they're transporting the telemetry that they're manufacturing inside the warehouse. Their MO is to build the technology in different places, then bring them all together to assemble the circuitry and explosives in a single location. Probably in the target country.'

Sean leant over the captain's table and passed a small covert camera to Jugsy. It was about the size of a bottle top. 'I've hidden these in their workshop, so we can see who's coming and going. I swabbed the place and the findings were positive for explosives.' He pointed to the mini mass spectrometer.

'What's your thinking then?' Jugsy asked.

'Well, it's a long shot, but I think this lot may be moving the parts to a site that also has the explosives. But that's where you come in Jugsy. Have a look at the covert-camera imagery, get some photo IDs of the bravos and follow them with your drones to wherever they're moving the stuff.'

'Type of explosive?'

'Pentolite.'

'Big stuff then. Moving into Europe or the Middle East?'

'Possibly being moved through the Balkans and into Europe, so that gives you a good steer to the north-west of Istanbul.'

'OK. I'll get onto that with Billy. I assume you've fitted routers to the cameras with an IP we can tap into from their Internet?'

'All done. Yes.'

'OK. I'll land the mini drone on the roof of the warehouse and use that as a repeater station. We can get close enough using our vehicle to cover the transmissions for a short distance. I don't want the big drones in the air for too long until we have something to follow.'

Sean paused and stood up to stretch. Each of the team stayed silent, knowing that when he stretched there was invariably a 'but' coming. It came. 'But the insertion last night didn't go totally to plan, and whilst I don't think I was compromised, we'll need to be mindful of that. Make sure our OPSEC is spot on and, Jugsy, start monitoring the cameras as soon as possible just to see if their activity is normalised or heightened after last night. One of their operators may have gone missing in action.'

'Shit,' Samantha said. 'May have? What the fuck happened?'

'Don't worry, it was taken care of. All you need to know is that they are missing one bloke, he won't turn up for work, will be presumed missing, but we have enough time on our hands to conduct the surveillance activities and get a few leads to follow.'

'Anything else you're not telling us? What about this bird Nadège?' Billy Phish asked, puffing on his pipe furiously now.

Sean explained the mission he had been given by Jack but omitted the part about getting her to turn, which would make it plain to them all how barking mad a mission it actually was.

'We think Nadège is leading this operation,' Samantha chipped in, looking to take control of this phase of the operation. 'She's due back into Istanbul tonight.'

'Do we know where she'll be yet?' Sean inquired.

'We do and it's all set for you and I to watch her tonight. Jack's source has told us which hotel suite she's staying in – she uses the same suite every time she visits Istanbul but it's regularly swept for bugs by her minder. I've got a CIA fixer making sure we have a room next door. And some tech kit to see what she gets up to.'

Chapter 16

Istanbul

S ean sat opposite the hotel, waiting to catch his first glimpse of Nadège in well over ten years. He watched her arrive in a silver Mercedes, which pulled up just in front of the large marble façade of the Çırağan Palace Kempinski Hotel.

The Çırağan Palace had formerly been an Ottoman palace located on the European shore of the Bosphorus in Istanbul and is famed for having one of the world's fifteen most expensive hotel suites. A beautiful marble bridge connects the palace to the Yıldız Palace on the hill behind, with the grounds protected from the outer world by a very high garden wall.

'NIGHTOWL at the entrance now,' Sean texted to Samantha, who was sat in the room next door to Nadège's studio suite on the second floor, which overlooked the magnificent palace gardens. NIGHTOWL, Nadège's codename, was to be used for all operational correspondence between the teams on the ground and for the technical staff back at The Court's HQ at RAF Bentwaters.

Because her minders had swept her suite, Sean couldn't fit listening devices and pinhole cameras directly into NIGHTOWL'S room so they had to make do with new technology in the room next door. Sean suspected that the first few hours of NIGHTOWL being in Istanbul would yield crucial intelligence from her meetings and telephone calls. These were the vital hours for his initial surveillance on the woman he somehow had to turn and convince to become a British intelligence agent. Yet everything in Sean's body told him she was loyal to her country. Or was she? What was her Achilles heel, he wondered?

'NIGHTOWL in situ,' came the reply on Sean's phone, giving him the signal to make his way to the room where they would

conduct the surveillance. He had verified that it was Nadège who had arrived at the hotel and would now check the covert CCTV imagery to make sure it was her who had entered the suite and not someone else. There could be no mistakes from this point onwards.

Sean walked past the long reception and made his way calmly to the lift lobby, which was crammed with an elderly American party waiting for the elevators to arrive. He checked his phone as he waited, noticing a text from Melissa back home.

'Can you call me tonight around 10pm – I'm beginning to find some useful information on Fletcher Barrington.'

The dodgy CIA officer, he thought, as the lift doors opened. He had wondered for some days about this man and the link to the missing FCO diplomat, Edmund Duff, but had been too busy focusing on this operation to delve into any detail on the kidnapping. He suspected something wasn't quite right about the ex-CIA station chief who Duff had been dining with in St James's, but didn't know how all this would link together. Had he known at the time he'd have probed Jack much deeper on the connection between these incidents.

Sean exited the lift on the second floor. He was dressed in a light grey suit with white shirt and red tie, making sure he was suitably dressed to follow Nadège wherever she went in the Palace Hotel. The Palace boasted a number of high-class restaurants, multiple cocktail bars and a casino, where he enjoyed the ambience of operating surreptitiously in one of the finest hotels in the world. He turned right and walked past a small table laden with a bulbous flower pot and a bunch of sunflowers in a separate jug. He glanced at one of the central sunflowers to check that his concealed covert camera was indeed concealed. Anyone entering the floor would be captured on this camera and viewed on his laptop in the surveillance room. He placed his room card on the suite console, watched the entry light go green and quietly entered the room. He closed the door, bolting it shut.

'She doesn't appear to have any minders with her,' Sean said, throwing the key card on the bed.

'Good. Now let me listen. No more interruptions please.'

Sean watched Samantha move her stethoscope probe on the wall in a circular motion – trying no doubt to get a better signal to listen into any activity in Nadège's room. Samantha had a set of small headphones on her head and was sitting in a chair with her back to the bed, moving her probe gently in small movements with her left hand.

In front of her was a long dressing table that normally had the television on it. This had been removed and replaced by three laptops. The first was used to capture any sounds and speech from Samantha's highly sensitive microphone. The second laptop was displaying imagery from the covert camera placed in the centre of the sunflower. It gave an excellent picture of anyone exiting or entering the lifts. And the third laptop had a very strange image on it consisting of what looked like a stickman in yellow, blue and red colours.

Sean sat down in front of the third laptop to monitor the movements of Nadège in the room next door. The screen showed a dark grey background with the stickman moving around, replicating the movements of the human body on the other side of the wall. It wasn't a picture. Rather it was a series of small circles and blobs, with the head showing as red, the arms blue and the torso and legs yellow. Astonishing stuff, he thought. The wires on the back of the laptop led to a series of ten or so probes that were nailed into the plasterboard. Just like acupuncture needles in the skin of a body.

The equipment had been designed by scientists to use artificial intelligence to teach a wireless device to detect a person's precise actions and gestures, even when they were behind cover. The signals received by the needles were able to analyse radio signals a thousand times less powerful than home Wi-Fi that were bounced off the bodies inside to create animated stick figures that walked, sat and moved their limbs on the screen in sync with the targets. A different way to see through walls.

'How's it work?' Sean asked pointing at the blobs on the screen that were replicating Nadège's movements as she walked around the room.

'A bit like aircraft radar. But instead of bouncing off planes and returning to the ground, the signal travels through the wall, bounces off her body, which of course is full of water, and comes back through the wall and into our detectors.'

'British tech?'

'No. American. The artificial intelligence associates the labelled body parts with subtle radio reflections coming back through the wall. This ends up with a human visualised as blobs, which correspond to points on the body such as her knees and shoulders. The AI then turns this into a stick figure that shows Nadège moving in great detail. Such great detail, in fact, that the system can identify individuals eighty-three percent of the time by first determining their unique features and movement style.'

'Nice tech. What's she doing now then?'

'She's heading for the shower by the looks of it,' Samantha said, placing her headphones on the desk. 'Can't hear fuck all but hey, you can see your ex naked soon as a stick woman.'

'She's not my ex Sam. Never was. Just a bit of a stupid fling.'

'Same as me then, eh?' Samantha teased, looking Sean right in the eye. 'Is that how you see us all, just a fling?'

Sean decided not to answer that and stood up. He walked to the large double-glazed windows with a balcony beyond overlooking the city. 'Who exactly is this source that's close to Nadège then? Jack's source? Any idea?'

'Don't change the subject. You always do that. You know, we might just find a little time together later tonight when she's asleep.'

Sean turned and smiled at her, rubbing his chin with his hand again. The pain had subsided, helped by the ibuprofen he had been taking for the last day. 'You know I have a girlfriend now.'

'Or is she just a fling?' Samantha proffered, putting her hands through her hair. 'You know I'm still pissed off she beat me to it, but I'll bide my time as you know.'

They stayed silent for a while. The kind of silence ex-lovers have when weighing up their situation in close proximity to each other.

Sean broke first, eager to get on with the job in hand. 'Come on, tell me about this source that Jack has. I need to get as much info as I can on Nadège before we plan how to engage with her.

I'll be dropping right back into her life as a gunrunner some ten years on and this doesn't help.'

'You mean BOLLINGER?' Samantha asked. 'That's the codename Jack gives me whenever he refers to the source that's close to Nadège. He has never said who it is at all. But whoever it is has been accurate so far with her movements and timings. But there's no detail being provided from that source on the operations she's planning.'

'Exactly the same as the GRU defector, Sergei. When I chatted with him at length, he too knew nothing of her operations, yet he was her GRU handler. She's a double agent you know.'

'So why doesn't he know what she's doing then?'

'Well the Russians keep their top agents highly protected. Sergei was only ever instructed to provide her with whatever she needed, and that included setting her up with people she needed to conduct the operations. I'm the latest one he's teed up. As a weapons smuggler.'

'So, is that what you were doing when you were banged up in Kabul? In that stinking jail? You never told me the full story.'

'Not exactly. But yes, I was involved with some dodgy people running weapons and drugs from Afghanistan across central Asia and into Europe. Nasty bastards too.'

Sean shivered a little, remembering the misery of his incarceration in the Kabul jail. He sat down and kept a cautious eye on the CCTV. The hidden camera he had placed in the plant had a small infra-red sensor that operated a small buzzing alarm if anyone triggered it when leaving or entering the lift. Nothing so far. 'OK. What about if she leaves her room and gets on the move? Are we sorted?'

'Tracking device on her Mercedes, and a CIA team prepped and ready to go outside the hotel. It's covered and I'll run the comms from here. You'll follow her wherever she goes in a car poised ready to go. Quite a cute-looking Yank driver actually.'

The CCTV alarm buzzed. Sean concentrated on the screen to see who it was. A blonde. A medium-height attractive woman wearing a cream two-piece suit and heels. It was only a fleeting glimpse on the camera but enough to see who was coming and going on this exclusive floor of only four VIP suites.

'Not bad-looking,' Samantha said, putting her headphones on. 'This could be fun,' she said, raising her hand signalling for quiet. Sean glanced at the stickman screen and watched the slow gait of yellow, blue and red making its way into the main lounge. They were on.

Sean tapped Samantha on the shoulder and pointed to the second set of headphones, which he quickly put on. They listened intently, watching the screen. A few moments passed before they witnessed the stickwomen hugging. Samantha glanced at Sean with a huge beaming smile on her face. She put her fingers to her lips and winked.

Sean watched both women walk towards him to where the bed was located on the other side of the wall. The stickwoman on the right made movements with her arms, suggesting she was taking her jacket off.

'I've missed you lots,' were the first words he heard. Then came the muffled sounds of lips touching and a gentle groan from one of the women. Not sure who. Finally, he watched both stickwomen move onto the bed and into a horizontal position, each set of blue arms entwined and the yellow legs enmeshed in a strange holding pattern on the bed. The arm movements were clear to see as the second woman, Nadège, made more movements, taking off whatever clothes she had on.

'Bloody hell, this is great,' Samantha whispered. 'Never expected this but I like it. A lot.'

'Sean took his headphones off and stood up, fascinated by the artificial intelligence technology that was providing them both with a show of digital voyeurism.

Chapter 17

London

Jack sat in the back of the security-service Jaguar and passed the Director General of MI5 a note outlining the situation report from Sean in Turkey. The A4 piece of paper was topped and tailed with the security classification and caveat: TOP SECRET / STRAP 3 / C-OPS / D Eyes Only. The C stood for Court operations and whilst it had a standard style of classification, C-OPS would not draw undue attention if the note got into the wrong hands.

D read the note whilst intermittently looking out of the privacy window, remaining silent. He asked no questions of Jack and kept his own counsel before handing the note back to Jack and remaining silent. Jack knew he would have memorised its contents and would use it as ammunition in the meeting he was due to attend at the Cabinet Office in fifteen minutes time. D peered out of the window again, clasping his hands tightly - Jack knew he was in the zone of complex thought.

This was going to be a very tense meeting for D, who was accountable to the government for all elements of intelligence relating to national security and the defence of the UK's shores. The meeting was to be held in the Cabinet Office briefing rooms in Whitehall with the United States National Security Advisor. The President's closest confidant on all matters relating to overseas and homeland security.

The newly appointed John Redman was also a hawk. And a neocon. A man with a very close personal relationship with the President which ensured his influence stretched easily to matters of foreign policy, particularly with Iran and Russia. Jack had done his homework knowing that Redman wanted Iran to be dealt with robustly and Russia kept fully in check with the President relying upon his personal advice on how to achieve that. For Jack, Redman's recent appointment as the National Security Advisor meant that the President's foreign policy team was now the most radically aggressive to surround an American president in modern memory.

Redman arrived twenty minutes late, giving Jack a chance to add some additional verbal briefing points to D. Jack knew all eyes would be on D today and most of the questions posed would be aimed at him.

Redman would be addressing the UK's Joint Intelligence Committee, a Cabinet Office body responsible for intelligence assessment and the coordination and oversight of MI6, MI5, GCHQ and Defence Intelligence. Each of the heads of those services was present, along with their senior staff officers, who sat in chairs just behind their principals on the main table. Also present was the chief of the London station of the United States Central Intelligence Agency, an able female of fifty-two summers by the name of Laura Creswell.

Jack had always liked her can-do, will-do attitude and made an effort to smile and acknowledge her as he walked behind D to take his seat directly behind him. The CIA chief of the London station had been attending the JIC's weekly meetings since the end of the Second World War and Laura considered it a huge privilege. As Laura recently put it to Jack: it was the highlight of her career as the London CIA chief. Jack admired that and had ensured he struck up a solid relationship with Laura as she bedded into her new post.

Jack glanced over to see the chair of the committee stand behind his seat, inviting the National Security Advisor to sit to his right. The chair, Hugo Campey, was a member of the UK senior civil service, and rumour had it he wanted to take over as the Director General of MI5 whenever D retired – or as a few close hands knew, died. Previous incumbents had gone on to lead MI6 but never had anyone from outside the ranks of MI5 taken the reigns as Director General. Hugo saw it as his destiny to break that mould, especially as he was a firm favourite of the Prime Minister, having served under her when she was Home Secretary.

After welcoming their most prominent guest for many years, Campey invited Redman to address the quorum. Jack perched forward in anticipation of what was to come, primarily to make sure his own predictions on the politics being played out were right.

'Ladies and gentlemen,' he began. 'Thank you so much for the personal briefings you sent to my team and of course your wonderful welcome in the few days I have been here. It is indeed an honour to address you all today as we face a difficult time ahead together.'

Jack watched Redman lean forward, elbows on the table, hands clasped. He was a strong orator and always right on point. Redman was known to be a fierce statesman, whose deep-set eyes and trademark grey beard gave him a steely aura. Jack sensed this would be some speech, one to get the British intelligence community on his side for what lay ahead.

'I'm here today to add some gravitas to the situation we all face and to call on your help. I know you are all doing a tremendous job and I suspect much of our work will remain firmly in the five-eyes community of intelligence...' A long pause. '...but predominantly this will be a two-eyes community effort...' Another pause. '...my country and yours. The UK and US intelligence communities operating together to cull the evil in our midst.'

Redman was now getting into the swing of his speech, and he cleared his throat before continuing. 'We must work hard. And we must work together on every single snippet of information we get about the Iranians. We need every available avenue opened, and very quickly too. They will strike us hard unless we get to the very crux of their inner operations, so your intelligence is vital to us all.'

Redman's voice was gravelly and unmistakable to those who had seen him speak strongly against Iranian aggression on TV over the last few months. Redman was enunciating every word and every syllable, but Jack felt it was partially contrived to get the troublesome Brits onside.

One of Redman's staff officers tapped a few buttons on the audio-visual console and a map of Iran appeared on the large screen at the end of the table - with a picture at the side of the map showing the mullahs who ran the country.

'I want us all to be clear why we are here and why this has come about,' Redman continued, standing now. 'Ladies and gentlemen, there is a basic rule in Iran's politics and in Iran's Supreme Leader's philosophy: *concessions mean weakness*. They see us as weak. If you show your weakness, they will take advantage of that or, as the Persian proverb goes, they will milk you to the end. We, the US, gave too many concessions, which allowed them to keep milking the cow. Iran's blatant aggression and provocative attitude over the last year reached unprecedented levels, ranging from launching ballistic missiles in the middle of the day, to supporting Syria's Bashar al-Assad, both militarily and financially, and galvanising the Shiite proxies to engage in war. This, ladies and gentlemen, was why we killed off the Iranian nuclear deal that has now led them to begin waging asymmetric war on both our nations.'

Jack noticed the murmurs of agreement around the room and, importantly, those who disagreed.

'So, you see, we have been caught with a dilemma,' the US statesman continued. 'We can prolong the milking of their cow, and the continual state-sponsored terrorism threat they have developed, or we can confront it and deal with it now.'

The mood in the room was sombre. Exactly as Redman wanted it, Jack surmised. He knew full well that not everyone around the table agreed with the US National Security Advisor and his President's approach to dealing with the Iranian threat. Indeed, most hadn't wanted to see the nuclear deal culled at all and preferred a longer-term plan to reduce the Iranian threats. As a result of the US President's sanctions against the country it now looked like the Iranians were intent on deadly revenge.

It was the Director of GCHQ who interjected first. Barbara Wainright, a woman immaculately dressed in white blouse and jacket with purple hair, and never one to be overawed by an occasion. 'I agree with your sentiments on milking the cow, Mr Redman. The chain of events easily leads to Khamenei, the second-longest ruling leader in the modern Middle East, mastering the game of negotiation and brinkmanship. A shrewd man.' She paused and looked around the room to check she was being listened to. 'Our signals intelligence helped capture their strategy so that we could help your staff and rationalise the situation. We are very proud of collecting that intelligence, which is unique.'

Redman nodded throughout her pitch, Jack thinking that she was showboating a bit early in the meeting. Cringeworthy even. Jack watched Redman stroke his beard and continue in his West Coast accent. He was firm and strident throughout. 'You're absolutely right,' he said, sitting back and opening his posture. 'You guys in GCHQ have been magnificent as ever. Your intelligence helped us understand the games they have been playing. Threatening to pull out of the negotiations if certain conditions were not met. Continuing to flaunt all the red lines we had about missile testing, still pursuing a goal of enriched uranium, and our former President sadly gave them more milk. Khamenei and the IRGC leaders wanted to milk the cow more. I believe there can be no more appeasement policies or bowing to the ruling clerics of Iran and giving them any more. Enough is enough.'

Redman turned towards the chair and thanked him for the opportunity to address the British intelligence agencies. In return, Campey suggested a short briefing from each agency on what had been done so far.

The discussions sparked the Cabinet Secretary to add the national security position. Sir Justin Darbyshire was also the British National Security Advisor and a favourite of Jack's. An old hand with a sharp sense of humour.

'Following on from the recent threat assessments, ministers and I have now stood up specialist military assets for counter-surveillance at all of our ports, critical national infrastructure sites, our core gas and power sites, plus our airports. This includes drone intrusion of course.' There was a ripple of laughter at this line following the debacle of 2018 when a small drone had brought Gatwick airport to a complete standstill for days. Jack smiled. Sir Justin had yet again made his mark on the most sombre of meetings and made sure he followed through with aplomb.

'So far, we've contained the media position so that the country is not overwhelmed by the threats we now know we face. It's proportionate and balanced at the moment whilst we await any further developments. And do be assured those developments are well underway with the best of our best intelligence assets.'

Jack knew immediately what was coming next. Sir Justin was skilled at manipulating such meetings to make sure he showcased MI5, their importance to national security and, of course, the investment they needed from central government. He was posturing that government needed to ensure MI5 were properly resourced in the coming decade to deal with the asymmetric and hybrid threats coming to Europe, the UK and the world. He had teed up the Director General of MI5 perfectly. Campey, the chair, looked less than impressed.

D remained calm as ever and simply posited that it was a huge joint intelligence effort at home and overseas, nodding politely to his secret intelligence service partner and close friend sitting quietly at the end of the table. The chief of MI6, C, rarely spoke unless asked to do so.

'Our intelligence tells us they will strike against us ladies and gentlemen,' D began. 'It's as much consequence management as proactive defence I'm afraid. Our friends at the Civil Contingency Secretariat have their work cut out as my friend the Cabinet Secretary has stated. Contingency planning for major national terrorist-related incidents and cyber-attacks is our most pressing need.'

Jack was impressed by how D had changed the position, putting the pressure squarely back on the Cabinet Office and the Civil Contingency Secretariat. Jack was a little worried about D's health though. He was coughing a lot and was always out of breath when walking – especially up a gentle incline, where he really suffered. Jack had helped him earlier that morning when he had a dizzy spell exiting his office and knew this was all symptomatic of a heart condition. Jack also knew something that D did not know. That contingency plans were being put in place just in case D did leave the world early, with the Cabinet Secretary leading those secretive talks. Unbeknown to the Cabinet Secretary, D had confided in Jack on a number of matters relating to the perpetuity of The Court's operation and some of the smaller aspects of his funeral. D knew himself that he wasn't long for this world and had insisted that all his own plans remained under lock and key in his safe. Not to be opened until his death. Jack was to be the custodian not just of his legacy with The Court's operations, but also his departure from the world he had left a huge mark on.

'What about these so-called Iranian sleeper agents? Are we sure they are active?' Redman asked D.

The woman from GCHQ chipped in before D could answer. 'We can't be fully certain, but we have picked up a considerable amount of traffic and chatter that we think is consistent with such an action. Seems they had a particular modus operandi for putting them into academia and local government, allowing them to sleep but collect intelligence through surveillance and cyber-espionage, spying on our critical sites with relative ease.'

'Absolutely right,' D chipped in. 'Similar to the Russian SVR agents, their role is to stay silent but collect vital planning intelligence in the lead-up to a major bout of attack activity. Jointly, we all feel they are in that stage of planning right now – not imminent attacks, but right in the deadly heart of planning them. We desperately need solid intelligence to mount interdiction operations against them.'

'What about the Russians?' Redman asked nonchalantly.

D took a long pause and Jack saw he was struggling for breath. He composed himself like any solid professional and took a sip of water. 'We know they are happy to use the Iranians as proxies to carry out terrorist actions but the one thing they are very careful about is being attributable for any activity, movement of arms or direct support that implicates them easily.'

Jack looked on acutely aware of how the Russians were playing a shrewd game under Putin's master hand. He had been incredibly successful in influence-and-disinformation operations across the EU and US, so much so that Putin's divide-and-conquer methodology was now seeing political affiliations implode and extreme ideologies take over. D went on to explain that, by using the Iranians, the Russians could tactically guide them on how best to defeat the West in hybrid warfare without providing direct weaponry. The Russians were coaching the Iranians to hold the US to ransom in a number of ways, including infiltrating their political system to undermine the hawks and neocons. For years,

US hawks had argued that the only effective way to deal with the Iranian nuclear issue was with bombs.

Jack wondered if the path they had created was now the one likely to bring World War Three – in a number of forms. His worry was that what might start as devastating cyber-attacks would escalate via trivial incidents, perhaps in the straits of Hormuz, and that such an escalation might lead to terrorist incidents that would then lead to direct war on Iran, Hezbollah and all their terrorist proxy groups across the Middle East.

Jack's mind drifted back to yesterday's conversation with D. He had told Jack how everyone was miscalculating the basics of political warfare. Jack had listened intently to D's astute analysis of the situation.

'You see Jack, the US intelligence agencies were moving well towards infiltrating Iranian life with the aim of weakening the ruling cleric government from within. Creating the conditions to eventually topple the mullahs. Now they are trying to push too many offensive fronts in one go. All because the neocons want to show the US public that their hard-line President gets results quickly. Iran is destabilised, no doubting that, the riots and marches last year have shown that. But to move so quickly to a new offensive front, kill the nuclear deal and start sanctions again isn't going to work – our US friends have miscalculated again. The time isn't right. It might not have been for another year. But now we have a marauding state hell-bent on destruction through revenge. It's bonkers. And we're left to try and sort it out.'

Jack admired the wisdom of D and his words were left ringing in his head that night after their casual exchanges.

'Be under no illusion Jack, the Iranians will hold us to ransom in some way, and it won't be a pretty ending unless you, The Court and Sean get some bloody quick results.'

The committee meeting ran its normal course after Redman had left, except that the chair asked the MI5 representatives to remain behind. The two of them were summoned to the front of the table next to the chair. Looking stern, and taking his spectacles off, Campey looked directly at D.

'What I'm about to say is off the record you understand,' he said, waiting to see the reaction on the faces of what was, to all intents and purposes, just two MI5 staff in front of him. 'Ministers have decided we will not play to the tune of the Americans in a way that escalates the chaos they have caused.'

'You mean ministers or yourself?' D said matter-of-factly.

Hugo Campey adopted a fierce look and decided not to answer the pointed question. Instead, he chose to recite the cock-ups of the Iraqi dodgy dossier, which had led to the blame being left firmly at the door of the JIC.

'I will not allow that to happen on my watch,' Campey continued. 'I don't want you holding back on any intelligence that comes your way. I'm the senior government-level assessor and for this operation I want early sight of everything you have. No shrouding, no question of we can't be sure and certainly no operations that I haven't given prior approval of. Cabinet is clear. We will decide very carefully what we share with the Americans and it will all come through me before I put it to committee and then ministers.'

Jack could see this was about control. Hugo Campey wanted full control of the intelligence being given to ministers and the Americans.

D remained unphased despite the volley of orders coming from the chair of the Joint Intelligence Committee. D stood up as if to say 'thanks for the lecture, but no thanks.' He knew full well that Campey knew the protocols of intelligence sharing. And that the bullets he was firing were more about being seen to be in control by the PM and the Cabinet Secretary, exactly the people who would decide his next promotion.

'I shall make sure my teams share very widely with you through the joint intelligence organisation as normal Hugo. But I'd advise you not to push too much. I hold all the cards here you know.'

'Or you may not,' Campey retorted. 'Either way, it can easily be the end of you if you fail on this operation. The spotlight of the nation is on you to solve this. And I can protect you from the dogs - or I can sink you.'

'Good day to you Hugo,' D said, steering Jack out of the door with a hand on his back. 'Keep up the splendid work as ever.'

As Jack accompanied D towards the exit they bumped into Sir Justin Darbyshire, who was buttoning up his coat close to the door and obviously waiting to hear what the chair had said to them. He was, after all, the Cabinet Secretary and National Security Advisor and, by default, was responsible for the civil-service aspects of MI5.

'Well?' Sir Justin asked D.

'Much ado about nothing Justin. Easily seen off.'

Sir Justin and D walked through the doors and out into the brisk afternoon chill of a marvellous autumn day.

Sir Justin stopped at the steps leading down to the street and turned towards D. 'What's next do you think? Any idea?'

'It will be a war on a number of fronts,' D responded, placing his trilby on his head. 'The political game is already kicking off and we'll need to watch that. Operationally, Jack has plenty in hand for us to work with. Quite soon I hope. In the meantime, watch carefully what happens amongst the neocons and Redman. I fear he wants intelligence to set Iran ablaze and steer a course for their next war. The telltale signs are there to be read. But that's why we're here. To steer and coach them to avoid uncontrolled mayhem.'

Jack walked down the steps, reflecting on the word 'uncontrolled', and held the door to the Jaguar open as D and Sir Justin finished their conversation.

Jack looked back in horror as D's legs buckled on the steps, causing him to land on one knee, holding his chest and breathing in short sharp rasping sounds. He ran up the steps towards D, watching his hat fall to the ground just as he tried to put his hands on the steps to stop himself from falling further.

But D collapsed suddenly, fell unconscious and died within minutes from a massive heart attack.

Chapter 18

Istanbul

'How long will it take to get a camera tracking the vehicle?' Sean asked, watching Jugsy build the launch pad for his unmanned air vehicle. 'Time is ticking, and they've been on the road for nearly ten minutes already.'

'When have I ever let you down before mate?' came the gruff retort. 'She'll be airborne in less than five minutes - just admire the scenery for fuck's sake and grab me the small black box with the letters 'LP' on it. You'll have eyes on the target vehicle soon if you shut up.'

Sean grabbed the box and watched Jugsy slot the ten-foot catapult launcher together in seconds. Neatly packed into a man-pack, the catapult was simple to construct and only needed a thirty-metre patch of land to launch the military-grade unmanned air vehicle into the air. Jugsy used a small chrome ratchet to wind the industrial-sized elastic band into position, placed a pivot into a slot to hold it taut and, with some ease, placed his C-Astral UAV onto the launcher.

The UAV had a V-shaped wingspan of two metres, was constructed from incredibly light advanced-composite Kevlar, produced zero radar signature and had been adapted to carry a suite of high-grade spy sensors on-board. The command and control consoles were neatly packed into a Mercedes Sprinter van exhibiting nothing more than a small tracking antenna protruding from its roof. The van was branded as a Turkish telecoms vehicle and contained a bank of five twenty-inch screens, allowing Jugsy to control the UAV up to 150 kilometres away from its target site. On-board the drone were two electro-optical lenses, one operating at high resolution for zooming closely into the target activity, and a separate gimbal providing telemetry to capture night-time imagery using infrared and radar sensors. The high-resolution pictures would be transmitted digitally, enabling Jugsy to capture and replay moving TV and still imagery for him to conduct detailed target analysis. Also on-board the UAV was a small box of signals-intelligence equipment. A payload inserted into the hub of the nose cone allowed the team to monitor communication transmissions, with the data being analysed by SIGINT operators at RAF Bentwaters.

The day had started with Billy Phish raising the alarm as he watched his bank of screens come alive with CCTV imagery showing four men entering the target warehouse at 8.25am. The covert cameras that Sean had placed had now started to beam images out of the warehouse via the small drone sat on the roof, with one camera picking up the shape of a small man entering the bomb-making workshop. He began to pull on the carpet that concealed the cache of IED componentry before stubbing out a cigarette in the ashtray on the table. The covert cameras picked up his facial features perfectly, allowing Billy Phish to transmit the picture back to Bentwaters for facial-recognition analysis. The man had moved the table, bent down to lift the lid and then started to bring the twelve small boxes out of the cache.

Within two hours the boxes had been placed in a wooden crate and loaded onto the back of a van outside the warehouse.

Sean now had a target vehicle to follow from the port warehouse. A blue Volkswagen Sharan. As Jugsy finalised his launch routine, which took under five minutes in total, the Volkswagen was just about to cross the Bosphorus bridge, heading north-west on the 0-1 highway. Nicely tucked in behind the blue Volkswagen was a small Fiat 500x being driven by Warren Blackburn – Sean's best mate, known to his friends as Swartz, and the most recent recruit to The Court. Swartz had managed to survive twenty-five years in HM Forces and had reached retirement intact. Or partially intact at least. He had lost two fingers on his right hand from a small explosion when entering a target building in Iraq, but of more concern to him was leaving HM Forces with his pension intact after a number of dodgy ruses with Sean. Swartz had conducted his fair share of deniable operations for the government, most often in the guise of a Special Air Service trooper and, eventually, an officer. He had finished as a major, after rising through the ranks, and it was Swartz who had managed to break Sean out of the Afghan jail he had been ensconced in a few years previously. Sean was indebted to Swartz and Jack had managed to tease him into operating for The Court on a part-time basis.

Sean continued to watch Jugsy prepare for the take-off. Jugsy lifted the lid of a black Pelco case, looked up to check that the flight path for the launch was clear and then flicked a rubber switch to 'operation' mode. 'Standby,' he said. 'Three, two, one, firing now.' With his right thumb he pressed down on the launch switch and looked up to see the UAV whir its electric engine, before seeing the elastic pulley whiplash to catapult the UAV into the air. The UAV flew on a gentle curve before it angled dramatically into the sky, reaching an altitude of 500 metres in less than thirty seconds.

'Impressive Jugsy, bloody good effort,' Sean grunted. 'Now let's get going sharpish.'

They sat in the back of the van on collapsible canvas chairs, with Jugsy punching in some coordinates for the UAV to home in on. The tracking antennae above them would steer the UAV onto the target vehicle and, once tracked, the telemetry of the optical cameras would 'lock' onto the vehicle to allow the UAV to automatically follow it.

'Swartz, can you hear me?' Sean asked, speaking into an encrypted satellite phone. 'Let's keep some running commentary going now.'

'Roger,' came the reply. 'Is it in the air yet? I can see the terrorists' vehicle about fifty metres ahead driving right on the speed limit. Two occupants. A stash on-board.'

'OK, that's great. We can see you on our maps right now from the tracker. We're good to go and should have eyes on the vehicle in minutes few.'

'Roger that,' Swartz replied. 'The key junction that will give us the vehicle's ultimate destination is the E-80 interchange about another eight kilometres outside of town. The vehicle can either go north towards Bulgaria or continue eastwards in the direction of Greece.'

'Roger, let's stay sharp now. We need a result here. Out.'

Sean was content that the energy needed for the mission was coming together. He had worked through the night analysing all the intelligence that Samantha had collected from the hotel's listening devices and Billy Phish's data that he'd pulled from the stand-alone servers inside the warehouse. Sean had managed to piece together a detailed picture of the Iranian operation, which involved the movement of bomb-making equipment from the warehouse to what he thought might be holding areas for further transportation out of the country. Today he would hopefully find out where.

He'd also managed to look at detailed intelligence on the servers, which showed that Nadège had been at the warehouse and was an active part of this operation. But what was she masterminding? He had thought continuously about that during the night. There was one small nugget relating to the names, addresses and contact details of merchants situated in Georgia, Azerbaijan, Armenia and Iraq. A list of likely middlemen and key logistics operators who acted as part of the wider network.

The other piece of information he had found was a gem. The documents had all been encrypted within the server, but Billy Phish had cracked them using a backdoor tool used by the Americans for Microsoft Office documents. The details showed an itinerary for Nadège. It included a reservation at a conference in Istanbul in two days' time. The warehouse was acting as a communications hub for the Iranian teams with servers that were air-gapped from the Internet to retain operational security and stop people hacking into their data. Billy Phish had infiltrated these stand-alone servers, revealing a wealth of intelligence, some of which was of immediate use to Sean, the rest needing further analysis back in the UK.

Jugsy's UAV was now firmly locked onto the Blue Volkswagen, tracking its movement from just over 400 metres with a standoff distance of about five kilometres. Sean relaxed for a while as he drove the Mercedes Sprinter about an hour behind the target vehicle, with Jugsy monitoring the target in the back of the van.

Sean glanced at the digital tablet fixed to the dashboard, where a topographic map showed Swartz's vehicle as a small blue dot moving slowly along the E-80. It was just behind the red dot of the target vehicle, with both sets of coordinates being relayed into the van from the UAV in the air. The red dot showed that the Iranian Volkswagen was now turning right at the E-80 junction and beginning to head north on the D-20, towards the dense forests and hills surrounding the town of Kemerburgaz.

Forty minutes later, the Volkswagen turned right off the D-20 and headed towards the village of Saaflan, where it eventually entered some woods and came to a halt. Sean parked the van in a layby, knowing they would now have to rely on the eyes in the sky. He took up his seat in the back next to Jugsy.

'Looks like a long linear track into the forest,' Jugsy piped up.

Sean watched Jugsy fiddle with the UAV console, directing the UAV into a holding pattern high above the target vehicle and then zooming the camera in on the vehicle with his right thumb on the toggle. Sean sat and watched the screen. He now had superb pictures of the vehicle at an oblique angle that had been zoomed right in on the windscreen and rear number plate. Jugsy moved the camera to look at different parts of the vehicle and, on a second screen, he manipulated the imagery to create full coverage of the area. He was using Avigilon digital software, which allowed him to create a mosaic of images on two screens from just a single optical camera. One shot gave a wide-area view, another the entrances to the track, another the vehicle driver's door. Another small screen showed the number plate, with the last picture showing the back door of the van. All from one single camera offset some 500 metres away.

'Bloody good imagery,' Sean said, impressed with the software, which was being showcased to its optimum capability. 'Can you cut another view of where they might have their cache?'

'Yep. But the problem, as you can see, is that tree canopy. If they go under there we'll lose them, and I'll have to switch to radar, which is just shitty blobs on a screen.'

'What's that?' Sean asked, pointing to a small vehicle moving towards the Volkswagen. Jugsy cut another view with his mouse, put it on target lock and zoomed into the four-wheel vehicle.

'That, my boy, is a bloody quad bike. Looks like they'll be shifting their stuff into the woods on that thing.'

Sean's eyes darted across all eight screens as he tried to make out what was happening on the ground - he eventually focused on the one that Jugsy was manipulating with the electro-optical zoom. He watched three men shake hands before one of them opened the trunk to transfer six small boxes onto the quad bike. Jugsy captured facial shots of the men, all of whom sported neatly trimmed beards.

The UAV was now in a holding pattern circling the sky at 400 metres with the camera gimbals firmly fixed to the target vehicle as the three men smoked and chatted next to the quad bike.

Sean watched the men throw their cigarettes to the ground before returning to the Volkswagen. The last package was retrieved with some difficulty - it made him shudder. It was a black body bag, which all three men had to struggle with before it could be dumped on the back of the quad.

Chapter 19

Saafalan, Turkey

Two hours later, Sean started walking down the track with Swartz. The two Iranian couriers had long since gone, but Sean was worried about the third individual who had turned up on the quad bike and was likely to be the custodian of the weapon caches situated somewhere in the woods. The custodian would be responsible for monitoring all the caches and observing any unusual behaviour in their vicinity, periodically visiting them to ensure they were secure.

During his time in the Balkans and Northern Ireland, Sean had often come across cache custodians who had direct oversight of the stash of weapons and explosives they were paid to protect from prying eyes and ears. On this occasion, Swartz had followed this man back to a small log cabin located a good six hundred metres away from the site.

As he was walking down the track, Sean thought about the body. They hadn't seen this large torso being moved in the warehouse when they were monitoring the CCTV cameras – so it must have been on the vehicle when it arrived at the port. Could it be the body of one of their team who went rogue? Or someone who had crossed them? Did it really matter?

Before Sean walked the site, he had tasked Jugsy with monitoring the log cabin and the approaches to the cache area using split-image technology that would allow the Avigilon software to monitor both sites from the single UAV stationed in the sky above. The UAV only had two hours loiter time left so Sean and Swartz had to act quickly to find the cache of explosives and fit tracking devices in them.

The light was beginning to drain from the day as Sean fiddled with his earpiece that provided the radio coverage from Jugsy, who was sitting in the Mercedes van about three kilometres away. Sean listened carefully to the gravelly voice coming through the earpiece as Jugsy guided him towards the exact part of the track where the men had either dug or concealed their bomb-making equipment. The radar signatures relayed to the imagery screens had showed three black blobs below a large tree canopy, which the optical imagery couldn't view.

Sean walked cautiously, checking the landscape for any telltale signs of hidden movement detectors or cameras hidden in the undergrowth or the trees. He was fairly certain there weren't any – his experience of doing similar jobs in the past told him that. But he couldn't be sure. Plus, he didn't know if booby traps had been laid near the caches, wherever they were hidden.

'Can't see any markers at all, can you?' Sean asked Swartz, who was following a few metres behind. The dirt track was lined with trees on both sides with wild grass and plants breaking up the natural undergrowth.

'Nothing yet mate. Keep scanning, we'll find a clue soon.'

The terrorists would have chosen this site carefully. Were the caches buried? Or were they concealed in the undergrowth of the small ditches?

Sean looked for any ground disturbance. For footprints. For unusual-coloured grass. Unusual branches or logs concealing a clue or acting as a signpost to a buried hoard. Were there any markers cut into trees, as he had once seen on a job in Kosovo? Or small blobs of paint, like in Bosnia?

'Let's walk it again,' Sean said. 'All I can see are footprints on the track but no sign of them ever exiting it.'

'They must be using indicators somewhere mate. What's the best physical feature they could use?'

'Something obvious that we're not seeing. We need to get a bloody move on with this light fading.'

Sean decided to walk down the extreme left-hand side of the track this time. He moved a few large stones along the way, noticing they would be useless as markers as they were too easily moved. Then he looked back at the trees. 'Come on you bastards,

I know you're somewhere. How have you hidden them?' he muttered indignantly.

Then he saw it. He was looking at the tree branches above head height. It was a marker alright. A small nick in a tree branch. Close to the core of the tree on the root branch itself. 'Fucking hell Swartz. Come and look.' It was two feet above head height and skilfully placed.

'Great bloody spot Sean. The hide will be just below the nick I bet.'

Sean looked for any ground sign or disturbance. Fuck all. Not a thing. He grabbed a trowel and started digging in the layers of grass just below a slight incline leading away from the tree. He scraped away the loose earth with his gloved hands, using the trowel occasionally and being careful not to disturb anything that might be a trap. Still nothing. He stood up, brushed his knees down and lit a cigarette.

'Look at this,' Swartz shouted, now standing about ten feet away and pointing at a different tree. 'Another fucker here. It's small - and this one is painted blue inside the cut.'

Sean wondered what was going on. He had been on operational search missions for decades. He had used different methods to search for the buried corpses of missing diplomats and murdered agents in Central Asia. But this was a first. A couple of tiny markers, a splatter of paint, but no stash? What was going on?

Sean moved to the second tree and looked below the blue marker. What was the significance of the colour? Explosives? Or weapons? Or cash? Then he remembered the body. They would have had to have concealed the body too. He looked at his watch. He knew he had precious little time before darkness fell and the UAV would be out of power, leaving him exposed without any top cover to spot anyone approaching their position.

'Have a look further down the track - find all the markers you can,' Sean said, grabbing another tool from his rucksack. A small hand-held metal detector. Back on his hands and knees, he probed the areas around and below the two markers. Not a fucking thing. No metallic content. Irritated, he stood up and wiped his brow. What the hell had he missed? He put his mind into that of the

Iranian terrorists. 'How would I have marked this up and provided an indicator?' he said to himself.

'Another two down here Sean.'

'Keep finding them – what colour?'

'One is unpainted, another is blue.'

'Strewth. What's going on?'

'Got it, you bastards,' he shouted, waving to Swartz. Sean walked to the other side of the track, turned around and lined the marker up with his eye so that it was perpendicular to the track. He looked down. No other markers on the ground. Then he looked behind his feet. Just the smallest amount of ground disturbance with a few patches of dirt and mud that were slightly different in texture and colour. Enough to explore further.

He used the metal detector again, hovering it an inch or so above the ground. It alarmed. A small beep. Then another one. Metal.

'Found it - they've buried the caches on the opposite side of the track to the markers.'

'Neat,' Swartz said cheerily. 'Now be careful for fuck's sake.'

Sean dropped to his knees and began to carefully feel around the area for any wires, or batteries or anything that might indicate an explosive booby trap.

Nothing. It seemed clear. Sean started pulling the top layer of mud away using a three-inch paintbrush to scrape away the last of the topsoil. His heart rate rose as he spied a blue circular lid. He scraped away the rest of the mud to reveal the curving lip of a plastic vessel below the blue lid – the plastic container had a half-inch metal band and a clip to keep the lid in place.

'Bingo. Check around the other side of the container, Swartz. We need to be sure there isn't a pressure-release switch on the lid – I'm not going to take the cover off until we're sure and we've checked every container.'

Finally, after checking all seven caches, Sean returned to the first one to remove the cover. It was intensive work. Patient work. Careful threat-assessment work. But now was the time for the cover reveal.

He lifted the lid carefully, holding his breath. He held it an inch above the blue plastic container, a fifty-gallon container, while

Swartz checked underneath it using a small branch, feeling for any wires that might cause a booby trap to go bang if the lid was lifted too high.

With a nod from Swartz, Sean lifted the lid and peered inside. Cellophane-wrapped boxes, just as he had seen in the warehouse.

He moved to the second container, where the blue notch was the marker. They followed the same ritual, lifting the lid and checking for booby traps inside. Cellophane blocks this time. Square blocks of explosives. Sean swabbed the container, the lid and the cellophane with his explosive-swab equipment to allow him to identify the type of explosive.

'Bloody hell, look at this one,' Sean said, peering into the third container linked to a green marker. 'Small fucking suitcases.' There were two of them. Each about two foot wide by one foot high. Black leather ones, similar to those used by airline pilots. Sean pulled one of them out and opened the two clips at the front. He placed it on the ground to study its contents.

He took a moment inspecting the inside of the suitcase and then took a few photos. 'I haven't seen anything like this before, have you?'

'Looks high-tech,' Swartz replied, peering over Sean's shoulder, both of them puzzling over the advanced componentry and struggling to fathom its exact working mechanism. Sean knew he'd need to get expert IED assessments – what he did know was that this was high-grade componentry, manufactured to exacting standards and that only state-sponsored actors could design, procure and assemble. An aluminium frame fitted snugly into the suitcase, inside which a single professionally bored cylinder sat. A silver container with a myriad of different wires connected in series to the cylinders and a set of electronic circuit boards. But Sean couldn't see a power unit. Maybe they'd add that before it was prepared for final targeting?

He began to check inside the device to see if there were any traces of explosives. It was a partially constructed IED with high-grade telemetry but missing the explosives and power unit.

'Pass me the DNA swabs please Swartz,' Sean asked, now using a pen torch to conduct his forensic work. 'Start fitting the tracking devices and I'll finish up here.'

Chapter 20

Istanbul

Nadège Soulier walked through the central bazaar of Istanbul, a conflicted woman. She was one of Iran's foremost spies, at the very top of her game and a genuine star of the MOIS intelligence regime. But she was struggling. Struggling to keep her emotions in check the older she got. For she suffered with emotional intensity disorder. A complex type of post-traumatic stress disorder that caused an affliction at the very core of her being. It bled deep into her soul. She knew the condition well, knew her triggers and even knew her route to salvation. But she could never grab it if she remained an MOIS commander of overseas intelligence operations. She needed another world in order to heal herself. A world of wealth, modelling and glamour.

Feeling trapped, she had self-diagnosed her condition over many years, recognising that she was a high-functioning example of people with the disorder. The type of personality that was often fast-tracked through the ranks to become captains of industry, political leaders and chief officers of many a large corporate. Such people excelled at winning. At hiding their traits, at hiding their disorders. Rarely would they stay in a relationship long enough for anyone to get close to them to see exactly what lay behind the mask.

Nadège was dressed in a white sleeveless dress that was cut tight at the waist and linked to a hip-accentuating bodice and a softly pleated skirt running down just below the knee. She wore a white headscarf, classically draped to show only part of her hair, with the front buttons of her dress done up sufficiently to ensure a modicum of conservative modesty as she graced the metropolis. She wore expensive perfume and her Chloé Marcie handbag matched her cream-coloured high-heeled sandals. For all to see, she was wealthy and classy.

Nadège meandered through one of Istanbul's indoor malls, slowly making her way to the end of the concourse, where she stopped to admire the expensive Louis Vuitton handbags in the window of a small family-run business. She checked her headscarf in the mirror, applied a little more red lipstick and ambled into the small store.

'*İyi günler*,' the elderly owner said, revealing a huge smile and two gold teeth in place of his upper incisors. 'How may I be of service madam?'

'I'm just browsing for my mother today. Nothing in particular.' Nadège turned to adjust her headscarf in the wall-mounted mirror and picked up a black handbag.

'The finest top-grain leather from Italy, madam. Would you like to take some tea?'

With time on her hands, Nadège felt she needed a little calmness, which in her life was rare. 'Thank you. I shall,' she replied. Nadège was shown to a small iron table with a crocheted tablecloth. Tea in a small glass was brought and a small plate of Turkish delight accompanied her drink.

Nadège had been born to a wealthy Lebanese family whose father was an Iranian spy. Her mother had been a devoted wife and mother of four, with Nadège her favoured and youngest child. She was the baby of the family and remembered her mother telling her year after year that the baby of the family would become the star. She did. She followed in her father's footsteps from a young age to be recruited into the MOIS as a teenager. Yet, despite this, she had never lived in Iran. Yes, she had trained there. Often in the mountains, often in military camps, often battling with brutal instructors in unarmed combat. Occasionally being beaten badly by instructors who took no prisoners. Nadège excelled and became the person in whom many senior officers put their trust. And yes, she did sleep with many of them.

Nadège shivered as she recalled her early days, sitting now in an Istanbul store wondering what she should do next. Can I continue? Should I run now? She was tired with all the confusion her mind presented to her on an almost hourly basis. The confusion of her condition haunted her. Why was she like this? What had caused this? She knew many of the answers, and had lived her life by controlling her emotions, but occasionally the triggers were so deep that they led to her most evil episodes, where she would retreat from life for weeks on end.

She knew her condition would one day kill her. Most probably by her own hand. She had to feed her narcissistic soul to keep a grip on her mind. Her vain inner self needed to be fed by being the best at what she did. Only total perfection would suffice. Addictions were the meat of her life and Nadège fed those never-ending addictions with shopping, drug-fuelled sex and a delicacy that gave her the most absurd gratification - killing.

Nadège sipped her tea and crossed her legs gracefully. She looked to all the world like a wealthy and happy woman. But she was burning deep inside as her affliction continued to plague her. She hated having to keep the facade up.

Nadège slipped her hand inside her handbag which concealed the silver trinket that held her anxiety pills. She opened the lid and took one out. A small yellow pill that she swallowed whole. She leant forward, placing a hand momentarily on the table, and took a piece of Turkish delight from a three-tiered silver tray. She drank some hot Turkish tea, and then ate another piece of Turkish delight. She took her hand mirror and looked at her face. A face characterised by immaculate make-up, perfectly groomed eyebrows and a beautiful light brown complexion. She turned her head from side to side, puckered her lips and gently applied some lipstick.

I'll finish this mission and then that's it, she thought to herself. No more. She had long planned her escape from espionage and the clutches of the Iranian regime, and her destination, if ever she could pull it off, was Ecuador in South America.

'*Teşekkür ederim,*' she said to the elderly gentleman. 'Thank you for indulging me.'

She looked at her watch, becoming impatient now as she waited for her contact. A contact who had been provided by her Russian handler for the next stages of a mission that would propel her into notoriety.

'Your car is waiting outside madam,' a voice said in perfect English. She looked up to see a man dressed smartly in a beige jacket and dark blue trousers.

'Shit,' she said, trying to contain her shock. She sat bolt upright, processing the familiar features of her contact. A man she had not seen for many years but who she recognised immediately as Sean Richardson. She threw the lengthy drape of her headscarf across her décolletage and marched briskly out of the shop.

'What the fuck?' she said, stopping to confront the man who had followed her outside.

'Hello,' the man said. 'I had no idea it would be you I'd be meeting.'

He looked shocked too, Nadège thought briefly. She stared with disbelief at a man she had not seen for over eight years. A former lover. A Brit. And there he was, standing right in front of her after all these years. Looking very sheepish.

'Blimey,' the man said. 'I never thought I'd bump into you again.'

Sean Richardson smiled broadly and offered his hand. Nadège looked at it and started to laugh. A barrage of memories flooded her mind. Given that her emotions were dysregulated, she really wasn't sure what she was feeling, or if she should feel it at all. Such was the confusion her mind produced on a daily basis. But she thought for a moment that she liked it. That feeling of meeting an ex-lover many years on.

Her high-functioning emotion kicked in. The darker, more suspicious, side came first. Her eyes narrowed. 'What are you doing here?' she asked, now grimacing, looking to find an explanation. 'Have you done this on purpose?'

She watched as the man bent over slightly, laughing and gesturing with his hands. She liked his smart haircut and neatly trimmed beard. And she always liked a man in a white shirt. He smelt nice too.

'Yes of course, I've come halfway round the fucking world to bump into you as a contact and I've been stalking you for years.' Nadège watched him hold his arms out, as if to say 'you caught me lady.' She didn't like the fact that he was still chuckling.

'What's more, I can see why you're suspicious Nadège. Especially as you did exactly the same to me by trying to recruit me all those years ago.'

'Touché,' she said, beginning to smile again. 'Yes, well, that was work as you well know. Is this your old work?'

'I don't work any more. I was sacked. I'm your contact for what you want now - and I now…' A pause. 'I, er, make a living in other ways.'

'What ways?'

'Erm, I sell stuff and my wares,' he said cheekily. 'Bodily wares.'

Nadège felt the redness spread across her face. She remembered how Sean had always had a way of doing this to her. Making her feel happy and alive with just the normality of life but having a good laugh beyond the treacherous world of espionage. He was teasing again. She could see it in his eyes. She felt her subconscious mind remind her body of the intimate and volatile sex life they had once had, a distraction from the highly stressful lives they led.

'Well, I'm not sure I want to buy any stores from you. It's bound to be a set-up. I must be getting on,' she said, marching down the street, eager to kill this off quickly. Far too risky, she mused, but could it be true? Maybe he had been sacked? She could deal with him, she thought. After all, it might be a nice distraction from the confusion she was living with.

'Hey, have you got time for a walk somewhere?' Sean said jovially. 'I can sell you some underwear instead if you don't like my big stuff.'

Nadège halted and turned on her heels. She caught his cheeky grin and burst out laughing, putting her hand over her mouth. She couldn't control herself. Sean had hit her funny bone. And she had now lost control of that normally controllable mask on her face. Beneath that mask was emotional torture, but the things that made her soul better, the ones that gave her some sense of worth, were laughing, alcohol and sex. Elements that helped to soothe her inner pain. A pain that she had lived with since childhood, and that could only ever be tamed by addictive behaviour. It was always spur of the moment – spending a fortune during addictive shopping sprees and having sex after drinking alcohol. Addictive drugs to help soothe her pain. Laughing and having fun to take her mind away from the incessant burning sensation of a soul that had two opposing voices, one of which told her she needed to self-harm. Suicidal thoughts were never far from her psyche.

'OK,' she said, 'we can walk to the Blue Mosque Gardens. But just for a short time you understand. I need to get back to work. I can't use you for what I need.'

Nadège slowed her pace and strolled towards the Blue Mosque, noticing that Sean was now being quite polite and attentive, walking slightly behind her and giving her some space. She felt those sensations again. Some control too.

The gritty English accent came from behind her. 'Anyway, I could never have pulled that off if I was still a serving intelligence officer you know.' She felt him approach her shoulder as Sean continued. 'You're too savvy. You'd have known immediately that this was some kind of scam.'

'Maybe it is?' she replied, turning her head gently towards his face but avoiding any eye contact. It was her turn to tease a little. 'Anyway, why did you get the sack?'

'Had a fling with an Iranian spy.'

Nadège laughed. 'I imagine your masters put you in suspended animation, as you Brits like to call it. But to get the sack would have needed something far, far worse.'

'I got posted out of front-line intelligence operations to the backwaters of the Foreign Office. Did a bit of close protection in Afghanistan, a secondment to the UN and then got arrested and jailed in Kabul.'

Nadège stopped walking. She turned to look up at him. She looked him in the eye to check his truthfulness. She felt the gaze return, piercing right into her eyes and through her veins to her heart. Somehow, she still had feelings. But those feelings had always been tempered. Neutered. Burnt.

'You ended up in jail? How long and what for?'

'I was running weapons illegally across Central Asia for an organised crime gang. The Don was a British copper. He framed me, and I got fifteen years. Spent a year inside and then started again.'

'Started again on what?'

'Selling weapons – and my body.'

'You're still selling weapons? I'll ignore the body bit. I don't really want to picture you as a high-class hooker.'

'It pays really well though. Both of them do actually.'

Nadège laughed again. 'Listen, I can easily check if you're lying. Your life is easily checked by my facilitators. So I'd advise you to stop lying now as this little entente cordiale won't be going much further.'

'It's the truth. I'm a weapons dealer who your facilitators asked to help you. I can get whatever stuff you need. How the fuck do you think they vetted me first?'

Nadège held this thought. She had two handlers: her Iranian boss, General Alimani, and her Russian GRU handler, Sergei. Sergei had never let her down yet, but how the hell did he get Sean Richardson to provide her with the illicit stores she needed?

Nadège felt curiosity get the better of her. 'Come on, I'll show you the Blue Mosque.'

Nadège always visited the mosque when she was in Istanbul. She wasn't particularly religious, but she liked to sit on the large carpets and try and find herself. She showed Sean the major parts of the mosque, explaining its varied history, and then took him to the huge internal space with enormous carpets where people could sit in reflection. She had covered herself with a white cardigan before entering the mosque and buttoned it up fully before inviting Sean to take a seat on the carpet.

Nadège sat opposite him with her legs crossed. She noticed Sean was looking around at the magnificent expanse of Islamic architecture, taking in the ambience and the staggering views of the old paintings that hung high on the walls. The murals grabbed her eye, and she spotted one of the Red Sea. That was fitting, given that it was where she had first been given the task of trying to recruit him all those years ago. To recruit him for the Russian GRU, such was her versatility and relationship with the Russian intelligence agencies. Nadège had been acting as a conduit for the Russian GRU, who were supporting her role in this, her final mission. One that would bring carnage to Europe, Britain and the US.

She asked Sean to sit in silence for a while. She wanted to spend some time practising her mindfulness.

Nadège's thoughts drifted back to her days with her mother and the love she had had for France. Those memories conflicted with her loyalty to the Iranian government. A loyalty instilled in her by her father. A deep loyalty to the state. And a deep loyalty to her missions. Nadège had never really rationalised these contradictions, in part due to her difficulty in processing her emotions. Her life had been ingrained with the sole view that she had of protecting her country against evil foreigners. She recognised the propaganda she had been fed, and how deeply indoctrinated she had become during her training, whilst she was what the Russians termed 'a young sparrow'. But her times with the Russians had made it clear to her too that Iran was being used to further Russian aims at the expense of her own country.

She wondered if her Russian handler was playing her? Colonel Sergei Yuronov of the GRU had provided her with detailed intelligence on a British Foreign Office diplomat, Edmund Duff, who they had kidnapped in London only a few weeks ago. An act that would allow her to seek revenge on another man who deserved nothing less than a painful death: Fletcher Barrington.

Sergei had repaid Nadège's intelligence by tracking down Duff and watching his movements. All in return for Nadège providing intelligence on the intentions of the MOIS regarding the Americans sanctions. That was when the GRU had ordered Sergei to conjure up a plot to use the MOIS as proxy agents for Russian gains. The gains of creating chaos across Europe and the Western world by using the Iranians as their non-attributable proxies.

Nadège had used Colonel Sergei to track Edmund down, investigate his background, check up on his friends and monitor his communications and movements for over ten months – including hacking into his many cloud accounts.

Nadège then ensured that she was introduced to Edmund at a glamorous art event in Holborn, bedded him and then spent many long hours in his company across the London political circuit, extracting as many Foreign Office secrets as she could between the bedsheets and during the plentiful cocaine-fuelled party sessions with Edmund.

On one occasion she had briefly introduced Edmund to her model friend and confidante, Petra. It only needed to be a brief meeting, which she had set up at the box office of the Royal Albert Hall. Just a momentary chance meeting at which eyes could meet. It was all part of the trap. A trap that Petra could one day finish to find her peace.

To keep him close and eager, Nadège also booked an expensive female escort, making sure they had a wild and crazy threesome. She only needed one piece of information from him and she used every method at her disposal to get it.

Eventually, Nadège became known as Edmund Duff's girlfriend, enjoying lavish nights out in Mayfair with many of his closest friends, including her main target – the egotistical Fletcher Barrington. Barrington was to be her kill. It was a plot she had worked on closely with Petra and one that Colonel Sergei didn't know about. It was a plot for enacting revenge on a group of men who deserved nothing less than painful death.

She reported all of the secrets Edmund had revealed back to General Sergei via the Russian Embassy. High-grade foreign office intelligence that was of great use to the Russians and allowed Nadège to keep getting the funding and support she needed from Colonel Sergei. It was a perfect deal.

She recalled the dead-letter drops she had made across London with the secrets that Edmund had revealed to her. Drops she was ordered to make the old-fashioned way with handwritten notes in code. The Russians preferred it this way because of hacking, which had now become a danger to everyone in the spy world. Reversionary spy tradecraft was needed.

She placed her secret notes in small nooks and crannies across London for a GRU agent to collect them. The latest one she remembered was just outside Waterloo station, where she had waited to see her handler approach from the fire station on Waterloo Road. She waited until he'd provided eye contact, then placed the note behind a railway noticeboard whilst having a cigarette. She walked off, allowing the GRU officer to approach the sign, slip a hand behind it and, within seconds, lift the encrypted note, which provided secret details of future Foreign Office operations in the Middle East.

Two days later, the GRU conducted the kidnapping of Edmund Duff outside Quaglino's - Nadège had made sure Edmund had put in a leave pass for two weeks, using this time to bribe him with demands for information she would use to conduct her revenge.

Nadège's plan involved a kill. A kill that the GRU did not know about. A plan that was now seamlessly woven into her plot of conducting the Iranian bombing campaign, assassinating two more men and then escaping to South America. The last act of her plan was to kill the ex-CIA chief Fletcher Barrington, making sure he would suffer first. This would be the murder that would avenge many people, and the last death in a group of men who had pained her and Petra.

With all her plans in place, the last thing she needed now was the distraction of an old lover fucking it all up.

'I was approached in London by your Russian contact,' Sean whispered, causing Nadège to break out of her trance. 'They tell me you need some very special equipment that I can supply you with.'

'What was the codeword he gave you?'

'*German Bight*.'

'And your response?'

'*Dogger*.'

Nadège stayed silent. Dropped her gaze. Then re-entered her state of mindfulness. It was her way of indicating that not too much discussion was needed here. Sean had provided the correct answers. Verification. How on earth did he know the codes used between her and the Russians?

She remembered how she had been required to memorise all the shipping forecast areas, and that the only way to verify an agent was to use an adjacent area. Dogger was right next to German Bight.

'OK. One final check. *Biscay*.'

She looked at Sean's eyes. Not a flicker as he answered immediately. '*Fitzroy*.'

Nadège started to twist her hair with her right hand, a habit she had when she was both nervous and attracted.

'Look, whoever your contacts are, they wanted the best,' Sean continued. 'I'm the best at this across the Balkans and Europe now. I can get you whatever you need, and they've already paid me half my fee before the costs for the goods. There is no scam here. I don't give a fuck who pays me any more.'

Nadège sensed this wasn't true at all and began to have suspicious thoughts about Sean again. What if he had been placed by British intelligence to try to disrupt her operation? How on earth could he know the GRU codes? Codes that were only used on her operations as a double agent with the Russians. Her mind focused again. She had a mission to achieve and this was too much of a distraction. She'd check Sean's background with General Sergei but sensed something still wasn't right.

Nadège raised her gaze again. Stood up. She quietly made her point. 'I think this is a very bad idea. It was nice to see you, but for me that is enough. I'll speak to my people and tell them you're off the case. I'll get someone else.'

Nadège glided gracefully out of the mosque and headed through the gardens to the river.

She didn't notice Samantha sat watching her every move, nor did Sean see the man sat on the park bench taking photographs of him as he left.

Chapter 21

London

Jack decided to walk along the embankment of the River Thames that morning. He felt a little sombre and was in a reflective mood given that it was the third anniversary of his daughter being diagnosed with MS. In some small way he had a sense of déjà vu. He felt the rumblings of a war coming. Every sense, smell and rumour he grappled with around Whitehall told him so. And the secret intelligence he was reading on the American position on Syria and Iran told him they were again gunning for a war. Why the gung-ho approach, he wondered? Jack was a master of the game in the duplicitous halls of central government, and certainly knew the deceptive tricks the Americans could muster when needed. But for Jack, and many others in HM Crown service, they were often their own worst enemy, using the wrong tactics at the wrong time in global affairs driven by a blindness where realpolitik was concerned. He knew that game well, and knew it often overrode the more surreptitious ways of achieving a goal – and Jack was a master at those too.

He walked down Whitehall, enjoying the magnificence of the government buildings. He spied the entrance to a building where he had been summoned by the Cabinet Secretary, Sir Justin Darbyshire. A man that he knew, for British civil service equivalence purposes, was comparable to a military general or a High Court judge. Powerful and influential were the words that fluttered across his mind. The death of D was occasion enough for Jack to be beckoned by the most senior civil servant in HM government.

Jack was very aware that the true influence of the Cabinet Secretary extended far beyond administrative matters and reached deep into the very heart of the political decision-making process. Unusually for a democracy, his unelected role also provided some authority over elected ministers, although his constitutional authority was somewhat ambiguous.

Jack glanced at the highly polished brass plates situated either side of the entrance of the imposing grey-brick building and walked up the few steps to the door. The plates indicated 70 Whitehall, The Cabinet Office.

Sir Justin was a huge man. A man of real stature and one with impeccable military manners. He had been an international rugby player in the '70s and a rare civil servant who had previously served with distinction in the Royal Navy. Jack walked into his outer office to see Sir Justin stood pretty much to attention, wearing a beige suit topped off in masterly fashion with a dazzling Prussian blue tie set against a pristine white shirt. Jack noticed him holding his jacket collar with both hands, moving up and down on his toes.

'Ah, Jack, I've been waiting. Good to see you young man. Come on in.'

Jack walked over to Sir Justin and shook his hand, watching this eclectic man signal to one of his two secretaries to bring the tea and cakes.

'A great time for grub,' he said. 'And some damn good company. Now take a seat over there Jack, and make yourself very much at ease.'

Jack sensed the military flow to the way Sir Justin lived his life. But he also knew that behind the mask of this charming and jolly fellow lay the fierce skills of manipulation and charm. Sir Justin was the only senior civil servant outside of Thames House who knew of The Court's existence, and the man who ensured it got all the support and funding it needed beyond the normal MI5 finance system. Sir Justin had been in post for nearly three years and was destined to remain in post for many more to come.

'I shall miss him you know Jack,' Sir Justin began, referring to D. 'A damned fine friend and a bloody good man for us all over the years. I assume you'll be at the funeral?'

'Yes, sir,' Jack replied, holding his cup and saucer above his lap.

'Sit down and have some buns Jack. Plenty of sugar and British tea is needed for this discussion. It's not one I really wanted to have.' Sir Justin took his jacket off and relaxed into a '50s-style lounge chair. A favourite of his, Jack surmised.

'You see Jack, we are in desperate trouble right now I'm afraid. And it's all down to that warmonger Redman. He is a thorn in everyone's side and has completely blindsided the President. He's a US national security advisor who is fanatical about war.' He paused, as if wanting Jack to engage. Jack took the cue.

'I had long chats with D about exactly this before he passed away,' Jack began, knowing pretty much where this would lead. 'We agreed there is now a huge danger of us being dragged into a war with Iran and no sight of victory, especially if he encourages the President into taking such action. He was a huge advocate of the seven wars in five years the neocons wanted. A very dangerous man.'

'Indeed. And now we have Redman in the Whitehouse, the neocons have their man steering a rekindled course for regime change through military means. You know, Charles Talleyrand once said, erm, do you know of him Jack? The legendary French diplomat? He famously remarked about the House of Bourbon that they had learnt nothing and forgotten nothing. The same applies to the neocons as they press for the West to intervene yet again in the Middle East. This time in Iran as well as Syria. Things could spin catastrophically out of control, so we need to act against this for the sake of us all.'

Sir Justin stood and ambled over to his desk, placing his cup and saucer on its dark red veneer. He pointed to some of his pictures of his service in the Navy. 'Don't get me wrong at all Jack. I don't mind a well-founded war at all. But the rules have changed and sadly our politicians are not good enough to see through all this smoke and mirrors and I'm fearful that, if the current Prime Minister is ousted, as she doubtless will be, we could politically be on a course of joining the President and giving the Americans the clout they need to unleash mayhem.'

'The problem is, sir, times have changed now. Our intelligence is showing that the Russians are pretty much running the Syrian War and are now commanding the Iranians too, as well as all of their proxy armies. Our assessment in MI5 is that Russia has co-opted Iran under its command and control and has taken charge of all the events we are seeing in Lebanon and Yemen, and the attacks by Hezbollah on Israel. They are now controlling Iran as they had no one to turn to when we cut off their supplies with the additional sanctions after the Americans pulled the nuclear deal.'

Sir Justin sat at the end of his desk, picking up his tea and placing his hand on a knee. 'What else have you got on the operational side Jack?'

'Well, we've direct evidence now of a Russian command bunker in Syria where Iranian Al Quds officers are under their command, alongside Syria's own officers. We've picked up on their concept of operations via our own Court operations. We are seeing everything now being commanded by the Russians, with Syria and Iran being subordinate to them. Cold war 2.0 has been underway for a long time, but this time the Russians have bolstered their assets and added two countries to their new union – a Russian Union. It's Putin's grand plan. But this time around he knows Russia can win cold war 2.0 once he makes it hot.'

'What do you think their next moves are?'

'It's a graduated ramp-up, sir. A graduated year-on-year escalation so Putin can get command and control in place. Subordination too. He conducts skirmishes to test our responses, both political and militarily, as well as watching our intelligence responses. Then he acts again. Until he has the full picture. He's a master at shaping the battlefield to give him the conditions to win outright. We've played right into his hands by taking the nuclear deal from Iran as they had no one to turn to for finance, for commerce, for selling their oil. The significance of the Russians developing banking and brokerage relations with Iran is an important factor in their bilateral trade and the economic cooperation has been staggering in its depth.'

'A fine assessment Jack. Astute to the core, as D always said of you. He had a fine second in command for The Court, that's for sure. The problem is, as you well know, the battlefields are now hybrid. Where is Putin at with all this chaos now?'

'Doing rather well, sir. But I fear he's about to open up his terrorism front with multiple arms. Whilst my assessment is that he would never provide nuclear material direct to Iran, he would help them tactically if it supported his strategic aims. He simply wouldn't allow one of his children to have those arms, which is why we think the Iranians are accelerating their own nuclear programme again – not that it ever stopped of course.'

'So tactical support it is? Anything new for me?'

'Well, not a great deal I'm afraid. But I do have a Court officer in Istanbul right now who has identified one of the Iranian command hubs that evidences their command and control right down to tactical level. It's staffed by Iranian MOIS agents who have full cyber and terrorist capability that they can channel into the Middle East and into Europe. I think it's been activated. They call it station fifty-four.'

Jack paused and leant forward to place his cup and saucer on the small round table sat on a Persian carpet. He watched for Sir Justin's reaction.

'So cold war 2.0 has new affiliations. An axis of evil, for want of a better phrase, consisting of Russia, Iran and Syria. Good God. The devil incarnate is amongst us and this path needs to be trodden well.'

'It's certainly a union now,' Jack said, looking up and putting his glasses away. 'Some commentators have irresponsibly spoken of a possible World War Three and all the conditions are there, sir.'

'What else should we be doing then Jack?'

'Well, we need agents in Iran now. We only have one or two of any note. I have my man in Istanbul looking to help us with that cause. If you can keep the Americans from going on a full-scale rampage and direct war, I can begin to establish a network of spies and agents within the Iranian system. My man is currently trying to recruit one of their highest-grade MOIS officers, which could lead to us finding their sleeper agents in this country, and I'm sure we can get collateral to get others inside their nuclear programmes but, importantly, inside the MOIS. We can then begin to see their wider plans with the Russians and disrupt them.

'Very good Jack. You know it's all a bit nebulous. A foggy war. We need better information, so keep up the tempo. I'll make sure that D's replacement is the man we need too. It will temporarily be the Deputy Director, who is familiar with your Court operations I believe?'

'That's really good to hear, sir. He is. And a good man for the role too.'

Jack watched Sir Justin button up his beige jacket and grab his lapels by both hands again. A signal they were done. He then watched Sir Justin rise up and down on his toes. A strange foible, Jack thought. An able man behind the facade. Whilst Jack hadn't given away his full hand of cards, it had been an agreeable meeting.

'Thank you for your time, sir. I'll keep the momentum up on our needs.'

'Splendid Jack. By the way, any news on that diplomat who went missing? Our FCO chap?

'Nothing I'm afraid. He just went missing and there's been no news whatsoever. He is however linked to one of America's main neocons and a key advisor to the White House. A man called Fletcher Barrington. It's all a bit fuzzy right now but I'll keep you informed as we unearth it all.'

Chapter 22

Istanbul

Sean threw his rucksack on the floor of the newly decorated bedroom in the villa, grabbed a bottle of water and strode onto the terrace outside his room to think. He wondered about the veracity of Iranian sleeper agents in Britain, about the destruction they could create and the lives they led hidden behind a facade of normality in British society.

The stunning views of Istanbul distracted his thoughts for a while, but they returned with vigour, led most prolifically by a profound suspicion about what was happening. Something wasn't right, he thought. Possibly a trap? Who knew? How the hell was he meant to get intelligence from this woman, let alone turn her into a British agent? Where on earth did Jack get that notion? What was he hiding?

He took a long drink, throwing ideas around in his head about what Jack might be up to. He needed to analyse all the intelligence he had collected so far and try to figure out what to do next.

He took his shirt off, threw it on a pile in the corner of the room and stretched out on the bed, arms behind his head. His jaw began to tense as it always did when he was anxious. Some people tap their foot, some people twitch. Sean tensed his jawbones, a habit easily seen by others when he was under stress. He hated it when he spoke out loud but found himself doing it again. As if it were some nervous affliction he had formed from years of living right on the edge.

He breathed deeply and then tried to piece things together logically in his mind. Something wasn't right with Nadège. She had a distant gaze, a detachment, as if she were existing in a state of suspension. Her eyes gave a sense of soullessness, of being lost.

He recalled something from all those years ago, remembering her long moments of detachment. It made him wonder what might be behind that mask. Then it came back to him. All those memories of odd behaviour she had exhibited when they were lovers, the push and pull of their relationship and the occasional moments when they had argued and she'd insisted, 'I never ever said that.' But Sean knew she had. It sowed deep confusion in his mind. Seeds of doubt. Gaslighting. What exactly was all that about?

He heard his phone vibrate followed by the sound of a single tone. A text. Groaning, he lurched to his feet and walked across the room to the dressing table. It was from Melissa in the south of France.

'How's it going? I think I've got a lead on the diplomat who was kidnapped. Quite odd. You didn't call me last night. I'll call at 10pm your time. How's the tart?'

Sean chuckled. 'Amazing how the tables turn,' he said, speaking to himself again. Instead of being hounded by Samantha from afar as his operations mistress, this time it was Melissa gently reminding him where his allegiance lay. He smiled at that. And texted back.

'Miss you. She's fine and all cool in that regard. Fear not. Steady out here. Chat soon.'

He'd decided to have a 'heads in' with the team before dinner to share what everyone had found so far. He'd already informed Samantha that they'd placed tracking devices within the boxes they had found in the weapons cache, and at least he had kicked off the ludicrous engagement with Nadège. But how the hell would he manufacture the next episode? He needed a lure. Something to entice her.

'OK, who wants to start then?' Sean asked as the team crammed around the glass kitchen table.

'I think I need to start with the big picture first,' Samantha chipped in, exuding her command status. Sean watched Jugsy's eyes roll: he preferred more informal chats to briefings.

'It's the beginnings of a complex jigsaw that we need to piece together,' she started. 'We now have tracking devices on the IEDs, and we know the warehouse is the central logistics hub. But what

I want to know is, who is the female that Nadège had sex with the other night? A hooker, or a long-term liaison? And how do we get more from that link?'

'Well the blonde hasn't returned to the hotel yet,' Jugsy piped up. 'I've checked the cameras this afternoon. No one has visited her either.'

Sean sat with his hands behind his head, listening and thinking. The blonde woman who had visited Nadège intrigued him. 'Let's find out who she is Sam. Get amongst the staff back home and get her picture circulated across the agencies. We need to find out more about her quickly.'

'Already done,' Samantha confirmed.

'Good. Anything from the warehouse servers Billy?'

'Yup. Quite a bit actually. Might be of use for the next steps.'

'Go on.'

'A couple of itineraries for NIGHTOWL and some payments. As they always say, follow the bloody money. The money is being paid out in vast sums all over the place. Plenty to drugs mules by the looks of it and to local facilitators to keep the smuggling routes open across the Balkans. And plenty of dosh going into Belgium too. But the curious ones are linked to Nadège. Money going into Lebanese and Qatari accounts.'

'OK, some great leads Billy. Anything on her next itinerary?'

'Yep, a cruise across the Black Sea. Fancy tagging along?'

'Nice. When?'

'Thursday at 9am. It's a conference cruise and Nadège was booked to attend about five weeks ago. I've got into the system and booked you and Samantha in for the two-day duration.'

Sean sighed, glancing at Sam's smiling face before inquiring further. 'A conference cruise you say? Any ideas what she's up to?'

'Nope. One for you to square away mate.'

Sean paused as an idea began to formulate in his mind. 'What have we got from her phones Sam?'

'Quite a lot of information actually.' Samantha pushed a piece of paper across the table to Sean. 'These are all the contacts and I've marked the ones she's been calling the most. We'll infiltrate those phones and see what we can find today.'

'OK, good stuff everyone. I'm speaking with Jack on a conference call soon and I'll brief him on where we're at. Try and get some more details on this conference Billy and a full list of names with any background that might spring a thought on what she's up to.'

'Probably recruiting nuclear scientists to start uranium processing again,' Billy Phish said sarcastically. Sean knew he probably wasn't far from the truth there.

Sean walked out onto the garden terrace to think of what to say to Jack when he called. He grabbed a file that Sam had printed for him and that had been sent by Jack as a SITREP from the wider intelligence gathering of The Court. He nestled into the deck settee and began reading. What he read concerned the threats beginning to increase across Europe.

UK SECRET C-OPS ONLY // NO DISCLOSURE // BW // OP LONGHORN //

An Iranian diplomat and members of an Iranian sleeper cell were arrested this week in Belgium, Germany and France, as they were allegedly planning to bomb a high-level meeting in Paris. The arrests came after a complex investigation by several European intelligence agencies and were announced by Belgium's Minister of the Interior.

The operation against the sleeper cell began yesterday when members of Belgium's Special Forces Group stopped a Mercedes car in Brussels. The car was carrying a married Belgian couple of Iranian descent. One of them was found to be carrying four kilogrammes of triacetone triperoxide (TATP) explosive and detonators inside a toiletries bag. The same day German police arrested an Iranian diplomat stationed in Iran's embassy in Vienna, Austria. The diplomat was driving a rental car in the German state of Bavaria, heading to Austria. On the same day, a fourth person, who has not been named, was arrested by the French DGSI in connection with the other three arrests.

The four detainees were in contact with each other and were working for the Iranian government.

Sean took a few deep breaths, realising the tide was turning fast. Where were the IEDs destined for?

Chapter 23

Istanbul

Sean booted up his encrypted laptop for the secure video call with Jack. He punched in a two-factor authentication code to enter the secure partition of the laptop and then used facial recognition to enter the secure app for the conference call.

A few minutes later he could see Jack clearly on the screen, noting he was sat in his office in Thames House. 'Hi Jack, hope all's well,' he began.

There was a slight satellite delay before Sean heard Jack's response. 'Not too good I'm afraid Sean. A few bad things have been happening – are you alone?'

'Yes, what's up?'

'First things first,' Jack began, leaning towards the camera. 'Sadly, D had a heart attack yesterday. A very serious one and he died pretty much immediately. Nothing we could do at all. A massive loss to us as you know.'

'Bloody hell Jack.' Sean hadn't expected to hear such shocking news. 'That's bloody awful: the man was a genuine legend and a bloody good bloke.'

'I know, and it's hit people quite hard back here. He was very much a loved man both in the service and obviously amongst the wider intelligence family. He'd been busy though in his last days and that's what I wanted to talk about.'

Sean didn't know about the deal D had with Jack, but he'd have been devastated to have heard about what D had been investigating. A case that went back to the cold war and one of only a few files he had ever held safely under lock and key in his office safe. The case was the unsolved murder of a female MI6 agent in 1986. No one had ever found her body. Her handler had ended up in a mental institution in Prague shortly after she was murdered, and he'd been unable to provide any clues to the murder other than that it was very brutal.

'D asked me to show you this letter regarding this case Sean. He only wants you to see it and I'll send it over by email now. I'll call you back in twenty minutes. It involves your mother, I'm afraid - and how she disappeared.'

Sean sat back, gobsmacked. He couldn't say anything. Dumfounded. He started to grate his jawbones.

Sean remembered how his father had explained to him that his mother had gone missing. It was in Berlin in 1986. The year of his exams at the Charles Dickens School on Dickensweg. He remembered that day like it was yesterday and a ferocious sweat came over his body as he struggled to hold the drawer in his mind from springing open. He felt that moment. The moment he had felt before – the intervening moment before total breakdown from internal trauma. A sensation he had known from multiple bouts of PTSD over his career. But this one? This one was bad. It hit his soul. It was his mother. And no one could ever answer why she had gone. He'd felt abandoned. Gone in his teenage years, when the bond he had forged with her was at its strongest. The moments when his child's mind was growing into a man's. And the reason he ran away from home.

He grabbed a beer from his fridge and sat at the laptop to read the letter from D. He began to well up.

My Dearest Sean,
I know what I am about to tell you will come as a huge shock. Because it concerns your mother's disappearance back in 1986. If you are reading this letter it is quite simply because I will have passed on from this world and would not have had a chance to tell you personally of the circumstances that I have investigated that led to your mother's death. From my point of view, that is my saddest moment. That I have been unable to share this with you face to face and completely solve her murder.

Your mother was a fine woman and a fine agent of the Crown. A woman you should be immensely proud of. What you perhaps don't know is the extent of her bravery and courage in the face of the enemy amongst hugely stressful circumstances behind the Iron Curtain. She reminded me of those splendid female operators from the SOE in the Second World War. I have now written up a report on her death and issued a note of the circumstances to the Lord Advocate with a recommendation she is awarded as a minimum the George Medal.

Sean tried to calm his nerves and keep his blood pressure down. He breathed deep and hard, getting as much oxygen into his lungs as possible. It was the best way to deal with the traumatic stresses which he knew at some point would manifest into physical symptoms. For him it was scratching intensely before headaches and running out of breath, which would eventually lead to convulsions. He tried to contain it through his breathing before continuing.

Your mother was killed by a spy who I believe was a double agent. A man named Fletcher Barrington and a CIA operative in Berlin who your mother worked with regularly. I believe she was killed on the East German border and in all probability buried at the site of her murder.

'Fucking hell,' Sean screamed loudly. 'Bastard.'

He drank his bottle of beer, then opened another. He had no idea his mother had been an MI6 officer. He drifted back to those dark days in Berlin where he had lived with his mother and father from the age of ten on Bronteweg. His father was a captain in the Royal Engineers and a specialist officer recruited specifically for his map-making and cartography skills. Sean had always been told they had been posted to Berlin as part of the British Mission in Berlin, BRIXMIS as it was known, because of his father - but now he could see that it was his mother who probably had the primary reason for such a posting. BRIXMIS was The British Commanders'-in-Chief Mission to the Soviet Forces in Germany and was formed in 1946 under the agreement between the chiefs of staff of the British and Soviet forces in occupied East Germany. The agreement called for the reciprocal exchange of liaison missions in order to foster good working relations between the military occupation authorities in the two zones.

He loved his teenage days in Berlin and often revelled at his father's stories of cold war spying under official cover and of wearing the British Army uniform wherever they went in East Germany. During the cold war, the right of the Mission to travel relatively freely throughout East German territory was used for gathering intelligence on Warsaw Pact forces based there. This included collecting intelligence on installations, troop movements, equipment, morale and weaponry.

He knew his mother was involved in BRIXMIS but he had no idea she had been an MI6 agent. He needed to find out more very quickly. This was family. Something he'd never really had over the years after running away. He needed to know much more. He needed to know what his mother had done in those days. Sean had kept in touch with his father on a few occasions, but he'd never had a great relationship with him. He knew he needed to find his own way in life after his mother had died so he joined the army at eighteen. He just wanted to be by himself. No family. A loner. And a man who would fend for himself thereafter. Up until that point, he had loved Berlin. He had fond memories of his school, where he played rugby and cricket, and of the Grunewald, where he would walk with his mother. He loved the stories of adventure told by his father, who told him of his forays into East Germany, when he had once been stopped by the Stasi police and detained until the local soviet officers came to release them.

BRIXMIS was a legitimate spying operation. Its missions into East Germany involved enormous risk for the men and women who conducted overt travel to collect covert intelligence. As the British Army's secret unit behind enemy lines in the cold war, incidents with Soviet forces were regular and at times brutal. Sean recalled how his father was allowed to take him and his mother into East Germany as part of cultural tours of the East. His dad had to wear service dress and not the combat dress he'd wear on operations, and Sean remembered visiting Leipzig and Colditz. Dresden remained etched in his memory because it was his mother's favourite city, and they went to the opera there on a few occasions. His father had told him that he enjoyed these trips because he didn't have to sleep in a ditch as he did on his normal tours across the border.

The BRIXMIS tours, as they were called, took place in Mercedes G-Wagens and the three-person teams would collect intelligence and, on occasion, even break into Soviet command bunkers. The tours were made up of a tour officer like his father, a tour sergeant and a driver. Sean remembered his father showing him pictures and telling stories of how they were self-sufficient, cooking their own meals and sleeping in the countryside, either in the vehicle, as the driver always had to, or, as the other two normally did, in bivouacs or one-man tents. His father had told him that once they had left the Mission house in Potsdam they were entirely out of contact with their headquarters and were left to their own devices to deal with any incidents, arrests, or even attacks against them.

The secure video app started to ring. It was Jack again.

'Hi Jack. I've just read it. What the actual fuck is going on here? It is utterly bizarre that this has come out after so many years.'

Jack looked quite white, Sean thought. No doubt nervous about having such emotional conversations over a satellite video link. He watched Jack hold up an old snuffbox. Quite an antique, Sean thought.

'Your mother placed an encrypted message in this snuffbox the night she died Sean. It was hidden in a dead-letter drop for her handler to pick up if anything went wrong.'

'What the hell did it say?'

'We still don't know yet. It's being looked into. What we do know is the man who collected it ended up in a mental institution and only recently handed it over to D. He lives in Prague, where D has visited him on a few occasions.'

'Bloody hell Jack. I need to get onto this and find out more. Where do I start?'

'I agree Sean. Which is why I'm taking you off this entire operation. I'm pulling you in and Samantha will take over.'

'Not a bloody hope. I'm staying right here.'

'That simply won't work. Surely you want to come off this job? You know as well as I do your mind won't be on the job and you can start investigating your mother's links to these modern-day events.'

Sean's mind was a mixture of confusion, fear, sadness and anger. It was the anger at the bastard who had killed his mother that festered the most.

'What about this bloke Barrington?' Sean asked, raising his voice.

'He was dining with the Foreign Office diplomat who was kidnapped in Quaglino's. An American, quite elderly now, but a former CIA station chief who is very close to the President's National Security Advisor, John Redman. He was in London at the meeting with D on the very day he died.'

'For fuck's sake Jack. This is bloody messy now. You're telling me this CIA bastard killed my mother and is now somehow linked to this saga we're all fighting?'

'Maybe, maybe not. We really don't know in what capacity. Melissa has been investigating the background of the FCO diplomat and this ex-CIA chief. She'll call you later with the details and I'll send a note out shortly on where D had got to. It's a big puzzle Sean. Melissa is expecting you home and you can work on it together from there.'

'Jack, you're not listening to me. I'm not coming in. I'm staying right here.'

'I can't allow that Sean, it's all been decided.'

'By fucking who?'

'The acting Director General, D's deputy. He doesn't want any conflicts of interest or distractions.'

'Well you can tell him to go and fuck himself. I'm staying, and I'll get this done with Nadège too. You know I don't just throw the towel in. I'll cope.'

With that, Sean clicked on the button to terminate the call.

What the hell was going on, he wondered? How the fuck was his mother's murderer linked to the FCO diplomat who had been mysteriously kidnapped? What was their connection? He finished his beer and paced the room vigorously. His mind was a mess. He couldn't think straight at all.

He decided to draw all the linkages on his sketchpad, just as he normally did to rationalise the relationships of people and their connections during intelligence investigations. Intelligence-linkage maps that he had been creating on every job he'd done for years. He started sketching, hoping Melissa could fill in the gaps during the call later.

He placed a circle in the centre of the sketch pad with the name of the CIA killer. BARRINGTON. Then he drew three circles. In one he placed the name of the FCO diplomat – DUFF. In the next circle he put the name of the US National Security Advisor, REDMAN, carefully drawing a dotted line to D, who had died shortly after briefing the man. Then he put Nadège in another circle using the codename NIGHTOWL, with a link to her blonde lover whose name he didn't know yet. He drew a few curved lines with arrows to a large blank space on the paper. He wrote the words *background connections*. He added the names of the Jews who were murdered in Chelsea, VAN DE LULE, wondering how their deaths were linked, if at all.

What is it that connects all these people, he asked himself? He simply didn't know. He remembered the mission at hand. To recruit Nadège and find the bomber she had recruited, wondering about the extent of her tentacles.

He drew a circle directly below Nadège with the name of the bomber – Wilson HEWITT. And finally he wrote the words BOMBER TARGETS at the bottom of the paper in large capitals followed by three question marks. He simply didn't know. Finally, he typed his sketch into the i2 intelligence software which displayed images of the people, their linkages and their backgrounds. He would add to this as the intelligence picture became clearer.

It wasn't long before he found himself reliving the images and memories of his times with his mother. Each image and memory starting to layer the trauma he had carried for decades. His mind was numb, his body exerting all the manifestations of severe stress. Scratching incessantly. Sweating in the groin.

He decided enough was enough and that he needed a good drink. Within fifteen minutes he was in a taxi heading into downtown Istanbul.

Chapter 24

Raffles Hotel, Istanbul

S ean started the night thinking just a few drinks would do the job before he returned to the villa the next day but, as ever, the second led to a third, and the third to a fourth.

He had booked himself into the Raffles Hotel. Pure decadence for a night of debauchery. A hotel rising elegantly above the hustle and bustle of the ancient metropolis, sat prominently in the expensive Zorlu Centre where high fashion, glamorous arcades and art galleries converged with gourmet restaurants. Having the spirit and design of its famous Singapore cousin, Sean chose the opulent Long Bar in which to bury his mind in alcohol. An old-fashioned bender as he'd call it.

Sean was at home with tradition. He sat in a lavish maze-like parlour of crystal, choosing a barstool in the far corner, from where he could watch the comings and goings of the night. The evocative nature of Raffles drove him to begin the night with a Tiger beer, followed by a couple of Singapore slings, which he demolished at speed.

He was reminiscing about his childhood days before taking a journey in his mind to the way he had entered the dark, seductive world of intelligence. He'd spent time on an east London building site as a hod-carrier for a year before joining the British Army where, many years later, he had majored as a Defence Intelligence officer. Despite not having a great relationship with his father, the man did have the fortitude to build emotional strength into Sean during his teenage years, knowing that one day he would need to draw on such resilience given everything the world would throw at him after his mother's disappearance.

Sean wondered how much his father knew of his mother's murder? Probably nothing. No one had known until now. How on earth would he break it to him now?

In-between his thoughts, Sean joshed with the bartenders, tasted different mixologist's potions, and watched them prepare a Yıldız Spritz inspired by the symbols of the Yıldız pavilions and the colourful collections in the Topkapı Palace. He picked at red beetroot chips and had the occasional gorge on tuna sushi to mop up the cocktails. It wasn't long before he had the urge for a bit of weed, and maybe a woman or two. A party, he thought. That would be good.

He needed to drown the sorrow of forever feeling abandoned by his mother, an irrational thought but that was how it was. He had never recovered from her loss, and yet here he was now, having just found out she had been brutally murdered at the hands of an American CIA agent. Murdered, for fuck's sake. By a Yank.

'Where do I get some good-looking women in Istanbul?' he asked the barman, who thought he was still joshing. He wasn't. Sean was still compos mentis, but only just. He needed something to take his mind off things and drugs and women were the forbidden fruits that would sort him out for the night. He needed to go wild for a while. Not for too long, just long enough to get some satisfaction and blow his mind a bit. He felt excited at the prospect as the barman gave him a card with a few numbers on.

Jack was fuming. He knew Sean would blatantly ignore his requests and if there was one thing Jack needed to make his complex plots work it was control – control of what was happening on the ground. He felt he was losing that control and Sean might now enter one of his renegade periods. Who could blame him though? He needed Sean off the case and taken out of the country before he caused any damage to the mission. His mind would be wayward from this point on and not suited to the vagaries of a complex mission – he began to wish he'd extracted him first before telling him who the murderer of his mother was over a wobbly video call.

'I want him out on the next CIA plane and into Prague as soon as possible,' he barked to Samantha over a secure phone call. 'I'll sort him out from there and within a few days he'll recognise it was the right thing to do.'

'But he's gone Jack. Vamoosed. No one knows where he's gone. I checked his room earlier and all his kit has gone too.'

'OK, I'll get onto Melissa and see if she's heard from him. You'll need to track his credit cards using the CIA station staff, track him down, hold him and get him on a plane before he creates a diplomatic fucking incident.'

Samantha had never ever heard Jack swear, and it caused her to wonder what the hell was going on.

'Why Jack? What's causing all this?'

'Let's just say his mind is about to go into meltdown. I know him.'

'But why? Is he in trouble?'

'That's the point Sam. We need to keep him out of trouble. His ability to deal with stress has been stripped bare over the last few years and he'll teeter over the edge again if we don't get hold of him quickly. I misjudged it.'

'OK Jack. I'll get the CIA station to help us if you can contact them now. It might get a bit messy as he's a stubborn bastard at times, unless of course he's totally drunk, in which case we'll find him and get him on a plane asap.'

'Make sure you do. I don't want him anywhere near Nadège as there's a danger he'll blurt everything out and blow the cover of my GRU agent. Then we're really fucked.'

Jack explained the background of Colonel Sergei and how he was the most important Russian agent MI5 had recruited in decades. Sergei was one of only four known GRU officers ever to have defected to the West in over fifty years and two were already dead – killed by GRU assassination squads on British soil. He didn't want a third on his hands. If Sean got drunk with Nadège, the risk of that now being high, he might inadvertently leak information that would put Colonel Sergei immediately under the microscope. It was Sergei who had made sure that Sean would be tasked as the weapons smuggler for Nadège, which was a crucial part of the deception plan Jack had conjured. A lure to provide her with the fissile material she needed to accomplish the terrorist mission. A high-risk strategy that Jack was now seeing could go badly wrong.

Jack sent a classified message to his CIA contact in Istanbul asking for all possible assistance, and making it clear that force could be used on Sean if necessary.

Sean knew when danger was lurking. He had an innate sense for it. Even when he'd been drinking. Sean had spotted the three men take a seat in the lounge area just as he returned from the toilet. An uncommon number, he thought, for a classy hotel. Couples yes, families yes. Three men, dubious. They could be on the piss, he thought, maybe even waiting for their other halves. He'd keep an eye on them anyway, remembering the SVR still had a contract on his head. He had no idea at the time that Jack was very serious about pulling him off the mission. It being an order, not a request.

Sean played out in his mind who they might be and how they might avenge him. How on earth could the SVR know he was here? He had not entered Istanbul through any formal port authority, hadn't shown any passports and had retained a suitable disguise that didn't resemble his appearance from two years ago when he'd captured the SVR's most prolific sleeper agent.

Might be an insider in the CIA, he thought. Their Special Activities Division were, after all, closely enmeshed with The Court's operations. It was possible someone had tipped them off. Or could it be Colonel Sergei? Christ, that would be a savage blow if it was. A Russian GRU agent right in the heart of MI5's most secretive operation. The permutations of that particular scenario were too devastating to rationalise in his semi-drunken state.

He'd have to put his night of debauchery on hold whilst he dealt with them and needed to lose them. He mulled the options over in his mind. He could easily lose them if needed in the meandering malls of the shopping centre, or trap one of them in the toilet to find out who they were. Or was he just being paranoid, and everything was fine?

He came up with a plan. He made a call to an agency and asked them to send their best two girls for the night. An overnight stay. Then he'd watch to see if any of the men decided to follow him. If they did, he'd exit his room, create a few counter-surveillance moves and take them out one by one. Bold and brash but the beginnings of a plan. If they didn't follow him? Well, he'd have that night of depravity instead. Simple, he said in his semi-drunken mind, knowing no such plan survived contact with the enemy.

Two hours later he sat in the room entertaining two attractive women, popping the corks on two of the four bottles of champagne he'd ordered and keeping an ear out for room service, which he hadn't called. If they came after him he knew they'd be armed but he planned on a commotion to subdue that threat. He told the women he'd be back in twenty minutes perhaps with another friend, if that was OK? The smaller of the mini-skirted hookers said it was. He left the room and turned left, heading for the lift. Sure enough, one of the men stood at the end of the corridor amateurishly looking at the room numbers on the wall. Sean clocked his demeanour. A bowlegged man with Mediterranean features wearing a black blazer and an identically coloured shirt and trousers. He pinged the lift and headed down to the ground floor, knowing the man would remain upstairs. Sure as mud was mud, the second and third men were in the lobby, tall with hard faces, but oddly they seemed to be chatting to another man with the look of authority. The security manager perhaps?

The suited hotel man looked Sean in the eye, but he continued to meander towards the exit, taking a cigarette from his Rothmans packet. The doorman opened the huge glass door and Sean popped out into the still air of the night, watching a black Porsche Cayenne glide to a halt in a layby on the mosaicked roadway. He drew on the cigarette, telling himself he was sober and could make this work. He simply needed an escape. Time spent on recce was seldom wasted he told himself, knowing he was now under full surveillance.

Chapter 25

Raffles Hotel, Istanbul

Sean tossed his cigarette into a sand-filled container and made his way back to the lobby, making sure his swaying gait was that of an inebriated man, just as he had done coming down from the hotel suite.

The men didn't seem to have any radios or earpieces, which told him they were more likely to be local thugs told to do a job on him rather than pros from an agency. Surveillance more than attack, he thought. He made a mental note not to use his credit cards again, and to rely solely on the wads of cash he had in his rucksack. The lift was open and ready to go so he stepped in quickly, prepared if one or both of the hoods followed him. They didn't.

He arrived at the fifth floor fully expecting the third hood to be stood bowlegged, lurching around and picking his nose with boredom. Sean exited the lift, turned right and walked straight up to the man, who was now gazing out of the window, admiring the Istanbul vista, with his hand down his jeans scratching his arse. Sean tapped him on the shoulder.

The bowlegged man turned with a jolt.

Sean smiled harshly at him, keeping just the right distance in case he reacted aggressively. Sean waved a handful of dollars in the man's face. 'Listen, whoever has paid you, I'll pay you more. Do you savvy?'

The man had retrieved his hand from his backside and was stood in partial shock, mouth slightly open and with a gait that told Sean he was indeed an amateur. 'It's pretty simple really, no one will ever know I've paid you. You just say you missed me leaving the room, but the door was left open, so you entered to see if I was in there with the women who you saw turn up earlier.'

The man said nothing but gazed oddly. Sean could smell a mix of cannabis and stale odour on him. He seemed lifeless and partially stoned. He wasn't an intelligence officer for sure, nor a military man. But Sean wanted to find out who he was, the languages he spoke and who he was acting for. This was a man who was used to taking instruction, not acting with initiative, and one ruled by money and drugs.

'*Ty panimayesh?*' Sean asked in Russian.

'*Da, spaciba.*'

'*Harasho*. Good. Come with me and we'll fix this' Sean replied, pushing some notes into his jacket pocket.

Sean steered him by the elbow, knowing full well the man understood a little English but didn't quite know how to respond in a language that was so foreign to him when he was in shock.

As Sean nudged the man into his suite, he smiled knowingly at the two women who had started to undress and parade around the room in matching black knickers and bras, just as Sean had requested on the telephone. One of them immediately handed the Russian a glass of champagne and began touching his balls. She encouraged him to text his friends to say he was fine, and that Sean was in his room with the girls.

'Yours for the next couple of hours if you want them,' Sean uttered in Russian. A glaze of joy came across the Russian's face. 'Let's have some fun,' Sean said to the girls, pointing to the champagne on the round glass table. He's a bit of a novice but very eager and willing.'

Thirty-five minutes later, Sean and the two women left the room, exiting via the western stairwell, pushed a fire-exit door open and jumped into the black Porsche Cayenne. Sean made sure he smashed the fire alarm on his way out and the mayhem of the hotel evacuation began within seconds. Sean and the two hookers had left the Russian strapped naked to the balcony railings of the suite overlooking the Bosphorus river, complete with a marble facsimile of the Blue Dome dangling from his penis.

As Sean drove past the exiting crowds of the Raffles Hotel he caught a fleeting glimpse of Samantha and Swartz stood by a silver BMW.

Chapter 26

The Black Sea

Sean walked with a limp up the gangway of *RMS Crystal*, which had been booked for the two-day voyage of one of the largest luxury travel conferences in the world. It was a conference held only every four years and the second time the international organisers had chosen to run it on a cruise liner. More than five hundred people from all over the world walked up the gangplanks that morning to a welcome from the ship's officers within the lavish surroundings of one of the world's finest cruise experiences. Sean entered separately, retaining his covert guise.

Sean was moody and had remained quiet for most of the journey to the ship. He really didn't feel like opening up to Swartz, who knew he was in a bad place. Sean had spent a day recovering from his hangover in a cheap Istanbul hotel, having endured a tortuous night before he finally plucked up the courage to give Swartz a call.

'What the fuck are you doing Sean?' Swartz had answered. 'Jack and Samantha are going spare at what you left behind at Raffles. Some poor Russian bastard was superglued to the rails for fuck's sake.'

'Yes, well. It was just a bit of fun, nothing more. Listen, I think those guys were sent by Nadège just to keep an eye on me. They weren't Spetsnaz or anything so handy. If it wasn't Nadège, then we have a leak somewhere. That could be fatal.'

'OK, what's your plan now then? They've got the CIA and every Tom, Dick and Harry looking for you. Jack is shit-scared you'll blow his operation apart with the state of mind you're in.'

'My mind's fine mate. I just needed a good blow out to get it out of my system.'

'That was probably not the right thing to do mate, you've pissed everyone off. I don't even know what caused you to go off the rails?'

'All in good time. Now, I need a favour. You need to get me on a ship and go and buy me a couple of suits.'

Sixteen hours later, Sean was sat in a car with Swartz, heading towards the port and the cruise liner that Nadège was due to sail on.

'Come on mate, give me an idea at least,' Swartz said empathetically. 'You know it helps to talk mate.'

Sean remained quiet, ignoring Swartz's offer of support. Sean rarely showed emotion. He liked to think things through before he did. And it had to be with someone he trusted implicitly. Too many years of being shafted had made him a cautious man.

'It's a bit complex, and bloody confusing,' Sean said wearily. He turned to face Swartz in the car and let rip. 'I've just found out who killed my mother back in 1986. I had no idea she was murdered, and it was quite brutal by all accounts. I need to find out what happened.'

Swartz gazed at him in astonishment. Nothing more was said for a while, but Sean could see Swartz's mind was trying to compute what he'd just disclosed. Despite them being the best of friends, Sean had never ever talked about his family to Swartz. He felt shamed by it all.

'Sean. Listen, I'm really sorry to hear about this. Will you be OK?'

'It's fine. I'll be fine.'

'There's always some mad thing going on in your life and I'm here to help, you know that. What did you find out?'

Sean explained how D had found out about his mother's murder and described the hazy phone call with Melissa, who was investigating the disappearance of the FCO diplomat. Sean didn't know the full extent of the linkage between the diplomat and Barrington, but Melissa was delving into every aspect of Barrington's life to unearth the clues.

'Something's not right at all with this, Swartz. Melissa found out that this CIA guy who murdered my mother had previously served as the CIA station chief in Bosnia-Herzegovina.'

'Go on.'

'It was back in 1995. He was also operating from the American HQ based in Tuzla during the Bosnian War. Melissa found out that Duff was out there too.'

'Might be nothing though. Lots of us who served on operations in far-flung wars have stayed in touch with each other.'

'I know, but what's curious is that the FCO bloke was a political liaison officer for the American HQ in Tuzla. And...' Sean paused to think through his words. '...there were some dodgy goings-on at Tuzla with the local Bosnian mafia. I'm not sure how, but Melissa found out that some of the Tuzla officers were caught doing deals with local gangsters.'

'Wow. How has Melissa found all this out?'

'She has some pretty good contacts in the world of journalism.'

'What do you think?'

'Might have been protection, drugs, I don't know. One or two got the sack, and the files relating to the cases have disappeared. I remember the Russians were also based at Tuzla as part of the US Division. They were always up to no good in the town.'

'Still. It might be nothing Sean. That sort of stuff happened in the Brit areas and in Sarajevo too you know. Christ, most of the United Nations police officers in Sarajevo were knocking off local prostitutes. There was big money being exchanged when NATO and the International Police Task Force went in.'

'I know. I remember it well. When NATO went in the local gangsters saw a market for selling anything at a price. But when I sense something isn't right it's normally the bloody case mate. This bastard has got blood on his hands, and Jack had an inkling he was operating as a double agent. Knowing his ilk, he was probably up to no good in Bosnia too, which is where the link with him and Duff comes in. Whoever nicked this FCO diplomat might be using him for some sort of extortion.'

'What for though?'

'I'll find out. No one in London has heard a dicky bird about any ransom demand, unless Jack is holding stuff back from me.'

'Well, he's pretty cute in running these types of ops. Can't blame him for that mate.'

'Well we'll see about that. The bastard has a way of using us to make things happen in Whitehall. Something is very odd here. I need to get to Barrington at some point and get the bastard to talk. I've got an idea or two forming.'

'Why don't you call it a day on this job then? Get back home and find out more about how your mum was killed.'

Sean thought long and hard on that question. He thought it might be the better way. By the time he'd arrived at the transfer point where a taxi would take him the final mile to the dockside, he'd dismissed the notion.

Swartz had done a sterling job with creating Sean's disguise to get him on board the cruise liner. He'd been told that two CIA officers would be monitoring those who boarded, whilst Samantha had been tasked to conduct surveillance on Nadège during the conference cruise. Sean was now fully bejewelled as a wealthy Hasidic Jew, complete with a kippah, wearing a long black suit reminiscent of Polish nobility in the eighteenth century and sporting a scraggly brown beard. The art of disguise had been taught to him by an expert held on the books of The Court on a part-time basis. A former MI6 officer, she had become the master of disguise during the early stages of the cold war and had been charged with helping soviet spies defect to the West undetected. She was known only as Pearly. Sean had been taught the skills of disguise by Pearly when she visited his bolt-hole in Italy to help keep his identity shrouded from the SVR agents and proxies who had been paid to track him down. She was also charged with helping current-day Russian defectors who lived in Britain with the many forms of disguise.

'The trick, Mr Richardson,' she had said, 'Is to imagine someone wrote a list of your own features and provided them to the police. You'd need to create a disguise that was completely the opposite of those features. You have grey flecked hair. Not any more. You walk with your feet open. Wrong. You have a scar across your left eye. Not with good make-up.'

Sean remembered how she had told him some amazing stories. Pearly had served in MI6 for twenty-five years, traveling to Russia, South America, East Germany, Czechoslovakia and places she said she couldn't reveal to Sean. She had specialised in exfiltration - getting friendly people out from behind the Iron Curtain.

Pearly had retired in 1997. The cold war was long over and she spent her days writing walking guides in The Cotswolds. She never assumed The Court would come knocking on her door in retirement, she had told Sean in long discussions on her past. 'I thought I'd be forgotten about and lost in time,' she said. 'Spying and helping spies was satisfying. But never expect any reward young man. Ever. Take your satisfaction from the good work you do, and steer yourself to a life you want. Not what they want.'

Sean admired her humble ways, recalling her wisdom. 'Being someone else is easy, if you take away every little bit of you.' Those words kept ringing in Sean's mind as he made his way up the gangplank clutching a walking stick.

Sean was shown to his cabin by a petite Bulgarian steward and gave her a twenty-dollar tip. He placed his suitcase on the bed and waited for Samantha to arrive, enjoying the anticipation of the sense of shock she would have when seeing an elderly Jew sitting in her cabin. He wagered that her first words would be an apology for being in the wrong cabin, before reprimanding him for being a twat when she found out. A cheeky grin began to grow.

The knock on the door came twenty minutes later, followed by the key being turned to open it. Samantha glided in and placed her suitcase on the bed, noticing that there was already a black carry-on suitcase on it. Sean stepped from the bathroom and watched her jump. She shook with fright.

'What the fuck?' she exclaimed in her haughty Home Counties accent. 'Who are you? Oh, I'm sorry… am I in the right cabin?'

'You are, mademoiselle,' Sean said meekly, taking off his long brown beard.

'Sean! You twat.'

'Yes my lover, how are you?'

'Fuck off. You've been a right prick the last forty-eight hours and now you'll get me in the shit.'

'You really don't need to tell Jack you know. Just you and me on a romantic cruise for two with the biggest double bed I've seen on a boat.' Sean played to her inner desires.

'You really are a mad bastard you know. Your mother would not have been impressed with your behaviour – Oh, I'm sorry, I didn't mean…'

A silence. And a sad look from Samantha.

'That's OK, don't worry. I'm fixed up now. Anyway, how the fuck did someone know I was at Raffles last night and put a bunch of hoods on me?'

'Nadège had someone following her all the time at a distance – a stand-off minder to report back to her if she was being followed. He was taking pictures of you all the way to the mosque and outside it. That's how they tracked you down. She probably has most of the hotel security managers in the city well and truly in her pocket.'

'OK, well let's get down to business. We've got a lot to sort out for this trip. I'm going to approach her again, but first off we need to know who she's meeting on-board.'

'Might be someone they've replaced you with – another weapons dealer.'

'Not sure, but this boat is now packed with some of the wealthiest captains of industry as well as corrupt government officials from across the globe. It's a spy's paradise.'

Sean chatted about his plan with Samantha, who had now calmed down. He'd talked her into remaining onside and not blowing it with Jack just yet.

'I warn you though Sean, if this ends up going nowhere I call Jack, and get you lifted out of the country, right?'

'Deal. Give me a shot at it though at least. You know it will be worth your while,' he said with a twinkle in his eye.

'It bloody better be,' Samantha said, placing an arm on her hip to accentuate her curves. 'You've deserted me for far too long, so yes you can have a shot you naughty bastard.' Samantha walked to the cabin door, dropped the deadlock and turned on her toes. Sean caught a slash of her thigh as she undid a button on her blouse, partially revealing her ample cleavage. Sean breathed in deeply. He had to think quickly on his feet to avoid her being intimate with him again.

Sean had always been shocked at the intensity of their lovemaking, remembering how wild it used to be when they were close friends many years ago. It was always intense and dramatic with Samantha always wanting more. She was not one to hold back. But this was not a time for deviation, he had a job to fulfil. A mission. He couldn't go back. He turned and started to check his communications equipment, conscious of the loud tut he heard behind him.

'Come on, we've got some serious work to do today. We don't have much time right now.'

Sean ignored the noise of Samantha slamming her palm on the table and muttering loudly. He swore he heard a foot being stamped too. After a lengthy silence, he eventually shifted her attention to the task in hand despite the glum look on her face. He began to explain how he would lure Nadège into trusting him enough to give him a shot at supplying the illicit materials.

He asked Samantha to find out where Nadège was quartered on the ship and who she had met or had discussions with. He knew if Nadège was here on business it involved espionage. And he bet they weren't the only ones involved in spying at this conference. Conferences were normally rife with national spy agencies looking to recruit potential high-grade targets from multiple countries. He knew from experience that the importance of a conference wasn't measured just by the number of top class speakers or government ministers it attracted, but by the number of spies. Foreign intelligence officers target conferences because they make great hunting grounds. Sean had done his fair share of recruiting at overseas conferences in the past, and he remembered the words of his intelligence mentor in the old War Office in Whitehall: 'Every intelligence service in the world targets conferences, and looks for ways to get people to conferences and recruit them.'

He wondered if Nadège was working someone already and was here to continue that process. The only common denominator so far on this job was her drive to buy nuclear material. Was she recruiting someone for Iran? Or for her mission? The device he had forensically investigated in the buried cache had all the hallmarks of acting as a receptacle for a dirty bomb. The golden thread running through this mission seemed to be the desire of Iran to build nuclear capability or simply just acquire a crude nuclear weapon and detonate it. A frightening prospect on both counts, Sean thought.

Sean tapped a message to Samantha on his phone.

'Have you found out where she is yet? Follow her like a hawk. Let's see who she's trying to recruit.'

For now, this was a waiting game. Sean sat in his cabin. Nursing his thoughts. Waiting. Reminiscing.

Ninety minutes later Sean was woken with a shock. His phone rang loudly, blasting out Tom Waits's 'Telephone Call from Istanbul'.

'I've clocked her,' Samantha said, whispering through her jacket microphone. 'Got a photo of the name card she's wearing too as I brushed past her at the reception deck. She's quite pretty you know.'

Sean rolled his eyes and heaved himself off the bed. 'Good stuff Sam, and yes I know.'

A picture came through of the name card. Mrs Felicity Price it said. Liberty Travel. New York.

'*Let's see who she bumps,*' Sean texted.

The exchanges with Samantha reminded him how good a surveillance operator she was. Sean looked at the conference booklet and the schedule of events. Organised by Marinex, he wondered if this was a front for the CIA? Maritime conferences like this would be perfect for them to try to tease government officials from rogue states into their arms. This place could be swarming with spies, Sean thought, flicking through the programme of events.

This brought Sean's mind to how Nadège might recruit her target. And the tactics she might use. He needed to be ahead of the game for this. It was crucial he understood her motivations and her own vulnerabilities if he was to get anywhere with her. Sean suspected that Nadège would use the normal approaches of a spy trying to recruit an agent. She was clearly posing as an executive and her first job would be to peel the guards away from whoever it was she wanted to connect with.

I wonder if she'll defect? Sean heard himself saying. What might her motivation be to act as a double agent? There must be something. He still didn't know which button to push with Nadège. Yet.

Chapter 27

The Black Sea

Having spent the best part of four hours in the cabin with his thoughts, Sean decided he'd go to the reception lunch and then attend the afternoon session of the conference. He'd keep his distance from Nadège and rely on Samantha providing him with updates on her movements and the connections she made with other people. The timing of their next encounter would be crucial.

But something kept niggling him. Like itching powder under his skin. Four hours of deep thought came back to one thing. Why is Nadège so important? That question led to deep seeds of doubt being sown in Sean's mind. Was he being used again? Was he being used as a fall guy here? He tried to shake off those doubts but couldn't – too many years of being lulled into duplicitous events had taken their toll. He rarely trusted anyone, but he trusted Jack, right? After all it was Jack who had saved his life last time round. But Jack had a propensity for using pawns in the game to achieve a more strategic objective. What the bloody hell was it this time, he wondered?

An equally puzzling thought was the murder of the Mayor of Sarajevo by Nadège and her accomplice. Her lover? The blonde on the wall in the ops room who had visited Nadège in her hotel room. The common factor was Bosnia. The ex-CIA murderer of his mother had served there as well as in Berlin in the '80s. Sean didn't believe in coincidences and made a mental note to check through the linkages of the Mayor and the ex-CIA officer as soon as he could. Given that Nadège was an international model flirting with the elite, there might be a common thread.

Samantha called. 'She's had a brush with a tall man with glasses. Looks Middle Eastern and very well dressed, cravat, the lot,' she said. 'It was a short brush at a coffee table, a two-minute chat at most. I'll send you a picture now.'

'Good spot Sam. Keep watching and give me a confirmation that he's the target. I'll be staying out of the conference but I'm up on deck 4 in the piano bar. You'll need to send the picture back to The Court as I'm not here, remember?'

Sean peered out of the huge expanse of glass that provided shelter from the vistas across the Black Sea towards the coastline of the Crimea and the cities of Sevastopol and Yalta. The cruise was destined to do a circular lap of the Black Sea, a region of the globe steeped in the history of arms and weapons smuggling as well as the recent annexation of Crimea by Russia. The sea was calm, and the sun shone brightly at its apogee. He enjoyed the views and the time to think. His mind drifted to the times he had spent in Abkhazia and Georgia chasing down illicit radiological sources to disrupt terrorists smuggling the materials across Central Asia, through the Caucasus and into Europe. This time, he had another mission to find nuclear material and a bomber. All linked to Nadège. But the targets for unleashing the devastation remained unknown.

He leant across the table and grabbed one of the conference magazines. Just as he did so, he spotted a face that seemed familiar. It was a man sat three rows down who was looking at his phone. Sean tried to remember where he had seen him before. It wasn't someone he instantly recognised, but more like a face he had seen in the crowds or amongst the passengers on the cruise. It alerted him. His counter-surveillance skills and observation were kicking in and it was a face he had seen at least twice. Might be nothing, he mulled, but he chose to go for a walk anyway to see if this bloke followed. Just as he stood up, he got a text from Samantha.

'Same man, five-minute chat at the back of the conference room during the twenty-minute break. Your woman is good. She's mixed with a few people but the only one she has chatted to so far is this man with the cravat. Nothing back from HQ yet.'

Ten seconds later another text. Sean sat at the bar on his way out of the room to see if the man had stood up. He hadn't. He looked at his phone's screen.

'I picked up on their latest conversation. They are going to meet at 6.30pm for a drink before dinner.'

Sean didn't reply but continued walking along the long external corridor towards the central part of the ship, where he decided he would conduct a series of moves to see if this bloke or anyone else was following him. He hadn't yet forgotten the events of two nights ago, or the SVR threat, and he'd changed his appearance back to how it had been that night.

He had it in his mind that he'd strike against Nadège's target that evening. But first he needed to be sure he wasn't being tailed. Detours, he heard himself say. Slow gentle detours around the ship like any other guest finding their way on a new vessel. He made his way up the escalators to the grand entrance of the ballroom and stopped to admire the decor and the views across the starboard decks. He chose a position that allowed him to see everyone pass him from the escalator exit. Nothing. He leant on the balcony that provided the view to the shopping mall below. A young couple opposite him were doing exactly the same and an elderly man was taking photographs of the ballroom to his right. Sean scanned the concourse leading to the main deck and swimming pools through a set of automatic glass doors. He was looking carefully for faces he had seen before. The guy in the bar. Still nothing. Maybe he was too uptight, had lost his touch maybe? Doubts. One last move. Let's tease them out. He strolled around the balcony to the main entrance of the gargantuan dining room and chatted briefly with a young woman behind the reception desk just out of view from the base of the escalator. That should have been enough to force a man to mount the escalator to check he hadn't lost his quarry. He chatted with the woman long enough to know that such a tail would be on the escalator, then turned on his heels sharply. He marched quickly into the gift shop next to the dining room, quickly enough that no one would see him unless they had someone else watching on that level. He scanned the escalator from a gap in the window display.

Sure enough the man from the bar was there. Exiting the escalator. He was looking over his shoulder and then backwards and forwards. Looking for someone. Trying to find his prey. Sean stepped out of the gift shop and casually made his way down the hallway. He had spotted a toilet at the far end of the concourse and would visit it. He walked down the corridor, stepped into the large restroom and made his way to the far urinal. He unzipped his fly. The man walked through the door while Sean glanced down at his non-existent pee. Quiet. He was sure no one else was in the traps behind him.

The man stood two urinals down and unzipped his fly. Just as he flopped his penis out, Sean sprung from his heels and started smashing the man's head against the white tiles. Blood from his now-broken nose dripped down the tiles as he groaned in pain, both hands protecting his vulnerable todger. Sean knew a man with his hand on his cock was easy prey and vulnerable. It was an old pub trick he had used on more than one occasion. He smashed his head a third and then a fourth time, before letting him crumple to the floor unconscious. Sean grabbed him under the arms and bundled him into the far toilet cubicle, heaving at his chest to sit him up on the toilet seat. He quickly checked the man's pockets and took a photograph of the man's face using his mobile phone.

Bang. The entrance door to the toilets had opened and shut with the loud noise of metal on metal. Was it a second tail checking on his colleague? Sean waited. And listened. A good crew would have a second. It went quiet and the door opened and shut again. Maybe he'd just knocked out an innocent bloke? No, he was a follower alright and he'd seen his face somewhere else, though he couldn't remember where. Subconsciously, Sean had clocked his face, but it was fleeting, non-specific, just a face in a crowd. But enough of a glance for Sean's mind to know he'd seen it before. He checked his pockets again. Top pocket, a slim Galaxy phone. Sean secured it in his right-hand jacket pocket before checking the man's trouser back pocket. He balanced the body awkwardly then grasped behind his backside. He took all his belongings – wallet, watch, phone, cigarettes – just like any mugger would do.

Sean took a breath. He checked his suit. Just a few flecks of blood on his shirt, which he could hide by buttoning his jacket. He looked at the man's face again. Mediterranean looks, clean shaven, dark black hair. Mid-forties, he thought. Where the hell had he seen him before? Had he thought longer and deeper, he'd have known it was the man who had been photographing him on his visit to the Blue Dome with Nadège.

Chapter 28

The Black Sea

5.20pm. Corridor 25 heading towards cabin D0386. Sean followed Nadège's contact along the corridor, loitering five metres behind him, poised to strike.

The well-dressed man was carrying an expensive-looking briefcase, swopping it from one hand to the other before he reached inside his right-hand pocket for the cabin key. Senses tightening, Sean increased his speed, watching the man place the key in the lock and then turning it twice to the right before pushing the handle to open the door. During those few moments Sean lunged forward, kicking the man in the back of the knee with an open foot and striking hard against the popliteus muscle. The man let out a cry before crumpling in a heap. Sean grabbed the man, swinging him with brutal strength to force him inside the cabin before kicking the door shut. In his mid-sixties, the man was no match for Sean's speed and strength, nor did he have any inclination to fight back. The shock of the assault made him totally submissive.

'Shut the fuck up and do exactly as I tell you,' Sean shouted, exerting pressure on the man's shoulder socket. 'If you do everything I tell you then you won't be hurt. Understand?'

'Yes, yes, please, hurting, stop. Please,' came the reply in patchy English, which was slightly muffled as his mouth had been floored.

Sean grabbed a bunch of plastic tie wraps from his jeans and began strapping them on the man's wrists. 'On your feet,' Sean barked, moving to bolt the door. Wriggling and rolling, the man eventually found his feet with some help, looking terrified as his eyes met Sean's.

'Turn around, forehead on the wall, feet apart.'

Sean quickly searched him for any weapons and, despite the man's age, he was taking no chances. He took a phone and wallet from his pockets, placing them on a bench next to the TV.

'OK, sit down over there and stay bloody quiet until I talk to you.'

Sean grabbed his phone and punched out a text to Sam. Two minutes later came a knock on the door. Samantha entered, looking ready for action. 'His briefcase is over there,' Sean explained, locking the door.

'What do you want with me?' the man said fearfully. 'What have I done?'

Sean dragged a chair and sat opposite the man, taking a few deep breaths to calm himself. 'It's not what you've done. It's what you are about to do for us. Now, what's your real name?'

'Javid. Javid Saaid.'

'Who are you working for?'

'I'm a retired scientist from the University of Karachi in Pakistan. I was for thirty-five years before I retired last year.'

'Teaching what?'

'Nuclear engineering. Is this about that woman I met today?'

'Yes. Now listen very carefully to me,' Sean said sternly. 'You need to tell me everything you have been told to do and what she is after. We are from the British government, working on a case of nuclear smuggling, and I can have you arrested and banged up in Turkey within seconds of giving the nod to the authorities. Do you understand?'

'Yes I do. But I was asked to do this by some government people. I think they were government.'

'Why do you think that?'

'After thirty-five years working on nuclear technology in Pakistan, you get a feel for who's who, believe me. They threatened me with the loss of my grandchildren if I didn't comply. Said they'd make sure I was found to be a paedophile. It's horrible.' The man took a moment to control himself. 'I'm just a courier and was told to meet this woman at a holiday conference in Vienna two months ago, which I did. She passed a note to me requesting some data on nuclear technology and I returned to

Karachi to tell these people what she was after. They told me to comply with her requests. I'm just a go-between and a scientist – I want to protect my family, you know. I never wanted to do this. They said I'd never have to do it again.'

'Why a travel conference though?'

'She said it would attract less attention, and I travel a lot with my wife on cruises. I'm retired now, but they obviously did their homework on me. I've been attending holiday and travel conferences for many years.'

Sean knew by now he had a complicit agent. He could tell. Someone that the Pakistani intelligence service, ISI, had probably got to. Someone easily corrupted by the Iranians or Russians to make sure Nadège got the technical details she needed. Sean needed the full story of what the well-groomed man was supposed to be doing here and why. He reached around the man's back and cut the tie wraps.

'What is it you need to do at this conference? I need to know everything.'

Samantha helped the elderly man drink some water, calming him, before he answered. 'I have to give her an encrypted pen drive at dinner this evening. Then, over the course of the cruise, I need to explain some of the technical elements she needs. I'm supposed to meet her at 6.30pm.'

'Good, what else?'

'The men in Pakistan told me to create the designs she needed and return to this conference with all of the details of a nuclear device laid out in plans and documents. She must already know someone who understands how nuclear fission works with explosives because she gave me some very precise questions laid out in the documents in Vienna.'

This was all beginning to fit for Sean. The rogue British Army explosives expert who had gone missing – could it be him? The background Jack had provided on him showed that he was an expert in chemical and radiological devices. This all fitted with the suitcases Sean had found in the woods in northern Turkey. NIGHTOWL was putting a complex plan together for building a nuclear IED. Sean had now confirmed it.

'OK, we don't have much time. Where's the pen drive?

'In my spectacle case inside my briefcase. I was told to place it on the table when we had dinner. She would put her glasses in it and take the case.'

'Good. Fire up your laptop and I'll take it from here. You'll do everything I tell you, OK?'

Sean watched the man's hand shaking as he retrieved a brown spectacle case from the briefcase. He opened the case, revealing a silver pen drive inside. Sean placed his laptop on the table, entered the password and let it run the security scans on the pen drive to ensure it was free of malicious code. He then placed it in the port of the secure laptop Samantha had brought with her and asked Saaid to enter the password. There were only two files on the drive. A Microsoft Word document and a PDF. He opened the twenty-four-page Word document.

The document contained a mixture of text and drawings plus a few mathematical computations and equations. Sean had no idea what they represented. What he did recognise was a drawing of a gun device. A drawing that showed how a gun device operated to produce a nuclear improvised device and of a type that the West had long been fearful would end up in the hands of ISIS. The gun device worked on the simple mechanism of firing a large piece of uranium-238 down a barrel at immense speed to collide with another piece of uranium and create a nuclear explosion.

Sean copied all the files and the entire hard drive of the Pakistani's laptop onto Samantha's. He returned to the original Word document and began to insert some code into its macro feature. A code that put a time lapse on the entire document before it would scramble itself into a bunch of unintelligible characters. It would slowly destroy itself by acting like a cancer to the words.

'Here's what we do Mr Saaid. You will carry out your task at 6.30pm, making sure you do not give anything away about the discussions we've had here. My colleague here will wire you up, and we'll be watching every movement you make. Do you understand?'

'Yes, sir. But what about my family?'

'If you go through with this your masters will be none the wiser about what we've done. I want you to give my colleague here your address and contact details. When you return to Pakistan you'll have a visit from an officer from the British Embassy. You'll help them with their inquiries into who tasked you for this work and you'll be well looked after by them. You'll be operating for the British now - they'll protect you and your family. What you have done today is a highly important act that could avert a major terrorist incident. You'll be looked after, but do not under any circumstances tell anyone else about this except the British officers who will visit you in Pakistan.'

Sean watched the man break down, holding his head in his hands as if it was a massive relief to his soul.

'Right, get yourself together, and get your head right for this. There's no time for emotion. We get this done, OK?' The man nodded, trying to control his shaking.

Sean now had a head start on Nadège. At last. A lure, and an inside track. He had uncovered their command and control facility at the port in Istanbul, found the hidden caches of bomb-making equipment in the woods and verified that she planned to deploy an improvised nuclear device, with all the carnage that came with it. He had found the next big piece in the jigsaw. He also knew that the most difficult element of planning such a nuclear attack using a gun device was to acquire enough uranium to make it happen.

And Sean was the man who had been sent to Nadège to provide the quantities of uranium that she needed.

Chapter 29

The Black Sea

The evening entertainment aboard the *RMS Crystal* consisted of a five-course Michelin-star dinner accompanied by a 1920s-style Dixieland jazz band led by a bandmaster and a banjo player. A full crew of waiting staff, dressed immaculately in black, darted amongst the three levels of the ballroom, whilst sequin-dressed women guided diners expertly to their tables.

Sean was dressed for the occasion in a beige suit, white shirt and cobalt blue tie with matching pocket handkerchief. His appearance had returned to his clean-cut short-back-and-sides image, complete with a well-trimmed but greying beard. He hovered in the large cocktail lounge above the main restaurant, where wealthy conference goers were jostling for position around the centrepiece bar. A small cadre of cocktail waiters and mixologists were in full swing, flinging and tumbling containers between themselves, launching bottles behind their backs and generally providing an exquisite show for all.

Sean meandered amongst the crowd, listening carefully to Samantha's commentary on his tiny earphone. Samantha had followed Saaid and was sat in the quiet lounge a deck above.

'It's quite cosy up here you know,' Samantha began. 'Dim lights, piano player, classy sofas and some wonderful aperitifs. I think we can have a quiet romantic moment here later when they're all tucked up in bed.'

Sean smirked. His eyes connected with the deep green eyes of a waitress holding a tray of champagne in front of him. He felt a tinge of attraction, coupled with a fleeting thought about having a night of debauchery again, but quickly reigned them back in. He lifted a glass, leaving a lingering smile for the waitress, before pressing the radio switch twice to signify he had received Samantha's message.

'They're shaking hands. Now he's kissing her hand. Proper gentleman. He's sat down next to her. She looks stunning by the way. Strapless green gown, full length with a split, and hair up in a bun. Stunningly petite, but deadly I'd say.'

'Is there a seat nearby that I can use?'

'Yes. Now listen into their conversation. I'm sat at the bar next to some very loud Americans. Saaid is playing it well so far.'

Sean pressed the switch twice, found a quiet corner and used a second earpiece to listen to the conversation Saaid was now having with Nadège. The microphone had been neatly sewn into his jacket collar but so far it was only picking up small talk about the conference, with no reference to the matter at hand. Once the covert pass of the pen drive had taken place, Sean would make his move.

Sean listened intently to Nadège talking. 'I'll need you to answer some questions for my friend over the next two weeks by email. You'll answer these questions in the drafts folder of this Hotmail account.'

Sean imagined her passing a card across the table to Saaid with a Hotmail address on it. She was using a tactic that had often been used by terrorists to ensure no actual transmissions ever took place, and one which allowed operators to exchange messages in the same draft folder.

'My colleague knows what he's doing,' she continued, 'but he's asked me to question you in detail about the documents and techniques you're providing.' A long pause and the sound of fizzy drinks being poured and ice clattering against glass. 'We can do that over the course of the next day or so but after that he will contact you using the Hotmail address. You'll have to monitor it every day at 2pm.'

Sean listened to Saaid agreeing with Nadège. Saaid then explained how he would guide Nadège through the technical elements of the documents he was providing and that he would be happy to help her protégé from afar. Sean knew this to be the British Army bombmaker given the codename FALLOWFIELD by Jack for this operation. Sean had read that this man was perfectly capable of building an improvised nuclear device but that such a feat could never be completed by a single operator. He'd need scientific support on hand to guide him with the technical intricacies. Any small imperfection in the design and the explosive energy calculation would render the device useless.

This new turn of events now provided Sean with the ability to communicate directly with the bomber. A massive bonus.

'Saaid has passed the glasses case. All delivered,' Samantha said over the radio. Sean's sense of adventure was now peaking as he slowly made his way up the long winding staircase to the quiet lounge. He took a few breathes, adjusted his tie and sprayed a small amount of Terre d'Hermès on his neck from a sample bottle.

Sean walked calmly into the lounge and thrust a hand out to Saaid.

'Good evening, my name's Calum,' Sean said, gripping Saaid's hand firmly. 'Don't stand up… please.'

He turned to Nadège. 'Good evening, do you mind if I take a seat?'

Sean watched Saaid helpfully pull a chair closer. Before Nadège had a chance to say a word, Sean was sat in it, smiling broadly at both of them. Nadège's eyes threw piercing daggers - she was fuming, no doubt about it.

'It's been really nice to meet so many new faces here. Here's my card by the way, I'm from London you know. What about you?'

Nadège couldn't exactly make a public show of her rage and Sean had made sure that he came across as loud and gregarious, enough to capture the attention of other people on adjacent tables. The risk was that she would simply stand up and leave. She didn't.

'We've only just met too,' Nadège said finally with a forced smile. 'I'm from New York and I believe this gentleman is from India. What exactly do you do then Calum?' She enunciated every syllable of the last sentence, making it very clear she was pissed off.

'Oh, well. I do a lot of things. I mainly sell. Everything from Sunseeker yachts to providing personal coaching sessions. Perhaps you're in need of a coach?' Sean made a grand gesture with both arms, raised his voice a tone or two higher and provided a few inspirational quotes. Enough to make out that he was an eccentric type, but not a bumbling one.

'Never let fear get in the way of your dreams is my motto,' he said, gently tapping Nadège on the arm.

Nadège retracted her arm swiftly and sat forward. Her eyes were burning with rage. 'But why are you here Calum? This conference isn't about selling boats or coaching is it?'

'Of course madam, or is it mademoiselle? I do sell other things too you know,' Sean said sarcastically, knowing that Nadège liked it when a man flirted with her. He sat back in his chair, smiled at Nadège and threw her a look as if to say 'your turn next.' He placed his hand on his chin, watching as Nadège tried not to laugh. She had been soothed.

Saaid, dressed smartly in a three-piece checked suit and red bow tie, and sporting an expensive Rolex watch, stood to leave. 'Please forgive me for a few moments, I need to make a call to my wife. Mr Calum, a real pleasure to meet you.'

Sean turned to Nadège, smiling. 'I knew I'd get a reaction out of you there. You know it makes sense to have a night with me.'

Nadège regained her composure but wore a scornful face that wanted to take control of the situation. Sean launched in first. 'I have something you need Nadège. Just hear me out quickly. You need what I have, and I need your money. This is a massive sale for me and I've done a hell of a lot to get this set up for you. Did you check me out?'

'I did. Seems you're telling the truth for once but it's a story that could still easily have been concocted too. I'm simply not interested in using you. I've started to look elsewhere.'

'Listen. I need the money, and I'll be upfront with you. I've got a price on my head at the moment. Fucking Albanians have got a contract out on me and I need an out. I think they might be on the ship. Look at this.'

Sean showed Nadège the picture of the man he'd smashed in the toilets, knowing it was probably her man, but that it provided a good twist to his own story.

'He's my man, you bastard.'

'Oh?'

'Yes, and you nearly killed him.'

'Well he was following me. I didn't know he was yours. How did he find me?'

Nadège leant forward and touched Sean on the arm. She smelt divine. 'I know everyone in this city. Everyone, you understand? Police, ministers, army officers, security managers. I pay them a lot and they provide me with information. You were seen at Raffles and then again at that shithole of a place you bunked down in for the night.'

'OK. Your city then. Good skills. I was slack and, to be honest, not in a good place.'

'Why?'

'I'd just heard some bad news about my mother and gone off the rails. Needed a night out I guess.'

'Well listen to me now. You hurt my man bad. I'll have you killed if you keep pestering me. You're being a real pain in the backside. Just forget it. I'm not using you.'

Sean grabbed his champagne and slumped back in his chair, letting the moment ride to take the heat out of the situation. Nadège seemed in no rush to leave though. He waved for a waitress.

'Let's have another drink at least. Like old times? I could do with another good night out.'

'I most certainly do not want that,' Nadège replied haughtily.

'Come on Nadège, you know it makes sense. You have absolutely nothing to lose at all here really. Here, let me show you something.' Sean waited until the waitress had finished topping up their glasses and then took two photographs from his jacket pocket.

'That's me in the Kabul prison last year. Grim eh?' He watched Nadège take the photo showing the dingy cell in which he had been incarcerated. The picture showed a couple of rusty bunk beds bolted to the wall with the cell splattered in globules of phlegm and excrement. Sean was sat shaven headed on the bottom of the bunk.

'Taken by the British Consulate rep before I was released. Now look at this one. It's in Uzbekistan.' He passed the second photo showing him stood above five wooden cases of automatic weapons and grenades with a second man, a Westerner. 'This was the man I killed because he framed me before the Afghan police banged me up. It was all over the British press that he was murdered.'

'OK, but why show me this now? I've completed my checks. It doesn't matter to me. I'm not taking the risk of working with an ex-British agent.'

'Well you've been taking a risk with the British Army bomb-disposal officer you're using, haven't you?'

Nadège sat bolt upright. Her face dropped, and she lurched forward. 'How the fuck do you know about him?' she demanded.

'I did my own checks. He's been recruited the same way I was – via some young Syrian bloke, probably linked to the Russian mobs in London I'd have thought. It wasn't that difficult to find out once I got hold of him and threatened him with a knife against his throat. Pretty easy actually.'

'What exactly do you know about him?'

'I did a few checks with a few ex-bomb disposal men he worked with. It was all hushed up but he went mental and started a bombing campaign against his own army units. Proper nutter. I'd keep an eye on him if I was you.'

Sean was grateful for the intelligence Colonel Sergei had provided on the entire operation. He'd explained how they used Syrian and Greek gangsters as the link to the Russian mobs and then through to the GRU. It allowed money to be laundered and operations to be mounted without them being attributable to Moscow. Sean had just skewed the story a little further to suit Nadège's inquisition. She was cornered now. She could either have Sean killed, as he knew too much about the operation, or use him for a while. That would be enough time for Sean to probe further in a risky landscape of deep deception. She could have him killed at any time from this point forward.

Nadège sat back and went quiet. Stunned. Sean passed her his phone with an enlarged photo on it. 'This is what you're after and I have it Nadège. It's weapons-grade uranium, just what your bomber friend needs. I've been paid to get it for you. What have you got to lose?'

Nadège looked at the picture. 'Where is it?'

'It's a helicopter flight and a jeep journey away. You can have it in your hands within two days of leaving here. Your bomb man can have it within three, but you'll need to arrange your own transport to wherever he is. I have a flight ready to go for 8am on Saturday and, after the deal is done, I'll be gone again. It's as easy as that. Meet me back here after dinner at ten o'clock and I'll give you the details.'

Nadège stood up to leave for dinner and held her hand out to shake Sean's. 'I'll think on it,' she said, smiling a little. 'I'll make a call or two and we'll see. Maybe you are right. Perhaps I don't have anything to lose. I'll find out.'

Sean felt confident the lure had worked. Two and a half hours later, sat at the end of the bar with a whisky, Sean watched Nadège glide into the room. Their eyes locked.

'Just one quick drink Sean,' she began, 'then you can come to my room for a while. We have a lot to discuss.'

Chapter 30

London

Jack thought long and hard about what he was about to do. But he knew the time was right. The time was right to put some explosive evidence into the right hands. Some Kompromat.

Kompromat material that would change the American's foreign policy for many years and in a way that HM Government would approve but could simply not do themselves.

His cause was true. His planning impeccable. But despite his confidence in the plan, he wanted to think it through in a bit more detail as he left his office, destined for a rendezvous with one of America's most powerful women in Europe.

He opted for a long stroll from his regular MI5 office on Millbank, deciding to walk along the Thames embankment before traversing Trafalgar Square to arrive at St Martins Lane. It was a wonderful day, nothing more than a slight breeze with the clouds parting occasionally to reveal bursts of a hot summer sun. He felt a little anxious but no more so than with any of the other ingenious plots he had previously handled for his old boss, D. The fresh air would cement his thoughts and rekindle his vigour.

Jack had been temporarily promoted to Deputy Director and was instructed to report progress to Sir Justin Darbyshire, for all Court operations. But for this piece of work he chose not to. He knew it was the right thing to do to change the course of political events over the coming weeks and months, so he chose to do it alone, knowing full well that his deceased boss would have approved.

Jack carried a black under-arm briefcase that contained a number of highly secret documents he had rescued from D's old safe in The Court's offices. He thought about its contents. He even thought about his family as he walked. These were high-risk stakes for the country and for Jack's career and he was about to put his life on the line. He knew there was one man in the world who could change political events in the blink of an eye. The President of the USA. His ultimate but indirect target of the Kompromat.

He walked through Whitehall Gardens and stopped to look briefly at the imposing statue of Sir Henry Bartle Frere, a high commissioner of South Africa who was recalled to London to face charges of misconduct and was officially censured for acting recklessly in 1880. Jack pondered the same fate if he got this wrong.

Shaking off any self-doubt, he made his way to the Strand and finally into St Martin's Lane before entering his favourite restaurant, Asia de Cuba.

He nodded to the maître d' and was shown to his regular leather bench seat nestling discreetly in the far corner of the restaurant. Jack sat, checked his phone and then propped his briefcase on its end against the seat's wooden balustrade. Inside was a dossier. A dossier he had compiled from many hours of investigation following the disappearance of the FCO diplomat, Edmund Duff. The dossier had sat in D's safe next to the file on Sean's mother. The only legacies of D's world destined for final actions by Jack. Actions to square the circle.

'Hey Jack, so nice to catch up again,' the middle-aged woman said in her loud Californian accent. 'Great place for a late lunch I'd say. I had a bit of downtime for some shopping too don't you know.'

'So glad you could make it Laura,' Jack said, standing to greet her. 'You're looking really well as ever.'

'Oh I am Jack, never better,' she said, kissing him on the cheek. 'I'm betting a few of the staff in here are on your payroll then?' Her jovial manner reassured Jack, as did the glancing wink she threw him. She was right of course. Jack had used the restaurant for many years as part of The Court's operations when wealthy targets had been recommended to eat at the restaurant. A healthy ploy. A ploy normally used for the visiting elite, when the waitresses would listen in to discreet conversations with mistresses, wives and friends. The Greek waitress serving them was from Thessaloniki and was superb at striking up breezy conversation with target diners, who would be shown to one of the six tables she managed.

'Great news that you're staying on as station chief Laura,' Jack ventured, referring to his friend's role as Chief of the CIA at the London station. Laura Creswell was known to be a superb leader as well as a hugely talented spy after many years working the Middle East circuits. It had been a highly acclaimed career with only one blip – when she was asked to leave Berlin as station chief in 2014 after her teams had placed surveillance bugs on the German Chancellor's phone. London was due to be her respite before being lined up for the top role as Director of the CIA in Washington.

She had an active personal interest in Jack's Kompromat. They had been friends for many years and Jack trusted her like no other CIA officer. He rarely trusted anyone in the American intelligence community, knowing how much they leaked and that they leaked often.

'I'm enjoying my work here Jack and I'm so glad we could help you with your current overseas job. It's my pleasure as always you know.'

Jack smiled, knowing exactly how the Kompromat would act as a major lever to de-escalate the US–Iranian aggression, but also allow Laura to firmly position herself for Director of the CIA in the not too distant future. An added bonus in Jack's world of deception. The Americans, just like the Russians, would always stockpile compromising material on their political elite until such a time it could be made use of. The material Jack would hand to Laura would be a piece of Kompromat that would be dynamite in the American intelligence community.

Kompromat is a tactic historically used by the Russians to blackmail anyone in powerful positions. They had used such dark methods for decades. But now that the US media had released a dossier compiled by a private intelligence company containing unverified allegations that the FSB had a video of the US President with prostitutes in the Moscow Ritz Carlton in 2013, America had entered the dark world of the Russia's modus operandi – the use of explosive Kompromat on their politicians. Jack was about to add to this on a grand scale.

'The material is exactly as we discussed Laura. Fully attributable to the individual and damning. But when I give this to you, you must agree to use it only in the way we discussed. Only you and I know about its content at this stage. It must be used directly against your National Security Advisor, John Redman.'

Laura took a moment to take off her navy blue blazer, catching a glimpse of the Greek waitress perched discreetly next to the circular book stands, awaiting Jack's instructions. The restaurant was empty except for a middle-aged couple sat at the cocktail bar.

'You know Jack, these are bad, bad, days for us in the US. I know you British well of course, and as ever you want to coach us to do things in, well...' A pause. 'A more considered way...'

'With stealth,' Jack said, interrupting.

'Don't you know it Jack. I'm on your side and many others back home are too. There are many ways our intelligence communities can bring Iran to its knees, but not in the way the current administration is going about it. There are better ways to stop them arming Hezbollah, and better ways to induce an internal coup instead of escalating into a direct war with Iran.'

'It's as bad as I've ever seen you know,' Jack said, pouring Laura some spring water.

'You Brits do love an understatement. It's war Jack. Just over the horizon. Do your Joint Intelligence Committee ever listen to me when I come to those wonderfully British meetings?'

'They're not used to having such a feisty female from the CIA you know.'

'Ha. I have them in my bosom, that's all they ever bloody look at.'

Jack laughed, and the unlikely couple reminisced about some of their previous forays across the globe. They dined on cumin-dusted tuna, with a white bean and chorizo salsa, and treated themselves to a bottle of French Chateau Lestrille wine. Jack suggested that the hawks had got to the US President and that, whilst the Iran nuclear deal was bad, it did at least create a holding pattern whilst other covert methods could be used to create a coup from within.

'I'll get to Redman, Jack. Redman will be forced to get the President to back off but I'll have to think carefully about how I lay the ground for this to happen.'

'We need time now Laura. Time to stop what's coming next. A massive head storm of Iranian terror and a hybrid war. Get us some time and use that magnificent influence of yours amongst your people.'

Jack was quite clear about what he wanted to see happen. Using the Kompromat, Redman would be coerced into getting the US presidential administration to adapt the sanctions on Iran. This would buy enough time to stop the imminent terrorist strikes and allow for a resetting of the strategy. Russia were using Iran as their proxy to cause chaos and the President had fallen into the trap set by Moscow. Jack and Laura both agreed it would be cleaner if the US put all their efforts into creating the conditions for an internal coup in Iran to let the people rise against the mullahs. The compromising material Jack had in his briefcase was volatile enough to get their National Security Advisor to adjust his stance, and that of the President, via bribery and coercion. British politicians would be delighted if such a change of position occurred to buy the time needed to change course.

The lunch was agreeable, and they chatted briefly about their last operation together in Afghanistan in early 2004. Jack fielded Laura's questions about Asia de Cuba, and why he chose this as his go-to place. He showed her the four round pillars that held hundreds of books, intermittently adorned with old black and white pictures of Cuban people. 'You're very much our man in Havana, Jack,' she said whimsically, thoroughly absorbed in the enchanting decor. 'A quirky and secret place for lovers I assume?'

'Very many,' Jack replied. 'We've managed to hook the odd diplomat or two in here on many an occasion. Some very helpful Kompromat to oil the wheels on many a job we've handled in London. It's highly recommended you know.'

Laura laughed and finished her wine. 'A fine place Jack. Very much you. Recommended for being chic, sophisticated, witty and, above all, fun,' she said flirtatiously.

Jack chuckled at her flamboyant nature and let the moment go. He loved listening to her loud but melodic Californian accent and enjoyed her brash banter. He held the pause for a while longer and then made a request. 'I do of course need something in return for this Laura. A contingency.'

'Go on.'

'We may need your NEST teams on standby to help across Europe. We can handle it here in the UK, but if we see things begin to go crooked on the continent, we'll need some help.' Jack had briefed Laura on the intelligence Sean had uncovered in Istanbul but not on the potential for an improvised nuclear device being built by the Iranians. He now needed some level of support from America's Nuclear Emergency Support Teams.

'Bloody hell Jack. NEST teams? You waited this long to tell me?'

'Forgive me. It's only just been confirmed by our man in Istanbul. Your CIA teams have been a huge help for our Court operations.'

'What's he found?'

'Verified intelligence of a nuclear plot. It's a bit tricky as our man is somewhat on the edge right now.'

'Wobbly or fucked up in the head Jack?'

'He's bloody good but suffering a bit of both I'm afraid.'

'You what? You mean you have a mentally unstable individual providing you with intelligence of a nuclear plot? Jack, come on man.'

'That's why it's tricky Laura. His intelligence has been fully verified and I'm monitoring him right now. I just need your help if it goes haywire.'

'My special activities teams are fully involved in your Court operation, right?'

'They are, but up to now purely in a supporting role.'

'OK. I can have a look at the NEST teams but, from hereon in, we operate as a team on this op, OK? I'll play ball with the Kompromat, you play ball and give me full disclosure on the intelligence for this op. Deal?'

Jack raised his glass to Laura. 'Deal.'

'Right, let's go and get them, buster.'

'Just one more thing Laura. We need to play the Kompromat with a bit of skill.'

'Fine. What's the angle I need to use?'

'It will start with a letter to Fletcher Barrington, saying that the Russian GRU have kidnapped his best friend. Our FCO Diplomat, Edmund Duff.'

'Who exactly has got him then?'

'I have him Laura. Or at least, access to him. He's nicely tucked up generating all the evidence I needed - which is now in the dossier. The Russians lifted him but I have access to the information he's providing them.'

'Unbelievable! You're a real intrigant Jack. Your mind never stops plotting eh? What's this all about though?'

Jack waved at the Greek waitress. 'All rather simple really. And hopefully effective. Redman's best friend is Fletcher Barrington and they have a nasty secret they've vowed to keep silent. Edmund Duff knows all about the circumstances of that incident in the Kompromat – you see, he was there too. As was your National Security Advisor on one or two occasions. All three of them were in it together. They now need to believe it's the Russians who have compiled the Kompromat, and that Duff will be killed, their nasty secret revealed to the world and their lives in ruin if they don't comply with the instructions we give them. Far easier for you and me to bribe these bastards by acting as Russians you know.'

'Genius, Jack. So, we play this one out as Russians then.'

'Indeed.'

'Nice basket Jack. Good job.'

Jack watched the Greek waitress place the bill on the table in front of Laura. The bill was purposefully placed in a novel entitled *Playing with the Grown-ups* by Sophie Dahl. The restaurant always presented bills to its customers in one of the hundreds of books on their shelves.

Laura looked across to Jack in amusement. 'Very apt,' she said, hardly hiding her admiration for him. 'A coming of age.'

Jack nodded. 'One chapter at a time, so to speak. We have a few to deal with now but have a look at the fifteenth chapter.'

Laura turned the pages to Chapter Fifteen. Then she read. It was a chapter with encrypted instructions from Jack on how to take the Kompromat operation forward in precise detail. He loved books and he knew Laura did too. A riddle wrapped in a mystery, inside an enigma. A present.

'I'll send the cipher key separately for Chapter Fifteen. The photos of Duff being held by a couple of Russian thugs are in the dossier, and you'll need a good Russian émigré to hand the note over to Fletcher Barrington. He's in London for five days until Saturday.'

'This is wonderful Jack. Thanks so much.'

Jack held Laura's blazer by the arms. She kissed him, turned and slipped her arms in. She adjusted her collar before picking up Jack's briefcase.

'Just one question Jack. How are you going to stop this terrorist plot?'

Jack put his hand on Laura's back and steered her to the exit. 'Well, there's an old Armenian saying that I often use. "The honey is sweet, but it hurts those who eat a lot of it." I'll keep you posted if I get stuck.'

'Love it when a plan comes together,' she said chirpily.

Jack nodded at the waitress and they left.

Chapter 31

Armenia

Sean watched Nadège peer out of the round porthole in the fuselage of the aging MI8 helicopter. Below them, the Turkish landscape changed from the metropolis of Istanbul to the flat lowland plain of the coast of the Black Sea as they sped eastwards at 150 mph. Executive travel it was not. Once east and north of Istanbul and into Anatolia proper, they were steaming along over orchards, holiday villas and lush landscapes as the aircraft hugged the coastline. It all passed in a blur as they headed east towards the Turkish city of Kars, the gateway to the abandoned Armenian city of Ani.

To their north-east lay the fertile lands of Abkhazia and the glistening peaks of the Greater Caucasus mountain range in Georgia, but the most prominent feature they saw out of the porthole was the Crimean Peninsula and the environs of its capital, Sevastopol. Sean had been assured that a vehicle would be waiting for him when they landed near the Armenian border and that he would be required to drive the remaining two hundred kilometres to their rendezvous with the nuclear smugglers.

The inside of the MI8 was sparse. It had two very long bench seats either side of the fuselage and rusty grey seatbelts which neither of them used. It was designed to transport up to thirty-five soldiers but only Nadège and Sean were on-board. Sean wondered who Jack had recruited for this part of the mission. He would have needed to prime and pay several facilitators on the ground to make this deception work. This was a massive operation – the acquisition of an MI8 helicopter, a ground team in Armenia and the right people embedded in the smuggling gang's wider operation. Lord knows how Jack had conjured that up. But Sean was pleased that his lure had worked, and that Samantha had persuaded Jack to give him a crack at making the complex ploy work.

Sean now had the prospect of plenty of time with Nadège over the next forty-eight hours, allowing him to take the operation to the next level, although he had to be cautious. The lure had worked but inside the mind of his prey was a committed and dangerous woman. She could have him killed at any moment, but he needed to get inside that mind of hers. What exactly was she committed to? What was the vulnerability that might cause her to turn?

His mind whirred like the rotors above him as the two-hour journey gave nothing but time to think. He had spent the previous night researching the puzzling parts of the mission. He had searched for a list of all Bosnian-born models in an effort to find out who Nadège's blonde lover was, and to identify their historic connection, as well as how they may have met. He knew Nadège's cover as an elite model would probably have been the way they had met, but who exactly was this stunning blonde? He had looked at the pictures he had placed on the noticeboard in the ship's cabin, which now resembled that in a police murder room, with the photos of the various protagonists displayed prominently across the board and walls, each linked with a dotted line if they were connected in some way.

On the board, he had placed Nadège smack bang in the middle, with lines drawn to her blonde model lover and also to the missing diplomat using a dotted line with a question mark. What was the link to the missing diplomat, he wondered? The puzzle wasn't complete, and Sean had asked Melissa to find the names of the officers who had served with the ex-CIA officer in Bosnia. The link was Bosnia, but what criminal activity had they been up to?

Eventually, after trawling model websites for more than two hours, he found her. He found her on an obscure Montenegrin website for models who were for hire in the glamour industry. She wasn't a mainstream elite model – rather a part-time photo model called Petra. It was definitely her. Sean looked closely at the picture of her in the Istanbul hotel they had captured on his covert camera before she had met Nadège on the first night she arrived back in the city. Yes, her hair was short in the pictures, but it was her OK. Dazzling blue eyes, a perfectly symmetrical face and now a beautiful white complexion with long blonde hair. Sean was intrigued that Nadège had a female lover, but why this recurring Balkan connection he wondered? He sent the picture and name back to The Court to get them to verify her real name and background. By morning it had come back. Her real name was Petra Novak.

Petra was thirty-four years of age and had been born in Tuzla, Bosnia-Herzegovina in 1985. She was born to a Croatian father who had been killed in 1992 at the outbreak of the war. The town of Tuzla was not spared the atrocities of the Bosnian War and her father was killed in an attack by the Yugoslav People's Army on 15 May 1992.

The report Sean received didn't provide any further details, but he knew there was a big link here. The HQ of the United States Army during the Bosnian War had been in Tuzla. Moreover, the kidnapped diplomat and the ex-CIA officer who had killed Sean's mother were also stationed there during the war in 1995.

He sent a mail via the dark web back to The Court's HQ at RAF Bentwaters. He asked for more details of the life and background of Petra Novak, his curiosity piqued.

Sean stepped away from the helicopter, put his sunglasses on and spied the surrounding wastelands. The morning sun was searing, the landscape giving him a sense of myopia as he looked across the dusty, arid plains. There was nothing. No hut, no airfield terminal. Just undulating dust-and-gravel plains.

Sean turned to offer his hand to Nadège as she started disembarking the aircraft on a set of rusting ladders. She tutted and threw him a look. The pilot shut down all the engines to give his aging beast of a machine a well-earned rest.

Sean grabbed a GPS receiver and sat on his rucksack fiddling with its buttons. They had arrived in the Eastern Anatolia region, an arid and remote wilderness deep in the wilds of eastern Turkey close to the borders with Iran and Armenia. The nearest town was Pasliner, some five kilometres away, and Yerevan, their destination for the rendezvous with the smugglers, was another 170 kilometres away.

But where was the vehicle? Jack had promised Samantha that everything was set up and that there'd be no delays or problems. Samantha had told him that they would be travelling under the guise of tourists on a jeep safari, making their way across Turkey and crossing into Armenia before heading for Azerbaijan and then northwards into the Georgian mountains.

Sean grabbed a flask of cold water and raised his cap to watch Nadège amble around the area. She lifted her head to get the early-morning sun. She was dressed in denim shorts, a yellow crop top and a wide brimmed sunhat with her black hair tied in a bun underneath. Sean had succumbed to her allure once again the night before. An impossibility to resist. A fatal attraction. He knew he had to put his head in the mouth of the tiger to win it over.

Out of the dusty haze, Sean saw two distant vehicles hurtling across the rolling hills towards them, blowing a trail of dust in their wake. As they got closer he could just make out two red safari jeeps – open-topped with black roll bars and huge off-road tyres.

The first vehicle skidded to a halt on the small rocks and a large bearded man with a beaming smile swung from the roll bar to exit. 'Good day to you both. Sorry we're a bit late but this is your vehicle. Plenty of provisions on-board too.'

Sean was shocked to hear what appeared to be a South African accent which perfectly matched the man's gold and green rugby jersey with a springbok on its right breast.

Sean shook his hand tightly before the man handed him a small white envelope. 'All the details are in here. You'll be met on the other side of the border in Armenia by our contacts but it's your job to get across the border at the precise location given inside the envelope. You have a GPS receiver, right?'

'Yes. I've got a couple just in case,' Sean replied, knowing it would be illegal to cross into Armenia. The strained relations between Armenia and Turkey following the Armenian massacre in 1915 had never been truly repaired. As a result, the border between the two countries had been closed for many years.

'Good. You'll meet the big boss man just outside of Yerevan tonight. You've got dollars and whisky to show goodwill?'

Sean nodded and paid the man $500 for his time.

'The spare tyres, water and toolkit are all in the back. Call me if you get stuck. Bon voyage.'

The vehicle sped off into the landscape as the rotors of the MI8 roared into action.

'Time for a bit of adventure then I suppose,' Nadège said, waving a colourful bamboo fan across her face. 'Just like the old days with my dad. 'Illegal border crossings, dodgy mafia deals, money mules and awesome scenery.'

'You love this adventure, don't you?' Sean said. 'You must tell me about your father one day.'

'He looked a bit like you actually. Acted like you too.'

'What do you mean?'

'He was as much of an arse as you are at times.'

'Cheers. Jump in and don't you dare complain about my driving, which will be mad and bad.'

Sean threw his rucksack in the back, checked the tyres and fuel gauge and then fired up the jeep. He raced the engine a bit, checked the brakes and then sped off along the bumpy track down towards a plateau, before heading eastwards along what seemed like a never-ending ridge. He had punched in a series of GPS waypoints that would navigate him all the way to the ancient city of Ani.

Sean revelled in travelling in some of the most remote parts of Asia Minor. Remote highways, narrow and bumpy back roads, dusty unknown towns. They travelled in silence for the first twenty minutes or so, taking in the stunning scenery whilst Sean skilfully navigated the bumpy tracks and huge potholes. To witness the borderlands approaching Armenia and Iran was a mesmerising experience for both of them, Eastern Anatolia being a rarely visited region. The sparse, biblical landscapes that sprung from the Tigris and Euphrates were enthralling. On their travels they witnessed the first civilisations. The ancient settlements of Göbekli Tepe and Mount Nemrut, the exquisitely decorated Great Mosque of Divriği and the ruined city of Ani.

Sean made sure it was a wild ride and a chance for him to get into the mind of Nadège.

'What's next for you after this thrill?' he asked, tapping his fingers on the steering wheel.

Nadège grappled with her rucksack in the bouncy cab, trying to rescue a bottle of water. She passed Sean a few dates and twisted the bottle top. He glanced at her, noticing she had put on a headscarf to protect herself against the driving winds in the open-topped vehicle.

'Probably the Americas,' she said. 'You'd never find me or anyone else for that matter. I can disappear from this world and give up modelling and spying. It's my destiny.'

'Well, why don't you do it sooner instead of going through with this mayhem? You could get properly nailed on this one you know.'

'I'm locked in. I can't retreat from it. I don't want to talk about it. We get this job done and that's it. Stop probing.'

'You mean they have something on you?'

Sean looked at Nadège with a face of concern and a tone of empathy. 'Are they bribing you to do this? I had no idea you wanted out. I could help you know.'

Nadège held her hand up to shield the wind from her face and pushed some strands of hair back under the headscarf. 'I told you I don't want to talk about it. You know what our lives are like. They crush us. Then they spit us out. I'm done with all the killing after this.'

'I used to feel the same. I'm free now, don't forget. Making a good living, especially if this comes off nicely. Then I'll be gone too. With a fair wind and your dollars, I'll be setting up a little artists' shop in Tuscany.'

The silence crept back. Sean bided his time. There was definitely something amiss with Nadège. She was pained. But why? An evil killing machine inside, maybe she'd seen the light and her inner traumas were too much to handle any more. He got that. He had lived it. And beaten it.

'Are you a double agent?' Sean shouted out, turning again to look directly at Nadège as he rode the next set of potholes. 'Working for the CIA or something? I don't want to be banged up again if this is a fucking stitch-up. I just realised this could all be a set-up you know. And you've bloody well changed.'

'Don't be so bloody stupid,' Nadège retorted. 'I hate those American pigs.' Nadège lurched forward to hold the dashboard with two hands as the road got bumpier, before leaning back in her seat again as they hit a small stretch of tarmac. 'Don't try and turn the tables with me Sean, it's me taking the risks by hiring you for fuck's sake.'

'Did anyone else try to tap you up to try and turn you into a double agent then? Only happened to me once. With you.'

'Russians. The Russians are always after me, but it's hardly worth my while. I had a British female agent hit on me once, if that's what you mean? I mangled her with my mind though. Great sex, and she was easy prey – I don't think she ever found the courage to take it through to recruit me though. The sex was enough for her at the time.'

Sean laughed. 'Evil and naughty, no better mix in my mind. I pity the poor bastards that you've suckered in and spat out.'

The dusty and barren flatland began to change as they approached the Armenian border. Sean knew that the hardest part of the journey would be just getting near and over the border. He hoped the vehicle was up to it.

Eventually, just as the sun was at its highest in the forty-two-degree heat, he spotted the city of Ani, where he had planned a short stop. The views of the approaching ruined walls were staggering. The size of the ruins was immense. This was a UNESCO World Heritage Site and the home of an ancient civilisation. Yet there was not a tourist in sight.

Sean parked next to a ruined archway that was once the entrance to the city. He grabbed his rucksack, placed his black baseball cap on his head and ambled through the gateway. It was once the capital of the Armenian Empire and had been one of the world's great cities around the year 1000. In this part of the world, only Istanbul and Baghdad could hold a candle to the opulence, magnificence and architectural artistry of Ani. Rome? Sacked. London? Not even close. Ani was the greatest city no one had ever heard of. Citadel, former capital and heart of the great Armenian empire. These days, Ani is in Turkey and is an ex-city. Abandoned. Desolate, remote and largely forgotten for over seven hundred years. But not entirely forgotten. Especially not by the Armenians.

Sean was now located in what was once Armenia Minor, but the Kingdom of Greater Armenia had been squashed like a wet sponge into the tiny area it now occupied by centuries of warfare.

'It's an Armenian city, you know,' Sean mentioned to Nadège, as they sat in the shade of what looked like a ruined monastery.

They looked at each other knowingly. Sean rolled some fresh herbs and ham into a piece of flatbread and offered one to Nadège.

'Like my country, Armenia is a land of staunch chivalry and machismo,' Nadège said, passing the water to Sean. 'I've never been here but my father told me plenty about this place and about the Armenians. He said that, whenever Armenians visit it, they cry.'

Sean revelled in the magnificence of its history and grabbed a small drawing pad from his rucksack. He started to delicately sketch the remains using a variety of lead pencils to capture his version of the city beyond its remains. One day he would turn it into a painting.

The roads leading up to and away from the border were mostly gravel, and so severely potholed that travel in the jeep would be at less than 10 mph. To get to his designated border-crossing point, Sean needed to slowly navigate narrow tracks perched atop precipices with cliff edges dropping hundreds of feet into the ravines below. Only the smugglers knew of these winding border tracks and the driving was now becoming treacherous.

2pm. An hour before the rendezvous time at the border. Sean used his binoculars to try to find the river crossing below that he needed to traverse. He spotted it. It looked a bit hairy. He scanned the other side of the border. He could see a small hilltop barracks, not too dissimilar to the one he had passed twenty minutes ago on the Turkish side. He knew they had to be cautious now to avoid any border patrols. To be caught now would be a travesty.

Sean drove down the steep-sided valley that doubled back to the border crossing some distance below. They passed the remains of long-since-abandoned Armenian hamlets, visible only by way of red-stained grass and soil and crumbling rocks.

It wasn't long before Sean found the river crossing. He looked for an easier route across the raging river. Nothing. He spotted a route across the river with an island in the middle and decided it was a case of bursting through the waves and hoping for the best. There was no other option. Just as he jumped back in the jeep, he spotted a waving arm on the other side of the river. Just a single man, who now waved with both arms and then picked up a large wooden pole. He held it in his right hand and pointed to the route Sean needed to take. Sean pressed the accelerator, grabbing the steering wheel fiercely.

'Hold onto your bits, this will be fun,' he said, as he crashed into the first wave and rode the rocks below.

The water broke across the top of the windscreen, soaking both of them. Sean struggled with the steering wheel as the rocks forced the wheels to judder and the chassis to lurch. He kept the momentum going, glancing across to see Nadège standing up holding the front roll bar. It was exhilarating, great fun and a breathtaking experience as they traversed the island, laughing and shouting, egging the vehicle on.

The vehicle lumbered across the final thirty metres into Armenian territory, where the man was waving his arms towards an exit route up a mud bank. The man ran ahead, guiding the route for Sean to take.

As Sean eased the jeep to the top of the bank on the crest of the brow he let out a sigh of relief, pushing the steering wheel and groaning to get the jeep firmly onto the plateau above the river.

He lifted his eyes to be greeted by three blue and white Land Rovers, each of them regimentally parked alongside the next one. Two policemen were pointing AK47s straight at them.

'Fuck,' was all he could muster.

Chapter 32

Buckinghamshire

'When will you release him?' Fletcher Barrington asked the Chief of the CIA London Station. Laura Creswell simply narrowed her eyes and ignored the question.

Jack heard the words perfectly through the ceiling-mounted loudspeakers in the CIA safe house located just outside Stokenchurch, an hour to the north-west of London.

Jack looked at the CCTV monitor to watch the reaction of Barrington, who was sat at a table in the small kitchen.

Laura, a fierce CIA interrogator, looked at Barrington with utter disdain before leaning across the table to confront him.

'When this is all over, chances are you'll walk free, never to hear from me again. But only if you do exactly as I tell you on a daily basis. If you play this right with your friend Redman, you'll continue to live and be free of the shame I could drop on you at a moment's notice. You will make sure the National Security Advisor does exactly as I want him to. Do you understand?'

'What about Duff? You need to let him go free first.'

Laura sat back and applied some lipstick before screwing up her face. 'You know exactly how this works,' she began. 'I have got you by the balls, you asswipe. Don't worry about him. Worry about yourself. You do as I say from this moment onwards - you'll never see or hear from your bum chum Edmund Duff again. Remember the last time you met him in London at Quaglino's the night he was kidnapped. Remember his face. Savour the memory, but you'll never ever see him again you fucking despicable man.'

Jack watched Barrington pick up the photographs again. His face was as white as a sheet and he was now quivering. He pulled out a small sleeve of tablets and took one, washing it down with the single glass of water placed on the table.

'Your man Duff has been a silly boy,' Laura continued. 'He's been giving British secrets to the Russians, who found out about your own little secret that you vowed to take to the grave together. So, the Russians have you nailed to your filthy mast with your ass hanging out. Which is why you'll do everything I tell you.'

The Kompromat had been delivered. The reactions were just as Jack had expected. This was a moment to savour as he revelled in seeing the leader of an evil cabal suffer. There was no escape for Barrington – he was in the clutches of MI5 and the CIA for as long as he was useful. Useful for coercing US foreign policy in the belief that the Russians held the Kompromat.

The only matter that Jack would need to handle was that three people now wanted Barrington dead: Nadège, Petra and Sean Richardson.

Jack knew that his plan to manage this messy affair needed more work and that there was more to play out in the coming days - but for now, Barrington and Duff were fully ensnared in Jack's net. A net that he would bait and use to trap the right-hand man of the President of the USA – his National Security Advisor, John Redman.

Chapter 33

Armenia

Sean stepped out of the jeep with his hands held high – an act of surrender to the men pointing AK47s right at his chest. He told Nadège to do the same. A tall gangly man approached both of them with a pistol in his hand. He wasn't wearing a uniform. He wore a faded grey T-shirt with the words 'American grown, Armenian roots' on it.

Sean hoped that this was not a fuck-up. Jack would have been careful to ensure the operation was watertight, but what if someone had leaked information to the authorities? Was this all part of the planned deception? Or would they be kidnapped and sold as spies? The T-shirt resonated with him. Many Americans were proud of their Armenian descent but was he actually American?

The man stood in front of Sean with his legs positioned in a strident manner. 'You want to trade with Armenia?' he said nonchalantly. Sean reckoned he was probably nearer seven feet than six and felt a sense of relief when the codewords were used.

'Just for one day,' Sean replied. 'I'm looking for discount though.'

The man walked forward, put his pistol in the back of his jeans and shook Sean's hand wildly before giving him a painful bear hug.

'My name is Charlie and I'm here to take you to the big boss. He's expecting you, but first we must socialise with the border guards. They are expecting some reward.'

'That's fine,' Sean replied. 'Which part of the States are you from?'

'New York born and bred, but my home and heart is here in Armenia,' he said, placing his open palm on his heart and banging it twice with his right hand. 'Have some dollars ready and be prepared to drink lots. Follow me.'

Sean looked at Nadège, who was now sat in the jeep with her arms folded. Sean could see she was not overly impressed by the expected charade. 'This better not be a stitch-up,' she muttered. 'I can see what's coming a mile off you know.'

'I'm more worried about you stitching me up for fuck's sake. I thought that was it for a moment. Isn't it about time we worked together for a change? We could be a great bloody partnership making big bucks you know.'

Nadège tutted, fiddled with her headscarf and adjusted it so that it covered her hair, shoulders and breasts. She foresaw the macho world of Armenian hospitality.

Armenia is one of the oldest countries in the world on the famous Silk Road. Traders and merchants were the most mobile and active people in Armenian society and the country had been at the crossroads for a number of different trading routes into Iran or northwards into Russia. From time immemorial, Armenia was the smuggling capital of Asia Minor and, today, Sean was being treated as one of those smugglers, knowing full well that the border guards had to be paid off first.

Inside the small barracks, Sean and Nadège were taken to what appeared to be an old guardroom with a kitchen and dining facility. Five border guards sat around the rectangular table and T-shirt man offered Sean and Nadège seats at opposite ends of it. Sean spotted a well-worn 'anti-corruption' poster on the wall. The guards were young, casual and attempting to speak English, with the exception of the older gentleman in the well-worn uniform, whose job it was to receive the money for the illegal Armenian crossing. A type of visa transaction.

The officer passed T-shirt man a piece of paper. He then passed it to Sean and explained. 'These are what the transactions are for. It's part of their rules you know.' T-shirt man explained each line, indicating that Sean was paying all the fees needed to enter Armenia with a vehicle. The fees were for highway taxes, eco-charges, which made Sean smirk, customs brokerage and a few other odds and ends. There were about eight numbers written down, totalling about $900. Sean was told there was a large surcharge for using dollars, leaving him with no option. Sean played the game and rolled out the dollars on the table.

'Do you have any cognac?' the chief officer asked.

Sean smiled and, smart as a whip, placed his rucksack on the table.

'Cognac? Vodka? Whisky?'

The chief clicked his fingers and, within minutes, meat, vegetables, soup, bread, olives and grapes appeared. Iced tea, Coke and Fanta also came. Sean and Nadège were treated to a long late lunch with the border officials as T-shirt man's birthday was toasted, many, many times. Two hours later they departed to meet the big boss.

Sean followed the vehicle of T-shirt man to their final rendezvous. A location that had not been shared with Sean. He was now in the hands of nuclear smugglers and very aware of the implications of this all going wrong. His thoughts briefly relapsed to the time he had spent in the Kabul jail, which had nearly killed him. He didn't want a repeat of being banged up abroad ever again. He needed to keep his nerve and trust that Jack had everything in place.

Sean had done his homework though. He had read various dossiers on the worrying episodes of nuclear smuggling in Armenia and the propensity for the country to be at the very heart of such gangs' activities. Armenians had been particularly active in smuggling efforts across the region, with numerous arrests of their criminals, who had crossed into neighbouring Georgia to try and sell nuclear materials. This activity had increased in the past two years, with the latest event occurring just two weeks ago on the border with Nagorno-Karabakh and Azerbaijan. Eight Armenians had been arrested in the last twelve months for smuggling caesium-137 and enriched uranium-238 that could be used in an improvised nuclear device.

'Tell me about the agents you've been running then Nadège,' Sean asked, with an impression of insouciance.

'Which ones?'

'Oh, you know, the network of agents you've been running over the years. I'm interested to see how good you are – or were.'

'Piss off. I'm still a master at this game and, unlike you, I'm still in the game.'

'Oh, the life of a glamour model eh? Easy pickings then at the clubs and parties of Mayfair?'

'A few, yes. Don't forget I've been living and working in Britain for nearly fifteen years and it's fertile ground given the stupidity of the Brits in power.'

'Kill any of them?'

Nadège glared at Sean before running her hand through her hair. 'That's enough now. No more stupid questions please. Concentrate on the bloody road.'

Sean noticed they were approaching the outskirts of a major conurbation. Probably Yerevan. He was enjoying the experiences of Anatolia and Armenia. He caught a glimpse of a family picnicking peacefully on the bank of a narrow river and caught sight of a man driving his cab-less tractor on the verges of the road, dressed, somewhat bizarrely, in a blue suit. Sean was surprised by the differences between Armenia and Turkey. It was noticeable how clean and well-maintained Turkey was in comparison to Armenia, which had some of the ugliest post-Soviet-era apartment buildings imaginable. He also noticed that road signage did not exist to track his route.

T-shirt man slowed right down and put his arm out of his jeep to tell Sean to slow down - they were at the rendezvous. Sean turned right onto a small potholed track and spotted a set of double metal gates that gave entry to a huge compound with a large house inside its perimeter wall. The gates opened to reveal two men with assault rifles draped over their shoulders, each opening one of the gates with symmetrical efficiency to allow the vehicles to enter. Sean parked next to T-shirt man under a draped awning and jumped out of the vehicle.

They were immediately searched by another man dressed in shorts and a hoody. A muscular man. Pumping himself with needles to bulk out, Sean thought. The man searched each of their rucksacks thoroughly and then conducted a search of the jeep with T-shirt man.

'This way guys,' T-shirt man said, waving his arm over his shoulder. 'Bring your kit. You'll be staying the night.'

They were chaperoned into a large office. A great office, Sean thought. Worthy of a big boss. Sean spied the hefty wooden desk at the end of a large space suitably decorated with objects of war such as swords and guns. And then then were photos on the right-hand wall of soldiers' faces. A shrine? Were the photos perhaps of old soldiers the big boss man had fought with?

'I hope your journey was pleasant,' the man behind the desk said, standing up to greet his guests. 'Please take a seat.'

Sean and Nadège sat on two antique wooden chairs with a small table in front of them. 'You are my guests and, as is my custom, I have prepared a feast for you this evening. Make yourselves comfortable please.'

Sean watched the man's demeanour. He was a short, stocky man, perhaps with a military background judging by his style and manner. Now he was presumably a warlord and chief smuggler. Jack had not given him any background whatsoever, so Sean was still unsure how this would all pan out. The man had a crew cut, numerous grubby tattoos on his arms and a small scar across his forehead. The big boss certainly acted as such. No handshakes. Formal and welcoming, but taut. Sean watched him wave a hand to his assistant.

'Before we do business I have a small gift for you both. We are very welcoming people in Armenia and we like to look after our guests.' The assistant presented a silver cigarette lighter and a silver trinket case to them. Nadège saw it fit to hand the lighter to Sean and the big boss laughed. Nadège's relaxed impetuousness during the gift swopping was an icebreaker for the new business friendship, providing Sean with some relief.

'My name is Oleg and I served for many years in the Soviet Army. I can find and sell anything. What about you?' he asked, pointing a long arm at Sean.

The office, located on a sliver of land along the River Hrazdan, was the base for one of the world's most notorious nuclear smugglers, Oleg Achenco, a dual Russian-Ukrainian citizen nicknamed 'Kapitán'. He was a fugitive wanted by the US and Moldovan authorities for attempting to sell weapons-grade uranium to Islamist terrorist groups in 2015 and 2016. One of his middlemen had been caught and shot in 2016 in a Moldovan sting operation, during which police had found the blueprints for a dirty bomb in his home. But the Kapitán escaped and set up shop in Armenia.

'My name is Sean and I was a civil servant. I buy good-quality items now. I have brought a gift for you too.'

Sean leant into his rucksack and pulled out a full bottle of Isle of Jura whisky. 'One of Scotland's finest,' he said, placing it on his desk.

'Thank you. I like. Now to business, my friends. My team have confirmed me the deposit has been placed in my bank account. I need assurance you will place remaining fee once I show goods. You will not be able to depart until funds are in my account. Do you understand?'

Sean nodded, fully understanding his mispronunciations of the English language, delivered with a guttural Russian accent. 'When can we see the product?'

'Tomorrow morning,' the Kapitán said, lighting a cigar and opening the whisky. His assistant brought glasses for everyone. 'A mere mortal cannot just get his hands on this stuff you know. I needed multiple people in military to get this item. I'm glad it will be put to good use.'

Sean was glad of the walk-in GRU agent setting this up through his sources. Now that Sergei was a double agent for The Court, it opened the door to multiple operations for Jack to manage and exploit. Could this be his finest, Sean thought?

'If you don't mind me asking, where did you manage to get the product?' Sean asked, knowing it was a bit brazen. But nothing ventured, nothing gained.

The Kapitán took a sip of his whisky and drew a long breath. 'Aaah, a fine drink my friend. I shall tell you a story and you can decide if it is true.'

Kapitán Oleg explained how his Ukrainian background and the war in Ukraine had allowed him to purloin a number of 'products for sale', as he called them.

He had military contacts at the Pervo Maysk strategic missile base located in the middle of nowhere and a long way from Severesk in Siberia. The base was miles from any population in the quiet Siberian tundra, surrounded by sunflower fields and, like an iceberg, above the surface Pervo Maysk showed only a hint of what lay beneath. Oleg explained that there were a few light-weight fences, some electrified rusty barbed wire and a small collection of buildings disguising a real, cold war-era, underground Soviet Union nuclear base. It was from here that he acquired his special stores. True or not, Sean had a deal to make. He needed to take the operation to the next level and track and trace the bomber and any other bombs he had built. It was a sting operation but one that could feasibly take down Nadège's entire logistics network and, hopefully, reveal her sleeper agents in Britain.

'Now you will witness the world-famous Armenian barbecue,' Oleg said, as he chaperoned Nadège and Sean to the large yard. 'We will drink and eat and be merry. Pissed, as you say in England I think.'

The yard was huge. It had a mixture of large potted plants, a few raised herb beds, a large grassed area with two open-sided marquees and colourful lights twinkling up high. Sean spotted a strange-looking barbecue in the corner of the yard where numerous men had gathered to talk. An Armenian tonir barbecue. Each man wore thick chains, huge crosses and several solid-gold rings. The wives and girlfriends sat in one of the marquees, smiling and laughing whilst four or five small children played on the swings and makeshift climbing frame.

'First you must meet my wife while we wait for big chef to arrive,' Oleg said.

Sean sensed this could be some night – he knew how the people of the Caucasus liked to party. The women were all dressed smartly in Western clothes and summer dresses. Some even in glitzy T-shirts and tight-fitting jeans. Sean had read much of Armenian family values and how Armenian women were often regarded as the most beautiful and striking in the Caucasus region and beyond. They are famous for their dark hair, brown eyes and curvy figures. Think Kim Kardashian as an Armenian. Think Cher. The women Sean met were indeed striking and incredibly polite. As were the macho men to their partners. Respect was a golden thread of Armenian culture alongside their food and cordiality. Nadège joined the women with some ease and was offered a variety of locally made organic wines. Oleg cracked a bottle of Armenian wheat beer for Sean and they clinked bottles.

An entrance. The big chef. The men walked forward to greet a small portly man who was rolling his blue denim sleeves up. Tightly cropped black hair, a beaming smile with a gold tooth, unshaven but with a trimmed beard. A large gold necklace. The big chef was enjoying his starring role and shook hands wildly with the men, placing his left hand over each hand he shook. The main man had arrived. Sean wandered over to watch with intrigue how he plied his trade. One of the other men told him he was one of Armenia's strongest wrestlers, drove a truck during the day and was hired at night to cook tonir barbecues for the wealthy.

One of the men pointed the chef to two large plastic tubs full of meat that had been marinating all day in beer. Lamb and chicken khorovats. Shashlik on skewers. The chef fired up the enormous barbecue and stepped to one side to clean the huge iron skewers with a metal brush. He scrubbed them hard, banging them, turning them and soaking them in beer as he went. A beer was passed to him. The men crowded around the barbecue to watch him work and to chat about wrestling with him. The beer was now flowing, and the distinct smell of ale and charcoal wafted through the air as the evening light began to drain from the day. Sean began to enjoy this very amenable social occasion and he made sure that Nadège's wine glass was always topped up, so she never knew quite how much wine she had been drinking. This was an opportunity to chat socially and to allow the alcohol to penetrate her mask.

Sean chatted with the men around the barbecue and was offered a cigar by T-shirt man.

'My father taught me how to make these,' he said to Sean. 'Try one. They're legendary over here.'

Sean lit the hand-rolled cigar, puffed on it a few times and watched T-shirt man start to play the decrepit white piano positioned centre stage in the garden. The kids began to crowd round. Remarkably, the piano was perfectly in tune.

Nadège had joined them at the piano and Sean offered her the cigar. 'It's really smooth.'

'Haven't smoked one of these since I did a model shoot in the vaults of an old club in Moorgate. Promoting Coronets. Mmm, really nice.'

Sean put his hand on her back and chaperoned her to the middle of the garden for a quiet chat. They were both grinning with the alcohol, enjoying a brilliant party with authentic people in a marvellous part of the world.

'I'm loving this,' Sean said, clinking his bottle against Nadège's glass. 'You?'

'I love it – they're really great people. And boy, look at this home-made wine. Apparently Oleg has a number of vineyards and this is gorgeous stuff. I'm gonna party.'

They drank in silence for a while before Sean moved closer to her. 'You know, I had some bad news a few days ago. About my mother.'

'Why, what happened? You never told me about her.'

'I know. I just found out how she died when I was fifteen. Her death has lived with me every day and is probably a major cause of my own troubles through life. She was killed by the CIA in Berlin. She was a spy too you know.'

'Bloody hell Sean. How? What happened?'

'I don't really know the detail but I'll find out when this is over. I'll hunt the bastard down and kill him. I know he's still alive.'

'But how? Who told you all this? How do you know it's true?'

'Her handler in Berlin. Immediately after her death he went mad and was committed to a mental institution in Prague, where he had retired. He had a massive breakdown over her death, it was probably the final trauma of many he'd been carrying. You know what it's like.' Sean explained how the encrypted note had come into the hands of a good friend of his in a snuffbox. He left out the fact that his 'good friend' was the Director General of MI5.

'By all accounts, some of her handler's memory has now come back to him but I'm not sure how long he's got to live. I want to find out more about the detailed circumstances of her death. She worked for MI6 and was their expert in getting defectors across the border.'

'Wow. Respect to her.'

Sean chaperoned Nadège towards one of the garden sofas, where they sat for a while. 'What about your parents?' he asked, topping up Nadège's glass.

'I might tell you one day,' she replied. 'But for now, we should dance. I'm feeling it.'

'Feeling what? Feeling free at last?'

'Yes, very much so.'

'Good. Don't think for one moment I haven't seen those cuts across your wrists and arms.'

Sean looked at the shock in her eyes. They were bloodshot, and she was merry. But she was trying to grapple with her emotional control. He was hitting buttons she preferred weren't pushed. But she was also playing with her allure. He needed to get to her inner self and see how far he could push to find her motivations and weaknesses. She was tired of this double life. He could feel it. But he needed to coax her more.

'The MOIS have something on me that keeps me going. It's my last run out you know.'

Sean noticed the pain in her face. 'Wow. This is really bad then. You know I can help you, right?'

'You can't. I'll do what I need to do and then leave for South America. You can help by getting me what I need.'

Oleg called everyone over to the centre of the garden, where the tables were now placed in a square.

'*Bari galust im hyurerin*,' Oleg said, raising what looked like a goldfish bowl of Armenian red wine. 'Welcome to my guests. We shall eat, drink, dance and sing.'

A veritable feast. The tables were packed with kofta, harissa, organic tomatoes in dill, mante dumplings and unleavened lavash bread. Four hearty bowls of khash, a traditional dish of boiled sheep's feet, head and tripe, took centre stage on the side table. Sean winced but knew he would have to give it a go. Armenians put great emphasis on hospitality and generosity.

'Thank you for your excellent hospitality and friendship,' Sean said, raising his own glass of red wine. 'Armenian hospitality is the best. I salute you all.'

The men began to place the huge khorovats on a large rack on which the meat hung from a rail and the children and women began to help themselves.

Within the hour, Nadège and Sean were dancing. Dancing closely. T-shirt man played the piano, and the chef was now getting very drunk and dancing with all the women. No one refused. He was revered. Oleg was drinking whisky and playing a duduk, a wind instrument cut from an apricot tree. The Armenians called it the soul of the apricot.

'There is one thing you need to know Sean,' Nadège said, as she held him closely, leant back and looked into his eyes.

'Go on.'

'I had your child many years ago. Our child.'

Sean stopped dead. He couldn't believe what he was hearing. He was astonished. Was she lying? Was this a ruse? Yes, he had had a crazy fling with her for a number of months. But a child? His own child?

'I know you might not believe me, but I had to tell you. You're definitely his father. He's nine years of age now and looks like you.'

Chapter 34

Armenia

Morning. A cold breeze blew through the open windows. Nadège looked over at Sean, who was still sleeping, with just a white sheet covering his lower body.

Nadège was conflicted. She really wished Sean hadn't opened up to her about his mum. She began to feel a pang of empathy and she hated it when she felt like that. She now wished she hadn't told him about their child. It was too much now. Too confusing and too complicated. She just wanted peace with her inner soul and for the pain to stop. She was on a journey to self-destruction. Had been all her life. Emotional intensity disorder was killing her slowly and she winced at being unable to control her emotions after the wine.

Her mind always heard two voices. The empathetic one telling her to be kind and good. And the evil voice telling her to hate Sean and to kill those who had pained her or her closest friends. She was in a trap. A death trap.

In relationships Nadège would swing from idolising someone like Sean and desperately wanting to be with them to despising them and wanting to hurt them badly. In her relationship with herself, Nadège exuded swings from arrogant narcissism to self-hatred and disgust, which always led to her self-harming, most normally by cutting but sometimes by burning herself.

Cognitively, this meant constant split-personality responses. Nadège continuously mismatched the experiences of herself and others, which created confusion about who she was and what she wanted, resulting in feelings of frustration, anxiety, depression, emptiness and hopelessness. Her behaviour was at times deliberately self-destructive and dangerously impulsive. This was why she could kill with impunity, be reckless and self-harm, all within hours of each other. She was at war with herself. And at war with anyone else who tried to get in the way of her primary target. Herself.

Nadège jumped in the shower and began to think. Today she would get her hands on the nuclear stores she needed in order to succeed and then her journey to freedom would begin. But first she had to put a number of things in place. A plan. A means to get to the finish line. The steaming shower brought her soul back to life and she stepped out, memorising the text she would send on her phone. Sean had gotten too close for comfort and she now had to deal with the fallout from that and get her mission back on track. She felt uneasy but committed. Just as she had felt with the assassinations she had committed for her Iranian handler and for Petra, her lover. She missed Petra and longed for the time when they would be free together in South America.

Two hours later, Nadège and Sean stood over the nuclear casket. A nuclear shell. Nadège's prized possession.

A Russian shell at that. Nadège glanced over to see Sean put his rucksack on the floor, unzip it and pull out a black machine – a Geiger counter she assumed.

She knelt down next to the shell to inspect it. She touched it. Almost a full stroke. Then she twisted her head to try and read the black Cyrillic writing stamped across its belly. She had no idea how it operated, never mind how it was projected. All she knew was it held the uranium that she needed. She stood and admired it, feeling a sensation of ultimate power. What she was looking at was an artillery shell known as the Kleshchevina. A nuclear shell fired from a Russian self-propelled Pion 2S7 – the largest and most powerful track-mounted howitzer in existence. This cold war-era howitzer looks like a tank but is twice the size and carries a range of 203-mm artillery shells, including the tactical nuclear shell.

'Where's the uranium?' she asked, turning to watch Sean screw a long stainless-steel probe onto the end of the Geiger counter.

'There may not be any,' Sean replied, a strained look on his face. 'I need to make sure this is a genuine Kleshchevina and that it is indeed a tactical nuclear shell. If it is, then we're protected from the radiation by the lead casing. It's a bit big to transport back to Europe though. What's your plan?'

'Keep your voice down Sean. No one needs to hear us talk about this.' She threw a nod towards the wooden door, on the other side of which stood the Kapitán with his cronies. 'Let's just get this checked and we'll be on our way. You get paid, and I can get on my way.'

Nadège felt good. She was on a high. She revelled in the power she was holding and the drama she would create across Europe with this artillery shell. Her final days would make her a global icon. She would go down in history: not for being a beautiful playboy model but for the deaths she would unleash as the most notorious terrorist ever.

She watched Sean approach the shell with his equipment. He was a handsome man, and a strong one. Her inner desire for this man conflicted with the emotions in her dark mind telling her she had to deal with him. Soon. The dark side of her dysregulated mind was not providing any sense of logic, but instead a desire to blacken him. There was evil in him and he needed to be neutered to stop him interfering with her life and mission. Her mind couldn't process the thought that the man she wanted gone was also the father of her child. There was no empathy, no emotion for a good man. A man who, if she had a sane mind, she could turn to for help. She shook off any thoughts of caring for a man, avoided them as she always did. Because I don't know what they mean or what they are, she said to herself.

'It's pukka,' Nadège heard Sean say. 'Full-on nuclear.'

She knelt to look at the digital reading he was showing her on the small LED screen of the radiation equipment.

'What's it mean?'

'It means the reading I'm getting is roughly the same as it would have been when it was manufactured in the early '90s and it confirms it's a Kleshchevina shell. The uranium-235 is enriched and has a half-life of thousands of years. It's good to go.'

'Excellent. Anything else?'

'Only one thing. How on earth is your bomber man going to use this? That's the zillion-dollar question.'

'Like I said before, you've done your job now. This is where I take over. Let's get the thing on the jeep.'

Nadège and Sean had been led by the Kapitán to a remote vineyard earlier that morning. They had driven for an hour to eastern Armenia's Ararat Valley, which has been notably likened by wine experts to California's Napa. They drove by newly built wineries, some modern warehouses and ancient wineries hundreds of years old. The Kapitán had told them with passion of Armenians' pride in their winemaking skills and of how he had bought two such vineyards many years ago.

The Kapitán had taken them to an old, dilapidated wine warehouse. Nadège's breath was taken away by the stunning vistas surrounding the vineyard - the landscape with its precipitous cliffs, caves and ancient monasteries was the perfect setting to seal the deal with the Kapitán. The arid mountains were peppered with bright spots of cultivation, including the Kapitán's main vineyard, which was situated a mile to the south of the old winery. A collection of now-extinct warehouses where a once-thriving vineyard had stood. The smell of fermented grapes still hung in the air as they walked into the large wooden shack. The old grape presses were still there, slowly rusting. The Kapitán led them to a room where the wine once fermented naturally under the large concrete floor. A huge wine vat where the grapes were once mashed was below them. A concrete vat. Not temperature-controlled, as in modern vineyards, but an old-style vat that had once held over four million quarts of wine.

Nadège's anticipation peaked as she watched the Kapitán open a double-hinged trapdoor to reveal his secret hideout for the nuclear shell he would sell her.

She watched as two men jumped inside and attached a set of chains to a large crate with iron lugs on it. Nadège watched Sean and the Kapitán heave on the chains through a pulley that was attached to a wooden beam straddling the ramshackle ceiling. Slowly the crate began to rise until it emerged fully. She watched as all four men began to lift the crate onto the floor and start to dismantle it. Inside was an artillery shell neatly cocooned in a grey cradle for protection. The original cradle that Russian soldiers would have lifted into the Pion howitzer. Sean began to unscrew the cradle to enable the men to lift the four-foot shell out of its housing.

At that moment, Nadège sent a secure text in Farsi to her minders. Minders who had been tracking her every movement from a makeshift control room located just over the Turkish border in Kars.

Nadège had initiated a preset plan involving the MOIS.

Chapter 35

Armenia

Nadège stood by the jeep, watching Sean and the Kapitán's men steer a small cart with some difficulty through the open warehouse and down a gentle incline towards the jeep. The sun was now beating down fiercely, some of the men wiping sweat from their brows, and there was a tricky moment when the weight of the shell buckled one of the cart struts, causing a bit of a commotion.

Nadège stood scanning the environs of the abandoned vineyard some 1600 metres above sea level, where the Areni vines were growing wild amongst the boulders and walnut trees. She turned on her heels, as if searching for something in the sky. Then she witnessed the final moments of the crate being lifted into the back of the jeep, watching its suspension springs lurch with the weight.

The men were dusting themselves down, passing water bottles amongst themselves and laughing at T-shirt man, who had ripped a large hole in his trousers from the exertion of heaving the crate onto the jeep. There were a few high fives and Sean was revelling in the hard graft with the Armenian gangsters.

Eventually, the men walked back inside the warehouse with the cart, Sean leading and carrying the fabric straps they had used to help manage the heavy load. Nadège followed behind them and watched the Kapitán light a cigarette, offer one to Sean and pat him on the back.

Sean then helped T-shirt man close the hatch. He turned his head to look at Nadège. Just as he did so, she pulled out a pistol from the back of her jeans. She saw the terror in T-shirt man's eyes as she lifted the barrel until it was parallel with the ground, placed her left hand around the casing to provide a firm grasp and then fired one round right into his chest. T-shirt man's eyes remained glazed in shock as he crumpled to the ground. With her feet apart to provide a solid stance for her next shot, she turned her shoulders towards the man helping Sean. He was in a kneeling position, looking over his shoulder and about to get to his feet and run. Just as he rose, she shot him, the bullet piercing his neck. Nadège glanced at Sean. Just for a millisecond. To check his reaction. He was solid. No extreme movement. She lowered the pistol and then raised it again to flex her muscles and get a perfect stance for her shot at the Kapitán, who was now stood with his arms aloft. She fired. One shot straight through the heart.

'Don't even fucking think of doing anything,' she shouted to Sean. 'I'll kill you without a thought.'

Sean raised his hands and dropped into a squatting position. 'Why the fuck are you doing this?' he shouted. 'These guys didn't deserve that, you bastard.'

'Shut up. Just do exactly as I tell you and you might just live.'

Nadège checked each man was dead whilst keeping her pistol raised and focused on Sean. Their eyes locked. It was a moment where both knew what each other would or wouldn't do. She relaxed. She pulled out her phone whilst kneeling over the Kapitán, noticing that Sean was shaking his head, sat on the ground with his hands between his knees.

She punched out a text to her minders and pressed 'send'. Then she placed the phone in her back pocket and rose slowly to her feet. She walked towards Sean, holding the weapon firmly in her right hand alongside her thigh. She then raised the weapon, pointing it at his head from about five feet away to check his reactions. Nothing.

'Push all these bastards into that vat,' she said, nodding with her head at the trap door. 'I can shoot you now or you can play ball like the nice man you are and do as you're fucking well told.'

'Seems like I have no choice,' he said, rising to his feet.

'If you want to live to maybe see your son one day, you'll do everything I say, understand?'

'You mean you have a plan for me to see our child? Or is this just your mind playing with you again? I still don't believe for a minute that you had my child.'

'Shut the fuck up.'

'Look, you know I could have dealt with this and got you out of this mess, but you just want to make everything happen the hard way. The tortuous way. You can still pull out you know.'

'Not a chance.'

Nadège checked her phone. A text. Help was arriving within minutes. She watched Sean push the last of the three men into the huge concrete vat, each landing with a loud and echoing thud. Sean closed the trapdoor, one door at a time, placed the padlock on the rusting bolts and threw the key across the divide to Nadège.

Chapter 36

Armenia

Sean was gobsmacked. He knew there were risks to this part of the job, but he hadn't expected Nadège to pull the trigger on it all at this point in the operation. Yes, it was risky stuff trying to work her and turn her, no, he didn't think he had failed up until this point and, yes, he did think she might pull a trick or two a bit later on as they worked on leaving the country with the warhead.

How had he let his guard down yet again? What on earth was she thinking now about his son? Their son. Some sort of reunion or was this all just a ploy to keep him firmly in place? The nagging doubt in his mind still told him it wasn't true. Just a trick. But what if it was true?

Sean gazed across the trapdoor to where she was stood. The weapon was back by her thigh. She was not shaking, she looked calm, but her eyes still showed that trauma. Behind the eyes was a mind that somehow he had to work on now to keep his life intact. He scratched his forearm. Extreme stress caused him to scratch – and scratch a lot. His mind was racing but, for the hell of him, he couldn't work out what would come next. Until that is he watched a silhouetted figure enter the warehouse with the gait of a serviceman.

The man walked with a swagger. Feet turned out, striding confidently and with purpose. As the muscular figure came closer, Sean could just make out the chiselled features of a white man with a pale face and ginger hair. He was wearing jeans, desert boots and a black T-shirt. Sean immediately knew he was a British soldier. Or, more precisely, a former British soldier. The bomber. The man named Wilson Hewitt.

'I'm surprised,' Hewitt said. 'I'd have thought you were a scammer and it would be a dud shell. Just trying to make a quick buck. But from what I've just seen register on my equipment it's the real McCoy. Nice.'

Sean turned to look at Nadège, who was stood smiling only a few feet away from him. He looked back at the bomber. The triumvirate was fixed - but he was the odd man out. How the fuck could he now deal with this? He scratched his arm again. 'You're the bomber I assume?' he said, glancing back at Nadège.

'A little more than that,' she replied, walking across to Hewitt. She placed the palm of her hand on his chest as if to make the point to Sean that he was now nothing more than a package, and that Hewitt was her man.

'For fuck's sake. This just gets worse,' Sean said. 'Do you pair think you can just fuck off into the sunset, plant a nuclear bomb, detonate the fucking thing and you'll both be happy ever after? Do me a favour. Jeez.'

'Mate,' Hewitt said. 'We're both pros. We can do whatever the fuck we want and do it pretty fucking well. You know that, right?'

Sean shook his head and raised a smile. 'Ammunition technician then? 11 EOD? Or a sapper?'

The bomber laughed. 'Do me a favour mate. Sappers would never be on my level.'

'I know - they're not that fucking stupid.'

The bomb-maker smiled, revelling in a bit of banter. 'What mob were you then?' he asked Sean.

'Intelligence. Now a weapons dealer.'

'Is that right? Well thanks for your business with us. Seems like you came through after all.'

'You still might need me to get stuff across Europe you know. I have my contacts.'

'Who said anything about Europe?' the bomber said, shrugging his shoulders and turning to Nadège. 'We don't need anyone's help, thanks. Nice try though. Won't work.'

Sean didn't like Hewitt's arrogance. It was a stand-off. Two old soldiers with fierce rivalries that didn't bode well but Sean thought he'd push it a bit further. He had nothing to lose.

'I still don't think you've got the skills to convert that shell into a nuclear device you know. It's not a simple thing and, even with your training, you'd probably need others to help you get it right.'

Sean watched Hewitt tense and begin to clench his fists. He knew he'd hit a nerve. He watched Hewitt pull a pistol from the back of his jeans before pointing it squarely at Sean's chest and replying. 'Mate, don't try and bait me. You won't ever win on any terms. It's like this: you can play ball or I can make you go away now.'

Sean shrugged his shoulders and made a face. 'Fair enough. What's the plan now?' he said, watching Nadège turn and walk towards the exit.

'She wants you alive,' Hewitt said, pointing his weapon towards Nadège. 'Fuck knows why but you might, just might, come in useful at some point. Follow her.'

Sean started to walk slowly, deciding to goad Hewitt one more time. 'You know, you'll probably kill yourself with the radiation inside that casing as soon as you open it.'

'Keep walking, we've got a long journey ahead.'

Sean was glad he'd prodded the bomb-maker's ego as he walked slowly towards the jeep, trying to tease more and more information out of him. He certainly wasn't shy about explaining how he would go about his deadly mission. Hewitt started showing off.

'Cut the casing open, remove the uranium in safety gear with the right levels of lead shielding, place it in a transportable casket to move across the world. Easy-peasy.'

He was brash and confident about his abilities and Sean didn't need any more evidence that this man was a real-and-present danger. But what the hell had Jack been up to? How could Sean now let Jack know of the danger and that Nadège and the Iranians were now entering the last stages of a nuclear terrorist operation?

Sean walked out of the warehouse into the bright sunshine, holding his hands over his eyes to shield them. Just as he did, the bomber grabbed him from behind, smashed him to the ground and held his arm tightly behind his back.

Sean turned his neck, spitting out blood as he watched Nadège plunge a needle into his thigh.

Within thirty seconds he was unconscious.

Chapter 37

London

L ondon was baking hot. It was a blistering afternoon that saw Parliament Square and Westminster bedevilled with throngs of tourists clogging up every pavement that Jack tried to navigate. Parliament was now resembling a mini-fortress, with a multitude of steel barriers placed around it to protect the home of democracy from lorry bombs and terrorist attacks using vehicles. Even Big Ben looked tired of it all, its torso now firmly draped in scaffolding and tatty white-plastic covers. Jack winced at the prospect of the green lawns of Parliament Square being ripped up to make way for a new concrete eyesore that the London Mayor had recently proffered.

Something had gone badly wrong with our country, he thought to himself, as he walked past the main gates where, two years earlier, a lone, unarmed policeman had been stabbed to death by an Islamist terrorist. Jack still couldn't quite comprehend how the entire gated area had been left in the hands of a lone policeman, with no armed response at the post, and that the terrorist had simply driven across Westminster Bridge and hurtled into pedestrians before crashing into the gates and finally stabbing PC Keith Palmer. Jack stopped briefly to survey the scene. The police post now had four heavily armed CO19 police officers, each carrying an MP5 carbine with a Glock pistol holstered on their thighs.

What if the Iranians had this place as one of their targets, he thought? Or one of the many shopping centres in London? What if they were successful with multiple attacks on London over days? Or weeks? The country would turn into a nation under siege and at war. A dark war, with the public having no idea how a state-sponsored threat might materialise, and with the Russians and Iranians potentially acting together to create mayhem.

The British public were not used to direct war or never-ending attacks on home soil. Yes, they witnessed it from afar on their TVs from places such as Yemen and Syria, but could they survive such ongoing attacks? Could the British psyche win through, despite being subjected to military lockdown and martial law? Food in short supply, cyber-attacks on critical national infrastructure crippling lighting and heating in homes, cashpoints not working and Tubes grinding to a halt. These were the thoughts of Jack that day. Thoughts that would haunt him if his plan went wrong. It would leave the nation belly-deep in a hybrid war that he had failed to curtail. Such was the burden he bore.

'It's a little bit worse than that, sir,' Jack said, as he answered the first question the Cabinet Secretary threw at him. Jack had been asked to meet Sir Justin Darbyshire on Birdcage Walk to update him on the strategic and operational strands that Jack was running.

'I assume you have things under control right now Jack?' The question had been posed whimsically. By 'things' he meant political damage and no further risk to the security of British citizens from Iranian strikes on the UK. By all accounts, the Joint Intelligence Committee and its Chairman had assured ministers that everything was under control and that no immediate threats to the UK mainland were prevalent in formal intelligence reporting.

Jack squeezed his lips and stopped when he heard the last sentence. 'As I said, sir, it's a little worse than the formal reporting at the JIC.'

'Much worse, or a little worse Jack?'

'Much worse I'm afraid.'

'Mmmmm. Well, let's walk and talk about that. Campey has been comforting ministers. He likes to keep control of matters without making ministers panic.'

'A fair approach if he hasn't got any substantial intelligence I'd say.'

'I agree Jack. Now. When do we share your intelligence my boy? I am seeking your advice on the way forward now.'

Jack pondered on that question as they walked silently for a moment or two. The circumstances were so grave now that the impending threats couldn't just be spun away without the nation preparing properly. Jack knew he held the highest grade of intelligence, which the other agencies didn't yet have. And he didn't have enough actionable intelligence to bring interdiction operations to bear against the protagonists. But he did want Sir Justin to prepare the government for what might emerge from under the hybrid cloak of the Russian GRU and the Iranian MOIS. He was worried, however, that Sean had gone quiet because his burst transmissions from Armenia had stopped.

'I think you'll need to get Number 10 alive to the fact that they need to make some more immediate preparations,' Jack said, awkwardly trying to evade the low sun over Sir Justin's shoulder.

Sir Justin was a tall man, a good six foot four, and was now draped in his winter beige coat with black collar. A very civil service type of attire. Their own uniform. The autumn sun and the glistening leaves falling from the trees drew Jack's eyes to Buckingham Palace as he prompted the senior civil servant to speed up for the appointment Jack had made at the MOD building.

'How bad is it Jack? I'll start to coerce the right people, the trusted ones that is, to get things in place.'

The invitation Sir Justin had extended to Jack had simply said a catch-up chat, nothing more. But Jack had responded and suggested that they should walk first before having a look at PINDAR. This fitted with Jack's plan to start getting the nation prepared. PINDAR was the country's most top-secret bunker, located right below the gargantuan Ministry of Defence building on Whitehall. This was the opportunity Jack needed. The chance to brief a high-ranking civil servant, knowing full well that Sir Justin had the charm and skill of a mastermind, someone able to shake things up in government and make things happen with speed at Number 10.

'D used to bring me here occasionally,' Jack said, as their autumn walk, with dark shadows trailing behind them, came to a halt at the MOD entrance. 'He liked to make sure all of our equipment was maintained and working, and that we were prepared. I can't be sure that the UK is a main target but, trust me, sir, I believe the Iranians are about to unleash hell on someone and, if it's us, I want us all prepared.'

Hundreds of tourists and commuters walk along Whitehall in central London every day, from the House of Commons to Trafalgar Square, past Downing Street and the imposing Ministry of Defence headquarters. What these passers-by did not realise is that, beneath the pavement, deeper than the London Underground's District Line, is a huge bunker, kept secret for over four decades, and codenamed PINDAR.

MI5 had a secure area of operations within this colossal bunker to enable it to continue to conduct its missions and provide direct intelligence to senior generals and ministers. If Sean's ground operation failed, and the Iranians successfully detonated an improvised nuclear device in the UK or Europe, it would be from here that Jack and Sir Justin would operate. The thought made Jack shiver.

PINDAR took five years for the bunker to be completed in 1992, fitted out with the latest communications systems, including a huge situation room with video-conferencing equipment designed to protect its inhabitants during and after a nuclear attack or during civil unrest.

Jack entered through the first of a series of huge bomb-proof steel doors, which were held open by multiple iron hooks. There was a small cadre of staff keeping everything running and performing their own day jobs. The day-to-day custodians of the bunker.

'I assume you've had the tour, sir,' Jack asked, as he walked through the narrow corridors to the main briefing room.

'Yes, but a long time ago Jack.'

'You'll remember the bunker is fitted with bunks and accommodation for hundreds of staff and there are catering facilities on each level all designed to support operations for many months.' Jack turned right at the end of the corridor, past a breakout space nicely surrounded by greenery and plants with a small running-water wall feature just beyond it.

Jack led Sir Justin into the main briefing room, which had been upgraded to include the most modern elements of digital communications, all linked by satellites and with images displayed on multiple large screens around the room.

The centrepiece was a 3D model of Whitehall and its environs sat on a long table draped in a blue cloth. This was placed in the centre of a U-shaped set of tables that could fit thirty senior staff around it, with seating behind for another forty staff. In front of the U-shaped tables were two lecterns for presenters and behind them were a cluster of six high-definition screens that could simultaneously display live imagery from satellites or drones, and a series of high-grade maps that included overlays showing nuclear radiation or chemical plumes from terrorist CBRN strikes or bombing raids.

Sir Justin took his coat off and leant forward, placing his elbows on the table. 'OK Jack, it seems you've plenty to get off your chest, and I've got one most important matter to cover with you. No better place than a nuclear bunker eh?'

Jack smiled, unclipped his briefcase and placed a dossier in front of Sir Justin. The Kompromat dossier.

'I hope you'll allow me some time to brief you, Sir Justin. I'm afraid we're at quite a critical juncture in my operation right now and it's quite important that you know the lion's share, so that we can agree the next steps.'

'Call me Justin, for God's sake man. Good news and bad news I assume?'

'As always, Sir Justin. Bad news first is probably best.' Jack stretched across the table to grab the remote control for the digital projector, which he switched on. He tapped a few buttons on the audio-visual console, which displayed a map of Turkey and the Middle East on the top-left screen and a picture of Sean on the lower-left screen. He tapped another button and a picture of Nadège appeared too. Next came some flashing dots hovering on the maps. The yellow flashing dot looked to be smack bang in the middle of the deserts of Kuwait, and a second cluster of flashing blue lights were centred on Munich, the capital of Bavaria.

'As you know, all our Court operators are deniable,' Jack said, watching Sir Justin scrunch into his leather chair, deep in thought. 'If we take down any of the terrorists it will be non-attributable, allowing you to keep the political trust of our allies.'

'You're using mercenaries, you mean?'

'Well, everyone else calls them 'cut-outs' or 'proxies', but yes, mercenaries if you like. I like to refer to them as loyal veterans who have given, and continue to give, great service to our country.'

'I see,' Sir Justin said, clasping his hands. 'And the flashing dots? Terrorist cells or tracking devices?'

'The cluster in Munich represents bomb-making equipment. It's where the Iranian cell have moved their equipment before transferring it to their target cities. Our operator, who you can see on the bottom-left screen, is a former intelligence officer leading a Court team to track and trace the cell. His codename is CHIMERA. His mission was to try and find details of the sleeper agents lying in wait in this country and we're now watching to see where the bomb-making equipment moves to.'

'Any ideas on the targets?' the Cabinet Secretary asked, looking Jack in the eye. 'European cities? Brussels? Ourselves?'

'We're not sure yet, but their modus operandi has been to move equipment from Turkey, through the Balkans and onwards to their final destinations. My guess is that the operational cells will make their way to Munich to collect the equipment and from there they could move to a number of cities. My fear is multiple coordinated attacks across the EU. There are ten very sophisticated high-grade IEDs plus two suitcases that we think are designed to function as nuclear devices.'

Jack still didn't know if the Iranian cells had acquired other quantities of uranium beyond the sale of the artillery shell he had set up. There was enough uranium in that shell for two small suitcase devices. What he did know is that he had MI5 working day and night to watch all UK ports and airports to see who was leaving the UK and who might be arriving in Munich.

'We can't get this wrong Jack. If we have good intelligence we can bring lots of other nations in on this. We don't have to do this alone.'

'I'm afraid we pretty much do Sir Justin. Can you imagine the civil unrest, the uproar, the panic if citizens knew there were nuclear terrorists on the loose and planning a strike? There would be mayhem across the papers, and mass panic. What would you want to do with your family if you knew your city was the target? Now multiply that by millions of people. If this leaks out, it'll be chaos. And that's my problem. If we share this intelligence I can guarantee it will leak out quickly.'

'OK, I take your point Jack, you're right. But we need to be bloody sure we can handle this.'

'I agree, sir.'

'How then?'

'With trusted people. Our Court teams and a helping hand from some close friends over the pond. One of whom is ready to talk to you now.'

Jack flashed up a screen, ready to accept a video-conference call with Laura. He tapped the video button on the console and Laura's face appeared on the screen from the American Embassy in Lambeth. 'I can see you Laura, can you hear me?'

'Loud and clear Jack,' she replied, in her rapturous Californian accent. 'Nice to see you guys.'

'I've got Sir Justin with me Laura, are you able to give us a brief from your side?'

'Sure. Wait just one minute.' Laura disappeared from the screen as if she was picking something up from below her. She popped back up and said 'Hi' to Sir Justin. Then she held up a photograph of the American National Security Advisor – John Redman.

'We have him where we want him Sir Justin. For as long as he's in post we now have leverage on the way the US President will tackle Iran. The Kompromat that Jack unearthed is sealed and operational. The President trusts his NSA more than anyone else in the Whitehouse and now's the time for us to shape the landscape for the way we go forward. But we need you Brits working towards that too.'

Sir Justin looked astonished. 'Kompromat? What Kompromat?'

'I'll explain after the call Sir Justin,' Jack said, smirking. Sir Justin's face was now ashen with shock. 'What this means is that Redman will push the President to re-engage with the Iranians on the nuclear deal. That will give us more diplomacy to buy us time.'

'Exactly right Jack,' Laura chipped in, with a beaming smile on her face. Attractive and engaging, she had a way of getting senior politicians and civil service staff to come around to her way of thinking. She exuded trust, using compelling arguments. 'We're playing this with two very structured plans Sir Justin. If you'll allow me, I'll explain.'

'Thank you Laura,' Sir Justin said, in his agreeable Oxbridge accent. 'Any more shocks for me? I have a feeling I know what I need to do after this call.'

Laura laughed as she pulled her hand through her hair. 'I run the European and Asian operations for the CIA Special Activities Division and we work closely with Jack's Court team. We're going to run two strands here: a political strand and a tactical paramilitary strand. I only hope we have enough time to close down the Iranian terrorist cells before our political strand kicks in.'

The CIA Special Activities Division is one of the most secretive and potent organisations in the world. Within SAD there are two separate groups: the Special Operations Group, SOG, for tactical paramilitary operations, and the covert political action group.

The SOG is a department responsible for operations that include high-threat military or covert operations that the US government does not wish to be overtly associated with. Much like The Court's members, their paramilitary operations officers and specialised skills officers do not carry any objects or wear any clothing that would associate them with the United States government. If they are compromised during a mission, the United States government will deny all knowledge. Exactly the same as with The Court. SOG is generally considered to be the most secretive special operations force in the United States.

'Our political teams are not far away from creating the conditions to overthrow the mullahs of Iran,' Laura continued. 'We all prefer that option to what we are seeing right now. Cold war 2.0 is being used by the Russians to get Iran to create carnage across the West with its terrorist arms. It's bad all round and that's why we're going to use the Kompromat to get at Redman. The Kompromat allows us to continue with our covert operations to overthrow the Iranian regime and to start to get the US looking as if we're engaging diplomatically. It's a feint.'

'Bloody hell,' Sir Justin said, looking shocked. 'You're a pair of scheming rascals but I like what I'm hearing. I do however have a pension I'd like to keep so I'll need some assurances on all of this.'

'It's risky, but we have all our teams in place ready to go. Political and paramilitary. To be frank with you Sir Justin, if we go to other nations with this, they'll screw it right up.'

'I like your style Laura. Now, is all this deniable if things go pear-shaped?'

'Yes. That's why we're working with Jack using our covert teams to stop this. Two plans. One to interdict the terrorists using our teams, the second, if we fail, is to make sure conventional counterterrorist teams can deal with the aftermath. What we can't do is rattle the EU and get conventional intelligence agencies involved now. They'll fuck it all up.'

Sir Justin was mildly shocked but smirked at Laura's swearing designed to produce an effect. She was good. Damn good. 'OK, I get it, let's run it then. I'll get amongst our ministers so that they're saying the right things and make sure we're prepared if it all goes tits up.'

Jack picked up his laser pointer. 'I'm afraid there is one more bit of bad news Sir Justin.'

'Christ Jack, you haven't told me the good news yet. Go on.'

'Our primary agent, CHIMERA, has gone quiet and may well have been compromised. He's located here, in the middle of the Kuwaiti Desert. We have a tracker on him and we'll look to rescue him if needs be. He's deniable and has been dealing with our main adversary, this woman here codenamed NIGHTOWL. She's Iran's top female agent, who masquerades as an international model.'

'Bloody hell Jack, this is insane.'

'As is she. We'll take her down at the right time but our best avenue right now is to monitor the bomb-making equipment and strike at the right time.'

Jack was careful to avoid explaining that the dot on the screen showed a transmission from inside the casing of the nuclear artillery shell.

'Anything else you need from me?' Sir Justin asked Laura, as he inspected the red-labelled file in front of him. 'I get the political picture and Jack has just passed me what appears to be the Kompromat.'

'No, nothing from me Sir Justin. Jack and I are a good team with good operators on the ground. I have a NEST team available for Europe as and when they might be required.'

'NEST?'

'Our Nuclear Emergency Support Teams. If we lose control of this operation and can't interdict the terrorists, we can deploy them into Europe to search for and disable any nuclear device.'

Laura bade farewell and Jack turned the screen off.

'Seems we now have leverage for as long as Redman remains the NSA for this Republican administration Jack,' said Sir Justin. 'Good work as ever. D would have been as astonished as I am at how you've played this one.'

'Thank you, but there's a long way to go yet. I assume you'll coach ministers to work with the Americans now on the diplomatic channels and to be prepared for any attacks?

'They're a funny bunch this lot Jack. MPs of today have none of the guile needed to govern these days but, fear not, my team of civil servants is pretty good at this stuff, as you know. Now, this dossier. I'm not going to read it. Whatever you uncovered is yours. Get rid of it and hide the trails. You remember what happened with the Steele dossier a couple of years back? Don't let that happen here.'

'It's all attributable to the Russians, so we're good. Any evidence of that conversation with Laura is being destroyed as we speak too.'

Jack placed the dossier back in his briefcase, having predicted that the Cabinet Secretary would not want to view it. He tapped the touch pad on the console which triggered the screen to zoom in on the Kuwait map.

'Where CHIMERA has been taken is likely to be the bomb-making factory. We'll get him out at some point but the one thing you do need to know is that he is linked to the dossier.'

Jack touched his control pad, which prompted the screen to flash up a picture of the ex-CIA chief. 'This is the man who led us to the Kompromat on John Redman. His name is Fletcher Barrington. This guy and our FCO diplomat, Duff, were both involved in some pretty gruesome stuff many years back in 1995. Barrington is also the killer of CHIMERA's mother back in 1986. A bizarre coincidence.'

'Good God Jack. Does he know?'

'Yes. It was one of D's last investigations and he wrote to CHIMERA himself. A last act of loyalty to one of his foot soldiers. Fletcher Barrington was a CIA operator who worked with CHIMERA's mother in East Berlin during the cold war. She was one of MI6's best female agents.'

'I expect your man is fuming and looking for revenge Jack?'

'He is,' Jack said quietly, imagining Sean's pain. 'But I'll manage CHIMERA. We need Barrington alive for a number of years to come to keep our political Kompromat in play.'

'Splendid Jack. Now, as you know, I said I had something for you too.'

Jack looked at his boss, somewhat bemused and wondering what was coming next.

'There's every chance you'll become the permanent Deputy Director of MI5 now. No bad thing at all. We'll also run all the normal application processes for the Director General's job. But I want you to apply for that instead.'

'The Director General's job?'

'Yes. D's job.'

Jack didn't quite know what to say. He sat back and took a moment. Never in his own mind had he ever thought about doing such a thing. He'd spent many years as the counterterrorist operations director and took great heart in running The Court. It was an immense privilege to run global operations with retired operators from across all the intelligence agencies, sprinkled with military veterans across the world. Operations was his world, not the cut and thrust of political brinkmanship, although he was a devious hand at that on occasion.

'I'm not cut out for that Sir Justin. I'm an operational guy.'

'Nonsense Jack. The world is changing and, as D always said, we need to get sharper at hybrid warfare and shape our agencies to fight a new world order. You're the brightest spark we have in the box to take us there and, believe me, everyone will follow you. You're seen as a doer who makes the right things happen.'

Sir Justin leant forward. 'Have a think on it. Take your time. You'll have my backing to develop The Court's operations, although not on the mammoth scale of the CIA you understand. But we need to get bigger, better and sharper.'

Jack had a thought about his family and his ill daughter. She had battled MS for nearly five years of her young life. Maybe now was the time to either retire or take a bigger jump. He didn't quite know which way was for the best. He didn't know what would happen over the course of the next couple of weeks, never mind thinking about his lifetime's dream of becoming Director General of MI5. It was a move he had been mentored for throughout almost all of his career by D. It made his ambitious side begin to tantalise him.

'Of course, the following days and weeks will make or break my offer Jack. We'll also need to deal with the Chair of the Joint Intelligence Committee. Hugo Campey thinks the job is his already, so we'll need a plan to scupper that. Any ideas?'

'One or two,' Jack said, still somewhat shocked.

'Good. We need to put him out of the game permanently. Then you will become the youngest Director General of MI5 ever - if you make all this mess go away, deal with Hugo and succeed on this operation, it will be you.'

Chapter 38

Kuwait

The motto of the CIA Special Activities Division is *Tertia Optio*, which means 'The Third Option'. In the UK, intelligence agencies have an option of legal amnesty for agents needing to commit crimes for the greater good, known as 'The Third Direction'. Together, Jack and Laura had brought together all options through what they both called 'The Third Avenue' – an amalgamation of The Court's activity and the sheer might of the SAD to form the most potent covert partnership in the world.

Jack and Laura thought they had every option available to track and trace the nuclear shell, follow the terrorists and, when the time was right, kill them. These were seasoned intelligence officers comfortable with taking huge risks and who rarely made the wrong call. But this time their judgement was wrong.

More often than not, covert operations using the highest-grade intelligence apparatus and paramilitary forces will not go strictly to plan – and this was one such occasion. It all began to go wrong shortly after the helicopter transporting the nuclear shell with a tracking beacon inside it started to fly due south into Iran. That was not expected at all. That was not the interdiction plan. Their plan had been to use surveillance teams within Turkey and Europe, working on a hypothesis that the nuclear material would be destined for Europe.

The operational teams of The Court and the CIA were sat in a small Portakabin at Incirlik Air Base, with a Hercules airframe and two Black Hawk helicopters ready to go at a moment's notice.

Samantha had been watching satellite images of Nadège's helicopter and stared in astonishment as it entered Iranian airspace.

'Bloody hell. That's not what we expected. What the hell do we do now?' she asked Swartz, who would lead the interdiction operation to kill the Iranian terrorists and the rogue bomb-maker.

'You better ask Jack quickly, he'll be shitting it by now if he's watching back home.'

'Make sure you're ready to fly in case it diverts into Iraq – everyone's set to go right?'

'Yep. Aircrew in their seats, all the kit's on-board, including Jugsy and his airframes. All we're missing is ground surveillance wherever they land. Ram it home to Jack that I need that if we want to make this op work. Otherwise it will all go wrong from the get-go.'

Samantha mumbled a few words to herself and picked up the secure phone to call Jack. 'We've got three satellites on this operation courtesy of the CIA, so we should be able to steer you to the target. I just don't know how long Jack wants to play this out before we hit them.'

'Might not have a chance if the helicopter stays in Iran – we might never see the thing again and then we're properly fucked.'

The orders from Jack were explicit. 'We watch and wait,' he said over the phone. 'Just be poised and ready to go when I give the order.'

Jack and Laura had been sat in the operations room at RAF Bentwaters, monitoring the movement of Nadège's helicopter and listening to every radio transmission from the assault teams at Incirlik Air Base. They knew that the risk of losing the nuclear shell was immense and Laura had guaranteed that American military assets within EUCOM would be ready to be tasked to support the operation. She had the NEST teams at the ready, backed up by surveillance teams ready to fly out of Germany, one strategic drone and a high-priority tasking for imagery intelligence using US satellites. The problem was she hadn't placed anyone on standby in CENTCOM – the exact area of US operations where the helicopter was now flying to.

The small yellow dot on the screen showed the tracking beacon move southwards through Iran before it finally flew over the coastline and into the Persian Gulf. It then made a right turn and flew straight into Kuwaiti airspace, before finally landing in the middle of the Al Anbar Desert. The imagery-intelligence operator zoomed in to the desert complex where the helicopter had landed. The high-resolution imagery provided clear images of a large villa completely surrounded by a perimeter wall, with two smaller annex buildings and four vehicles neatly parked next to the entrance gate.

'Right, get moving Swartz,' Samantha barked. 'Ali Al Salem airbase in Kuwait. It's all good to go. There's a ground team being assembled now to watch the place. Go well.'

'I'm gone. Get me some more int before we strike for fuck's sake.'

Five hours later, the surveillance operation began to fall apart. A white Land Cruiser had exited the gates of the complex and was tracked by imagery-intelligence operators, who monitored its direction of travel from satellites situated 140 kilometres above the earth. The operations teams at Ali Al Salem airbase had cued three mobile surveillance teams onto the vehicle as it entered Kuwait City.

The satellite was locked onto the Land Cruiser, with Samantha watching it enter Kuwait City, where it stopped at numerous traffic lights before heading east towards the port and its final destination. It stopped at a set of barriers before entering a heavily protected Kuwaiti army base. Samantha watched it drive along the main barracks road before it disappeared into a huge military hangar.

'Shit,' she said, falling back in her chair. She was flabbergasted that the nuclear package had simply vanished into a military base. 'If they transfer the bomb to another vehicle, we'll never see the bloody thing again.'

Chapter 39

Kuwait

Swartz adjusted his ear defence as the helicopter rotors increased their speed ready for take-off into the cool Arabian air. He checked his seat belt, pulled it a little tighter, as he did religiously for all take-offs, and then checked that his Glock pistol was tightly locked into his thigh harness and safe. He placed his right hand on the grip of his MP5 automatic assault weapon and glanced across to his three teammates, who were looking primed and evil – ready to unleash hell on the target building and anyone who tried to stop them killing the bomber and any terrorists left inside the compound.

The last-known transmission from the tracking device had come from the villa complex in the middle of the Kuwaiti Desert and Swartz had been ordered to assault the compound by Jack. The assumption was that the site would provide vital intelligence to continue the operation, but there was also the possibility that Sean, the bomber and Nadège might be there too. No one knew who had driven the vehicle out of the compound, no one knew if the fissile material had been moved and no one knew if a bomb had been built and moved out of the complex. Jack knew only one thing. The deliberate plan had turned into a fiasco and he needed his team to assault the desert complex to find out more.

Swartz watched Phil 'The Nose' Calhoun give him a big thumbs up as the helicopter lifted off into the darkness of the desert night, followed by a beaming smile as they revelled in their adventure into the unknown. Phil was the team's bomb-disposal officer and would deal with any explosive booby traps they came across during the assault on the buildings and the subsequent search of its interior and grounds.

The intelligence was shit. It was meagre to say the least, making the assault a huge, but necessary, gamble. The entire surveillance operation was conducted by satellite with only two surveillance operators on the ground watching the gates of the complex. Swartz had no confirmation of the terrorist numbers inside the several buildings of the villa complex, no one was sure if Sean was there and he'd been told that Nadège and the bomber had not been seen leaving the complex. Only the Land Cruiser had left the complex in the last eight hours. If this was the best that Jack's deniable operations could throw up on such a vital mission he was bloody worried. The truth was that Jack couldn't wait forever to find out where the nuclear material had gone. Was it still inside? Or had it been moved in the Land Cruiser?

Had Swartz known at the time that the improvised nuclear device had indeed been moved in the Land Cruiser, he would have been horrified. Despite having persistent surveillance on the Kuwaiti Army barracks, there were so many vehicles leaving the site that it was impossible to know which ones to follow. Was the bomb still inside? How could he get operators into such a heavily defended barracks? Despite having the best of the American intelligence apparatus, they were now blind to where the nuclear device had gone. Was Nadège with it? What exactly was the link with the Kuwaiti Army? Swartz smelt a full-scale fuck-up coming on.

What Swartz had was inadequate for a fully planned assault, but he did have the best possible advantage – the act of surprise. He had studied the plans of the building, conducted rehearsals on makeshift layouts of the main villa and now had live imagery in place from Jugsy's UAV, which was currently loitering above the mansion relaying video pictures to Swartz's teams. The images were being beamed across the desert using encrypted line-of-sight technology to provide him with high-definition infrared imagery direct onto a ruggedised tablet. The daytime reconnaissance using two of the C-Astral drones had provided intelligence that there were at least five heavily armed guards patrolling the perimeter and the grounds, with two other Arab men occasionally leaving the main house to smoke shisha in the ornate courtyard. Swartz had two dogs in the second helicopter that would be launched into the stronghold, giving him the added aggression needed for his plan of using overwhelming force to take down the terrorists and conduct a forensic search of the complex.

Phil was not only the bomb-disposal expert, he was also the leader for the sensitive-site exploitation that would take place once the situation was benign and the terrorists were all dead. Phil's forensic and search expertise would allow the team to extract valuable forensic evidence from the site, which might lead to knowing what type of devices the bomber had built or at least provide some insight into the targets they were destined for.

Swartz remained pensive and pushed out a few breathing exercises as the chopper glided across the Kuwaiti Desert at low altitude, with less than ten minutes to its target site.

On too many occasions in his life Sean had felt the searing pain that comes from the shock of capture. It never got easier and, each time it occurred in his career, the anxiety levels forced him to scratch his skin until he ended up with open sores.

This time he had been drugged and flown by helicopter to the bomb-making factory in the Kuwaiti Desert – he remembered nothing from the moment when Nadège had inserted the needle into his thigh. He had been carried by four burly Iranian guards to the deep basement level of the mansion, chained by his wrists to the wall and left to fester until he regained consciousness in the tiny cell. He awoke with a stinking hangover, dizziness and a moment of pain that told him his right cheek was broken. Within minutes he was throwing his guts up, the incessant pain of stomach cramps causing him to retch in convulsions before the next batch of vomit was ejected from his body. The soiling of his pants told him his body had been violated by the drug and a deep feeling of helplessness returned, raging in his body as he grappled to retain his mind. The shock of capture had again hit him hard.

Everyone deals with stress in different ways, and the shock of being captured initiates severe strain in the body. For most, and certainly for those without the relevant training, the stress reactions are shock, numbness, anxiety, guilt, depression, anger and a sense of helplessness. For Sean the emotional anxiety always resulted in physical scratching and being nauseous. Surges of chemical imbalances had manifested into physical symptoms for Sean, who felt unable to breathe and had blurred vision when Nadège entered the cell.

'I didn't want it this way,' she murmured.

Sean had propped himself against the cell wall, his chains dangling over his shoulders. He looked up at her as she continued.

'We're leaving now but I'll let you live.'

'Thanks a bunch. Glad I could be of some help to you.'

'You've been a great help Sean, and my country would be proud of you.'

'You don't really want to go through with this, do you? I can see the fear in your eyes. What is it Nadège? What's fucked you up?'

Nadège squatted in front of Sean. 'Many things Sean. Too many things for you to understand. I have my way out now.'

'Why the fuck don't you let me fix this Nadège? Let me use the British. Turn to them, become one of them, for fuck's sake. I can connect you quickly and they'll have you secure like a shot. Save yourself.'

Nadège's face changed. She pulled back. She turned. Then she returned to kneel at Sean's eye level. 'My way will work. I've been planning this for years. It's guaranteed.'

'You know nothing is guaranteed in our world. Some treacherous bastard will shit all over you. And this time I'm betting it'll be that asshole bomber or whoever your handler is.'

Nadège stood and turned again. She paced the small cell, putting her hands on her head and pulling her fingers through her hair. She was becoming more and more histrionic, a demon inside. Sean sensed this was his last chance.

'Turn to the Brits Nadège. Change your life. You'll be on the run forever otherwise.'

'I couldn't kill you Sean,' she said angrily. 'It's too late now though. I'm going to go through with this. Once I've deployed the bombs, I get free passage to South America from General Alimani. It's all arranged. You're Maxim's father. I can live with lots but killing his father I cannot.'

'How can you trust this General Alimani?'

'I can't but there's no other way now. It's all set. My life is nothing, never has been. My soul was destroyed a long time ago and I want my son to be brought up without the toxicity I had to endure. My mother will make sure of that.'

'You mean 'our son'. And you can't just fuck off and kill yourself. That's defeatist and savage. Get a grip, for fuck's sake Nadège. Get me out of here and I'll get you full protection and a new life. It can be planned and they'd want you. You're more use to the Brits than I am but I can get you connected.'

'Don't be so stupid,' she said, dropping to her knees, quietly screaming into the cell, quietly raging inside whilst she started to dig her nails into her wrists, tying to harm herself.

'OK, calm down,' Sean said sympathetically. 'Why don't you tell me what's been happening? Tell me about all these killings you told me about in Armenia. At least leave me with the truth.'

Nadège sat cross-legged in front of Sean, holding her head in her hands, tearful and lost. 'It's all very bad,' she said, pushing her hair from her face to reveal her tears. 'Petra is special. A very special woman. My lover.'

'I know that. Go on.'

'She told me a secret she'd been holding onto since she was a child. She's a broken woman like me. She confided in me. She's the only person who can truly understand me. She's the same as me. We suffer the same nightmares, the same dark moments, the same harming.'

'Bloody hell. What was it that's bonded you?'

'An horrific episode in Bosnia that scarred her for life.'

'Abuse as a kid?'

'Worse.'

'Go on. At least confide in me now. I can't do you any damage any more. Look at me. I'm fucked again, and we now have a child, for God's sake.'

Nadège explained how she had met Petra. And how they became lovers. Petra had experienced similar traumas to Nadège, both having been sexually groomed and abused as children. But Petra had confided the precise details of her tormentors. They were American, Russian and British officers who had all been based in Tuzla in Bosnia way back in 1995. A bunch of senior and secretive officers who groomed young Bosnian girls, sharing them amongst themselves, and who had sworn to secrecy forever. They named themselves the High Chaparral. Senior officers who had been provided pubescent girls by a local gangster and politician called Franko Burrić, who became the Mayor of Sarajevo.

'I hunted them all down and killed them one by one.'

'Jeez.'

'They killed the souls of many young girls who they were sent to protect.'

'Bastards,' Sean said, dumbfounded at what he was hearing. 'How did you find them and kill them?'

'There were eight of them in total. Petra told me how they'd have their secret parties in Tuzla and that there were five girls who were raped and abused incessantly for more than a year. She told me about the local gangster, Burrić, who I trapped, and I went from there.'

'What about Petra?'

'Oh, she killed too. She helped me. It's helped to revive her life. She'll kill again soon. It's all planned.'

'Who's next then?'

'There are two left and they will be the sweetest kills. One is a former CIA chief and the other a British diplomat. It will be good to make them both suffer.'

'The name of the British diplomat is Edmund Duff, right?'

Nadège's jaw dropped. Her mouth opened. She went pale with shock. 'How the fuck do you know about that? How do you know about him?'

'It was splashed all over the papers in the UK. The kidnapping of a British diplomat when he was out drinking with his American mate. Lots of gossip about the Russians kidnapping him.'

'Mmmmm. It took me a long time to get that name. A very long time. Barrington was the ringleader but he was always hidden and was protected by the Brit called Duff.'

'Torture then? The Brit gave you Barrington's name?'

'None of your fucking business.'

'Listen, I'll bet there's people onto you already Nadège. They've probably been following your trail for some time, linking the killings, possibly even knowing about Petra. It's only a matter of time before they close in.'

'Maybe, maybe not.'

'Can't blame you both though. These are evil bastards who deserve to die. But you know what?'

'What?'

'There's more to that man Fletcher Barrington than you know about. He's also the man who killed my mother, way back in 1986.'

'Fuck.'

'So you see, we have a common purpose. A common aim. To kill this bastard. A bastard who does not deserve to breathe the air we walk in.'

Nadège started to relax, looking less fearful, engrossed now. 'Who told you about your mother then?'

'A very good friend. Was Barrington the kingpin in Bosnia then?'

'Yes. He ran two grooming rings. One in Tuzla and the other in Sarajevo. I killed the Mayor of Sarajevo who supplied the girls.'

'How did you get all their names?'

'I traced them over the years using my Russian and Iranian contacts. I love her Sean. I had to do right by her. I might be evil in my own way but at least I have a heart of sorts. These bastards killed these young women. They are all now psychologically scarred for life.'

'A little bit like you Nadège. I know you're suffering. I know you've had that trauma too.'

Nadège slid back, pushed her legs out and thrust herself forward to stand up. She paced around for a while before squatting back in front of Sean. Sean noticed that the fear in her eyes had gone, her face showed a grimace and she'd come back with a steely determination. Her volatile mood changed again.

'Listen to me,' Sean said purposefully. He raised both hands to pull them through his hair. The chains clinked against each other. 'You're suffering inside, and I have seen the signs. There are lots of them. Your emotional logic is shot and you're just not able to think the way your brain is designed to. Hand it over. Let me help you. We now have a common purpose: to kill this bastard and look after our child, for fuck's sake.'

'Fuck off and stop trying to diagnose me. Only I know what I have to deal with. No one else can ever know, so stop playing the doctor. I'm not completely fucked up, I'm more than capable of thinking logically and the logical part of my brain is telling me I should just slot you right now.'

Sean had prodded her right where it hurt most. Right in her emotional ego. Her emotions were dysregulated by the severe trauma she had suffered in childhood, which had conditioned her brain and emotions to defend her in the most bizarre, almost alien, ways. For her and many like her, it was a means of survival. She had a deep self-hatred, no self-worth, was hard-wired to function at an incredibly high level, but had an inner rage that led her to kill. All stemming from trauma in early childhood, from being abused as a young child, from being abused by her father.

Sean knew something was wrong. His psychoanalytical skills were good - but not that good. This was far too deep for him, but he wasn't far off the mark. What he didn't know was that her rage was turning black. Someone was sat in front of her and knew about her vulnerability, her inner scars, and now that someone was pulling back the cloak to expose her. That person was now turning into an evil being in her mind. The devil. Sean was taking off her mask, probing inside her mind, and that meant that Nadège saw him as the devil incarnate. It was a defence mechanism. She was blackening him. An effect that emotional intensity disorder sufferers use as a tool to protect themselves.

What Nadège would do now was anyone's guess – but Sean had no idea of the danger. He was oblivious to the depth of her hate for him. The worst thing he could ever have done was to call her out for the psychological illness she carried. She was exposed. From this point onwards she would rage internally against him.

Sean watched her stand and turn to leave. He noticed her face was red with fury. He knew he had blown his mission and his attempt at getting close to her.

'Tell me where Maxim will be. If it all goes wrong I can get to him and your mum. You know I'll do the right thing by them. Don't go off and bloody kill yourself.'

Nadège turned, drew her pistol from her jeans and fired a shot straight into the wall above Sean's head. She was furious. The noise in the small cell was deafening, causing Sean to shudder and put his hands to his ears. She took one pace forward. Sean watched her eyes. He watched her aim the pistol right at his chest. Then she fired again. Right into the roof of the ceiling. Then she walked right up to Sean and pulled her right hand down before swinging her pistol with a fierce whip-like action straight into Sean's face. He felt a searing heat as a massive cut ripped his cheek from his mouth to his eye.

'Don't ever hurt me again,' she said, turning to open the metal door. She pushed it open. Sean's ears were ringing. At that moment he didn't know if she would turn and kill him. Being only milliseconds away from death had made him forget about the pain in his face. A final shot rang out as she fired down the corridor.

He breathed a sigh of relief as he heard her final words. Words that told him her rage was a mask to protect herself.

'If ever you get out of here, and I'm dead, look for a place called San Pelayo de Tehona. Our child will be there.'

Chapter 40

Kuwait

Sean was left with nothing but his thoughts in the few minutes or so before all hell would be unleashed in the middle of the Kuwaiti Desert, as two helicopters made their final approaches to the partially lit compound in which he was incarcerated.

His mind juggled intermittently with the chaotic goings-on of Nadège and, more widely, with the background to his mother and her death. In a short space of time he had learnt of his mother's death and found out he had a child, and now he had a raging assassin on the loose looking to press the nuclear button and finish off a killing spree, with Barrington firmly in her sights. What's next, he thought?

His mind turned to Jack. What the hell was he up to back home? And when would he launch the interdiction operation to stop Nadège and her lunacy? He started to feel sleepy but, instead of nodding off, he found himself daydreaming, with his eyes closed and memories of his mother. It was the type of slumber where you have to make your mind work to dig deep and remember the years gone by, the small details, what she was wearing, what she had said and what images she had left in his memory of those younger days. He made his mind work hard, recalling his neuro-linguistic training for memory recall. Had he missed anything from those early teenage years? Or was it all just a blur? He delved deep into his memories, just as he had been taught to do all those years ago. It had worked miraculously with Melissa on his last job – one that led to him finding happiness with her. His mind drifted to Melissa. How was she, he wondered? Was she worried about him? What on earth would she say now that he'd found out he had a son?

Would he ever have a child with her? Those conversations had come and gone after the death of his wife all those years ago and he didn't want to reflect too deeply on having kids – he put those thoughts into his tidy little drawers. Closed them. But they kept bloody opening again.

Concentrate, man. Stop thinking of Melissa, think of your childhood and your mother. Why on earth had he never latched on to the fact that his mother was a spy? He'd been too bloody busy being a lazy teenager was his response. Oblivious to her heroism and fortitude – just like his dad's. God, he needed to learn more about his family – especially now that he too had a child. Or so he was told. For fuck's sake came the response, as a second voice sparked in his head. Was he going mad? Had the shock of capture sent his mind into overdrive? He knew how his mind often played stupid tricks with him when he was under duress. Dreams and imaginings all caused by severe stress.

Helicopters. Was he hearing helicopters? Was he asleep? Or in a stupor? He felt numb and sedated again. Why was his mother a spy and what on earth had she uncovered that was so big she had been assassinated? He was determined to find out if ever he got out of here. He had known there would be secrets in his family but, decades on, he wanted answers. Not stupid dreams rattling around in his head.

It was the sound of helicopters. Louder. He opened his eyes. He couldn't focus in the dim light of the cell. Then he heard the crack and thump of a firearm outside. A volley of controlled shots. Snipers? An assault? He listened intently. He knew he was awake.

Swartz watched the orange tracer shots stream into the grounds of the mansion located next to the main entrance of the huge courtyard. His night-vision goggles showed one man fall to the ground as a special forces sniper fired from a helicopter positioned about forty feet above the wall and at three o'clock to the main entrance. The sniper helicopter had flown in ahead of the other two air platforms and had smoked the ground at just thirty feet above the sand before rearing up at the last minute to rise sharply into the air, giving the sniper a perfect view of the two armed guards. Neither would have known what the hell had hit them until the last moment of their lives. They'd have heard the 'wocker, wocker' of the chopper blades for about ten seconds, but the low-level flying would have confused them. They'd have had no idea where the sounds were coming from until they saw the platform appear from nowhere and the tracer rounds were fired straight into their chests. The tracer gave the other helicopters a sight of where the action was before twelve elite soldiers fast-roped out of the airframes straight into the compound.

Jugsy was providing high-definition imagery from his fixed-wing drones, which had been loitering silently at eight hundred feet above the target location. The helicopter's navigator and snipers had perfect imagery of the target site on their ruggedised tablets as they approached, and it allowed the pilots to be steered directly to where the first kills would happen. Swartz watched the first two men fast-rope out of the helicopter and make their way to the target building. Phil 'The Nose' was standing in the gaping void, locking his hands onto the three-inch-diameter rope, ready to go next. Swartz watched the air loadmaster tap him once on the shoulder before Phil swung out on the black rope, dropping to the ground using nothing but the friction of his gloves to control the descent.

Swartz grasped the rope and twisted his gloved hands to form a lock and grip on it. He felt a tap on the shoulder and stepped out of the helicopter, feeling the rip of the downdraught from the rotors. He twisted his shoulders as he exited the aircraft and then accelerated his descent by gently releasing his lock on the rope. His knees were bent and spread to absorb the crush on his legs as he landed. He couldn't see anything below him and had to work on touch and feel as he pummelled into the ground at twenty-odd miles an hour.

The first thing that caught his eye was the sight of a Malinois attack dog being unleashed by a special forces handler and propelling itself, quietly and with no barking, at the lone gunman stood outside the main entrance. The poor bastard would be dead in seconds. The canine went straight for the man, who had now turned and started to run, but it was too late. The guard had no chance. The canine launched itself, striking the back of the man's neck, and he crumpled to the ground. The canine adjusted its head, furiously ripping at him before thrusting its teeth into his throat and killing him in seconds. The screams of death scythed through the still air.

Three down. Two by snipers, one by a canine, more to go. Swartz had no idea how many more men were inside, but he knew the dogs would find them.

The infrared imagery from the two drones sitting above the assault team allowed Swartz to receive direct radio commentary from Jugsy, who was now directing troops towards any movement he saw on his screens as he sat in the warm offices of an American airfield some one hundred kilometres away.

'One runner on the purple face of the building,' Swartz heard across the radio. 'He's heading towards a Range Rover with a red-hot bonnet. Looks like the vehicle is primed and ready to go.'

'Whisky two four,' Swartz barked into his helmet radio. 'That's your side of the building, take them down.' Seconds later he heard a volley of automatic fire smash into the vehicle before he sprinted into the open courtyard. He heard a rasping sound across the radio from Whisky two four, indicating that the action was complete and that two occupants had been killed. Five down. No real fightback. Swartz, sweating now, adjusted his helmet and then rode the adrenalin surge, knowing that the most dangerous part of the mission was about to come: clearing out the building and finding any occupants within. He had three teams of four assaulters, two attack dogs and two snipers hovering above the site to make the place safe before Phil conducted his target-site forensics. He wondered if Sean was inside.

Breathing heavily, he turned the first corner in the courtyard to lead Phil into the building. Two other troopers had already entered with two canines, leading the charge to find any gunmen left inside.

Swartz steered Phil to the white alabaster steps that led to the basement below the courtyard. The building plans had suggested that this would be the perfect location for the bomb factory to be. It provided safety and containment for a bomber mixing dangerous chemicals and acted as an underground sanctuary that would most likely be used to control access from prying eyes.

Just as they dropped to the first turn in the staircase, Swartz heard one of the canines barking. He turned the corner into the unlit corridor. Sure enough, right at the end of the corridor, was a dog jumping up and down at a large metal door. The dog could smell the human scent inside – the scent of Sean. Swartz took the lead from the dog's handler, who gave him a thumbs up. He put his hand on the door, sliding the small flap to its side, revealing a spyhole to look inside. He removed his night-vision goggles to peer through the hole. A night light inside the cell gave enough illumination for him to see Sean sitting in the darkness chained to the wall, eagerly looking at the door.

'Sean, can you hear me?'

'I hear you, who is it?'

'Who the fuck do you think? There's only one bloke who ever breaks you out of jail, for fuck's sake.'

Swartz smiled and turned to Phil. 'All yours now. Make it a clean one.'

Phil pulled out a length of plastic explosive from his chest pouch, moulded a couple of blobs and placed them on the door, close to where the double-locking mechanism latches engaged with the wall. He shouted through the keyhole. 'Sean. Can you hear me? Keep your head down for two minutes and stick your hands over your ears. Rattle your chains if you heard that.'

A rattle of chains and the fading sound of a barking dog being led up the stairs to the courtyard. Swartz watched Phil place detonators in the explosive gel, fix a wire into the remote-detonating firing device and crouch down, turning his back on the cell some fifteen feet down the corridor. Phil signalled to Swartz to turn away from the blast. Seconds later – boom!

The blast wave engulfed Sean as the door swung violently open, forcing a wave of overpressure down one side of the cell. The cell thundered with the penetrating blast, which rattled the entire foundations of the ceiling structure, and a piece of masonry whistled past his head, splintering into the wall behind him.

'Jesus Christ,' Sean spluttered, looking up to see half of the wall blown off where the dual-locking mechanism had once sat, securing the door. He looked behind him to see the pockmarked wall where the masonry had shot into the wall.

'Sorry about that,' Phil shouted, as he stood in the doorway silhouetted against the night light. 'Didn't want to fuck about with two or three goes. Are you OK?'

'Just about, you nutcase. That piece of rock nearly killed me, for fuck's sake. Don't bloody well use that stuff on these chains. Get a saw.'

Sean sat up, showing his hands to Phil. 'What's your plan for these then, eh?'

Swartz walked into the cell and shook Sean's hand. 'Another fine mess you've gotten us all into mate. Love it when your plans go to shit. I've been told to get you out and take you to Prague. You're late on bloody parade again.'

Chapter 41

Kuwait

Sean winced as Phil 'The Nose' began to cut into the metal wrist bands that had shackled him to the wall. It was a delicate operation, using a battery-powered circular saw about the size of a teacup – but with enough power to slice Sean's wrists right off if Phil buggered it up. He started slowly, with the aim of making just enough of a cut to weaken the metal and then rip it apart using metal shears.

'You carry a lot of bloody kit Phil. Whatever makes you think you'll ever need all this stuff?'

'With you leading us, you never know what's coming next,' he said, with his trademark chuckle. 'Now stay still - this might take a while and I want to know everything you've found out so far. Samantha has got everyone lined up for bombs going off across bloody Europe. What the fuck's going on?'

Sean watched Phil switch on his iPod as he always did when he was dealing with tricky manoeuvres - normally when he defused bombs. Next came the gentle sounds of Bizet's *Pearl Fishers* friendship duet. The calming notes of a tenor and a baritone singing of their allegiance to each other until death.

'Why the music Phil? You never did tell me after you defused that bomb around Melissa's neck in France.'

'Ah, well music is in my blood, in my veins and in my soul. I'm a Welshman, remember?'

'Keeps you calm then?'

'Yup. Now shut up and stay still. This is a tricky bit I need to cut.' Phil revved the saw up a notch or two, turning his music up even louder. 'You see, this is my favourite duet. Bloody good sing-song. It's about a chorus of men singing of the dangerous tasks that lie ahead - *Sur la grève en feu.* And a few rituals to drive away evil spirits. What evil lies ahead now then Sean?'

Phil was an explosives legend. He was only five foot eight inches tall but well built, with a very distinctive boxer's nose, wide shoulders and a trademark number one haircut. He was the font of all knowledge on bomb disposal and technical surveillance and had received many bravery awards during his distinguished career in the British Army.

'Bombs. Plenty of them, by the looks of it. The Iranians have been set up as proxies by the Russians to set fire to Europe.'

Phil held his shears in his mouth and stopped drilling momentarily. Sean saw the eagerness in his eyes as he looked at Sean with an unusually serious face. 'Do we know where? How many?'

'We've got tracking devices on most of them but can't be sure it's all of them. But, worst of all, they're putting together INDs. They have uranium.'

'Fucking hell. Improvised nuclear devices. That's massive. Jesus.'

Phil sat down, crossed his legs and took a break. Sean saw the shock in his eyes.

'Listen Phil. This is the building where the bloke put the devices together, but they've moved everything across the continent separately to assemble them just before they select the targets. We think there's enough uranium for two devices but I'm not sure if they acquired any more from someone else. We need to search the bomb-making factory, which is down here somewhere. It's probably booby-trapped from what I heard yesterday.'

'OK, I'll have a look once we get you out of here. Hold on, nearly done.'

'The bomber is ex-British military – guy called Wilson Hewitt. Do you know him?'

'Fucking hell. Any more shockers you want to tell me about? He was kicked out of the army about fifteen years ago. He was before my time, but a real idiot from the tales I've heard. He was an ammo-technician sergeant and got kicked out for using cocaine. He went nuts, went rogue if you like. He made a load of remote-controlled IEDs that he placed around army barracks in southern

England. Although he was never found guilty, that's the story that's been told. That it was him. He used anti-open, anti-tilt and magnetically sensitive booby traps on them all.'

'Shit. That's not good – he knows what he's doing then.'

'Yup, and he knows his plutonium from his uranium rather well so he's a bloody dangerous bomber capable of anything. This could be a long job dealing with the bomb factory.'

'We need as much forensics as we can Phil, and we don't have much time to muck around. We need to find out the targets quickly.'

'There. You're done. Let's go and have a look at this room next door then, eh?'

Sean explained to Phil what they had found in the buried caches in Turkey and how the suitcase bombs looked as if they were ready to be adapted into dirty bombs. He described the ruse in Armenia that had been used to try and lure and turn Nadège. A ruse that involved Jack providing an artillery shell to the Iranians, whose transmitter was still transmitting from the room that they were now stood outside.

Phil used his small torch to inspect the door fittings. There was no window. He lay on the ground to look under the door. No lights on inside. He then stood up and looked at Sean pensively.

'Tell me if I've got this right Sean.'

'What?'

'You mean to tell me we gave the Iranians a nuclear shell…' A pause whilst Phil grimaced. '…a shell full of uranium and we've gone and lost it?'

Sean didn't want to answer that, it was Jack's bag.

Swartz chipped in matter-of-factly. 'That's exactly right Phil.'

'And we now have an expert bomber on the loose?'

'That's about the size of it, yes,' Swartz answered again, this time sheepishly.

'Jesus fucking Christ boys.'

Sean couldn't hide his exasperation. 'What do you mean you lost it? How?'

'Cock-up on surveillance.'

'But Jack had all the US assets at his disposal, right?'

'Yup. Too big a job if you ask me. Too hard to control properly. Not sure what Jack's playing at to be fair.'

'Where did it go then?' Sean asked, flabbergasted by what he was hearing.

Swartz took a moment. 'Well, only one vehicle has left this location. We tracked it until it entered a Kuwaiti Army barracks right in the heart of Kuwait City.'

'Bloody hell. This has turned into a right fiasco,' Sean said, shaking his head before doing a palm slap on his forehead. 'Phil, can we get inside and have a look inside here? Let's get on with it, eh?'

'Maybe. Hewitt would have known how to extract the uranium so I'm guessing we'll find the shell inside here and the uranium gone. That is, if he has the right kit to shield himself from the radiation, which would debilitate him if he handled it without any shielding.'

'Best we have a look then, eh chaps?' Swartz chipped in. 'Let's get this job done, eh?'

'Not so bloody fast big boy,' Phil said, holding his hand up firmly. 'This place could easily be booby-trapped so I'm on a go-slow for this job. One bit at a time. And I want total quiet from both of you. You might as well sit down. This will take a while.'

Sean watched Phil place his rucksack on the ground and pull out a small endoscope. 'Here, push this under the door while I grab a look on the screen.'

Sean took the long wiry piece of equipment with a video camera as its probe. A strong beam of light within the lens allowed Phil to look into the room as he pushed it gently under the door. Sean heard more opera. This time Phil had switched on Borodin's *Prince Igor*.

'Up a bit. I can't see fuck all. This chorus is just like our own bloody opera. Trying to save the homeland - again.'

Sean twisted the head of the probe, allowing Phil to have a better angle to look inside.

'Fuck,' Phil said, looking over to Swartz. 'Here. Have a look at this mate. Is it what I think it is?'

Swartz had a look. Nodded. Then turned the screen to show Sean. A body slumped on the ground. A man. The face of the bomber. Sean looked back at Phil. 'What now?'

'Well if that's our bomber it probably means we have a nuclear bomb or two making its way across Europe without him. He's done his job and they've slotted him.'

'Nadège slotted him,' Sean said knowingly. 'The place might not be booby-trapped now then?'

'Not sure. But certainly less of a chance now. Let's have a look.'

Sean watched Phil and Swartz kick the door in. Two boots powered onto the lock did it. Phil leant through the doorway to switch the lights on, which confirmed the gory scene inside. Sean could see the body of Wilson Hewitt lying in a pool of blood, with what looked like a couple of shots to the back of the head. Behind him lay a highly technical laboratory.

'Stay here while I have a look around,' Phil said. 'I need to make sure it's safe before you loons come in.'

Ten minutes later, Sean wandered around the laboratory. Wilson Hewitt's bomb factory. What he saw astonished him. This was a well-financed operation that had delivered state-of-the-art machinery, hi-tech componentry, laboratory sinks with bottles of chemicals cooling in water and a plethora of electronic equipment. He gazed at the workbenches covered in pliers, electrical wire, duct tape, electrical tape and the odd calculator sat next to two laptops. A state-sponsored outfit and a hive of intelligence that would take days to exploit. But Phil would take care of that. What he needed now were some clues, anything to find out where Nadège had gone and where her targets were. He certainly hoped Jack was following her. Satellites maybe? What was Jack's plan?

He walked the length of the room, inspecting all the materials and equipment without touching anything. He needed the big clues though. Something that told him about the types of bomb that had been made. Sean made his way to where Phil was stood – next to a large glass box with a set of gloves inside it. The glass box was seven foot long and stood on a huge bench, the gloves providing access inside it. The artillery shell was inside the box. Cut open. A long fuse, a lining of high explosives within the casing, a plunger to initiate the shell and a copper baseplate that had been separated from the main shell.

'This is where he cut into the shell to extract the uranium.'

'How?'

'Super-fast saw, a bit of grunt and a final transfer to another shielded container – into his explosive device.'

'How the hell did he manage that without killing himself from the radiation?'

Phil shrugged his shoulders. 'Looks to me like he's transferred the uranium to another container whilst it was inside this box – he could work on the material and be shielded all the time.'

Sean wandered around the rest of the workshop as Phil inspected the workbenches, taking photographs of everything he saw, inspecting componentry.

'How on earth did he plan to transport the bombs?' Sean shouted out across the room.

'Over here mate. Look at this,' Swartz chipped in, stood next to a dishwasher.

'I see it,' Phil said, eagerly making his way across to look inside it. 'So that's his plan. Hide the device in a dishwasher, freight it in lorries or shipping containers and the job's done.'

'Shit, do you think one machine or a few?' Sean asked Phil.

'Just a hunch, but I think only one. I don't think he had enough uranium for any more.'

'Do you think it'll be on a ship then?'

'I'd say it's probably heading for a ship, yeah. It would be bloody hard to move these through borders in a road vehicle and there would be much less of a chance of it being detected on a ship. So yes, ship it probably is.'

'Giving us a good bit of time to find its destination, right?'

'Well a week at least if it's destined for Europe. That would be my guess.'

Sean wondered what Nadège's final solution was? Where was she headed? He wandered over to the corpse of the bomber. Sean checked his trouser pockets, then turned him over to check his shirt pocket. He checked his belt, and rummaged around, checking for a wallet or a phone. Nothing. Sean looked at Hewitt's boots. A pair of Caterpillars. He took a few moments to unlace them before taking them off to inspect them. Didn't seem like anything untoward. A small cavity in the sole. Then he saw the leather had been parted on the top of the boot. Just a small void but big enough for a piece of paper to be concealed. Sean ripped open the leather and retrieved a tiny piece of paper.

It was a map. A map of the British Isles with the shipping forecast areas. Thirty-one areas, with odd names such as German Bight, Biscay and Trafalgar. The shipping forecast areas that Nadège had been using as codewords to verify the agents that had been recruited for her by the Russian GRU. Exactly as Colonel Sergei had told Sean back at The Court's operational base at RAF Bentwaters. Sean had been told to memorise every single forecast area and which ones were adjacent to them. Hewitt had kept the piece of paper on his person to memorise them.

The difference though was that Hewitt had now drawn on the map a few additional shipping forecast areas for the Atlantic. Only one of those areas was shown in capital letters. The name CANTABRICO.

Chapter 42

Essex Countryside

In a secluded and obscure piece of farmland in the Essex countryside, far away from any local villages and an hour from London, a woman unlocked a rusting metal door that led to an underground bunker. A special bunker built for the cold war, the only indication of its provenance being a battered sign above the door with three letters in red on a black background: ROC.

A man in handcuffs and a white forensic suit sat inside the Royal Observer Corps bunker, one of 1,563 that had been built across the country to warn people of a nuclear attack during the cold war. The bunkers were built underground to a standard design, with a four-metre entrance shaft which gave access to two rooms: one containing a chemical toilet, and a larger, monitoring, room which was furnished with chairs, a table, shelf and cupboard space and a bunk bed to sleep two. The bunker was fitted with a ground-zero indicator: a pinhole with four holes facing outwards in north, south, east and west directions. A piece of photographic paper would become exposed in the event of an atomic blast, with one or more of the pinholes indicating the direction of the blast.

Petra Novak entered the bunker, switched the yellow lights on and secured the door. She was dressed in rambling gear, sporting a brown waxed jacket, blue jeans and a pair of scuffed Scarpa boots. She placed a small black rucksack on the square table, unzipped the opening and took out a grey paint can with perforations dotted around it.

Edmund Duff had been lying handcuffed to the bunk bed in the dark and was just stirring, shading his eyes from the bright lights, still curled up in the foetal position and draped in an army blanket.

'Wake up you dirty bastard,' Petra shouted, smashing the metal poles of the bunk bed with a tin mug. The racket startled Duff, who shook violently before pushing his feet to the ground as he struggled to get to a sitting position. The trauma of his incarceration was evident: his eyes were full of fear and his mouth mumbled odd sounds.

Petra pulled up a chair and sat facing him, wearing a face of scorn. She had no problem about killing this man but wanted him to suffer. Duff had been kidnapped by the Russian GRU outside Quaglino's on the orders of Nadège, who had a deal with the GRU via Colonel Sergei Yuronov, her Russian handler. Nadège had extracted Foreign Office secrets from him and passed them on to the GRU while she used Duff to confirm the name of the man who had acted as the elusive ringleader involved in the grooming of girls in Bosnia in the '90s. Duff had been brutally interrogated by the GRU agents and, after only a day, had revealed the name of Fletcher Barrington, the man that Burrić, the assassinated Mayor of Sarajevo, had never met. Colonel Sergei had leaked the name of Barrington to Jack and the Kompromat plot had begun. Duff was no longer of any use to Nadège and was a dead man awaiting assassination.

'You won't remember me,' Petra began, poking Duff in the face. 'I was one of the girls you raped in Tuzla, you evil swine. Not just once, but dozens of times.'

Duff groaned, saying nothing.

'Today you will die very slowly and very painfully, you bastard.'

Petra stood up and turned to hide the tungsten knuckleduster she was placing on her right hand. With a fierce blow, she punched him once in the face. It was all she needed. Duff fell backwards, banging his head on the bunk bed, his face smashed and bright red blood oozing from both nostrils.

The chemical device she had placed on the table would kill him slowly in the confined space of the underground bunker. The device comprised two separate vials of sodium cyanide and hydrochloric acid. The seal between the two would be broken by a small blast cap, causing the liquids to mix to produce deadly hydrogen cyanide gas, which would disperse in the room.

'You choked me, you slapped me, you strangled me, you violated me, you took my childhood. Now you will suffer.'

The air vents of the bunker's chimney were covered with downward-sloping louvres above ground, with sliding metal shutters below ground to control the airflow during contamination by radioactive fallout. Petra gripped the shutter's handle, thrust it to the left and locked the shutters firmly. She placed the rucksack on her shoulder, glanced back at Duff and smashed the plunger into the paint can.

Duff's face was stricken with fear as he tugged viciously at the chains holding him to the bunk bed, which was bolted to the wall. The effects of the gas entering his body would be similar to the effects of suffocation and his death was destined to be a slow one, before the final dramatic and rapid onset of heart failure would cause sudden collapse and then death.

Only Fletcher Barrington remained.

Chapter 43

Prague

Ever since he was a child, Sean had always found peace and tranquillity through art. Oil or watercolour, he didn't really mind, as both allowed his mind to wander, to create, to feel. Art took him to a world away from the stresses and strains of the day, led him to release his hidden emotions into a painting and to dream.

It was 5.30am on a cold summer's morning in Prague, the Bohemian city that appealed to his bon vivant nature, a city whose cocktail bars had held his attention for many an hour. He strolled through the brightly coloured streets and covered colonnades of the Old Town, following his nose to the river, where he would paint. Sean had been ordered to get on the plane to Prague to meet Jack later that morning, probably to be told off and informed he'd been sacked from the job again. So be it, he thought, sauntering aimlessly through the magical labyrinth of ancient churches, gates, courtyards and bridges. It certainly felt Bohemian, he felt Bohemian and the gothic towers that soared above him like a scene out of a Harry Potter fantasy made it Bohemian.

Sean had had a fitful night's sleep, an irritating and regular occurrence as the drawers in his mind, stuffed with his traumas, somehow sprung open and came alive to taunt him as he slumbered. He hated it. The ruminations never went away. Especially at night. The loss of his wife, Katy, a decade ago haunted him the most, as did the death of his best agent in Central Asia, which still played heavily on his mind. Now the loss and murder of his mother were about to be re-enacted by Jack taking him to visit her cold war handler later that morning and, to top things off, Nadège had told him he had a child. He still couldn't bring himself to believe that, knowing that she was simply nothing more than a dangerous psychopath on the run across Europe with a nuclear bomb in tow, for God's sake.

He had failed. Failed to recruit her, failed to protect his wife and his agents, failed his mother by believing she had just abandoned him and failed to obtain freedom for himself. He was trapped by The Court, had a price on his head from the SVR and carried shame for getting the sack from Crown service all those years ago.

The rising sunlight made little starbursts on the shiny silver boat gently cruising under the Charles Bridge as he set up his easel. Five paintbrushes. Ultramarine Blue oil. Linseed oil. A battered wood palette. The sun peered over his shoulder as he skilfully shaped the white crests of the wake of the boat below Prague's oldest bridge. He shaped the first curves of the bridge, sketched out the baroque statues and drew the magical sword of a Knight of Blaník being mysteriously pulled from the bridge by a hand emerging from the sky. According to legend, the sword is hidden inside the Charles Bridge and only when the country is in its darkest hours will the bridge crack open and the spirit of Saint Wenceslas will lead the Knights of Blaník to defend the realm.

Sean's imagination ran riot in those quiet hours. How on earth could he recapture the essence of victory, a vitality, a strength to stop Nadège? He started to make a plan in his mind. How he'd convince Jack that he was the one who needed to stop this carnage and that it was he who held the keys to unlocking the puzzle.

He sat with these thoughts, painting. He was pissed off that he'd lost his freedom, pissed off that he had to live in the south of France, a hunted man, and ashamed at losing his career as an intelligence officer so that now he was just a deniable mercenary who Jack could easily throw to the dogs, without anyone caring a jot. He was just a tool in Jack's box to be used. The years had once been kind to him, but now they were just layering crap after crap on him.

He took a few moments to clip two pieces of paper onto the right-hand side of the easel. Two heavily folded and thumbed pieces of paper. The first was his linkage map showing the characters and the puzzle he had to solve regarding Nadège, and those she had assassinated. The second was the shipping forecast map. Sean had entered a surreal world in which all his control, all his plans, the whole way in which his life configured itself through his own stupid behaviour was falling to pieces.

He committed himself in those moments to struggle against it all with all his might, hoping there might be a chance. A chance of redeeming his soul once again. A failsafe that would avert his own catastrophic failure.

'Good to have you back in one piece,' he heard from behind him. A pat on the shoulder came next.

It was Jack. The grey man from the Home Counties. The chief spook of MI5's Court. In a city full of spies, Jack was dressed for the occasion. British trilby, long mackintosh and a black gloved hand now offering friendship.

'Jesus Jack, you look like something from the cold war for fuck's sake. Do you never dress down?'

'Old habits I'm afraid. You know me.'

'Do I? Every time I take on one of your jobs, it ends up with me in the shit and you coming out of it smelling of roses and getting promoted.'

Jack laughed, suggesting that everything would be fine. 'May I?' he asked, pointing at a wooden stool that was home to Sean's flask whilst he stood painting.

'Fill your boots and watch the paint on your civil servant coat.'

'You know I had to get you off the job Sean,' Jack said apologetically. 'I had no choice. I could sense you'd go off the rails. I can't take big risks on this job now, it's gotten pretty serious.'

'Bollocks,' Sean said, placing his brush in the palette. 'You lost your nerve and you proved that you had fuck-all trust in me. I was in control all along.'

'So it would seem. It was a good regain with Nadège.'

'So how will everything be fine then Jack? We've lost Nadège, lost the bomb and it'll be on its way to Europe on a ship by now.'

'Maybe. It's tricky I know. And yes it's a bit of a cock-up but I'm certain we will find her and the device. I've got an American NEST team on it. They'll deal with it all from here.'

'Nuclear-search ninjas – wow. How the hell did you get them to play?'

'Let's just say an old friend is helping me out on this one. Bit of a favour being pulled in. Good partnership actually. It's a massive search and a big ask but I'm hoping they'll be up to it, else we're all pretty much in deep trouble.'

'A friend, you say? You and your friends in high places. I'm guessing you've hatched a plot to cull a few politicians while you're at it.'

Sean studied Jack's face, which now had a large smirk all over it. It was an impish look, telling Sean that there was a much bigger plan than Jack had ever revealed on their first meeting in Viola.

'Talking of friends Sean, I need to tell you about D's friend, who we need to get a hurry on to meet.'

'Go on.'

'His name is Karel Zatopek. He was first contacted by D in 1974 and became a mole of ours in the Czechoslovakian Státní Bezpečnos a year or so later. At that time, the Czechs were the most effective espionage organisation in Europe, better than us, better than the Americans, better than anyone else. He worked for M16 when he was stationed in East Berlin and was the man who provided all the information to us on those who wanted to defect from the Warsaw Pact.'

'A double agent whose cover has never been broken then?'

'That's right. Karel was the man who established a network of British-run spies in Czechoslovakia, right up until it closed down in 1990. He gave us access to every single piece of information inside the Czech StB and that included anything that the Russians or the East Germans shared with them. He was our highest-grade mole during the cold war and word must never get out that it was him.'

'What's the catch Jack?'

'Nothing. Except that he alone knows the story of your mother. He never provided any details to D, simply because his mind shut down after she was murdered. By all accounts he suffers from dissociative amnesia. He had memory loss for over thirty years.'

'Well, it will certainly be interesting to meet him. I bloody well hope he knows where her body is.'

'I'm not sure about that but I'll obviously help you with anything I can. This was D's final ask of me. They were great friends apparently.'

Sean nodded his appreciation and started to screw the lids on his paints. 'Now, what about me and this mission? It's a bloody long way from over right now.'

Jack stood up and answered matter-of-factly. 'Well, obviously you're off the case now Sean. Speaks for itself. We have the teams that we think can track and trace the bombs and Nadège, and I now think she's a lost cause.'

'What on earth made you think I could recruit her?'

'A hunch.'

'A fucking hunch. Bloody hell Jack, you're as mad as she is.'

A long silence as Sean packed the easel into a large leather holster. 'You can't take me off it Jack,' Sean said vigorously. 'I know exactly where the target of the nuke is – and I know exactly where Nadège will be.'

Sean folded up the shipping forecast map, slipped it into his inside pocket and started walking.

'You better keep up Jack. Only I know the entire plan, and I'll be the one to kill this off.'

Chapter 44

Prague

With a shaking hand, Karel Zatopek lifted the lid on a small antique silver snuffbox for the first time in thirty-three years. He was visibly upset as his daughter watched him try to take out the encrypted note, but he failed each time he tried. His daughter offered her help but he rejected it with a dismissive wave. Instead, he sat hunched in his wheelchair, taking solace by simply looking at the rolled-up note that had flooded his mind with memories he wished had never returned. A tear gradually fell from his left eye.

Karel felt very little these days; the severity of his Parkinson's disease had all but robbed him of his life. But he was happy that his memory had returned to allow him to make one last loving gesture to the British people he so loved.

The home and sanctuary of the reclusive Karel Zatopek was a small eighteenth-century castle that had been formerly owned by the Archduke of Austria, Franz Ferdinand d'Este. Zatopek was the last surviving male member of a long line of prominent aristocrats with German and Czech roots.

Sean and Jack drove past rows of tended orchards and vines and through rolling pastures where cows grazed before driving along a narrow ridge providing superb views of the River Vltava below. The small castle was a curiosity. Complete with two cylindrical towers, a fortified watchtower and a drawbridge, the French-inspired edifice was one of Bohemia's most secluded private castles.

The car crunched to a halt on the gravel outside a newly built annex, where a stout middle-aged woman stood awaiting them. Sean knew very little about the man he was about to meet other than that he was dying and was the son of a wealthy aristocrat who had spent his entire service working for MI6. An amiable man by all accounts. A man who had shared his secrets with D before the latter had died on the steps of the Cabinet Office.

The woman introduced herself as Zatopek's daughter and escorted them through the long corridors of the castle. Baroque paintings lined the walls and long Persian carpets lead the way past a number of Bohemian statues sitting proudly on circular oak tables. A door was opened by a butler, who invited them into an enormous reception room that gave access to the immaculate rose gardens and long manicured lawns of the castle grounds. Sean spotted the old man sitting behind an ornate wooden desk, gazing out of the French windows at the expansive views.

Sean exchanged a glance with Jack and they entered, curious about the man and his past. Zatopek sat in a wheelchair, a tartan blanket on his lap, dressed in an immaculate white shirt with blue tie and with an oxygen mask at the ready hanging from his neck. Sean noticed that the man's hands were shaking. The old man was gaunt, underweight and his skin badly blemished - but he had the face of a tough man. Bizarrely, he seemed to delight in smoking a cigar and he threw Sean a beaming smile as he came into his sightline.

'Thank you for coming to see me, gentlemen. Please be seated.'

Sean watched the man stub his cigar out, his motor skills far better when he was calm. Zatopek's daughter asked the butler to bring tea.

'Have you heard of the legend of Wenceslas?' Zatopek asked Sean, making a sweeping gesture and not expecting an answer. 'His crown, I was told by my father, once resided here. It contains a thorn supposedly from Christ's crown of thorns in its top cross and is said to have a curse on it. While the crown now belongs to the state, it retains the immortal spirit of Saint Wenceslas. He protects the Bohemian people by keeping unqualified kings off the throne.'

Sean was surprised by Zatopek's immaculate English. His articulation was perfect, and his mind seemed very able. Sean watched the man's hand shake as he leant forward to bring a silver snuffbox closer to him. Was this the box that D had written about in his letter?

'That curse, it seems, hit me for more than thirty years, as I literally went out of my mind. Bohemia is no longer a kingdom, I am no longer the man I once was and that blasted curse continues. But before I depart this world I want to tell you about your mother, young man.'

Sean glanced again at Jack, who nodded, suggesting that Sean should speak. He just didn't know what to say. A moment or two later all he could think of was to maybe say that he was glad the man had recovered. Sean felt unusually shy in this man's company. A man who, most probably, had known his mother far better than his father had. As her MI6 handler, he'd have known her soul.

'Thank you, Mr Zatopek. I'm very glad you recovered.'

'My memory recovered, my friend. Nothing else ever did I'm afraid. But my friend who led MI5 was most surprised when I told him of the contents of this snuffbox. It came as quite a shock to him.'

'I never really knew what happened to my mother. My father didn't really know what had happened either, so it seemed she had just left us. Thank you for sharing with me today. I really appreciate it.'

'Ah. Well she suffered a curse too. Perhaps my curse. I'm very sorry for your loss Mr Richardson.'

'Sean, please.'

'As you please. She was a wonderful woman. Her death broke my heart. Literally.' Zatopek opened the small snuffbox and his hand began to shake uncontrollably as he tried to take something from it. 'Damnation. Margaret, please help me.'

His daughter lifted the tiny rolled note out of the snuffbox as Zatopek's eyes narrowed and he continued his story. 'The tale of your mother is not a good one, I'm afraid.'

'I know. But I need the truth. No one ever told me the truth about her. I didn't really know her that well. I loved her dearly but, as a fifteen-year-old, I had no sense of her life and of what we were doing in Berlin at the time. You don't think like that as a fifteen-year old.'

'She was a brave woman, Sean. A fine officer. A fine investigator too.'

'You said that my mother was murdered. How do you know this?'

'Wait. Let me tell you what happened.' He put the mask on his face and took several breaths of the clean oxygen. 'It was 12 November 1986. Marcella had just turned forty-one. Something was irritating her and she wasn't herself at all that night - but she never told me what was on her mind. I've gone over the events of that night so many times. In the end it drove me insane. Because you see...' He cleared his throat with a weak cough. '...because you see, Marcella was the fifth of my agents who had been killed in less than four months.'

'I'm sorry to hear that. You were a brave man yourself, operating as you did behind the Iron Curtain.'

'Perhaps. I've been told by those wretched doctors that the layers of trauma sent me into a spiral and I literally went mad overnight. I never remembered anything of those days until thirty-odd years later. I was a mentally disturbed man, still am. But my memory awoke and it all came flooding back.'

Zatopek had suffered an almost fatal episode of internal trauma that had caused his memory to be shattered. He entered a world of disassociation, a world of amnesia. The levels of severe trauma he had faced had been the cause of his psychogenic amnesia. With this rare condition, Zatopek's mind rejected his thoughts and feelings from those days, and his memories became too overwhelming to handle. His mind shut down. In the end, he was diagnosed as one of the very few people in the world to suffer from psychogenic amnesia. The condition manifests as an act of self-preservation, where the alternatives for him may have been overwhelming anxiety or suicide. It was all a mystery to the medical experts. Throughout the decades he had been nursed and looked after by his daughter and a dozen or so mental-health experts and nurses.

'This snuffbox was your mother's,' Zatopek elucidated. 'A gift from me when she arrived in Berlin. She took it everywhere with her. I was sat in the very bar where she last held it, watching over her. She didn't know I was there, but I wanted to watch over her that night. I had a feeling that something wasn't right. Not right at all. I should have pulled her out when I had the chance. You see, at each location where she'd meet her contacts, we had a dead-letter drop for emergencies. A code to tell me if something was amiss or if she needed to call a halt to a defection plan. I assume you know your mother was the expert we had in Berlin to get people to the West?'

'I do, yes.'

'We had a team on standby that night to follow her and pull her out. But when I went to the dead-letter drop location in the garden the note inside the snuffbox insisted that the job was clean and that it should proceed.'

'So why did she leave the snuffbox there?'

'It was a safeguard in case she didn't return. A contingency. Her legacy, actually. She obviously felt there was a threat, enough of one to leave the box. But she wasn't convinced there was enough to abort.'

'And the note inside?'

'Well, the note and box are yours to keep young man. The encrypted note provided me with a location where she had stored all the files of an investigation that she had been carrying out for many years. An investigation into the ghastly activity of some very nasty people in Berlin at the time.'

'So, if I'm hearing this right, she wanted to give you these files in case she never returned. My guess is she knew there was a chance she might be killed or taken.'

'Oh she did. Her body language told it all. But, probably like you, she was a very determined and very brave person. A very independent woman. She hated it if I stepped in or acted as her minder. What she eventually uncovered were the corrosive secrets of a dark underground gang in East Berlin, a group of men who had revived the name and modus operandi of the Ringvereine.'

'The Ringvereine? Who are they? Some kind of mafia?' Sean looked at Jack to see if he had ever heard of them. Jack made a face to indicate he hadn't.

'The Ringvereine were prominent in Berlin during the Weimar era, but only one or two rings still existed in the '80s. Most experts had suggested they had all totally disappeared in the '60s. But they hadn't.' Zatopek paused and breathed deeply. 'You see, they were communities of like-minded convicts and members of the German underworld, who aspired to a petty-bourgeois lifestyle and, above all, to respectability. The East Berlin Ringvereine had re-invented themselves and were engaged in extensive prostitution, the drugs trade, the management of the city's nightlife and protection rackets.'

Zatopek paused again, his voice wavering quite a bit now. 'The Ring Brothers could be identified by the identical signet rings they wore and they were bound to absolute secrecy. Their criminal clubs had melodic names like the High Chaparral or Blood of the Apache. Their prostitution rings developed a sinister side that Barrington made use of – prepubescent girls. Underage girls. That's how he began his relationship with the criminal underworld of East Berlin – abusing and using teenage girls.'

'My mother uncovered all this? By herself?'

'Yes, and much, much more. The Stasi's links to the Ringvereine were strong and your mother knew she was entering dangerous territory investigating them. But she wouldn't stop. It was her doggedness that kept driving her on to smoke out the criminals and then hand the evidence to the CIA. Many young girls suffered at the hands of these elite gangs.'

Sean was astonished at what he was hearing, eager to know the full unadulterated story. He needed to know more about his mother. Barrington's linkage to the Bosnian sex gang was exactly the same evil that his mother had uncovered in East Berlin. Barrington had been doing this wherever he was stationed for decades. Sean took a moment to walk around the room, making a mental note to check out all of his overseas postings.

'Did she find anything else? I mean serious evidence of wrongdoing that can be used now?'

'It's all in the files. Jack, will you do the honours on my behalf?'

Jack reached into his brown briefcase and pulled out a dossier. 'This is what D had been researching for the last year,' Jack began. 'It was in his safe alongside the snuffbox when he died. It took me a while to join the dots, but D asked me to make sure this case was finished. You see, D came here to visit on quite a few occasions, having put together a case that could see Barrington charged under US law. Barrington is as evil an agent as we've ever known Sean. Truly evil.'

'He's a bloody dead man walking Jack, you know that. Justice for my mother and for everyone he's killed is coming. There'll be more we don't know about.'

'I understand. Let's keep that for later. Mr Zatopek will explain the other things we have found out together.'

Zatopek was now taking more oxygen, feeling the strain. His daughter pushed the wheelchair around the desk, so that he could sit next to Sean.

Sean looked the old man in the eye. They had an intense connection. Zatopek had pain etched all over his chiselled face and was riddled with guilt. That was for sure. Sean became emotional when the old man tried to reach out with a shaking hand to place it on Sean's. He didn't have the strength and his hand fell. Sean felt a twinge of sorrow at the man's pain. His dying days were punctured with the misplaced shame he bore.

'Where on earth did my mother hide all these files then Jack?'

'With a law firm in West Berlin. Under lock and key. Sadly, Mr Zatopek was never able to see the files as he became ill and lost his memory the day after your mother went missing. Once he realised your mother was not coming back from that last mission, he plummeted.'

'How on earth did D pick all this up? The whole story is heartbreaking on so many levels.'

'The snuffbox sat in this house for thirty years after Mr Zatopek retrieved it from the Berlin bar and your mother's files sat for the same period of time in the offices of the West Berlin law firm. It was only when Mr Zatopek's memory came back last year that he was able to tell D. To show him the snuffbox and tell him where the files were. We sent a team to break into the law firm's offices and retrieved the dossier.'

'Two safes, two huge secrets then Jack. You never cease to amaze me. What's next then?'

'Well, there are most certainly a lot of loops to close Sean. I propose that you and I retire to the city to discuss those.'

For Sean, the last few moments in the company of Jack and this amazing old man seemed to all go in slow motion. He watched the old man wave a shaking hand to his daughter, gesturing for her to bring one last item. Zatopek looked exhausted by the lengthy discussions and Sean could see that he was frail and very tired. He sensed that the old man would go to his grave a contented man now that he had finally been able to lay his guilt to rest with the son of his most favoured agent.

A map was passed to Zatopek. A map from the 1980s, showing the border between East and West Germany.

Zatopek looked at Sean, tears in his eyes, breaking down fast. 'This is where your mother died Sean. Marcella is buried somewhere here.'

It was while he was following the map being placed on his lap by the old man in slow motion that Sean broke down.

Chapter 45

France

At a train station somewhere in the south of France, a man and a woman casually walked the concourse pulling trolley backpacks. In a nearby airport, a number of highly trained detection officers provided a covert presence in the baggage reclaim hall. They were part of the US's NEST teams. Their backpacks contained radiation-detection equipment that Jack and Laura hoped would be able to detect a terrorist's nuclear device being moved across the country.

At the same time, located in a secret hangar somewhere on a sprawling US airbase in southern Germany, preparations were being made by the forward elements of the NEST team, who had transported over thirty tons of technical equipment from Nellis Air Force Base in Nevada.

'Maybe we should start with where you think the target of the bomb is Sean?' Jack asked, passing the wine list across the table at a Bohemian restaurant close to Prague's Old Square.

'Maybe you should tell me how the hell you lost a nuclear bomb Jack. It's not a good position we're in right now and your career as a civil servant looks like it's heading down the pan right now to be honest.'

'It's not a nice place to be in, I agree. You go first.'

The mystery of Jack never stopped giving. Sean wondered what else he had up his sleeve and if this was a ruse all along? He took out the well-thumbed map that he'd found in the bomber's boot, unrolled it and placed a couple of glasses at the ends of it to keep it open.

'This is the target Jack. Somewhere in the area of the Cantabrico. This is the Atlantic shipping forecast map the rogue bomber had on his person.'

'I see. The Biscay area on our British shipping forecast map.'

'Yes. You don't seem at all shocked.'

'No, I'm not. This piece of the jigsaw has just confirmed my own intelligence.'

'You mean you know the target?'

'Yes.'

'Bloody hell Jack,' Sean said, exasperated. He waved at the waitress, needing a stiff drink. He chose a Mâcon-Villages and asked for a beer as well. 'How on earth do you know?' he continued, making sure their conversation wasn't overheard as they sat at a discreet corner-table of the restaurant.

'Well, you're not the only officer I've had working this case Sean. There's been plenty of other activity too.'

Sean felt the nip of Jack's barbs. 'I always knew you had something up your sleeve Jack. But what exactly? What the fuck is going on?'

'The target is the G7 conference in Biarritz.'

'Wow.'

'Indeed.'

'Jesus wept. You're not even joking.' Sean felt embarrassed that he hadn't worked it out from the map. Now it was becoming clear. The G7 conference was taking place in three days' time, when the leaders of the world's seven leading economic nations would all be gathered in the same place.

'So, as you can see Sean, the only way we can tackle this now is by using the nuclear ninjas, as you call them. The NEST team are now in situ and searching for the bomb. It's a race against time.'

The highly secretive NEST teams were given the nickname 'nuclear ninjas' in the mid-1990s, after *Time* magazine ran a feature covering their secretive capability.

Jack continued. 'Yesterday, the equipment stored in containers was loaded onto military cargo planes and a small advance party flew to France to set up a command post at Cazaux Air Base. It's a safe distance away from the G7 conference should a nuclear explosion take place.'

'Should a nuclear explosion take place! How do you stay so calm and matter of fact? This is off the Richter scale.' Sean ran a hand through his hair and took a hit of his beer. 'Exactly how far have they got in finding the device? Any clues yet?'

'It's a huge operation Sean, and is now being handled by Laura and the CIA in conjunction with the NEST teams and US Special Forces. The fact that the US President is due to fly into Biarritz in two days' time justifies the operation and you'll be playing a part in it.'

'Why?'

'It's a long story, I'm afraid. I need you to lead the hunt to find Nadège and her Iranian master. You see, the whole grand plan has been designed by her Iranian handler, General Alimani, as an extortion plot against the US President and the G7 leaders over the Iran sanctions. An extortion plot to stop the crippling sanctions against Iran and get the Americans to back off with their military plans. It won't work and we must find them. They have their hands on the nuclear trigger but we don't know where. Alimani is the mastermind behind it all. The Iranians have gone for full-scale death and chaos across Europe and this nuclear extortion plot is their final act against the big Satan.'

'How on earth do you know all this Jack? This is pure fantasy stuff. Armageddon across Europe.'

'From my other agents. What I do know is that he'll go through with the plot and detonate the bomb if he has to. That's how he's designed the entire operation. Now let's enjoy the food and wine because we're up early in the morning and the Americans are flying us straight into France.'

Jack poured wine into Sean's glass and told the peculiar story of how the plot had come to his attention. General Ali Alimani, a high-grade Iranian spy and the Director of Kuwaiti military intelligence, was afforded regular access to the British and American Embassies and their defence attachés. He had inside knowledge of their foreign policy and their military plans for the Middle East and, even better, he had access to many of the Middle East's Western elite through his wife, a French national who worked in the French Embassy. General Ali would regularly be seen in the Embassy's bar dressed in Western clothing including a New York Yankees baseball cap, and was often seen smoking cigars outside the bar on the wooden benches. Alimani had been embedded into the Kuwaiti military as a young lieutenant but his Iranian masters, even in their wildest dreams, never expected him to reach the lofty heights of a general within their intelligence services. There are many Iranian agents in the Kuwaiti ministries, due in part to their Shia dominance – but Alimani's rise to fame was the stuff of legends. In the area of Qurain is a house that set him on a trajectory to being a national hero. He was one of eighteen members of the Kuwaiti resistance who made a valiant last stand against the Iraqi military might a day or so before the coalition liberated Kuwait in 1991. The Iraqis bombarded the position, heavy artillery killing eleven of the men. Alimani became the leader of those who remained and fought the last ground battle with the Iraqis, exhibiting bravery that would become part of the folklore of Kuwait. His rise to fame was rapid, and his escalation through the ranks of the Kuwaiti military was made on that soil.

'Your work tracking down the bomb-making equipment in Turkey was immense Sean,' Jack said casually, tucking into a starter of kulajda, a traditional South Bohemian soup. 'We now have teams ready to interdict the terrorists across European cities as they prepare to plant their bombs. Alimani's plan is to set off one or two bombs in Europe before issuing his extortion demands to the G7 on the first day of their conference.'

Sean was listening intently now. He began to realise the magnitude of what Jack had uncovered and what he had put in place. It was extraordinary. 'If you get any of this wrong Jack it'll be curtains for you and many others. How on earth are you going to stop this madman?'

'It's risky stuff. Bloody risky. But we have one or two things in our favour. Now, the bit I don't know is, where do they plan to detonate the bomb from? Where's the trigger? Where's their base? What is their escape plan? Any ideas?'

'Well, just one thing. Nadège told me that she had my child. Nine years ago. She's most probably lying, but she did say something about San Pelayo de Tehona after she nearly killed me by firing bullets into my cell.'

'She's not lying Sean. She did have your child. Why do you think I sent you to turn her? Only you could ever have got close enough to her. She still has feelings for you.'

'Bollocks,' Sean said, feeling his irritation rise. 'She nearly killed me twice. Once when I first met her, and the second time when I last saw her. She's a crazy assassin Jack and if I get the chance I'll slot her.'

'Maybe. First things first, we need to find her and find her fast. Samantha and the SIGINT teams are working with the Americans on that. Let me send them this location. San Pelayo de Tehona.'

Jack spent a moment tapping out a text to Samantha while Sean decided he needed to ply himself with more wine.

'How the hell do you know she had my child? How do you know it's true?'

'It came from a man who is now deceased. He was the British diplomat who went missing. Duff.'

'No way. What the hell happened to him? Nadège mentioned him when I was in the cell. Reckoned he didn't have long to live and was one of her targets for assassination.'

'Edmund Duff was kidnapped by the Russian GRU on Nadège's orders in return for her supplying intelligence she had gained from him. You see, they were lovers for over a year and he was purposefully targeted by Nadège. She was acting as a double agent with the Russian GRU, handled by Colonel Sergei. Sergei made sure Duff was fully interrogated by GRU agents before he was murdered by Nadège's lover, Petra.'

'Murdered? Why?'

'He was of no further use to them and he was the man who had protected Fletcher Barrington in Bosnia when they were connected with the sex gangs, which consisted of senior officers from Russia, America and Britain in Tuzla and Sarajevo. The bastards are all being killed off by Nadège and Petra. He was the last but one of the sex ring. Only Barrington remains alive.'

'That fits exactly with what Nadège told me when she was firing bullets around the cell trying to kill me off. But somehow she pulled back – she was raging like nothing I've seen before. How do you know she had my child though?'

'Nadège had been loose with her tongue when she was high on drugs and alcohol with Duff. She said she'd had a child after a fling with a British intelligence agent nine years ago.'

Sean was gobsmacked. His emotions started to play havoc in his mind. His gut told him he needed to find and kill Nadège, who deserved nothing less in his mind. But now Jack had thrown him a curve ball, signifying he was the father of her child.

But where exactly was his son?

Chapter 46

France

Cold dank space. The smell of aircraft fumes. Urns of tea and coffee on trestle tables. Rows of plastic seats and a series of projector screens hanging from parachute cords off metal beams. The cavernous voids of aircraft hangars always felt the same to Sean. He had spent countless hours waiting for Special Forces' operations to kick off in these types of spaces and they always gave him the same feeling. A sense of adrenalin, a sense of excitement, a real buzz.

Swartz tapped Sean on the shoulder, pointing to a row of trestle tables. 'Let's grab some tea and toast. This is going to be some bloody operation with the amount of kit they've flown in.'

Sean's mind still wasn't in the right place and he had trouble concentrating on any single thought. The ruminations were hounding him. He lingered behind Swartz, taking in the extraordinary sights in the hangar. It was a veritable hive of activity, the hangar full of military staff and tons of specialist equipment. A bunch of men in civilian clothes were setting up satellite-communications equipment, map boards were being erected and other uniformed soldiers were hanging signs throughout the hangar identifying which organisation should sit where.

Standing with a coffee that Swartz had poured him, Sean spied a few of the signs, trying to make sense of it all. Along one side of the hangar he could make out the words 'Metrology', 'Medical', and 'Geoint'. On the opposite side were signs saying 'Decontamination', 'Intelligence' and 'Detection'. The tactical command centre included a multitude of national experts, all of whom had been flown at a moment's notice from the US as part of the NEST teams. The operation also included the US Navy Seals, who had established their base in the hangar next door.

'No toast,' Swartz piped up. 'What kind of set-up is this where's there no bloody toast? I'm starving.'

'They do things differently here, by the looks of it, it's much bigger and certainly different. Our peculiarity for tea and toast hasn't quite made it across the pond yet mate.'

'Well, the last time I worked with these ninjas they couldn't get enough of us. Thought we were the dogs, mate.'

Sean managed to raise a smile at Swartz's exuberance, who was excited about what would come in the hours and days ahead. Dressed in desert wellies and jeans, Sean and Swartz stood drinking their coffee, gazing at the world's most secretive nuclear operators. They watched scientists and soldiers scurrying around, preparing their state-of-the-art equipment, trained and ready to deal with nuclear Armageddon and with the means to stop it.

It was impressive to see what some of the NEST teams' annual budget of twenty-five million dollars had been spent on. Sean glanced at a small fleet of nondescript cars through the partially opened doors of the hangar, ordinary-looking vehicles turned into radiation-detection vans. Men and women walked around the hangar with wireless earpieces, bomb-disposal robots were being tested and desk after desk of staff officers represented each specialist department for the operation. Right in the centre of the hangar were three semicircles of chairs and two lecterns with a projector screen located between them. The nuclear ninjas were in town and ready for action.

The NEST teams and FBI maintain a permanent force to respond to events in Washington and along the Northeast Corridor, whilst a second team trained to dismantle nuclear weapons is based in Albuquerque. Eight other teams able to diagnose radioactive materials are on continuous alert, ready to be deployed anywhere in the US or overseas if needed. The NEST teams have the ability to deploy hundreds of people to the scene of a radiological incident, but deployments are normally much smaller, generally involving around forty to fifty scientists and servicemen. On this occasion there were a good two hundred operators complete with a variety of equipment weighing up to 150 tons, along with a small fleet of aircraft including four helicopters and three airplanes, all primed to search for the terrorists and their devices.

Sean pulled up a green canvas chair, glanced around the room at the maps on the wall and shook hands with those around him. He was sat amongst twelve other senior members of the NEST and Navy Seal teams, waiting for the strategic command briefing. The quiet chatter around him shrouded the sense of intrigue within the room at an unknown face being amongst a cabal of US officers, all of whom knew each other. Sean was now sporting a full beard, neatly trimmed for the day, a grey T-shirt, Jeff Banks jeans and beige desert wellies which announced to the quorum that a Brit was amongst them.

Four individuals entered the room carrying papers and cups of coffee. Leading the way was a female, in her late forties, Sean thought, followed by three men, one of whom wore the insignia of a US general, the other two in civilian attire. They filed in behind each other and sat behind a long table at the head of the room. The muttering ceased and an air of expectation fell across the room. The last man in was Jack, who introduced himself as the British Intelligence Liaison Officer. The other three each introduced themselves to the twelve commanders who would turn their strategy into operational reality. The commanders had in front of them four individuals who they had never seen before on the many and varied NEST teams' exercises held within the US and occasionally overseas. Laura was the CIA's representative, General 'Big Al' Gordon was the United States Strategic Commander from European Command, EUCOM, and the final representative, Jim, was EUCOM's Political Liaison Officer. A fifth senior official, a representative of the US National Security Agency, had been delayed and would arrive later that day.

Brief introductions were made amongst the sixteen senior commanders before Big Al introduced Laura, the only female present, and invited her to provide the intelligence briefing to the men. Known for her shock and awe tactics, she was about to deliver a virulent and punchy briefing. Sean perked up and rid himself of any ruminations as Laura stood and launched straight into her speech.

'As a culture we focus on those finely balanced moments when, against all the odds, the stars align perfectly and great things are achieved. Gentlemen, we will achieve that great thing, but be under no illusion – our enemy are equally intent on those stars aligning to achieve their great thing. The decimation of thousands of people. Do not, under any circumstances, allow this moment to conspire against us so that they win, and our moment turns to utter shit.'

Sean marvelled at this no-nonsense woman, who was delivering one of the finest motivational speeches he had ever heard. He watched as Laura stopped speaking and looked every man in the eye. He could tell she would breathe fire and shoot brimstone. A sense of expectation cut through the men in the room like no other briefing he had ever attended.

'The conspiracy of circumstances that has led us to this moment is just so wildly improbable that you could probably live multiple lives and never see this again,' she uttered with pure conviction. 'It's a monster riding through a blue moon on Halley's fucking Comet.'

Laura paused frequently for effect. 'Unless you guys make a difference today, and the next day, and every day, these bastard Iranians will have burnt the souls of our ancestors and every good human being this side of the Persian Gulf. We must not fail. If you want a mission statement, that is it. You guys like a mission statement to be said twice. So here it is. You must not fail. You must not fail.'

The atmosphere in the room was tense and brittle. Sean wondered what the hell would come next. This was one feisty woman. Sharp and attractive too. Laura stood in a blue two-piece suit with white blouse, her dark hair neatly tied up in a bun. She was wearing flat shoes but, with her vernacular, they seemed like burning killer heels. Sean watched her with some admiration as she flicked a page of her notes laid on the table. He looked around him, struck by the effect this woman was having on some of the most battle-hardened men in the world. He took a swig from his bottle of water as she continued.

'I have no idea if there is just one improvised nuclear device or two or more. That's just the way it is. It's the intelligence I don't have and it's for you guys to find,' she said, nodding at the NEST team commander, a full colonel from the US Army. 'We need all our bases covered to find where the radiation is emitting from in the area of the G7 conference, and then we launch the operation to disable the bombs.' She turned briefly to introduce Jack, who was sat furthest away from her, the only man in the room wearing a suit and tie. Jack was adjusting his tie so that it sat perfectly in the middle of his shirt. 'It is the Brits who infiltrated the Iranian operation and I'd like to thank the man in the red tie from Her Majesty's security service for getting us here today. Without Jack and the man in front of me, death incarnate may have come to seven world leaders and thousands of innocent civilians.'

Sean briefly felt a tinge of redness rise through his face as Laura's finger pointed right at him. Her eyes were searing into his very being. She continued to point at him, speaking about the British operation, whilst murmurs of applause permeated the room. He hated it.

Jack stood and, with impeccable manners, gave the details of the intelligence that Sean had collected. 'My intelligence has verified that the mastermind of this operation has set up a command hub somewhere on the Iberian Peninsula and that's where the trigger finger resides to commence the Iranian attacks. My team will concentrate on finding that location with SIGINT and then we'll take him and his sidekicks down. In the meantime, gentlemen, you'll be finding and tackling the nuclear devices and taking out any terrorists protecting them. My intelligence shows that each device will be protected by armed terrorists, but we don't know how many or what kind of armoury they will have. Equally concerning is that the sensitive-site exploitation that my teams undertook on the bomb factory suggests more than one nuclear device. Our assessment is that there could be one or two, but it's unlikely to be more than that. Each of the devices is estimated to have a yield of about a kiloton. Our assumption is that the nuclear devices will be protected by armed Iranians prepared to die for the cause, and the location of his trigger point will be the same.' Jack took a step from behind the table and walked towards the wall, adjusting his tie as he walked. Sean knew he'd do that. Jack was always fiddling with his tie. It was a foible of nervousness from the impeccable master of intrigue.

'The Iranian mastermind is this man on the wall here, General Ali Alimani. His command-and-control hub, wherever it is, will trigger a series of catastrophic events across Europe that we have to stop and contain. Oh, and to verify our concern that there is more than one nuclear device, we found one more body at the bomb-making factory – the body of a nuclear scientist who had helped the bomber make the devices.'

Sean lurched forward, utterly surprised by this announcement. Jack caught his eye and simply continued.

'My operators knew about one single device, but until we completed the forensic search of the factory we didn't know that General Alimani had another one ready to deploy at the G7 and to attack with at the same time. What we now know is that his entire operation is based upon extortion. Extortion against the G7 which, if they don't do what he wants, will result in him initiating attacks in Europe to prove that his threats are credible. He plans to issue a threat of nuclear devices exploding unless the G7 agree to halt sanctions against Iran, as well as other more rigid demands. We assume this is the last stand of a regime in total meltdown. He even expects Iran's demands to be discussed right there and then at the G7.'

'Madman,' a voice called out from the periphery of Sean's view. 'An act of war,' said another voice.

Jack acknowledged the comments, knowing full well that it was the Russians who had agitated to get their Iranian proxies to this point and cause global chaos, which would then draw America into an unwanted full-scale war. 'Of course, he won't get away with it, but he is committed to the cause and extremely likely to explode the devices unless we find them all. Our assessment is that the nuclear devices have been concealed inside dishwashers and that they are viable.'

Sean felt the hairs on his neck rise as Jack mentioned the word 'viable'. All along, Sean had thought there was one device. Now it was becoming clear: he had been used as the lure to find the bomb-making factory and its single tactical nuclear shell. The intelligence indicating that there was more than one device had come from the detailed counter-IED forensics at the Kuwaiti bomb factory. The forensics that Phil had collected during the sensitive-site exploitation suggested that there were two dishwashers and enough uranium for two devices – but what about the two suitcases he'd found in the caches in Turkey? Where were they destined for?

Jack fielded one or two questions before sitting down, and Laura began walking around the room to where the maps were displayed on the wall.

'Gentlemen, your operational orders will follow this session. There are two aims and one mission. You know the mission,' Laura began, waving her hand around the map of France centred on Biarritz. 'Our assessment suggests they will deploy two devices around the G7 location which, in all likelihood, will include one in the Bay of Biscay on a vessel. We'll nail the maritime location I'm sure, but the other one needs some hard work. The second aim is to take down the command hub once we've found it.' She walked back to the table, picking up her notes. 'This is a two-eyes US and UK operation, kept from the public and the press using the highest levels of secrecy, meaning that every single person on this operation will not use mobile phones or disclose any element of this operation for years to come. Finally, a big thanks to the Brits today, who will lead the task to find the command hub. Any questions?'

The Navy Seal commander was the first to chip in. 'There's an exclusion zone two miles from the shore of Biarritz. What's the plan if a vessel ignores it and heads straight for the G7? I don't have enough men for multiple-vessel interdictions.'

Big Al stood up and walked to the map that showed the defence for the G7 conference. 'In case you're not aware, the G7 conference is the most heavily defended conference in the world. We've already got three or four rings of steel surrounding the venue and the French are providing the naval assets for maritime protection, which include two destroyers and surface-to-air missile defence. Add to that airborne early-warning capability and air defence monitoring the skies and we have all the necessary assets at our disposal. My role is to inject the threat and intelligence at the right time to make sure that, if our interdiction operations don't go to plan, we can bring air assets into play and sink vessels.'

The political advisor added to the General's words. 'Most importantly, we must not under any circumstances reveal that there is a nuclear threat to the conference. We cannot have a panic-stricken public across Europe; the fallout would be unmanageable.'

'What about other European targets?' Sean asked. 'Are they contained or are the threats non-nuclear?'

'A very good question Sean,' Laura replied, with a smile. 'Jack, can you answer that?'

'Yes of course. We've tracked the suitcase bombs and are ready to interdict them with conventional assets. They are sat in London and under surveillance. The intelligence suggests they are dirty bombs. Radiological dispersal devices. The other conventional, but high-powered, IEDs have been tracked and traced to Paris and Brussels.'

Sean nodded, knowing that tracking devices were on each device, making interdiction much easier. 'OK, thanks. What's the plan for hitting the command cell?'

'You led us to the bomb-making factory and uncovered the plot – this is the moment we have all been waiting for so we want you to find and take down the command hub. You'll have a British SAS team and military assets ready to help once we've found the site and you have a plan.'

Chapter 47

Asturias, Spain

S ean leant on the wooden balustrade of the upper decking of a split-level chalet, gazing at the glorious view across the meadows to the quaint river below. A herd of cows and the gentle chime of their bells broke the silence across the remote valley that lay below him, the gentle trickle of river water providing the backdrop to Sean's thoughts. San Pelayo de Tehona would be the perfect place to return to once he'd fixed the domestic problems in his life, he thought.

His mind drifted to many places that morning. What to do with Nadège when he found her? The chances were she'd be killed in any assault on the building anyway. How would he feel if that happened? Probably a mixture of relief and grief. What about her son? Who would bring him up? Sean was beginning to become overwhelmed by the new drawers of trauma that were being added to the ones he'd already kept firmly shut in his life. Why me, for fuck's sake? I just want peace now.

His mind tried to focus on the assault planned to take place that evening. Samantha had been flown into the French airfield and had set up a small team of SIGINT operators to scour the Iberian Peninsula for any communications traffic that would identify the terrorists' command-and-control location. Swartz had made sure the arrival of two SAS teams had gone smoothly and he had briefed their commander on the mission, without providing the full background to the wider operation. Jack was insistent that any forces brought in to support the operation simply needed to know the bare minimum. Terrorists inside a stronghold that needed to be eliminated was all he'd imply. Sean wasn't so sure about that being the implicit mission. He had thoughts of dealing with it in some way other than death and carnage if he could.

Sean remembered the words that Samantha had shouted to everyone in their small ops room in an annex to the Navy Seals' hangar. 'Got the bastards!' Her voice reverberated outside the hangar, where Sean and Swartz were chatting through the mission. Sean threw his cigarette away and ran inside to the ops room. Samantha was stood next to a SIGINT screen, holding her arms in the air like a champion boxer.

'Found them myself,' she shouted to Sean, hardly containing her excitement. 'You coconuts better get ready to move quickly, we've less than twenty-four hours before the US President is due to fly in.'

'Where? Show me.'

'I've tracked them to a wooded farmstead near La Morgal airfield in the Asturias, not far from Oviedo. Right next to the runway. It's a private airfield and the only signatures that are connecting regularly into different parts of Europe. It's definitely a command hub, not linked to Spanish infrastructure or government communications. Right next to a fucking runway ready for escape by private plane.'

'Good work Sam. Swartz, get the helicopter pilots in here now. We're going to move on this quickly. Sam, get your team to find me a base somewhere close as a bolt-hole. Use your imagination and get Jack to clear airspace and warn off local law enforcement. We're going to need large outer cordons in place and back-up from their military.'

'On it now.'

'I want this all moving quickly, team. Let's get this nailed and make sure we have all the kit we need. Sam, we'll need to take down all public mobile communications in the area at a moment's notice and I'll need the entire building locked down with RF jammers. Can we fix that?'

'Phil's your man for that. He's got portable stuff to block all the signals emanating from the place. And he'll deal with any explosive booby traps too.'

Sean had the basis of full capability to deal with General Alimani – two SAS teams, a small high-risk search team with Phil

'The Nose' as the bomb-disposal officer, the Spanish Army on standby to support the operation and Laura providing the requirements for satellite imagery back at the National Geospatial-Intelligence Agency based in Washington. The ground operation for tactical imagery would be steered by Jugsy, using two unmanned air vehicles, and the political gateways would be smoothed by Jack and EUCOM's political advisor. The first men on the ground were tasked to provide ground surveillance on the farmstead whilst Sean and Swartz developed the attack plan. The farmstead was right next to the runway, with one major house complex, three small outbuildings, a barn and a small ruin nearest to the airfield. If it all went wrong, there was enough clear ground around the complex for a military assault and air attack if needed. Sean had no idea what defences the General would have in place, but he knew he'd be well prepared.

Sean felt Swartz's hand on his shoulder as he waited for the results from the ground reconnaissance team. Sean knew he wasn't himself and it was always Swartz who had the uncanny knack of snapping him out of it.

'It'll be OK mate. You know she has to be killed if she's in there. There's no option. You know this is the right thing to do, so don't dwell on it too much mate. We're here for you and you'll be OK.'

'Maybe. Maybe not. Too many fucking drawers stuffed with all the shit in my life mate.' Sean turned and shook Swartz's hand. 'Funny how the branches of life take you on their merry journey, eh? The good thing is that I now realise how fucked up I was when I lost my mum at fifteen. No one has any idea how vulnerable you are at that age. It shaped my idiocy for life. I just didn't know it until now. If I'd have had a sound family upbringing, you know, with Mum and Dad always there, maybe I'd have taken a better way in life instead of all this killing and carnage. It's just anger inside me every single day. Rage and anger.'

'That's how it works mate. You know that. Life experiences define us. Mould us. Eat away at us. For God's sake man, look at what you've done for the good of many. Saved lives and put away those who are pure evil. You and I were destined for this shit mate because of the teenage years we had. Built of steel, just bloody flaky inside trying to hold it all together now, you know.'

'Mate, as ever you've nailed it. Always bloody rescuing me. Right, let's get this done and dusted. By the way, when this is all over there's another job I need to settle. I've asked One-Eyed Damon to set a few things up for me in London when we get back home.'

'Ah, fuck. Another bloody ruse. My pension and freedom in the balance again. What's the kill method this time? A bloody torpedo into the man's house party?'

Sean laughed and gave his best mate a man hug. 'Much more fun than that, I can assure you.'

Chapter 48

Asturias

Three hundred and twenty feet of cold steel. A vessel badged with the flag of Malta, built in 2005 and powered by Chinese engines. Four eighteen-foot Rigid Raiders trailed the vessel, each carrying eight men who would be the first of many to board this ship at 2220 precisely. They would await the order to attack the terrorists once they had boarded the vessel and hidden themselves.

The Americans were now coordinating simultaneous attacks on a vessel, a target location not far from the G7 conference and General Alimani's command-and-control complex in Spain. The coordination had taken less than forty-eight hours to plan the interdictions. Now was the time for precise action, at precise times, with overwhelming force. The terrorists at each site had been trained to die as martyrs, trained by the Iranian Islamic Revolutionary Guard Corps, who were now about to face the best of the US Navy Seals and the British SAS. The Iranian terrorists were all former soldiers of the Al Quds force, which had been labelled a terrorist organisation by the Americans and was the body responsible for many British and American deaths in the Second Iraq War as it had supplied high-tech IEDs to the Iraqi militia. Iran's overseas war machine, their state-sponsored terrorists, had been active for decades, and had been the thorn in the side of the US during many global campaigns – was their time about to end?

The 1300-ton container ship travelled steadily at twenty-five knots per hour as the Rigid Raiders approached the vessel before two peeled off to hug the ship's starboard side, whilst the other two slipped into place on the port side, all of them hidden from the view of the bridge. The coxswains steadied the raiding boats alongside the ship, whilst the assaulters awaited the final signal to climb onto the vessel. Then they would wait.

They call it green Spain, but the verdant trees and pastures of Asturias are only part of its spectrum. On the northern coast between Cantabria and Galicia, fanned by Atlantic winds and bolstered by fertile soil, this stretch of land encompasses the beach-strewn Costa Verde, smart towns and a wild interior that belies its diminutive size. All Sean could hear was the trees being gently combed by the breeze, while a lone bat skilfully navigated the building's rafters. Come morning, this would all be over, but what branch of life would this event lead to for him?

Late-evening drizzle. A night for a kill. Sean was lying in deep mud as he watched Swartz crawl up alongside him, each of them making gradual progress along the ditch to their assault start line. The farm complex gave them perfect cover as they covertly moved into position. Numerous dilapidated walls surrounded the farm, multiple trees and hedge lines provided close access to the four buildings and a few tin sheds close to the main building would be used to spring the SAS assaulters.

Surprisingly, Jugsy had not picked up any activity from his airborne drones in the eight-hour period before the assault and neither had the ground surveillance teams. There were two cars parked on the muddy driveway but Sean had no confirmation of who was actually inside the main house. The detailed target analysis Jugsy had prepared showed a large square building with brand-new red tiles on its roof, two entrances, one each at the back and front, two floors and six windows on each face of the building. To its rear was a small meadow and towards the road was a slanting tiled roof that appeared to be a newly built annex for a large laundry room. There were no CCTV cameras, no passive infrared-initiated external lights and absolutely no indication of any defences that would warn the residents of intruders within the grounds.

'I'm not sure about this Swartz,' Sean whispered, looking through his night-vision goggles from behind a three-foot-high wall. 'This could be some radio ham and his family and we're about to assault it based on SIGINT alone. Not a bloody chance.'

'Well, it's down to you and me mate. The troopers are all primed and ready. How do you want to play it?'

Sean knelt down behind the wall and reminded Swartz of the drawing they'd made earlier. The drawing was marked with the four faces of the building. Their approach to the face in front of them, which was the back garden, was marked as the purple face, the front was amber and the other two sides were grey and blue. 'You take the amber face Swartz, I'll take purple. Thirty minutes should be enough to meet back here.'

The slight wind rustling through the birch trees provided useful background noise as they started their recces. They both wore night-vision goggles strapped to their heads on top of their black balaclavas. They each carried a Glock pistol in a thigh holster with endoscope equipment strapped to their waists on black belts. Small drills and toolsets were attached to the rear of their belts.

Sean crawled the last few metres from the rose bushes to the corner of the building and then stood up slowly to stand against the side of the wall. His first target was the large room facing the small meadow, which he suspected was the living area. The lights were on, but the curtains pulled to. Sean placed his endoscope through a tiny air gap in the patio doors and looked at his two-inch chest-mounted screen, which was shrouded with a black veil to hide the light and disguise his presence. He twisted the head of the camera using the toggles on his chest controller to look around the room. No one inside. He then carefully depressed the door-handle to see if the door was open. To his shock it was.

He checked the visual inside the room again. This time, when he adjusted the focus, he immediately saw movement in the dining room. It was Nadège.

Chapter 49

Asturias

The entire joint operation across three target sites in France and Spain, plus multiple terrorist interdictions across Europe, was now firmly in Sean's hands and it was his call to spring attacks on them all.

Sean knew that each operations room would be awaiting the moment when the assault on the house had been successful and the command and control of General Alimani's operation had been thwarted. There was no room for error, there could be no cockups, no miscalculations and certainly no indecision. The precise actions of Sean and his team were being monitored by dozens of radio operators, who were just waiting for the codeword to launch their assaults.

Sean's mind wandered to Jack and what he had uncovered. Jack would be the most nervous of those listening in to the radio traffic, and Sean's penchant for doing things differently would probably be occupying Jack's mind by now. Sean smiled at that, remembering the words of one of his commanding officers decades ago on intelligence operations, when he was being berated for completely ignoring operational procedures. It had been a two-minute interview with the most senior British intelligence officer in the Balkans. 'You're going to take this bollocking Sean, and take heed of it. You fucked up. Don't do it again. And for the avoidance of any doubt within these four walls, you're a bloody maverick. Some people don't like mavericks. Do you hear me?'

Sean had simply agreed with everything the Brigadier had said. That razor-sharp man had already saved his career on a few previous occasions. 'Now, get back out there and keep being a fucking maverick. You have an uncanny knack of making things happen, now scoot and keep doing what you're doing.'

Sean remembered every word his boss had told him that day and the beaming smile he had worn on his face as he had left the Brigadier's office, having been given licence to carry on making things happen. That was the type of leader Sean liked. Ballsy.

But here he was now, with the world looking in at him, hoping and praying he'd make the right decisions. It was a venerable responsibility that he could not shirk from. But for Sean, gut feel was always the way. He knew what was right and what would work. This was one of those gut-feel occasions where he would bend every operational order and rule that had been thrown at him in that hangar. The orders from the American General had been simple: assault the house, kill the terrorists inside, find the initiation mechanisms and give the codeword for the other assaults to begin. The codeword had not left his mind. CLAYMAST.

Sean whispered into his radio, waiting for Swartz to respond in his earpiece. 'Go ahead,' he heard. 'Send.'

'Swartz, get your ass round to purple face quickly. I'm going in and you're gonna back me up.'

'What?' was all Sean heard, as he ignored the rest of Swartz's advice. 'Just get around here now.'

Sean had watched the room for fifteen minutes and seen no one else inside. He had observed a huge open-plan living space with two sofas and a row of desks to his left with three computers and a raft of monitors, some mounted on the walls, some on the desks. He spotted several mobile phones on the desks – was that the way the General was communicating with his teams? Was it as simple as that? Or was Nadège in charge of this? Was the General somewhere else?

What no one knew was what would happen if General Alimani was killed. Had he put other contingencies in place to allow the explosions to occur? No one quite knew the means of initiation for each of the explosive devices. Would they be remotely detonated? Possibly. On a timer? Highly unlikely if this was the extortion ploy. By a trigger in the hands of the terrorists at each site? No one knew. What the NEST team had found was the location of the second dishwasher. Exactly as assessed, their radiation equipment had found one device on a ship steaming towards Biarritz, with the second identified as being on a cargo transporter parked at a service station on the D260. With these two tactical nuclear devices, the devastation of the entire G7 location was guaranteed. Despite every inch of the conference locality having been searched for bombs inside the rings of steel, these were all placed well outside the cordon and two security zones. The NOTAM, a Notice to Airmen and Women, for creating the sterile airspace above the G7 was guaranteed and French fighter jets were available at a moment's notice to move to take down any threatening aircraft loitering in the area.

Despite all the known unknowns, and the high-risk nature of the coordinated operation, everyone knew that the General would provide the first attack order - and the kill chain would follow from that. To alleviate such a threat, the joint US and UK operation had decided that, once the command cell was taken down, they would take no chances and would assault each location, aware of the risk that the terrorists could detonate the devices themselves. There was no room for error at either site. Overwhelming force was needed to stop the bombers and then render each explosive device safe, all within precise timeframes.

Swartz tapped Sean on the back. 'I hope you bloody well know what you're doing.'

'I do. I feel it. Listen. You and I have taken down this kind of threat before. This is doable without a full-scale assault. We watch for another ten minutes then I go in with you covering my back, OK?'

'You're having a laugh mate. If this goes pear-shaped on your gut feeling it's not just us that's fucked. It's a helluva risk mate.'

'On my call, Swartz. Trust me. Get the lads to be prepared if it goes wrong and, when I give you the signal, be prepared to give the codeword over the net.'

'You and your bloody gut could kill us both. Are you just gonna walk in there?'

'Yes. That's my plan. My orders were to kill the terrorists, not everyone in the building.'

'But fucking around like this will put our lives at risk. We need to go in hard and fast. No fucking about.'

'That's what we're used to doing but this needs a bit of stealth mate, not a full-on attack. Watch and shoot, watch and shoot.'

'Jeez.'

'Ten minutes, then we go.'

Had he seen the panic and commotion going on in Whitehall, Sean may not have chosen the path he had decided on. The entire security apparatus of the United Kingdom had gone into overdrive.

'What do you mean, we can't strike against the terrorists now?' Hugo Campey had said to the National Security Advisor. 'We know where they are, we have people ready to go against them, so why not?'

'Jack will explain,' came the response from Sir Justin Darbyshire who also acted as the UK's National Security Advisor. 'It's a very complex operation, with many lives at risk.'

Jack was about to inform the entire congregation of the British government's emergency response committee, who were sat in PINDAR, having been alerted by intelligence from the CIA that multiple attacks were about to take place in London, two of which were assessed to be radiological devices. The threats were imminent, they had been told by the CIA.

Jack peered into the webcam, knowing he was being beamed live into the depths of the PINDAR bunker to personally brief the Prime Minister and her crisis committee. There was no time for introductions to the others sat around the U-shaped table that evening, but Jack could see a full house on his monitor. Sat around the table were twenty-six individuals and they included, amongst others, the Commissioner of the Metropolitan Police Service, the Chief of MI6, the Director of Defence Intelligence and the Chief of the Defence Staff. Twenty-four hours before the PM was due to fly to the G7, and perhaps only thirty-odd hours before General Alimani would issue orders for his attacks across Europe, Jack knew he had to nail this briefing with rigour. He fiddled with his blue Charles Tyrwhitt tie.

'Jack, can you hear me?' Sir Justin said.

'Clearly, yes,' Jack said, sitting in a secure room at the French airbase. He placed a finger on his earpiece, which would ensure that he clearly heard the dialogue in London.

'You have ten minutes and no more to tell the Prime Minister and everyone here exactly what your assessment is. Then we have a fifteen-minute briefing from the CIA followed by a thirty-minute call to the White House. Do you understand?'

Jack nodded firmly, then began. 'One single man, an Iranian spy, known as the General, will provide the orders to attack London in less than thirty-six hours,' he said. 'The Republic of Iran will implicitly deny he is acting on their orders and, quite simply, there is very little evidence to connect their government with this plot. It is state-sponsored terrorism, expertly put together as a fully deniable operation. They'll be able to blame the Russians for the attacks and, likewise, the Russians will be able to blame the Iranians. It will create a vacuum of international confusion.'

Jack paused, waiting to see if anyone responded to that bombshell. They didn't. All he saw on his screen were several people behind the Prime Minister scurrying around, passing notes and whispering into people's ears. 'The Americans, as you know, are leading this operation, but we have one single agent who has uncovered this plot. He's on the ground with the Americans, alongside a small team from our Special Forces. We know that two improvised nuclear devices have been placed around the G7 location, with two known suitcase bombs sat in London that are potentially fissile. Our chief scientists have stated that the suitcase bombs are unlikely to be large enough for a nuclear explosion, but we should proceed on the basis that they may well be dirty bombs. They are radioactive dispersal devices, or RDDs.'

Jack watched Sir Justin Darbyshire raise a hand. 'Jack, forgive me for interrupting, but you should know we have raised the threat level here in the UK to CRITICAL, we've mobilised all of the SAS and SBS counterterrorist units and have placed all military bomb-disposal units under operational command to provide military aid to the civil powers. We have planned for multiple attacks across London, and not just chemical or radiological attacks. How sure are you that these attacks will take place and what about the threat from plots we don't know about?'

'I'll be brief and to the point on this, sir. Firstly, we must not strike against the suitcase bombs until the coordinated order is given by the Americans. That's my first recommendation. Quite simply because, if we attack one without attacking the others, word could get to the General and he'll order all strikes to go ahead. We must strike against all four locations simultaneously. Secondly, the Iranians have activated their sleeper cells within the UK. My judgement says that, if the General initiates the nuclear devices, that will be their code to attack other targets across the UK. If he doesn't set off the bomb, then his demands will have been met and they will stay silent.'

The Chief of the General Staff, a former SAS commander, chipped in. 'What about if we take them all down, at each of the four locations, and kill the threat off? The sleeper cells will attack us across the UK once they know about this, right?'

Jack stayed silent, watching the conversation spread amongst the committee members. He sensed he'd made his play and, with his and the other briefings they were about to get, he hoped they'd all agree on two things: to strike against the suitcases at the same time as the nuclear devices in France and to be prepared for any other attacks that might come from the sleeper agents that Nadège had been commanding in Britain.

'The sleeper cells won't attack if we take down this plot,' Jack said confidently. 'They'd operate only from the Iranian central command and, once the plot is taken down, the Iranians will deny all knowledge and go back to their planning table.'

The Metropolitan Police Commissioner put her hand up. 'Any idea how many Iranian sleeper agents there are in the UK Jack? I had no idea they existed.'

'We've been trying to infiltrate their cells for some time and what I can say, here and now, is that we're not far off that. Numbers are unknown, but I do know that the General will look to set the first bomb off in Paris or London to show he is credible. But he won't do that until he's issued the extortion demand to the G7 countries. We have some hours to play with.'

'You could well be wrong though, couldn't you Jack?' came the voice of the Chairman of the Joint Intelligence Committee, who was agitated and clearly peeved he wasn't in the know. 'If you're wrong, and we get this wrong, the future of this world could be thrown into chaos.'

Hugo Campey was stirring looking for support across the room.

'And the Americans will go big,' the Chief of the General Staff boomed. 'They've been itching for a full-scale war with Iran for years. This is now an act of war for them.'

'An act of war, yes, but verified as being ordered by the Republic of Iran, no,' Sir Justin replied.

'This is insane,' Hugo Campey said, throwing an arm in the air. 'Our role is to protect this country, and we now have two suitcase bombs ready to explode. We have to act now and not wait.'

Whilst not in the room, Jack could fully sense the agitation and nervousness, and a fear of making the wrong decisions. He watched as Sir Justin began to command the room, just as he had hoped.

'Prime Minister, we can control the Americans and their urge for war. We must be very careful here and Jack is the man on the ground who we should always listen to. I shall brief you separately, but we have some collateral now with the White House. Some collateral that I can assure you the Americans and their President will listen to. I'm afraid it's highly secret and cannot be shared in this forum right now.'

'What?' came the thundering voice of Campey sat opposite Sir Justin. 'I cannot allow that. We are all equally vetted to hear whatever is needed at this time of national crisis.'

'I'm afraid you're not,' Sir Justin replied aggressively. 'You, sir, better than anyone in this room, should know that, when there's a need to know, it remains need to know.'

Jack couldn't hide his contentment at seeing his competitor for the role of Director General of MI5 being put firmly in his box by Sir Justin. The Kompromat might just play out well, he thought.

The Prime Minister spoke quietly for the first time. 'Jack, you seem very calm about all this. We have to go now, but we're entering the endgame and can't afford for anything to go wrong. Do you think the Americans can pull this off in France?' The PM paused to look at her notes, as silence filled the room. 'And my second question is, do you think your agent who is on the ground has got all this right and will be able to take down the General?'

Jack took a moment, his mind drifting to Sean's friable nature. He experienced a moment of concern but it was overridden by his confidence. No time for indecision, he kept telling himself. 'Yes to each of those questions ma'am and, yes, I'm fully assured this can be done if everyone goes with the timings and sticks with the plan the Americans have come up with.'

'Splendid Jack, well done. Now, I'd like to speak with Sir Justin alone before we move onto the call with the CIA.'

Jack sighed and breathed out with a huge sense of relief, hoping that, amongst all his hopes, Sean would stick with the plan.

Chapter 50

Asturias

$\mathbf{S}$ean peered into the living space of the target building and could clearly see four suitcases at the far side of the room: Two large blue ones and two small carry-ons. He had been watching the room for nearly ten minutes and had seen only one person. Nadège had been sitting on the sofa, occasionally getting up to walk to the kitchen and sometimes checking her suitcases and placing the odd additional item inside them. Swartz had briefed the SAS team commander on Sean's new plan and the men were stationed at every ground-floor window, ready to strike.

'Still no sign of the General,' Swartz whispered to Sean. 'For all we know he could be sat in the middle of the Kuwaiti Desert ready to trigger all this.'

'Anything from the guys at the other windows?'

'Nothing. No one else has been seen inside.'

'Shit. Hang on, who's this?' Sean cried out. 'It's Petra. With the General. Fucking hell.'

'We take him down straight away, right?' Swartz asked, flicking the safety catch on his Glock.

'No, he's not armed. None of them are armed. I want you on my shoulder with a team going straight upstairs to take anyone out. This room stays ours - no one shoots unless needed. Make it happen quickly Swartz.'

Sean adjusted the endoscope to get a better picture, with all three of them together in the frame. Nadège and Petra were walking towards the large dining table at the end of the room and the General walked behind them and placed his mobile phone on a sideboard. He stopped and stood at the table, pulling out a dining chair that he leant on with both hands. They were talking. No phones, no firearms. Sean wanted this done stealthily. The General was not in any shape to fight him, had a huge beer belly and looked unsteady on his feet. It was risky but doable, Sean told himself. They won't run. If they do, I'll shoot. It was high-risk stuff but something inside him told him it would be OK.

'We're good, on your call,' Swartz said, tapping Sean on the shoulder. 'I'm right behind you.'

Sean took a few deep breaths, pulled his Glock from his thigh holster and gently turned the door-handle. He pulled the door open, calmly moved the curtain to the side with ease and walked straight into the room, his weapon at his side.

The General had his back to him, as did Petra. It was Nadège who spotted him first and their eyes locked for what seemed like an eternity. He continued walking until he was in the centre of the room, Swartz taking up a wide position to his rear on the right, pistol down by his side. There was still no movement from any of them, with Nadège looking spaced out, gazing at what was happening in front of her eyes. Sean's breathing calmed and his body tightened as he watched the General peer over his shoulder. The shock of seeing a man in full black kit, a weapon at his side and a death stare on his face had fixed him to the spot for what seemed like an age but was in fact only tenths of a second. Sean calmly drew his pistol until it was aimed right at the General's head.

'No, no,' the General shouted, grappling with the chair as he tried to get to his feet, stumbling as he made a run for his phone on the sideboard.

'Stand perfectly fucking still General Ali,' Sean barked, in a voice that would have commanded instantaneous submission from most. 'Turn around very fucking slowly and put your hands on your head.'

The General's shirt buttons were undone, his belly flopping over his loose jeans, his face ashen with shock. Only Nadège would have seen the four SAS soldiers quietly move around the curtain and up the stairs, tightly bunched together, MP5s pulled into their shoulders, barrels held high. Sixty seconds later Sean heard the familiar sound of an MP5 double tapping bullets into someone's body upstairs. He didn't know how many were upstairs, but he trusted that if they were terrorists they were all dead now.

'You,' Sean barked at Petra. 'Yes you. Stand up now.'

'Don't shoot, we're not going to hurt anyone. It's him, not us,' she said, pointing at the General.

Sean waved his weapon at the General, indicating to him to move away from the women to the right-hand side of the room, where Swartz had his pistol aimed at his chest.

'Not really true, is it?' Sean replied. 'You've both been on a killing spree across the globe so don't fucking say it isn't you. You're both part of this shit and we're here to fix that.' He stopped and put his finger to his earpiece, hearing the words 'rooms clear' come across the radio.

It only took a millisecond for Sean to recognise movement as the General ran towards the sideboard, where his phone was. He didn't make it. Sean shot him in the thigh and the General slumped sideways, letting out a scream before crumpling to the floor. He rolled over, tried in vain to crawl towards the phone, then slumped into a foetal position, clutching his leg. Sean walked over to stand in front of him.

'We've got all your bombs,' Sean said impassively. 'And your men are all about to be killed. It's over mate. Properly fucking over.'

Sean turned to Swartz and gave him a thumbs up. 'Make the call now.'

Swartz clasped his radio, pressed a switch and released a series of words that the ops room in the hangar had been itching to hear. 'Hello Zero, this is November Four. CLAYMAST. CLAYMAST.'

Chapter 51

Biarritz & London

The bodies lay still, some in the seats of their vehicles, blood dripping down their faces, others prone on the bridge deck of the Maltese-flagged vessel and, in London, two bodies had folded into each other as they ran towards their SAS aggressors.

Near to the D260 just outside Biarritz, two snipers had chambered their rounds into the breeches of their McMillan TAC-338A rifles, each squinting through their sights before controlling their breathing. The two terrorists sitting in the articulated lorry didn't stand a chance. The shots were released simultaneously from two different locations that afforded the best sight of the men charged with detonating the nuclear device in one of the dozen or so dishwashers in the trailer. The shots hit both of them square in the head, punching a fist-sized hole in their skulls and slamming them hard against their seats. Within fifteen seconds the NEST team had arrived and begun their entry into the side of the lorry. A large canopy was drawn over the vehicle and the nuclear support team began their operation to mitigate the effects of any explosion from within. One hour later, the improvised nuclear device had been rendered safe.

The most complex assault that night took place on the vessel, which began with two stun grenades being lobbed onto the ship's bridge before four Navy Seals entered, killing four men within seconds. Two US Navy helicopters hovered above the decks of the vessel, releasing twenty-four more assaulters who fast-roped onto the decks before making their way to every part of the ship to hunt down any terrorists within the voids, engine rooms, galley and cabins. Within thirty minutes, speeding in on the mistral, the second wave of helicopters arrived, carrying the NEST team specialists who fast-roped onto the vessel with boxes of hefty bomb-disposal equipment. Specialist high-risk searchers began the hunt for the nuclear device as the ship turned and headed back out to sea. Three hours later, a dishwasher inside a thirty-metre container, was found and the device made safe. The final words of the senior NEST team commander were heard across the radio as everyone held their breath, hoping to breathe again. 'Standby. Ready to make safe.'

In London, a bomb-disposal officer with six tours of Afghanistan under his belt made his way inside a small lock-up located below the arches of a railway bridge close to Waterloo station. He had previously made the lonely walk to defuse dozens of high-tech IEDs in Iraq, Afghanistan and Northern Ireland but had, to that day, never dealt with a live dirty bomb. His record tally was thirty-three bombs during his first tour of Afghanistan and he hoped to rack up his first and only radiological device. He wore a brand-new Kevlar bomb suit, fifty-odd pounds of ballistic and blast protection and a black helmet with a visor shield across his face that received cooling air from its internal system. He walked past the two corpses, noticing how one man had fallen with his face in the groin of the other. He then made his way to two suitcases that he had previously seen having studied the diagrams of what lay inside provided by a couple of intelligence operators, who had looked inside them whilst they lay in a cache. He was mightily grateful for the drawing and photographs, which provided him with an indication of what he had to defuse.

Behind him, a whirlwind of activity had been taking place. Eight SAS soldiers had stormed the lock-up, killing the two occupants with less than eight shots fired. In the PINDAR bunker, the Prime Minister and COBRA officials watched live imagery of the SAS storming the lock-up, followed by a number of high-risk searchers from the Royal Engineers. Finally, they watched the Royal Logistic Corps' bomb-disposal expert enter the garage, a man known as 'Glynn H' they had been told.

When 'H' eventually looked inside the first suitcase, he saw the advanced telemetry of an Iranian-built dirty bomb. He inspected the device by eye, noticing the advanced-level electronics, a frame that held the radioactive device and two mobile phones that would act as the command hub to initiate the bomb. For the second time in his life as a bomb-disposal officer, he shuddered as one of the phones started ringing. The LED screen was illuminated and he stared into the abyss, knowing that, if the second phone went off, it would be curtains for him. It didn't. Nothing happened. He lived.

The forensics investigation would later show that the device had been built inside the lock-up and the cobalt source inside it had originated from Kazakhstan. The investigation would take over a year to identify where it had come from, but it could never be linked directly to the Iranians.

Just as that investigation was concluding, fourteen months later, Glynn H would receive the George Cross from Her Majesty the Queen.

In London, the issue was how to provide secret intelligence that would neither be leaked by the offices of 10 Downing Street, nor ignored for what it was. It had been an Iranian attack on the G7 and, by default, an act of war against many nations. The hotline between the President of the US and the United Kingdom was red-hot. Missives were flying around the inner sanctums of the White House and Number 10 about how to treat this catastrophic situation and staff were furiously working up different political and press options.

Chapter 52

Asturias

'How many bombs has he planted?' Sean demanded, looking at Nadège. 'You're next to get slotted if you don't comply.'

Nadège looked perplexed, a vision of blankness. She just stood there, no emotion, no soul. Was she in shock? What did it matter anyway? She had conspired to kill thousands of people by leading the charge to unleash evil across Europe.

Nadège ignored the question but Petra responded as if she were her advocate. 'There are two, and she was forced to put all this together. He's the bastard you want, not Nadège.' She pointed to the General, who was now propped up against a sofa, blood oozing from his thigh.

'Pass me a towel. Wrap the wound up: please, please,' implored the General.

'Shut the fuck up,' Sean blasted. 'You will die anyway at some point. You deserve nothing.'

Nadège finally spoke, breaking her haunting silence. 'You will never understand my life, will you Sean?' She threw him a cutting glance then slowly drew a Makarov pistol from the back of her jeans, casually biting her lip and keeping her eyes firmly fixed on Sean's. Sean tensed, knowing Swartz was behind him, probably with two hands on his weapon, knees bent and aiming right at Nadège's head.

'Give it a rest. I'm not here to get mind-fucked by you ever again. You're a dead woman if you pull that trigger,' Sean ventured, frowning.

'I'm a dead woman anyway,' Nadège replied, taking a pace forward, now smiling. Sean studied her face, now beginning to see that what was behind those inhuman eyes was a cloud of pleasure. Was she drugged? Before his mind could process that thought, Nadège slowly moved her arm to the left, lowered the barrel a fraction, pulled her other hand onto the steel grip and fired a single shot directly into the head of the General.

Sean raised his hand to stop Swartz from firing, watching the General's last gasps of air suck into his lungs before he slumped onto the carpet, blood oozing garishly from his forehead. The smell of cordite lingered in the air. The look of relief on Nadège's face was palpable. Sean was stunned.

'He's the bastard who ruined her life, he's the bastard who killed her,' Petra shouted, before breaking down in tears, hands firmly clasped to her head.

Sean looked across to Nadège, who was now bawling at him. 'If you ever listened, if you ever looked inside me, you'd know,' she said wearily. 'I bet all you ever thought was that I'd strap myself to one of those bombs and kill myself, eh?'

Sean calmed himself. 'That thought did cross my mind. What if I cash in my chips now and call this fucking charade a day?'

'What do you mean?' Nadège said defiantly.

'You tried to kill me, twice. You tried and failed to kill thousands more than just the bastards who abused young women in Bosnia, and you don't give a fuck about anyone except yourself.'

'What is with you Sean? You succeeded. That's all that you're about. Yourself. You're as cold a killer and as evil a sociopath as I am.'

'What?'

'Yes, you are. You're as fucked up in the mind as I am. Only you never want to see it.'

'I'm not the mass killer here, remember?'

'Enough. Let us go. We're leaving and you're not going to stop us.' She turned and began to pull the nearest suitcase, the wheels squeaking harshly on the wooden floor.

Sean shouted at the top of his voice, exasperated and raging. 'Stop moving. Stop right there and stand still, you piece of fucking shit.'

'What, are you going to shoot us both?' Nadège was agitated now, her sharp features frozen like blood run cold. The anger inside her was rising and Sean knew his own was close to boiling point too.

'Just stop. It's over for you. You're going to jail for a very long time. Don't make me kill you now.'

The silence spread torpidly across the room. Three guns, four faces, one body, four suitcases. Sean looked around him, each person looking scornfully at his face, which was now twitching uncontrollably with anger. At that moment he saw sadness everywhere. He felt out of control.

Nadège looked down towards her training shoes, releasing her hand from the suitcase, looking drawn. 'I had a job to do, a job he made me do to release me from my own shackles.'

'You made my life a shithole,' Sean replied furiously.

'You were my only male friend. My only true male lover.'

'You didn't let me in, never, you were just cold.'

'You hated me.'

'I don't hate anyone.'

'But you do Sean. Look inside you. Unravel it all.'

'Fuck you. You fucked me up.'

'I did, but in my heart, you were close to me,' Nadège murmured, taking a moment before pointing to the General, her hair now flopping over her face. 'He burnt me, made me the way I am and threatened I'd never be able to leave and take my family away from his dirty hands unless I did all this. For years he owned me.'

'Why didn't you just kill him?'

'She couldn't, she just couldn't, could she?' Petra now shouted, her mascara dripping from her eyes. 'Can't you see?'

'See what?'

'He was her captor, her father figure, her saint,' Petra shouted back.

'What? He abused her?'

'Yes, but he's not the only one. Her father sent her on that traumatic journey as a child. That bastard lying there just took advantage of it and became her emotional captor. Mind-numbing control. Stockholm syndrome, I think you call it.'

'What?' Sean asked again, shocked to the core and unable to process his confusion. He turned his head towards Swartz to see if he had made any sense of it all. He'd gone. Where was he, for fuck's sake? Bloody hell. Then came a voice from the stairs. Swartz's voice. A calm voice encouraging someone down the stairs.

'Sean, hold up for a minute mate,' Swartz called from up the stairs, out of view. 'Just wait. We need to sort something out.'

To Sean's astonishment, Swartz turned the corner at the bottom of the stairs with his hand placed around the shoulder of a young boy, with an elderly lady following. Sean studied the boy. A small boy with wispy brown hair and a face of distress. A face like his own. Hair like his own. The same square jaw and chiselled features as Sean's father. The same features that Sean bore. It was haunting.

A deep chill ran through him, a lingering chill that drove right through his body. His mouth went dry.

'All these years, it's my life that's been a sham, not yours,' Nadège whispered in a calming tone.

Sean turned. He gulped twice then raised his hand to his mouth. His eyebrows narrowed. 'All this time… I'd have done anything for this boy.'

'I know.'

'My son.'

'But you're MI6.'

'Not any more. I'm not sure who I am any more.'

'Let us all leave Sean. I need to run away and make a life for this boy, not be stuck in jail for years. I'll never abandon him.'

That hit a nerve for Sean. Abandoned. The word 'abandoned'. How he had felt when his mother disappeared. How would his son feel growing up thinking that his father had abandoned him?

'I hate the Iranians, I'm done now. Let us leave. We all love each other, and the plane is waiting now.'

Sean didn't answer but turned again to face his son.

Nadège whispered again from behind him. 'Do you know Colonel Sergei, my Russian handler?'

'No.'

'Well I think you probably do. He's the only man who could have leaked on this job. But it doesn't matter now. I'm free, the job was done, Alimani's dead. I want to leave with the three people in my life who love me. Surely you'll let that happen, right?'

'OK, so I know Sergei,' Sean replied, turning again to face the mother of his child. 'So what?'

'Well, I left something for him in a dead-letter drop just outside Warwick Avenue some time ago, just in case the Iranians found out I was working for the Russians and had me killed. My Syrian facilitator who helped me recruit the bomb-maker will give Sergei the directions if I'm killed, and it's something that will be of use to you. You see Sean, you nearly convinced me to go to the Brits, and so did Petra. She's been trying to help me escape for a long time, but now it's here – my escape is here - and our destiny lies in your hands. There isn't much time. I don't need anyone to help us any more, we just need to get that flight to South America and be gone.'

Sean's shoulders dropped, his agitation lessened. He nodded at Swartz, knowing this was the right thing to do. He wasn't being a maverick this time, he told himself, just human. It was an act that might just one day see him find the solace he was seeking. In a sense, he was envious of Nadège. Envious of her freedom but gutted that his son would leave too.

Nadège walked past him, pulling her suitcase. Then she stopped, her back facing Sean. 'Here, take this,' Nadège said, turning to face Sean and handing him a note. 'He's a young man from Syria, not associated with any intelligence services and he was my helper. Nothing more. You'll need to give him the codeword. Use FITZROY. He'll know what has happened.'

'Then what?'

'He'll give you the location of the dead-letter drop that contains the full list of Iranian sleepers in your country.'

With that final pass of a note Sean watched his son walk out through the door he himself had entered some fifteen minutes earlier. Sean's eyes welled up and he imagined a drawer in his mind that he'd never ever close.

Chapter 53

London

'Can you find a derelict place somewhere around London?' Sean quietly asked One-Eyed Damon. 'It will need to be a place that no one would think of entering for a while after I've committed a crime.'

One-Eyed Damon shrugged his shoulders, drank his pint of beer in one long swig and nodded. 'Any specific plan you have?'

'Yes, an interrogation followed by a death. Here, take this: this is what I'm after. Within the next week would be good.'

One-Eyed Damon leant across the table and rolled his one working eye. His face narrowed and his shiny false eye glinted, revealing a lens with an RAF roundel in red, white and blue. 'You are fucking joking, right? This is insane.'

One-Eyed Damon stood and asked Sean if he wanted another pint. A quiet nod. He dwarfed Sean. He was a gargantuan man and had been a second-row rugby forward in his prime before he was shot in Iraq. One-Eyed Damon was Sean's go-to man for operations in London. He was a Northern Ireland and Iraq War veteran and a legend of the veterans circuit. A surveillance and weapons expert who, even with only one eye left, was still one of the best operators and a man who had contacts across the UK who could fix up anything that was needed. Break into a law firm, Damon was the man. Provide a weapon or plant some bugs, Damon was the man.

One-Eyed Damon returned with three pints. Two for him and one for Sean. 'Can't be arsed getting back up again waiting for you to drink your pint, you snowflake.'

'Thanks. Love you too.'

'Now Sean, this will cost a lot of money,' One-Eyed Damon said, looking at what Sean had written on the note. 'I know a man who has a place like this but why, for fuck's sake?'

'I thought it'd be a good idea.'

'Sadistic I'd say.'

'Slow death though,' Sean replied, chinking his beer glass against Damon's.

'How do we find this bloke then?'

'He's due into London tonight and I want you to follow him everywhere. Let me know every moment of the day where he is, who he's with, what he's doing.'

'OK, who's gonna help me?'

'Swartz and Phil 'The Nose'.'

'Great. Samantha involved?'

'No, she's tying up a few loose ends in France mate.'

A huge grin began to form across One-Eyed Damon's face. He had once been a very handsome man, many said he still was despite huge scars across his face and skull, the result of dozens of operations to save his life and make his future more palatable. Somehow, this Northern icon had survived. 'Money upfront please. Can I frighten him a bit first?'

'No, but you can interrogate him a little. He'll talk if you're dealing with him.'

One-Eyed Damon smiled affably. 'OK. Now, when do you want me to lift him off the streets?'

'Once the site is all prepared and good to go. We need to capture as much information as we can for the American investigators who will take this on.'

Three hours later, Sean emerged from the Tube station into the thunderstorms of a gloomy London evening. He felt depressed at seeing his son in the flesh and was deeply disturbed by the thought of never ever seeing him again. Feeling sluggish and dejected he wandered past Marble Arch, heading towards the Victory Services Club. It was a time of calm contemplation that would bring finality to this case, and he quietly wondered what the future held for him next before he slipped away back to France. His hair had grown long enough to carry a small ponytail, and he'd spent the last hour taking a sauna and trying to get his head around everything that was swimming inside it. He chose to wear a dark grey suit, white shirt and club tie for his meeting with Jack, which he sensed would reveal the forlorn puzzle behind the operation.

Once an American servicemen's hospital, the Victory Services Club sits proudly in prestigious Seymour Street in the outer heart of Marylebone, a haven for veterans.

Sean entered and was shown to a small window table in the bar, where Jack was reading *The Times*. Sean glanced at a TV in the corner of the room which showed that the G7 conference was underway in Biarritz.

'It's gone ahead then I see,' Sean said, shaking Jack's hand tightly.

'Touch and go I'd say,' Jack replied, pointing to a picture on the front page of *The Times* showing the PM arriving a day late for the conference. Mechanical delays with the airplane, the newspaper suggested. 'There was a lot of activity between Washington and London, deciding if it was safe,' he continued.

'Should be some conference discussion now then. How on earth have you stopped them going to war over this then?'

Jack passed Sean a glass and nodded at the bottle of Bordeaux. 'Not one of my finest operations, if I'm fair, but luckily you eventually played a blinder.'

They both smirked, and Sean felt a little more at ease. Jack explained to him how the Brits now had a hold on the way forward with the Americans over Iranian aggression, and that snippets of intelligence would soon be leaked to Western nations showing the extent of nefarious activity between Russia and Iran. In time, Jack surmised, sanctions would bite, the tide of diplomacy would turn against Iran and Hezbollah and the mullahs would be overthrown.

'But what about that artillery shell Jack? You had a live one on the go from the outset?'

'Wasn't viable though. It might have registered on a machine as being so, but it wasn't high-grade enough. Plus, we fed Hewitt some confusing information using the Hotmail address from the Pakistani scientist. He's fine by the way, and we'll be allowing him to come to the UK with his family.'

'Smart,' Sean said, thinking that Jack would have had a failsafe plan somewhere. 'So, I guess the second device must have caught you out then?'

'That was always the risk, and one that was always at the back of my mind. None of these operations are perfect Sean, as you know. But using you as a deniable asset to find the bomb-making factory was key. It was the start we needed, even though there were still risks we didn't know about. It was a big bonus to get that list of sleeper agents though. The services are mopping them up one by one.'

'Love it when a plan comes together, eh? What's next for me then?'

'Probably some sort of big thank you from the Director General I'd have hoped. The new one will be appointed in the next few months, but we owe you a lot Sean. We now have the list of sleeper agents on our turf thanks to you. And we have a bit of a swop planned which might work out in your favour.'

'Go on.'

'We're going to do a swop with the Russians for the female agent you captured a few years back. She's been in jail for a while now, but it does at least mean the Russians might cancel that contract on your head.'

'Wow. Who for?'

'The Russians have agreed to release a senior GRU officer who we recruited in Copenhagen but was convicted of high treason and sentenced to eighteen years in a Moscow prison. He made a number of basic errors and was arrested when he returned to Moscow to visit his mother. The case is very similar to Colonel Skripal, who was poisoned with nerve agent last year in Salisbury.'

'Well if it gets the SVR off my back, all the better.'

'Of course. And if it all goes well I have a plan where I want you to work with Colonel Sergei and this guy over the coming months and years. The GRU have been sloppy over the last year or so and I want to exploit that a lot further. They really hate that we know more than they do at the moment, so let's see how it all pans out, eh?'

Sean glanced out of the window, wondering how Jack found the time to continually plot. Jack poured them both more wine. 'You've certainly been busy Jack, but how on earth did you manage to blindside all these ministers from the shit that was happening with General Alimani?

'It had to be deniable Sean and, what's more, I needed to get the right civil servants on-board with my plan. We'd have got nowhere if ministers had found out.'

'How though?'

'No names, no pack drill. You see, mandarins operate behind a wall. Eventually you will find a door. But it only opens from the inside. And when, after receiving well-evidenced advice, ministers make a decision, it's the duty of civil servants to execute it. But you may be surprised to learn that, amongst civil servants, this often doesn't happen. That's how it works in Whitehall Sean and I had to exploit that with one or two of them. It's the powerhouse. We knew we had a problem with the Iranians and, after a bit of observation, we had to act, but not be constrained as D often said to me.'

'Brilliant Jack. What about Nadège then, what's happened to her?'

'I'm really not sure yet but we'll find out. Now, I must leave soon but I want you to come and meet someone on Friday before we fly you back to France. Her name is Pearly. You may remember her from your training days at Fort Monkton. She was our disguise expert.'

Chapter 54

London

Fletcher Barrington was a man of ritual and habit. This had helped One-Eyed Damon immensely in the three days he had been following the man across London. Time spent on recce was seldom wasted, he hummed to himself, as he sat for dinner in Kaspar's seafood and grill restaurant at London's Savoy Hotel.

One-Eyed Damon had a table for one and had been assured the very best of hospitality as he arrived at the restaurant, prodding with his white stick and tapping a few chairs and tables to make his entrance known. He'd made sure he'd eaten there on the previous two nights and he'd become very friendly with the maître d', who had ensured he'd received the very best of Savoy attention. Fletcher Barrington sat at his normal table next to the centrepiece bar, where uniformed chefs would mingle with the customers. But it was the large table in the centre of the room that caught One-Eyed Damon's working eye. Positioned next to thirteen diners was a two-foot statue of a black cat on the table, with a napkin around his neck and a plate in front of him. This was Kaspar, the most famous occupant of the hotel. Kaspar's story began in 1898, when a diamond magnate held a dinner party for fourteen guests at the hotel. One dropped out at the last minute, reducing the number of diners to thirteen and prompting a diner to predict that death would befall the first person to leave the table. Weeks later that diner was shot dead. To this day, you won't find a table of thirteen anywhere in the Savoy's restaurants. Instead, diners are accompanied by a black feline sculpture, which becomes the fourteenth guest.

Within the hour Barrington had paid his bill and exited the hotel into Savoy Court to start his walk up the Strand to his favourite pub, a ritual One-Eyed Damon had observed on each of the last two nights. One-Eyed Damon walked right behind him, carrying his white stick, and tapped him on the shoulder. 'Excuse me, sir, can you see a blue Mercedes van parked anywhere near? The driver tells me he's parked here somewhere but my eyes aren't what they used to be.'

Barrington, somewhat shocked to be confronted by the battle-scarred face of One-Eyed Damon, hesitated before realising he had a civic duty to help the blind man.

'I'm a war veteran, lost my eye in Iraq,' One-Eyed Damon continued.

'Thank you for your service,' Barrington replied, almost bowing to the huge beast of a man in front of him. 'There's one at the end of the road parked on the wrong side - can I assist you?'

Barrington held One-Eyed Damon's arm and walked him across the hotel's small roundabout.

'Would you mind opening the side door?' One-Eyed Damon asked as they approached the vehicle. 'The registration is HNY, right?'

'Yes, it is. I'm sorry to ask, but do you mind telling me how you got your injuries? I was in the CIA a long time ago.'

One-Eyed Damon watched Barrington slide the side door open, revealing two bench seats inside the privacy-screened rear cabin. Swartz lay out of sight, ready to deal with the package that would soon enter the vehicle. He cussed as One-Eyed Damon decided to overplay his role by continuing chatting to the man.

'Long story, but I'd just rescued six soldiers who had broken down in Basra,' One-Eyed Damon began, handing Barrington a business card with a Blind Veterans' logo on it. The conversation had all the air of normality on a balmy summer's evening in the heart of London. 'I put my head out of the wagon and got shot by a sniper.'

A bullet had entered One-Eyed Damon's left cheek and exited through his right, shattering both cheekbones, destroying his left eye and severely damaging his right. Damon was rushed to nearby Basra Palace for emergency treatment, where he was given a lifesaving tracheotomy to let him breathe. Then he was airlifted by helicopter to the base hospital, where he underwent the first of many operations to rebuild his face.

'Half my face is now titanium,' One-Eyed Damon explained with a smile. 'Here, have a look at my eye.'

One-Eyed Damon leant over the man, who was now utterly mesmerised by the story of a hero and whose horror-strewn face intrigued Barrington.

'Looks like a reindeer to me,' Barrington said, peering into One-Eyed Damon's left eye.

'Spot on. It's Rudolph the Red Nose,' One-Eyed Damon said, tilting his head backwards. The headbutt to Barrington's nose that followed was so quick and brutal that no one would have had any time to think anything untoward was going on. Barrington flopped backwards and was assisted by a huge pair of hands, which bundled the body neatly into the back of the van. One-Eyed Damon casually folded up his white stick, walked around to the passenger seat and nodded once at Phil 'The Nose'. 'Drive on please young man.'

Chapter 55

London

Sean knocked on the door of Jack's office in Devereux Court, just off the Strand. He wasn't quite sure what to expect from this final meeting of the operation and certainly wasn't prepared for the surprises that followed. Curiously, he'd received a text from Jack an hour earlier stating that Pearly was ill and couldn't make the meeting. But he had someone else Sean should meet.

Sean knocked again, just as the door began to open.

'Sean. Great to see you. Come on in.'

Sean followed Jack into D's old office, the decor of which threw so many nods to the cold war it made him catch his breath with surprise. The second surprise was sitting in a high-backed chair opposite an antique oak desk that Jack walked towards. Sean caught a glimpse of the blonde hair of a woman who didn't turn to greet him. She sat with her legs crossed, leaning gently on the chair's arm, her hair flowing along her shoulders and down her sleeveless arm.

'Let me introduce you to Petra,' Jack said knowingly. 'I believe you have both met once.'

'Christ Jack, what on earth is she doing here?'

'Take a seat Sean and all will become clear.'

Sean gazed at Petra's face as he crouched to sit in a battered and beaten high-backed chair. He immediately grabbed its arms with both hands and began fiddling with some twine that had come loose on the right arm.

'Petra is one of us Sean. She's one of The Court. Coffee or water?'

Sean was stunned. His mind couldn't compute what Jack was telling him. She was Nadège's lover. Or was she? Why on earth had Jack used him to try to turn Nadège when Petra was already embedded right in her arms? Sean studied Petra's face. She was smiling and now offered a hand across the divide between the two high-backed chairs. Sean reached over and gripped it.

'I bloody well knew there was something about this woman Jack. Incredible. Tell me more.'

'Well, as you know it's a little complex, but the crux of the matter is that Petra was failing. She was failing to convince Nadège that her life would be better if she turned to us. You see, Nadège wanted to keep her professional and love lives fully separate. Never would she burden Petra with her missions or her formal role in the MOIS or drag her into the killings she conducted as part of her Iranian terrorism. She loves Petra and wants to always protect her, especially given what happened in Bosnia. So Petra asked me for a little extra help. Two people influencing Nadège and changing her mind would work better than just her lover. And that's where you came in and succeeded.'

'So where is she now then?'

Jack nodded at Petra, indicating that the question would probably best be answered by her. 'She's safe, courtesy of your British intelligence services. Eventually, she agreed with my view that we'd all be much safer as a family under British protection instead of being on the run forever in South America. She's quite ill at the moment but in a private clinic where me and Maxim can visit her.'

'And Maxim? Is he OK?'

'Your son is fine and will grow up to be a wonderful young man now his mother is getting the right medical treatment. Nadège collapsed because of the traumas of the last few weeks, but you'll never see her again I'm afraid. I'll be caring for her from now on, along with the people Jack's assigned to us.'

'Petra will still be working for us,' Jack chipped in. 'She has connections in the Balkans that are gold dust for us and you'll be assigned to help her over the coming months as the Russians are beginning to play around there I'm afraid.'

Jack explained how he was concerned that the next phases of hybrid warfare would begin in the Balkans and how the Russians had already established the conditions for tensions amongst the nations there to grow. He also explained how Petra was not trained or able to penetrate Nadège's varied communications equipment but provided details of her movements and contacts, to help Sean on the mission.

'But how did you recruit Petra then Jack? What's the story?'

'You remember when the Mayor of Sarajevo was killed? Burrić?'

'Yes.'

'Well, on his deathbed, he told his best friend about the two women who had trapped and shot him. His best friend was one of our agents permanently established in the Balkans and linked to a number of paramilitary and drug-running gangs. He's still there but we used his information to explain to Petra that she could either work for us or go to jail for a very long time. She's a very bright woman and has been a perfect star for us ever since.'

'By that time my life was in absolute tatters,' Petra said, looking at Sean. 'The best way to describe my life was as a whore being bought and sold by sex-trafficking gangs in Bosnia and across the Balkans ever since the arrival of NATO and the UN police monitors in 1995. Nadège pulled me out and rescued me some years ago. Then we made a plan to kill off the ones who had trapped me in a life of hell.'

Jack and Petra spent some time explaining the background to her tragic story. From 1992 to 1995, thousands of women and girls suffered rape and other forms of sexual violence during the conflict in Bosnia and Herzegovina, including abuse in rape camps and detention centres scattered throughout the country. With the signing of the Dayton Peace Agreement in December 1995, violence against women and girls in Bosnia did not cease. The grim sexual slavery of the war years was followed by the trafficking of women and girls for forced prostitution. Worst of all, many of the trafficked women were exploited by some members of the International Police Task Force, who were often complicit in supporting underground operations across the country.

'Trafficking first began to occur in 1995,' Jack explained. 'The estimate was that as many as 2,000 women and girls from the former Soviet Union and Eastern Europe found themselves trapped in Bosnian brothels alongside local girls. Petra was one of them.'

'We were all held in debt bondage,' Petra chipped in. 'Forced to provide sexual services to the police and clients, falsely imprisoned and beaten when we did not comply with the brothel owners.'

In dozens of interviews with Human Rights Watch, women and girls, mostly from Bosnia, Croatia, Moldova, Romania and Ukraine, described brutality - including physical violence and rape en route to Bosnia and Herzegovina - at the hands of traffickers. Their testimonies proved that most of the purchasers were local Bosnians, like Burrić. But, in many cases, women and girls were purchased by members of the UN, Western contractors and members of the International Police Task Force.

'Burrić, Barrington and Duff were one secretive part of a much bigger problem,' Jack said quietly. 'Despite the detailed investigations by Human Rights Watch, everything was covered up by the international organisations operating in places like Tuzla.'

Petra added more to her story. 'After Burrić released me, Duff sold me to their High Chaparral club. After he left the country I was then sold to another American contractor who lived in Dubrave near Tuzla. He told me he had paid $2,000 for each of five girls. My movement was completely restricted. I could not go anywhere. In one club, two or three UN policemen were very often there. Every time we refused to work we were beaten and threatened with being sold to Serbia. It was horrific.'

Trafficked women and girls reported that brothel owners forced them to provide free sexual services to UN police, and particularly to officers employed in the unit responsible for issuing work and residency permits. Brothel owners received tip-offs about raids and document checks from local police, allowing them to hide the trafficked women and girls before a police sweep. Human Rights Watch investigators also found evidence that some NATO contractors had engaged in trafficking-related activities. There was evidence that some civilian contractors employed on US military Stabilisation Force bases in Bosnia engaged in the purchase of women and girls. Not one foreign contractor ever faced prosecution in Bosnia or their home countries. Instead, when they came under suspicion, they were returned to their countries and their crimes were hushed up. Such brisk repatriation precluded Bosnian prosecutions and prevented NATO contractors from serving as witnesses in criminal cases against the traffickers.

'So, what's next then Jack?' Sean asked. 'I need to deal with Barrington first and I have him nicely tucked up.'

'Get as much information as you can from him Sean. All of his connections, his postings and the extent of the sex gangs he operated across the globe and everywhere he was posted.'

'How much do you already know about his activity?'

'We have enough to push this to Congress for a full investigation. Laura is setting it up through her channels. Petra has provided Laura with details of many of the women who were abused during that period and it will be handled by reopening the Human Rights Watch investigation with new evidence and material. The original evidence was never acted upon by any nation involved and it was effectively shoved under the carpet when Human Rights Watch completed their reports in 2003. But there is now enough political will to push this to Congress and to expose the nature of corruption on the part of US contractors, police, diplomats and soldiers.'

'Christ. Whose idea was that then?'

'Laura's of course. She'll hand it on to the relevant diplomatic and Justice Department investigators, but it will be well known that Laura will have uncovered all this and fed it into the right places.'

'Presumably with a promotion then?'

'She was always destined to become Director of the CIA Sean, it was just a matter of time after a couple of previous fuck-ups.'

'What about Redman?'

Jack stood up and walked over to the safe. He'd always wanted to kick it like D used to so he toe-punted it once before turning to explain. 'There is a lot of incriminating evidence in here Sean. Video and photo evidence against Redman when he visited the

High Chaparral. Your mother's evidence from her encrypted note will also expose significant members of the US government, the CIA and the US Army and reveal their nefarious activity when they were stationed in Berlin. We also have a host of Kompromat we can use against Redman to ensure we can still exert influence at the White House.'

'Good. It will be nice to see all this in the US press. I assume I have permission to use some old fashioned leverage on this last piece of work with Barrington then?'

'Not my preferred option Sean but hey, why don't you pair go for a walk for an hour and get to know each other? Discuss it a little bit. It's a beautiful day out there.'

Chapter 56

London

'**D**o you want to kill him?' Sean asked Petra.

'I suppose it depends on what you mean by 'kill',' she replied. 'Is it to slaughter, or is it a decisive act that conclusively secures something?'

'Well, we have trapped him I suppose. He has no life to live, whichever way we choose to go with it.'

'I vote we watch him suffer in court. Feel his humiliation, watch his pain slowly kill him.'

'OK, I'm with you. It's a bloody good kill in its own right. Conclusive. We win. He loses. We get justice.'

Sean and Petra sat on a wooden bench in nearby Lincoln's Inn Fields, the largest public square in London and the scene of several important executions in the sixteenth and seventeenth centuries. It was a fitting place to finalise their kill, a carefree space surrounded by the Inns of Court, and a place to find their minds amongst the well-manicured lawns and in the shade of trees. It was a time of contemplation and a time to plan the execution of their captive.

'Who do we hand him over to?' Petra asked, punching a text into her phone.

'Probably an American diplomatic investigator but Laura and Jack will probably decide on that. We'll just warm him up for it first and get as much information from him as we can. Do you still have witnesses that will testify?'

'Lots of women, yes. Jack has made sure they'll be well looked after. The evidence he's accumulated alongside the testimony of the witnesses will be overwhelming.'

Sean was relieved in a way. It felt good to share his thoughts with another victim of the same evil perpetrator. Petra had experienced the most horrific depravation and abuse, but here he was, sharing his inner thoughts with a woman he'd only met once under gruelling circumstances, but one with a common purpose: to see the man who had killed his mother and propelled Petra into a life of sexual abuse publicly shamed and slowly killed through the justice system.

Sean had set up plans with One-Eyed Damon to have Barrington incarcerated in a small grain bin on a dilapidated farm in the countryside south of London. One-Eyed Damon had begun his interrogations and Barrington had been threatened that, if he didn't comply with the questions and provide the names of witnesses and perpetrators, he would quite simply be killed. Killed in the slowest, most brutal way. Sean had asked One-Eyed Damon to provide a grain auger with a conveyor belt that would slowly fill the nine-foot-high bin with corn. Barrington was strapped to a chair directly below a hole in the roof. The corn would fall on his body and slowly consume him. Drowning in corn would be a suitably slow death Sean had surmised.

One-Eyed Damon had demonstrated how it all worked to Barrington and took pleasure in watching his face as the corn entered the grain bin and began to settle firmly around his stomach and torso. Once trapped in the corn, the kernels locked Barrington in like hardened cement. One-Eyed Damon continued to interrogate him from outside the bin, peering in through a hole above head height. He explained to Barrington how his body would react once he was encased in corn, as the kernels kept falling.

'In water you drown by inhaling water which floods the lungs and replaces air. In a corn drowning, the pressure of those kernels on your rib muscles and diaphragm will become so intense that you won't be able to breathe at all. You don't want that now, do you?'

One-Eyed Damon had explained to Barrington the deadliest part of a corn drowning: suffocation by kernels blocking the nose and mouth. He would feel an overpowering urge and desperation to inhale, but it would be impossible. A terror-filled one to two minutes would follow.

Barrington squealed, and never stopped talking. Fear permeated every part of his body and he talked for over forty-five minutes. He provided names, places and the grizzly details of his sex-gang activities in multiple cities across the world. Enough for investigators to probe and verify.

Sean felt a tap on his shoulder from Petra. She pointed into the far distance across the grass towards the central bandstand. Out of the trees walked an elderly lady with a small boy, who was carrying a football.

Couples lay on the grass in front of Sean enjoying the summer's day. One man popped a bottle of Prosecco and a group of small children were playing with their dolls as a small cairn terrier ran around them chasing a tennis ball.

Petra placed her hand on Sean's forearm. 'You won't be able to see Nadège again, but I'll make sure you have plenty of access to your son. That's Maxim there. Walking across the grass.'

Sean felt cold shivers run down his spine and goosebumps on his neck, the result of the adrenalin that was now flooding his circulation. His hands started to feel clammy. He stood, hoping that Petra had not heard him gasp. He looked at Petra, impressed by how skilfully she had managed Nadège and how she had now helped him find a way forward. He turned, not knowing what to do next.

'I think thirty minutes will be a good start Sean. He knows he is meeting his father today. Play a little.'

Sean caught Maxim's eye as he approached, both of them showing nervousness at the prospect of such an awkward but humble first meeting. Sean stepped forward to shake Maxim's hand, knelt and asked him if he liked football.

Minutes later, five passes of the ball had been made and a bond had slowly begun to form. Sean wiped a tear from his eye and they both laughed as he chased the ball that had zipped through his legs. A nutmeg by his son. The first of many, he hoped. He was immersed in the calm joy of having fun in the park with his son.

Epilogue

Helmstedt, Old Inner East German Border

Four men. Two dogs. One vehicle. All moving across Germany with a range of search equipment on-board and a secret legacy that would bring some closure to the world of pain that Sean had endured over the last couple of months.

Sean sat next to Jugsy in the rear of the vehicle while Billy Phish sucked on his unlit pipe as he drove the specially adapted Toyota Hilux with a large rear cabin where two cocker spaniels sat sleeping their way through the journey. Billy Phish's human-remains dogs were the forensic specialists who would help Sean locate his mother's final resting place. Sean peered out of the window at the German countryside, happy to have his friends accompany him on this final pilgrimage to pay homage to his mother and hopefully recover whatever remains were left of her.

Swartz sat in the passenger seat, navigating the multitude of small roads between Helmstedt and Bartenslebener Forest. Each man remained quiet as they approached their final destination. Time had passed, but Sean finally felt able to take his team to search for the body of his mother, which had lain close to the old inner East German border for over thirty-two years. He glanced at the map that Zatopek had handed him. He knew that the decomposition of her remains would mean there would be very little left except for her skeleton. He'd wondered about how to organise her funeral, how to tell his father and who to invite. He was determined to make sure he crafted a suitable obituary that was worthy of a national hero from the cold war, and he hoped to hang a picture of her in the Special Forces Club in Knightsbridge, alongside those of many other female heroines from the Second

World War and after. Maybe one day he'd even write her memoir. He wasn't sure.

He had two special items in his small canvas shoulder bag: his mother's antique snuffbox and a cutting from the *Washington Post*. He'd pass the cutting to each of the men before they commenced their search in the woods. He passed it to Jugsy first.

It read:

Fletcher Barrington, a former Central Intelligence Agency station chief, has been indicted by a federal grand jury in Washington with one count of murder committed in Berlin in 1986 and four charges of rape and imprisonment of girls in Bosnia-Herzegovina in 1995. He was further charged with the attempted murder of two witnesses and with conspiracy relating to the Bosnia cases.

Barrington, 67, will appear in the Federal District Court in Washington and could face up to 30 years in prison for murder and additional time for the other charges. Further charges are expected to follow from Justice Department investigations relating to his service in Algeria and Oman.

The prosecution's summary that had been prepared for the trial had been written a week before the charge, and had stated that there was overwhelming evidence that Barrington had been involved in sex trafficking, imprisonment and the rape of women and girls whom he had bought and owned as chattels in numerous cities across the globe.

Washington and New York were awash with rumours of dozens of sealed indictments that related to Barrington being the leader of sex rings in Berlin during the '80s, when a number of diplomats, military officers and intelligence personnel had been part of a secretive gang that had bought and abused young girls. Sean had been assured by Laura that these sealed indictments would lead to multiple convictions as a result of the secret investigation that his mother had carried out during her time in Berlin as part of the BRIXMIS team and as an officer of MI6.

Back in London, Jack was wondering whether to continue with his application for the role of Director General of the security service as Sir Justin had suggested. He still wasn't sure it was him. He heard the wisdom of the former Director General singing out loud in his mind as he fiddled with his tie whilst pacing round his office. His coach and mentor had driven the words into him whenever a situation was nebulous. 'There is no time for ease and comfort. There is a time to dare and a time to endure.'

Jack sent Sean a quick text.

'Best of luck with the search. Your mother watches over you, proud of your achievements.'

Sean replied.

'Just reading the Washington Post. *Who was it who collated the evidence for Barrington's murder charge in Berlin?'*

Seconds later, Sean's screen showed that Jack was typing a response. A lengthy reply finally came through.

'It was a woman called Pearly. She was your mum's best friend and worked on her disguises in Berlin. When she retired she spent every working day tracing Barrington's accomplices down. She interviewed them all. Did her own casework. Over 15 years of investigations which, by a stroke of luck, only came to D's attention when he had dinner one night with her in London. It was a casual conversation that revealed that her best friend had been your mother. D didn't know that. He took up the case when Zatopek finally recovered and tasked a team to break into the lawyer's office to retrieve your mother's investigative files. Between Pearly, D and your mother's encrypted note in the snuffbox they amassed the evidence that will see Barrington convicted of your mother's murder. Your mother's note has incriminated many more diplomats and military officers. I think Pearly may have taught you the art of disguise once, not that she knew you were Marcella's son at the time. She's sorry she had to cancel our meeting with her, but she was ill that day.'

Sean took a moment to process this astonishing information. It was a tale worth telling in his mum's memoir. He decided he would write it, hopefully with the help of her best friend. He made a mental note to go and visit Pearly soon.

Within the hour, the canines had detected the scent of a body in a shallow grave amongst the bracken and between an expanse of spruce and larch trees.

Sean knelt down with a trowel in his hand and broke down as a torrent of emotions flooded his mind and soul.

There was a quiet moment before three hands were placed on his shoulders. The comfort began.

***

Acknowledgements

It's been a wonderful experience writing this novel, which has been a mixture of fun, serious challenge at times, and long periods of thought creating the story arc and plots. I hope you enjoyed the story and were able to immerse yourself in the world of these curious characters who have given me so much pleasure to develop. It's been fabulous to take them a stage further from my first novel, The Failsafe Query.

I'm indebted to a number of good friends and family for encouraging me to write this second spy thriller, and top of the list is my wife, Rebecca, for her selfless support and enduring inspiration. She has been an amazing stalwart of my work, a critical friend and enthusing guide. A big thanks too, to my mother, sisters, and my wonderful children, who have all played a major role in encouraging my new journey and adventure as an author.

Thank you once again to my editor, Derek Collett, who provided superb advice throughout, and to some amazing friends who helped in many aspects of finalising the story: Mary Liddell, Michaelyn Yare, Bryan Miller, Nick Milne, Liane Hard, Neil Lancaster, Jessica Belmont and Trevor Foster. You have all been wonderful. Also, a huge thank you to Alan Gordon for providing some amazing insights during my research elements of the book. A special thank you to my great friend and mentor, Brigadier John Almonds, for his wise words and mentorship of my life and careers, and his unswerving support in all I do. I only wish my late father had met you John!

Finally, to you all. My wonderful supporters and readers who continue to inspire me with the wonderful feedback I have received, the letters, and the encouragement. The third novel is now well and truly underway because of you all. Thank you for your generosity and support.

Michael Jenkins MBE
London
June 2019

Did you enjoy this book? If so, I'd be delighted if you would take the time to submit a review on Amazon and Goodreads, which really helps make a difference to authors. Honest reviews are our lifeblood and are so helpful for readers and authors alike. I'm very grateful to every one one of my readers and supporters, who inspire me to write more.

Other novels by Michael Jenkins:

The Failsafe Query

You can follow me or join my readers club at:
www.michaeljenkins.org

Featured author on www.londoncrime.co.uk

Manufactured by Amazon.ca
Bolton, ON